The Seven Lands

Seventeen Siblings

George R. Mead

assisted by

Zakke L. Zacog

E-Cat Worlds Press

LCCN 2014937213

Mead, George R.
Seventeen Siblings /
George R. Mead assisted by Zakke L. Zacog.
p. cm. – (The Seven Lands)
ISBN-13 978-0-9890927-2-2
1. Fantasy. 2. Seventeen Siblings Title.

E-Cat Worlds established its publishing program as a reaction to the large commercial publishing houses currently dominating the book industry and the smaller intellectual clones. It is interested in publishing works of fiction and non-fiction that are often deemed insufficiently profitable or commercial or that are not necessarily reflective of current literary trends and fads.

E-Cat Worlds, 57744 Foothill Road, La Grande OR 97850
www.ecatworldspress.com
SAN 255-6383

In the middle of nowhere - Creativity.
First Edition:
Printed in the United States of America

Nonfiction

A History of Union County
The Ethnobotany of the California Indians, 2nd Edition
A History of The Chinese in The West: 1848-1880
Yachats. The Town Called "Dark Water at the Foot of the Mountains."

Fiction

From Grandeville.

Portal
Lair
Search
Not Again
And Again.
Magiwitch
Rebirth
Offspring
Holiday
Treasure
E'Nilt
Braidna

A Tale of The Feyra

Jonathon and Dee
Dee Of The Fontala
Dee and The People
Dee and The Golden Cartouche

The Seven Lands (assisted by Zakke L. Zacog)

Seventeen Siblings

Something.
        Nothing.
It stirred.

Here.
        There.
It stirred.

Wanting.
        Needing.
It stirred.

The Battle That Began It All

The Heart Of All.

She stood on the top platform of the high tower, a black stone finger pointing upward from the grey stone wall that guarded the main gate, constructed from the dense black wood of The Tarna Tree harvested from the Forest of Sighs. This tower of the Guard Wall was called "The Tower of The Soaring Dragon," and was centered above the great entry gate to the town called The Heart of All. She watched the distant edge of the grass and waited for them to enter that vast meadow stretching from the base of the great walls to the edge of the forest that covered the southern end of this continent, did The Queen of the Seven Lands.

Just two hands of days past she had been The First Princess of Nu'vern designated to someday replace The King. Just two hands of day past when The Summer House had exploded in flame, killing The King and The Three Queens, thrusting The First Princess into her new role. She and her twin brother and The Third Twins had been staying in the more formal Royal Quarters in the central town and had thus survived as had all the rest of her siblings who had, in the many seasons past, scattered into the other lands.

Now he stood on the top platform of this highest tower of Nu'vern and watched as the gentle breeze flowing from behind her and her companions gently stoked their hair.

From the great gate running straight across the light green grass of the meadow and into the dark green, shadow dabbled forest, the small group could watch the wagonway called Aydel's Track. It was the only entrance to the vast agricultural lands behind the watchers. The wagonway disappeared into the thick forest and began its sinuous passage to the edge of The Dismal Sea where it joined the narrow wetway often called The Folly of Franbandan for the many lives lost in the construction of the wagonway along this uptrusting spine connecting two continents.

The early morning sun cast the shadow figures of her, her companions, and the tower across that dense meadow grass. The multicolor of her hair seemed to glow in the early morning sunlight. The three colors of her hair, this first born child of the First Twins of the First Royal House, were an expression of The Gift: white, black, and orange in bands as neat as if they had been dyed. At her right side stood her twin brother, also so marked, Zak'ke Elias'dea Noriyon Zacog, nicknamed "Shadow" by his sister.

The Twins were tall, slim, and fair-skinned. Moderate to tall stature and fair-skinned was normal for the folk of Nu'vern. Tall and slim was normal for those of the First Royal House as were soft grey eyes.

She wore the golden circlet of the Queen, gems sparkling in the sunlight and from something else deep within them. Her robes were the soft pastels of The Royal Weave, deep red and a lighter green. Her brother wore a narrow band of gold incised with stylized creatures twisting around one another, their heads seeming to peer forward to observe whatever he saw. The scale armor he wore was a soft brown and green.

On the Queen's left stood the Avelerain Tha'a'da warrior, Viana Tivean Tru'ert of Clan Veronji, a lethal friend and companion, dressed in the flat black garments favored by all of her clans, loose blouse and trousers draped over boots of supple black leather.

The Queen, at twenty three seasons, the youngest for many generations, leaned the great Lance of Power, her father's lance, against a pediment and bent into the notch between the great weather stained stones to stare, soft grey eyes now hard, at the shadowed edge of The Forest of Sighs. Something moved at that edge, something vague that wished to remain hidden.

Sar'al Rada'doa Noriyon Zacog, The Queen, frowned at that something vague out there and sighed softly. She was *The Queen* because The Gift had expressed itself in the multi-colored pattern of her hair and that of her twin. Unfortunately, her father, The King, and her mothers, had died in that raging inferno without passing on the knowledge and training that Royal parents usually gave their children. Her parents had assumed that they had plenty of time to do that before that eventual event arrived when she would become the Princess-Queen. Now, here she stood, high above the gateway that led into her homeland, Nu'vern, the gate closed and barred against whatever it was that the gate guards had felt was a threat out there.

"The demons approach, My Queen." Viana pointed one of her glistening blades at the figures beginning to assemble just beyond the forest edge. She glowered at them and thought that she might die in the brawl to come, but many, many of them would be sliced into quivering pieces before that happened.

The term "demons" was a derogatory term used by all the Avelerain of the three Bera'ar'andar, the clan organizations on the three continents where the Avelerain lived, for the deep dwellers in the denseness of The Forest of Sighs. These deep dwellers called themselves The Azkar, "The Ones of The Forest," one of the Hidden Ones. None of the folk of the Seven Lands now dared to enter that shadow shrouded place with one exception. That exception was Aydel's Track. This passage had been held immune, a safe passage for all with scattered openings for camping, temporary camping, for those passing through The Forest of Sighs. Trader-Merchant caravans, and all others, traveling along Aydel's Track always left behind food and items desired by the Azkar when they decamped from each safe spot. It was a long standing and understood "fee for passage."

Something had happened out there, something

unknown to the small group watching ever so carefully. But that something had caused the Azkar to surge to the edge of their domain bearing weapons.

The Queen nodded and waited and remembered how it had been when all she had to concern herself with were those things that a girl of less than fourteen seasons had while living among the Avelerian Tha'a'sa of The Silent Woods on the continent Shar'daine. It was shortly after her arrival there that she met the young Viana who had come to learn from her "cousins." Over the seasons they had become very close friends.

Her brother had always visited at the stroke of midnight earning him his nickname. He had learned how to do this, "travel," but was sworn to those who taught that arcane art to never divulge either the skill or the name of those who had taught him. It was during these visits that the pair had agreed to always be together, to be honest with each other, and to die together. Even at this early age they were beginning to feel the weight of the task that they would now have to assume.

He had trained elsewhere in the warrior skills, the very lethal skills necessary for one who would always be standing close to his Queen, prepared to prevent anyone, or anything, from bringing harm to her. As far as Zak'ke was concerned, he had a much simpler and a very straight-forward thing to do than she did. She, his twin, had the truly difficult job. She had to make decisions that could affect everyone. All he had to do was kill whatever might need killing. He smiled at the thought. Doing that didn't take very much planning at all. Although, it appeared at the moment, that there could be many, many things to kill. Perhaps too many. He gave a mental shrug. It was a warrior's life.

Continent Shar'daine, a land of rolling plains and scattered woodlands, was separated, in the main, from the other continents by wide oceans and narrow seas. Six of the seven continents were connected at some point by one or more land bridges, known collectively as Wetways, some long, some rather short. Shar'daine was connected to Nu'vern, one of the great land masses, mostly covered by vast and highly productive farm lands with scattered fishing villages here and there along the coastal edge, and to An'darl, with a great mountainous interior. An'darl connected across narrow straits to the desert lands of Farza, and a long and wide peninsula to Mart'den, a vast place with twisting valleys within the sinuous mountain ranges drained by streams and a great river. The heavy jungle forest continent of N'Farza was joined to Farza via a very long and narrow sand tongue which was awash at all times other than at the most low tides. In N'Farza were the lands of the Avelerain Tha'a'ea. The seventh continent, Adna'arl, a never visited place, sat in isolation far to the west. It was a great interior basin surrounded by a high ring of mountains and volcanoes which kept most of the moisture in the clouds from reaching the interior. At the base of these forbidding ranges, on the outside of the ring, there was a very broad band of green vegetation and wide sandy beaches.

So, for many nights and weeks and months of seasons the young pair far from their home, one the mirror image to the other, talked about their large number of siblings, their father had three wives. The folk belief, held by some of the Royal families, called The Ten Houses, was that the first born of the first wife of the King with hair like the twins had would be an ill-omen for all the lineages. Royal mythology suggested this in the many tales from an unwritten past when such rulers did bring unwanted events to The Kingdom.

Today Zak'ke stood there, close to his sister-twin, a quiet warrior, called The First Blade, great scarlet Honglar sword hanging on his wide belt, crafted from the dark-metal mined and forged in the mountain vastness of the Lands of the Honglar, Continent An'darl, craftsmen of weapons and armor for all the lands that would buy or trade. That metal was called "dark," not because of its color but because of the lethal qualities it gave when made into weapons. On his back Zak'ke wore a great quiver that matched in artistic detail the deadly Avelerian Tha'a'sa crafted short bow held in his left hand. Additional bundles of long shafts tipped by shining razor sharp arrowheads were waiting in buckets next to his left side.

"Speak the words, Priestess Sister Queen," he urged. "The Jewels of The Sun are needed." Hopefully those things of myth were real and would be helpful. If, in fact, Sar'al had really been trained to be able to call them.

She nodded and retrieved her lance, covered with runes and winged beings curling from butt plate to just below the two feet of polished and razor sharp dark-metal point. Pausing, taking a slow calming breath, she began the chant never before used. It had been one of the few things her father had taught her during their short training time together. The soft words, the call, took wing, glittering gold and black against the deep blue sky. The call flew outward, the request of Priestess to Priestess. *Come*, said the call, *come to our aid.* It had felt rather untrained to her.

The call flew outward and outward and outward until it eventually drifted into her chamber, rousing her from her deep slumber. As she stood and yawned and stretched, she wondered why that young one had used that voice.

She strode from The Beyond, slipped through The Inbetween, and out into the Audience Hall of the Crystal Palace, a rather short female of delicate features and form, dressed in soft robes of a deep blue color.

The Crystal Palace was perched on the peak of one of the highest mountains on the Continent An'darl. It gleamed with and refracted the always bright sunlight into multicolored bands on the floors, walls and ceilings.

The ever present cloud layer of this mountain

range was held away from the palace by a great circle barrier, cast by the one who now stood here, admiring the beauty and elegance of the structure she had brought into being here on this mountain top many long ago.

In this form she could appear to be much like the population of any of the lands she might visit, except for her eyes. The slanting, large oval eyes, filled with the azure of the sky above, were the eyes of her true form.

Many thousands upon thousands of the inhabitants time cycles ago she had come to this small world just to see what the two-legged sapient species were doing. Intrigued by them, she gave them a new thing, a special capability. And watched them, every once in awhile, to see what that capability would become.

That early population had grown and spread and settled in various of the joined continental environments. There they developed separate and independent cultures as well as the physical forms and shapes of their populations. And as season followed season after season the capability would express itself, now and then, in ways unique to one of those populations.

Her gift had expressed itself most strongly in one family line, passing from parent to offspring.

Now it was time to see what a current daughter of that family line had to tell her. She had called, a very cumbersome call, but it was a call none the less. It felt as if this one had not been very well trained.

On top of the tower, The Queen spun to one side, snatching the great lance from where it had been resting, and stared. A short young woman had suddenly appeared, dressed in robes of a unfamiliar cut and design, colored a deep blue.

"Dragon eyes!"

The woman nodded at her. "A term of ancient mythology and folk belief. But not exactly correct, Sar'al Rada'doa Noriyon Zacog. For what reason have you send the call?"

Viana stepped past her Queen, glistening blades held in each hand. "What are you, creature with dragon eyes?"

Zak'ke's hand jerked to the hilt of his sword.

"Na dragon, Avelerain Tha'a'da! Behave!"

Sar'al held out one arm, cautioning, restraining both Viana and her twin. "You are one of The Jewels?" Soft grey eyes peered into the azure ones reflecting the question asked.

The woman smiled at her, and shrugged. "A much better sounding name, Fair Queen, but not exactly a correct one either! Answer my question."

"We wished for . . . aid? How do We know that you are what We sought?"

"A wise question to be asked by one so young." The woman nodded, stepped away, and clothed herself in a wide, whirling column of dense fog which quickly hid her from sight.

Sar'al stared, took two careful steps forward, and listened. It seemed to her that she could hear from deep within all that swirling fog the rasp of talons on the stone of the platform.

The fog began to collapse and spill into the interior space of the great gate structure. The trio stepped back, and back again, watching carefully, clenching their weapons in unsure hands.

Immense wings stretched and stretched, wider and wider, dark blue scales glistening in the early morning sunlight. Then the great head was slowly lowered on the end of the long neck until one large oval azure eye could look into Sar'al's face.

"Why . . . did . . . you . . . call?" asked a gentle voice. "I have come a long way."

"The Azkar threaten Our people, a thing never before seen nor written down." She pointed at the vague masses still gathering at the forest edge.

"And?"

"We would have your aid, We would."

"Most regally spoken," laughed the great thing.

Sar'al stared at her, a dark frown forming on her face. "You refuse?" Her eyes squinted at this being. When Sar'al had learned the call, she had been told that the one called could not refuse.

"What aid do you wish, glowering young Queen?"

"Kill them!" hissed Viana, dark brown eyes flashing anger, a battle ready glare, ready to attack.

"Why? Fierce warrior trained one."

"We are but three and they are many!"

With a puff of laughter the beast became a small woman dressed in robes of a unfamiliar cut and design, colored a deep blue.

She frowned at Sar'al. "Just you three? Where are your Armed Masses, Queen of The Seven Lands?" It seemed to her that this Kingdom hadn't put any thought into its own self defense.

Zak'ke laughed, a very soft laugh. "The Seven Lands have not had such a thing stretching back into the long past days of Kant'ald'dentar, self-named The Mighty. It was during his struggles with all the lands that a great peace was achieved. Or so the tales say! He assumed the title of King of The Seven Lands, warranted or not, obeyed or not. It has been passed on ever since." He nodded at Viana. "Although in some of the lands, clans often still settle disputes among themselves in a rather, ummmm ah, violent manner. But as long as they keep this between themselves no-one else expresses concern." He shrugged.

"Then you three are all that stand between that great horde out there and your people and perhaps others in the other lands as well? Ummmmm?"

"Indeed," replied Zak'ke. He grinned, a happy warrior's smile, and waggled his free hand toward the distant forest. "We do appear to be greatly outnumbered."

"BROTHER!"

Zak'ke bowed to his sister. "My Queen?"

"This is not a joking matter!"

Zak'ke shrugged. He thought that her very Royal glare ought to be cracking the stone they stood upon.

"Oh, I do agree." He shrugged again. "But facts are facts, are they not?"

Sar'al looked at the short woman and pointed toward the forest. Then she stated as firmly and Regally as she knew how. "Kill them! That is the aid We request."

"I will not."

"WHAT! You dare disobey!"

"Only in the means, not the intent, Young Queen-In-Training." A long finger aimed toward the throng gathering at the forest's edge. "The Azkar have been soul-twisted." She waved the pointing hand in a loose waggling motion. "There! They will begin returning to their camps now."

"Soul-twisted?" Soft grey eyes searched those azure ones.

"Most so. Whether you know it or not, the lands have a great enemy, Fair Queen. A great and hidden enemy. Think on this, Sar'al. You wear a circlet which proclaims you as The Queen of The Seven Lands. BUT!" She waggled a finger at Sar'al. "Perhaps this is merely a belief of those who live here in Nu'vern or of your ancestors. Have any of you Royals ever traveled and visited all the folk out there to find out whether you are their Queen in fact?"

"No," came the soft response. Sar'al's shoulders slumped. She had never had a need to do that nor had any of her parents ever suggested that would be the duty that a Queen would have here in Nu'Vern.

"Perhaps there was no reason to do this as a Queen in Nu'vern? However you who are named *The Queen of The Seven Lands* will need to help these lands overcome this menace before that threat becomes more than any single folk will be able to withstand by themselves. And you will require their help as well. The Azkar are now safe from any more tampering of that sort."

"But . . ."

"Ah, ah, ah, ah, ah, ah, ah! Being The Queen of The Seven Lands will be hard and difficult work. I will not do this for you. Your brother twin and this other warrior will help in all the ways that they are able to do. But, the Queen must make decisions for all of her folk, for the good of all of her folk." Her hand waved. "Including such as the Azkar and perhaps some of the other Hidden Ones as well."

She bowed deeply to Sar'al. "Young Queen, you are about to embark on a hard and a dangerous and a frustrating chore, the saving of all your people, whether the folk know that they are your people or not. They are still your people! You will need many, many to join you in order to succeed. You will have to convince them to join with you, to accept you as their Queen!" She grinned as Sar'al. "Think of it as a learning experience, appropriate for a new and young Queen."

And was gone.

"Oh my," sighed Sar'al. "Now what? Search for Hidden Ones?"

Zak'ke laughed, softly. "Is that a command, My Queen?"

Viana hissed at him, frowning darkly.

To Begin. To Travel.

The Heart of All.

The understood history of the town was said to have been begun by Kant'ald'dentar as the place for the King and the government to live. In his case, he felt that the King and the government meant him. His son, after taking on the mantel of government, asked the more influential members of the several towns in Nu'vern to form an advisory council. This action reduced a large amount of the grumbling and the discontent among the folk.

It was his son that agreed to help underwrite the activities proposed by Zelar Aydel, that is, to construct a wagonway to the tip of the continent where the wagonway would join the wetway. At this time there was only a narrow horse trail down one coast to where it connected to another horse trail on the wetway leading to Shar'daine.

With the financial backing of the ruler and the business interests of the several towns, Aydel was able to hire a sufficiently large enough crew of workers to push the project forward. His crew were mainly those who sought work other than in the vast agricultural fields, at least for the duration of the project. The planned wagonway started at the edge of town, crossed the Pinch, a very narrow place that almost severed the continent into two pieces, traveled down the great meadow and into The Forest of Sighs. As the southern forested section of Nu'vern had never been adequately mapped they hoped that they were truly headed toward the far distant tip of land.

Some time into their labors, with the wagonway having to take a jog here and a sharp bend there around obstacles unplanned for, they met the Azkar, much to the surprise of the construction crews and Zelar Aydel. No one had mentioned that such a population lived this deep in the forest mainly because no-one had ever traveled this deep into the forest. The coastal horse trail that Aydel wanted to replace was the only route to Shar'daine and it wandered along the very edge of the continent, mainly on the beaches at low tide.

As things sometimes happen, Aydel turned out to be very capable at diplomacy, much to his surprise as well as to that of his crew. And after some prolonged and nearly unintelligible discussions, the "fee for passage" system was agreed upon. Soon after this the wagonway builders saw the last sight of the Azkar they would ever have.

Seasons later, after Ban'da'ta Franbandan had completed his wagonway on the wetway connecting Nu'vern to Shar'daine, the then king of Nu'vern started the construction of the Guard Wall and the gate across Aydel's Track at The Pinch. This king also started the expansion of the town itself. He felt that it ought to be the seat of the kingdom as he defined it, it being, mainly, Nu'vern.

His successor reinforced the Guard Wall and build directly over the gate a watch tower high enough that anyone standing on the top platform could see to the very edge of the great meadow and the spot where Aydel's Track entered The Forest of Sighs or in the other direction, the vast agricultural fields stretching to the distant edges of the continent. It was during this time that those folk who could read became wildly enthusiastic about stories that contained dragons in them. They began to call the great tower, "The Tower of The Soaring Dragon," and the name stuck. A common banner of the time as well as the large one on the pole on top of that tower often held a creature that was often called a "dragon" as well as other fanciful names.

In the early morning light of the present time, a number of days since the strange visitor, Sar'al stood just inside the gate in deep conversation with Rau'ke and Cant'al, the last set of the twins that had been born to the First Wife, formally called The-Third-Twins-of-The-First. The three were discussing the final details of local governance and others matters needing resolution. It would fall on the backs of Rau'ke and Cant'al to begin the process of recruiting and establishing the Armed Mass for Nu'vern.

Sar'al had in the past days send Fast Riders on urgent matters requiring the beginning of accords dealing with acquiring of the necessary equipment required by an Armed Mass.

One rider was headed on the long trip to the Lands of the Honglar, those that manufactured the arms and armor for all the lands requiring such. The other rider accompanying him would stop at the first village of the Avelerian Tha'a'sa of Shar'daine and discuss the need for large quantities of short bows and arrows.

Rau'ke and Cont'al bowed very formally to Sar'al, and to Zak'ke, who stood with them, a silent observer to the discussion, and then walked swiftly into the main building, the Royal Quarters, to begin the process of all that they had been charged to complete. As they walked they discussed all the things that had to be organized, all the planning that it would require. The Kingdom had never faced such a chore before.

Sar'al, Zak'ke, and Viana now wore traveling clothes, those loose fitting common clothes of greens and browns, utilized by all the Trader-Merchant caravans as they traveled from continent to continent.

The trio's fine clothes, head gear, etc., were packed neatly in their mount's saddlebags. All the camping gear, food, and other things necessary for the journey were bundled in the neat leather bags on their pack animals.

"Are you sure you really want to do this?" Zak'ke looked at his twin.

Sar'al nodded and each of them saddled up and led their spare horse and a string of pack animals through the now open gate and down Aydel's Track toward the cool environment of The Forest of Sighs, so named for the sound that the deciduous leaves made in the more or less constant breeze that blew across this part of Nu'Vern. From here to the first village on Shar'daine was a considerable distance, a journey of many days.

The Silent Woods.

The two Fast Riders had ridden hard, as they had been instructed to do, changing horses frequently, each had two spare mounts as well as pack animals, and were now resting themselves and their animals near the village called Grey Thicket deep in The Silent Woods on Shar'daine. It was the home of Clan Zalanal of The Avelerain Tha'a'sa.

After two days rest, one Fast Rider had headed north on the long ride to The Lands of the Honglar in An'darl.

The other now sat in the large grassy circle, The Discussion Circle, with members of the four clans and handed his documents to the most Elder of the women, sitting on his right side. She carefully read them, pursed her lips, and passed them to her right.

Slowly, ever so slowly, as it seemed to the rider, the documents were passed from hand to hand, carefully read and handed on. Finally the documents were handed back to him, stained and crumpled, but still quite legible.

The Elder stood and held one of her hands over his head. "Uh huh, uh huh, uh huh. In two suns we will meet on this spot and talk." Silently the circle dispersed, members walking into the woods on various of the paths and disappearing from sight. As The Elder strolled toward her dwelling she wondered what Sar'al was up to.

The two huts for the riders had been quickly constructed on this spot when the pair had arrived. He stood, stretched, and nodded to himself. He would get two more days of rest and relaxation. It would be good for man and beasts. All had plenty to eat and to drink.

The Forest of Sighs.

They settled around the third camping spot, a wide grass covered section next to the wagonway munching on their dinner, dried foods from various of their supply bags.

Sar'al sat, crossed-legged as she chewed on something, consulting a thick volume in her lap. She had taken it from one of her saddle bags.

Zak'ke looked up from his rummaging around in the dried fruit bag. "A little light reading?"

She shook her head and swallowed. "Not at all. This is the most recent edition of *The Travelers Guide to the World*, issued by the TMA."

"By what? A guide?"

She nodded and unfolded one of the many maps bound into the book. "The TMA. The Trader-Merchant Affiliation. This book contains maps and descriptions of every wagonway, wetway, secondary and tertiary trails, seen by traveling Trader-Merchant caravans on the continents. The book is updated every so often as those who keep it up to date feel that it is necessary. Every Trader-Merchant outfit sends in changes and additions and corrections as they see things on their travels."

He sat up and tied the top of the dried fruit sack closed, a long brown stick of something stuffed in a corner of his mouth, and smiled as much as he could while he chewed on one end of the object. She always seemed to be reading something.

"It was in the library," explained Sar'al. "We, ummm, borrowed it."

He yanked the stick from his mouth and laughed. "Sounds usual."

She straightened up and frowned a Royal sister frown at him. "We are The Queen, We are. It was in the *Royal Library!*"

He ducked his head.

Viana suddenly straightened up and held a cautionary hand loosely over her mouth, and whispered, "We are being watched."

Zak'ke stood, stretched, and strolled nonchalantly over to his still saddled horse and stuffed the dried fruit sack into one of his saddle bags. They hadn't started unloading and making camp yet, just taking a bit of relaxation before doing that. He took his sword belt from the saddle horn and walked back, lazily swinging it in one hand. Plopping to the ground, he leaned sideways and murmured to Viana, "Where?"

Her eyes flicked in the direction of whatever it was, toward the edge of the shadow dappled forest just at the edge of the wagonway in the direction that they had planned on going.

Sar'al marked her place in the book with her finger and said very loudly, "THESE CAMPING PLACES ARE CONSIDERED SAFE SPOTS!" She folded the map, set the book to one side, and set one hand on the lance lying by her side.

Viana stood and wandered over to check one of her pack horses. When she returned, the hilts of her blades rose above each shoulder, the two hilts angled outward. Neither Zak'ke nor Sar'al had seen her put her weapons on.

"So, now we wait," said Zak'ke, in a low tone of voice. He smiled and watched that spot from the corners of his eyes, the direction indicated by the stick that had been slowly pushed into place by Viana's foot as she sat near.

Finally, ever so slowly, ever so carefully, ever so silently, their visitor slipped from the nearby shadowed patched trees and became obvious. His garb was a confusing pattern of greens and browns that faded him into the surrounding vegetation. He was quite wide.

Sar'al slowly eased herself to her feet and bowed. "Warm greetings, dweller of the forest."

The other stopped advancing and bowed awkwardly. Then he walked closer with soft and silent steps, leaving not a mark on the ground as he approached. Nodding his head to Sar'al he worked his mouth, apparently struggling to speak their language.

"Qyreem," he rasped. He pointed down the way

they would be heading from this camp spot, and wobbled his head. "No not, urmmmm, tree . . . val more. Ba'da!" He held one hand as high above his head as he could reach. "Ba'da! Lur . . geh ba'da!"

Zak'ke stared at him. "You are Azkar?"

The man waggled the thick cudgel he held in one hand, the end studded with great nobs of dark wood.

"Yeeee . . . sssss."

Sar'al looked at the others. "The guide book has a long word list in it. Ba'da means a great danger, ummmmm, of an unnatural sort."

"Yeeeee . . . sssss. Ba'da!" One arm pointed at the forest, away from the wagonway. He tapped his chest and stepped that way, turned, and nodded at them. And gestured violently.

"Amat! Amat! Amat!"

"Hurry, hurry, hurry," stated Sar'al. She did, and soon had her animal string ready, her horse's lead firmly held in one hand. She started after their guide.

In moments, a long line followed him deep into the forest, headed west.

The Azkar led them at a walking pace, not too fast, not too slow, just a pace that they could maintain through the rest of the day, that night, and a part of the next day, as they slipped through the trees, the lighter green of the deciduous trees intermingled with the darker pines.

All were not exactly stumbling as they entered an area, surprising to them, expected by their guide.

Great grey-brown boulders stood in clusters in

and around the growth of tree and bush. The boulders were twice as tall as they were and equally as wide. When their eyes became accustomed to what they saw, they could pick out four low structures constructed from the same but smaller rocks that lay in all directions, in and around the site.

This place, explained their guide, hissing, snarling, growling, coughing his way through the trio's language, was the place where they would rest. At next light they would continue on.

Prime Shield.

Ran'dyal, Secretary-Treasurer of The Trader-Merchant outfit whose main offices were located here in the town that was the organizational center of The Honglar of An'darl, looked up from the last invoice and the appropriate ledger entry he had just made and then out the window of his small office. He could see that yet another long tedious day was ending.

Outside the shadows were lengthening as various members of the staff were wandering toward the main gate and their homes.

He filed the invoice in the correct folder, slid the brown leather bound ledger into its slot on the nearby shelf, arranged various items on his desk top back into their proper order, stood, and walked down the short hall to the outside door.

He strolled through the twilight coolness toward the small food establishment that he preferred, The cost was moderate but the quality was high and the service quiet and discrete, all aspects of dining that he preferred.

As he stepped inside the rather nicely furnished main room, pale brown wood paneling on the walls, slightly darker wood for the floor, he was greeted warmly by the owner and led to a corner table, the quiet corner table that he preferred.

After he was seated and the table was set, he and the owner discussed various of the selections for the day and had come to an agreement.

Now, Ran'dyal sat relaxed, taking a sip, now and then, from the beverage that he always ordered.

He sighed, not very loudly, and thought, not for the first time, about his position and the probable direction his employment would take him in the Trader-Merchant world. It was not what he thought that it ought to be, or what, he truly believed, was what he deserved. But so far he hadn't found a way to do something about that.

So, as he sipped and pondered once again the injustice of his position and his life and wrestled with how he might affect a positive change in that situation, a tall man walked over and sat, uninvited, at his table.

Ran'dyal frowned darkly at him. This was an inappropriate and most unmannerly thing to do, especially to one of his current status and position, high enough, but not high enough.

But, before he could call over the owner, the stranger slid a thick stack of the local currency across the table toward him, and smiled, a dark smile.

"I wish," he said softly, "to make you a, uh eh, business proposition, Ran'dyal. This proposition, I believe, will address all your personal concerns."

Then he explained.

Ran'dyal would never see him again.

Three Drinks Green.

Den'tza the Gross stood in the central spot, clear and smooth in the brown and red sand and rock, and banged his shark-toothed weapon against his shield. He stood a head taller that anyone else in his troop. Everyone in these lands was tall, he was just a bit taller. He banged his shield again, and looked at his troop, The Troop of The Fierce Countenance, just to insure their attention.

Inadat the Dower looked up to see what Den'tza wanted, now. Inadat had just finished filling the last of the water skins from the largest of the three pools of clear water around which their dwellings were built. The pools produced a patch of green growth in a sea of brown and red desert.

All around in that green wandered the White Wirt-Whitel Soar-Wings, nibbling at the grass, keeping it well mown and removing whatever might be crawling around in it.

Only on very rare occasions did any of the troops take one of them for eating and feather harvest.

All on Farza knew that these fliers migrated to Farza and then back to wherever they spent the bad weather portion of a season.

The troop appreciated the utility of the fliers as they kept the growth mown close all around the troop's pools and dwellings. They believed that if they took too many of them that they would not return. The troop members felt that catching one of the fliers for any purpose had to be an activity that occurred less frequently than once a season.

The children and the glar-dogs learned at very early ages to leave these fliers alone.

This troop, as did all the troops of Farza, had a tendency of naming that was mostly fanciful rather than accurate. This may have been a result of living in what would seem to outsiders to be a stark desert, the desert of their homeland. No-one really thought about that, either stark desert, or, naming conventions. What one was named was just the way things had always been done.

Den'tza was all muscle and no fat, as typified a troop leader. The troop, men, women, children, glar-dogs, were, for the most part, contented and happy. Fierce countenances were rarely seen other than in the sdnabal-brawls with other troops, an infrequent occurrence, often over wife bartering. Of course, no-one in the troop could recall ever seeing a smile on Inadat's face.

Den'tza thumped his shield again and selected those he would taking on the meat-hunt into the dense jungle forest of N'Farza. While they were gone the rest would visit the shellfish grounds and tidal pools, now becoming visible as the extra low tide slowly went out, and gather quantities of the tasty morsels found there to be added to their stored food supply. Inadat nodded, a very tiny nod. It was about time.

The selected ones began to run behind Den'tza as he headed out and onto the long sand spit beginning to appear as the tide allowed. The hunters could run for hours and great distances. From a young age everyone ran, regardless of the distance.

Now the distance was great, very great. The land they were headed for was a vaguely seen grey green shadow hidden in the fog mists there were perpetual around N'Farza.

Inadat ran at the rear of the line, carrying the gift box, and watching for sea-raiders. He always did this.

The gift box, woven from the blue sea grass, contained highly polished shell ornaments made from those shells that had been gathered from selected stretches of beach. These were highly prized by those whose lands they were hoping to get permission to meat-hunt in.

The sea-raiders were long bodied beasts with large mouths filled with rows of teeth. All the troops of Farza had lost members to these feared creatures, most frequently members gathering food during the low tide. But it was wise, and sometimes helpful, to have someone watching for them.

A meat-hunt on N'Farza was an all too infrequent occurrence, one that could only be undertaken during a very low tide. Only when this occurred could a party expect to cross the long expanse of exposed sand in both directions successfully.

So they ran.

South.

The hunt had to be quick as there was little time before the group would have to head back, on the long run back, a race against the tide that would soon cover the only link between Farza and N'Farza.

If their gift box was looked upon favorably by those they traded with, they might receive meat already prepared for transportation, which they could sling from the long poles they carried with them.

Such a quick exchange was desired. Troops had lost members, in the past, sometimes most of the selected ones had disappeared, from dallying too long on N'Farza. The rising tide would swallow the wetway and the laggards alike.

So, they ran.

South.

The Cave of The Dark Fates.

Dark Shadow walked.

He walked from the cave mouth and blinked in the bright light of early morning.

The cave was located at the very headwaters of the great river An'unl'dur that coursed from the high northern country across Mart'den to the southern delta.

A soft tremor had shaken away the debris and talus that enclosed the cave's mouth. And he had awakened, not from sleep, but from dormancy. The tremor wasn't felt in the downslope village, it was that soft.

Long seasons past, before the folk had developed writing, a male had stumbled to this cave, The Gift glowing around him, and he had created Dark Shadow and was gone. The cave mouth was suddenly covered by debris and talus that hid his creation.

Now the awakening event had occurred.

Dark Shadow started on his long walk south from this most distant northern edge of Clan Nu'Anji, Tha'a'da, territory.

He was dressed in armor over which a long robe was pulled. The hood covered his head. A large shield was slung on his back, over the robe, a great sword hung from his belt, hidden by the robe. Everything was black. So was he, almost. Dark hair, dark eyes, dark skin. All brown, dark, dark brown.

He walked down the trail. He strolled down the trail. He strode with the fluid grace of a trained warrior, of a beast of prey.

The Gift guided him. Toward his goal. It was a long way away, was that goal.

But neither distance nor time was a concern, only the act of getting there.

A young woman gathering basketry material looked up the trail and saw him. She bolted downhill toward the village.

She quickly told The Elder what she had seen, this thing of their most ancient myth come to life. Word quickly spread through the village and all closed their doors. Runners raced down the trail to spread the word.

IT comes!

HE comes!

The Tranatal of earliest myth, "Walking Death!"
Great danger was approaching the villages.

The Elders would have to gather and decide what this portent signified and what the Tha'a'da should do. This was a new thing, never before faced.

The Wild Fields.

Cloud Spirit, archer/scout-guide, sat patiently and quietly in the very organized work room of Palata, Master Craftsman, as a new bow string was fastened to his great long bow, and tested for strength and the proper length. The need for a new bow string had been one of the causes of the many uncomplimentary comments said about Cloud Spirit by the Master Craftsman as she had made slight repairs to Cloud Spirit's great long bow. Cloud Spirit had just returned from a go-about of a short season.

He was the most senior of the archer/scout-guides and had returned to rest and to have his most prized possession looked after, his great long bow.

Cloud Spirit, as did every child in The Wild Fields of Shar'daine, had begun practicing with the bow at an age when children could hardly bend the bow sized to fit them.

As the children grew, in strength, stature, and ability, they were carefully observed at the annual competitions.

A few of them became Craftsmen, even fewer

Master Craftsmen, the terms applied to males and females alike. A select skilled few in their early adulthood were asked to join the ranks of the archer/scout-guides, still a minority among the scout-guides. This was so even though for many sessions past the scout-guide numbers had been in a steady decline. Long before the development of the wagonways and most of the horse trails, the scout-guides had been those who led parties from place to place, across the continents. Now the scout-guides mostly occupied themselves with creating ever more accurate maps for their usage.

If they chose to do so, join the archer/scout-guides, male and female, a great long bow was made to fit them, constructed to match each individual's stature and capabilities. Each great long bow, unstrung, was a head taller than the one for whom it had been built. Those few chosen to join the ranks worked as apprentices in the Master Craftsmen's shop while the bow was constructed and finished as well as the first quiver of arrows.

Then in a great public ceremony all the new archer/scout-guides were "married" to their newly created weapons. The men always spoke of their bows as "her" or "she." The women spoke of "he" or "him."

Of course, archer/scout-guides did take spouses as well.

He watched Palata stand from behind her large work table, then step close to him to nod and smile, an ever so gentle smile.

"She is back to her true beauty, Cloud," Palata said as she placed the great long bow in his outstretched hands.

Cloud bowed his head. "Great benefit to you and your's."

Palata sat on the bench beside him. "One hears unusual tales from some of those who return, one does." She handed him a spare bow string. And wondered at his bother.

Cloud Spirit nodded. Since he had returned, he had been talking to each archer/scout-guide as they visited The Small Gathering Hall before traveling on to their homes in one of the Stoneholds, each Stonehold built on top of one of The Eight Hills.

Cloud nodded and looked at her. "I have told each to remain and to prepare. Many will do so. Such tales sound to me that each Stonehold must ready itself. As each crop is harvested, the great storage structures within are to be filled with all that keeps for two seasons. All trades are now to sleep inside the high walls in their Stonehold homes. All towers to be double staffed, all eyes to watch the far distance."

Prime Shield.

In the fading light of day, the apparition staggered through the main gate of the most southern town of the Honglar and into the open space of large white paving stones that was surrounded by grand structures constructed in varying shades of stone. The gate staff stared open mouthed at it and wondered how any of the folk could get into that condition. The battered figure, a male clothed in shreds, clenched a sword in one hand and held the remnants of a shattered shield in the other. He lurched to one side, stumbled into the great door of Origin Hall, managed to open it just wide enough, and disappeared inside, forcing himself to complete his assignment.

He was observed.

He was observed by those whose wish for power and status served The Dark Wind, an organization unknown, at the moment, by those of all the lands. That one, it was noted, was one step from death.

But, The Great One had spoken. Soon they would take and have the control throughout the lands. Now, they waited and watched, appearing to be the same as all those they lived among.

Prime Shield was the first town built by the Honglar, the center of knowledge and governance of all their trade. It was located not far from the long ago abandoned grey stone quarries.

Inside the short hall, the figure staggered along, canted heavily to one side, his sword tip dragging a narrow gouge in the highly polished wood floor as he lurched his painful way toward the light ahead. In the central space, he crashed to his knees, and toppled onto his side, shield remnants clattering across the floor.

Night Staff rushed up. One tried to remove the sword, but this male's grip was stronger than the staff member's.

The Senior Night Staff pointed at one of those

gathering around and barked, "Quickly, to The Place of The Others. There is a healer there. Fetch! Hurry! Hurry!"

That one rushed away while another of the Night Staff rushed up, basin and towels in hand, and began to wipe the grime from the face of whoever this was. She thought that it was probably a waste of time.

As the Night Staff continued to argue about what else they ought to do, the great outer door swung wide and they walked in, their footsteps silent as moonbeams.

The Senior Staff jumped to his feet as the others stared and slowly stood.

The two females strode toward the body on the floor, ignoring all else, trailed by the one sent to fetch them.

Their garb, a strange cloth of silver and white, seemed to radiate a soft sheen, a cloud of light around them, obscuring details. But it appeared that they wore loose jackets and billowing trousers. The pair's skin tones and hair were a dense grey almost black, made all the more dramatic by the contrast between that and their costume. The pair stopped and peered at the mess on the floor.

Then one looked at The Senior Staff, who blinked and began to sweat. Red eyes bored into his pale brown ones. Lips are red as her eyes twitched at one corner of her mouth.

"This one is Soft Touch, a One Who Saves." Her hand casually indicated the other. "This one is Final

Touch, a One Who Does Not." Her voice was a soft and deep velvet, deeper than most of the Honglar, softer than any.

She dropped to her knees and placed her hands on either side of the figure's head. "A spark, a trace, a life there is!"

The staff stared and watched carefully to see what she would do. She didn't seem to do anything. Nothing that they could see.

The man shuddered, sucked in a great breath, his eyes popped open, he looked up and blinked hard to focus his eyes.

"A forever debt," he rasped as he squinted. Then his eyes fluttered and closed.

She stood, stepped back, and pointed at the figure lying so still.

"This one, a pale skin of Nu'vern, requires long rest and vast quantities of nourishment."

She turned to go. The Senior Staff stepped toward her, one hand out to grab her arm. "Where do you come from?"

Her companion stepped between them, a short silver and gold scepter held in her right hand, unnoticed until now. It had a soft yellow glow.

"Do not tempt death," whispered the soft, deep voice.

The Senior Night Staff leaped backward, crashing into another staff, knocking her off her feet.

"The Heart of Darkness," came the deep soft sigh reply to his question from the other.

Final Touch spun and walked with her companion down the hall and back to their quarters in The Place of The Others, a large sprawling structure, one built in each of the large towns. The Honglar made all non-Honglar stay there when visiting any settlement above a certain size.

The Temple of The Dark Fates.

Now there were only the remains.

Buried for the most past by the dark soil and the rank vegetation.

Here, in this small, mostly unknown and rarely visited, box canyon were the remains. Walls, roof, supporting and decorative columns, statuary, all tumbled and broken, mostly no longer visible. Over here, a stone hand reached for the sky, over there a large section of a white marble column resting at an odd angle on a large boulder.

The temple was gone. Mostly.

A single alcove, the single remaining, untouched, in a manner of speaking, alcove, carved into the mountain flank, remained. The roof was long gone. The alcove was now only a curve cut into the mountain side containing a pedestal, and the statue of a woman standing on top of it. Everything else, all of the temple, was tumbled and broken.

As the early morning shaft of sun crept across the small canyon floor, it reached over and touched the pedestal and then the statue.

The statue shrugged.

A tinkling, chiming cascade of tiny shards rained down and pooled on the ground around the base of the pedestal.

She stood there and looked around, blinking in the bright sunlight.

She was dressed in flowing robes that moved around her as she stepped to the ground, moved around her as if they had a life of their own. The robes were heavily decorated, black design on black material.

She held a long, black staff in one hand. The toes of black boots poked from beneath the hem of her robes.

She peered from the hood of her robe at the remains of the temple from dark brown eyes framed by dark brown hair, cascading around and framing the skin of her dark brown face.

She flowed, predator smooth, across the ground, her stride that of a warrior.

With a casual wave of her hand, all the tangled dense brush, blocking and obscuring the tight crevice that allowed exit from this place, crumbled into dust. She stepped through the crack and started down the narrow, twisting canyon, here in the northeast corner of An'darl, just north and over a few mountain ranges from Honglar'a'at, the Land of The Unique Warriors.

She and the temple had been created long seasons past, long before the folk developed writing, by a woman who had glowed with ability.

Now she, Clear Shadow, strode toward her goal, the far distant goal.

It was why she had been woken from her long

dreamless existence.
       Striding south.

Siblings

The Great Blue.

The upwelling was slow but steady. It was greater than any other on Farza. The water seeped into the surrounding sands until it became nothing but vapor. But before this happened a wide band of green drank deeply and flourished here in the very center of the vast desert.

This place was the home of The Troop of Many Fingers and the One Who Spoke For all, Vachannal The Insignificant. Here would all gather, all those who spoke for their separate troops, to meet and discuss matters of concern for every desert dweller. It was a large scatter of low structures around the wide, clear pool of water.

In the not too long ago, stood Vachannal on The Stone For Those Who Spoke. He had thought long and hard about this stranger and her gentle nature, a strong contrast to the way his folk saw things. He looked at all those gathered and told them about The Stranger Who Burned, the young woman, the slender young woman with the pale grey eyes from the green lands, whose fair skin was never altered by the blazing sun. This one was now to be considered as Bar'Farza!

Troop leaders, including the troop leader of this place, Kranz the Limber, jumped to their feet and stared at Vachannal and then at this person who stood so still to one side of the gathering spot. She wore flowing robes made from the cloth woven of the fibers of the Yellow Sea Grass, a grass whose stems stood taller than the tallest of the Farza. The females of The Troop of Many Fingers were the only ones allowed to weave cloth from these strong and smooth fibers, smooth as the skin of a newborn child. This person, with the fair and pale skin, grey eyes, and the light yellow hair from the green lands, was now Bar'Farza, the one who must be welcomed everywhere she chose to walk. The symbols that circled the cuffs on the wide sleeves and the hem of her robe proclaimed to one and all that this was so. She was now a member of no troop but a member of all the troops. The same as Vachannal.

Word had been spreading from troop to troop of this young female from the green lands who walked untouched by the desert. Now the Troop Leaders looked at that one and wondered what she was exactly.

Then, in a great explosion of noise, they crashed their weapons against their shields, and shouted as one "BAR'FARZA!"

She smiled into the tumult and wondered what The-First-Daughter-Twin-of-the First would think about this.

Clerian'tra, First-Daughter-of-the Second, had been on an aimless wander of discovery, the thing she had been set upon right after The Gift had spoken to her during her fourteenth season. She had rambled into The Plains of Singing Grass and had met and camped with Soft Rain, an archer/scout-guide. Soft Rain had explained to her their cultural concept, that of the go-about.

Clerian'tra had thought that it sounded like a fine thing to do, to go-about.

Two days later they had parted company, the one striding toward the setting sun, the other leading her string of animals toward the far horizon, north toward An'darl.

She had strolled along the wagonway and followed it through the Honglar town of Prime Shield and then west into Iron Hammer, the town that was the gateway to Farza.

There she had talked with various of the folk, Honglar and others, about the desert lands beyond the gate and the wetway and those who dwelled there.

As she strolled here and there she could feel eyes watching her, unkind eyes. But try as she might, she could not pick out who those folk were, the ones with such dark thoughts.

After some time, curious about what she had been told about Farza, she sold her animals, bought a large backpack, stuffed it with foods that keep, and headed across the wetway to see a very different place. A land of folk with brown skins, brown eyes, brown hair, and a zeal for battle.

Two Swords.

The trio wandered here and there through the vast marketplace of this northwest town of The Honglar, the gateway guarding the wetway to the north, to Mart'den, the northernmost of the continents, as odors of cooking food and just harvested fresh vegetables billowed around them, beckoned to them.

The market place was bordered on one side by the broad wagonway that led to the north or to the south from here.

Their mother, the Second Queen, had sent her triplets here to study at a small house of Adepts who had been given permission by the Honglar to have such a dwelling outside The Place Of The Others in this town. Being sent here had happened right after The Gift had spoken to them during their fourteenth season. Their mother had recognized what it was and knew where they should go.

The two girls looked identical to each other but not like their brother. Most times they were seen as twin sisters and a brother. He had been born before his sisters by a short moment of time. As the three newborn had settled in their mother's arms, she had pronounced them triplets, and so it was. Their training had bound them even tighter to each other, tighter than just being triplets would have done.

The three of them, as close as triplets could be, didn't care one way or the other about whether they were triplets or not.

Caevelos gently poked her sister in the ribs with a careful elbow, pointed at the purple yellow fruit cluster hanging in one of the booths, and smiled. She felt hungry.

"Let's," she suggested.

Cer'alda tapped her brother, the brother with the long name, a joke shared only by the three, on the elbow. "Verd?" she asked, jerking his attention to what his other sister wanted.

Verdorios-elvershair, usually called "Verd" by his sisters, nodded. "We could," he said. If either one had used "Shair" he knew that he was in trouble.

Cer'alda purchased the fruit cluster and walked between them so they could easily reach over and pluck their choice loose and pop it into their mouths.

So they wandered, three folk dressed in dark green with light green cuffs on sleeves and trousers, among the varied colors of costumes of the folk gathered here.

They were enjoying a rare "free day," free from their studies. Otherwise, they were involved every day, and often at night, learning the rare and difficult skill of merging their mental abilities into a focused whole for "special" purposes. Many of those purposes were rather destructive in intent and effect.

They had agreed, among themselves, that this was the most difficult thing that they had ever tried to learn. But they had been determined to succeed regardless of how long it would take them to master this skill.

But today, on this "free day," they were going to celebrate and enjoy their twenty-first season day. They had been hard at work for seven seasons. In fact, they had become very accomplished at their collective skill.

"We are being spied upon," said Cer'alda. She was glaring around the marketplace. Some folk or things needed correction in their behavior.

"Eh?" asked Verd, watching her face carefully.

"By what or who?" Caevelos carefully peered around as they continued walking along.

"Unknown," answered Cer'alda. "But it is true." She waggled one hand, the other still held some of the fruit. "They are very careful, very good at not being seen. But it is true! I can feel them, those not very nice thoughts."

Verd nodded and glanced at her. From her expression it was just as well that she couldn't identify them. It would not do to have gore and bloody body parts flying about the market place.

He and Caevelos smiled. They knew that their sister had developed such an ability, something that had only developed in her during their very long training.

Each of them had developed abilities unique to themselves. It was handy and it added to their whole.

The Runes of Huroma.

She stood on the highest balcony of the great spire and gazed out at the rolling plains stretching to the far eastern horizon etched as a dark black line by The Dismal Sea, the broad water separating Shar'daine from Nu'Vern. And as she looked outward she looked inward and thought about the history of the Royalty of Nu'vern and of the Ten Royal Houses as recorded and understood by The Adherents of Huroma. She had been puzzling as to the why of her many siblings, a unique event for a unique generation. In all their history it was a never before event.

The third king after Kant'ald'dentar, who self styled himself The Mighty, had taken two wives who had given him five children of whom only one survived into adulthood, a daughter. In that very long ago time, life had been hard and the healing arts primitive. The daughter, at a young age outlived her parents, married a cousin, had a son, and had secured the royal line.

Subsequent kings, several in the long line, had taken two wives, but had greater success in producing offspring that survived into adulthood. This was primarily due to a greater and more varied diet as well as an improvement in the healing arts.

From the offspring of the various Kings had come the development of The Ten Houses of Nu'vern Royalty.

Four kings back from her father, The Gift expressed itself in King Dentar-shair The Studious. In his fourteenth season his hair changed color from the light brown of his previous seasons to black with startling bright white streaks.

Each of the successive kings had the same thing happen to them during their fourteenth season.

Her grandfather, Har'ta The Studious II, realized that in only three of the other Ten Houses were offspring showing signs of The Gift. These three Houses had been affecting things for seasons.

It was her father, Zerta'ald'ver The Observant, that took the step that seemed obvious to him. His action produced her generation and the full flowering of The Gift in House Noriyon Zacog.

Zerta'ald'ver married the First Daughter of each of the other three gifted houses and produced a great number of children with them. And it was he who set the firm, unbreakable policy/edict that when The Gift was expressed during their fourteenth season that his offspring must travel outward, away from Nu'vern, to develop and to survive, hopefully, the expression of what they had received.

When his first wife birthed the three sets of twins, he watched the first pair carefully. When they had but a few seasons, he set out with those first twins on a long journey from which only the king returned. Little known prophecy had driven him to do so. It was the only exception to his rule.

And for nine seasons all the other offspring wondered whether their father had killed those twins for unexplained political reasons.

Now Verin'yashi, First-Daughter-of-The-Third, two seasons younger than Sar'al and Zak'ke, wondered what life would bring to that pair. After all, the history of the Royals of the ruling line had been one of great struggle and, often, short life spans.

Staring down at the small cluster of dwellings below she wondered whether that pair would visit. She smiled. Few from anywhere ever did. Few ever came to this small village and ancient temple. No wagonway terminated at their gate, only a slightly utilized horse trail. But it would be good if the First-Twins-of-The First did come here.

She laughed. The lack of visitors was all due to a shift in the wide spread folk beliefs and twisted mythology. Many long ago the place name here had changed, not because here desired it to be so, but because as the stories were orally passed from the teller of tale to the teller of tale, from the believer in mythology to the believer in mythology, a slight change in a single word happened.

Now, here was called by those outside, "The Ruins of Huroma."

The Plains of Singing Grass.

Wind Sky, archer/scout-guide, stood on the slight rise, a somewhat short and compact female, and listened to the grass sing a soft evening hum song as the day breeze began to fade away with the light. It was a pleasant time of the day.

Like all scout-guides and archer/scout-guides, she was accustomed to solo travel anywhere in The Seven Lands but she favored the great plains over all other environments.

She tramped down the patch of orange Carla Grass to make a soft cushion to sleep upon. The garments that she wore would provide all the shelter that she would require. It was standard archer/scout-guide gear, jacket and trousers of many pockets and multiple adjustments, all of a soft brown sturdy material.

Finished with her sleeping mat, she knelt to gather the multihead kernels from the beaten grass. They would make a fine First Meal at dawn. She stood, tied the small sack closed and stuffed it into her carry pack.

Then after carefully wiping her hands on the flattened grass, she lifted the great bow in the palms of her outstretched hands and sang to him one of the night chants. She thought that he enjoyed it.

Setting him carefully on her carry pack, Wind Sky slowly turned for one last scan of her surroundings, a final check, and gasped. In the far distance, inside the tall yellow Martha Grass, way over there, just within bow shot, something glowed with the orange color of flame. The greatest terror on The Plains of Singing Grass was a fire on the loose. She watched it carefully. It did not flicker. It did not grow larger. It did not make smoke.

As she watched she saw, far to one side, a cluster of Nuapar slipping through the tall grass.

The grazers wandered in small clusters of one or two males and three to six females. While the cluster grazed one of the males, if there were two, watched for the one that preyed upon them, The Grass Larpa.

The clans of the Tha'a'sa took a very few of them, now and then, mainly when their supply of leather for boot making was running low. The leather of the Nuapar, after proper treatment, made extremely comfortable, and extremely wear resistant boots.

These grazers, the size of small horses, were hairless. Their hides were pebbly in texture and adjusted their coloring to match the grasses they were standing in. When they were standing still they were very hard to see.

As The Grass Larpa were sight-hunters, a nervous Nuapar that decided to run would shortly become a meal.

Wind Sky smiled at the sight, and then, finally, satisfied that whatever was producing the glow was not some form of combustion, lay down, curled around her carry pack, and fell asleep, one hand lightly resting on him.

She woke, as a faint trace of light and the cool breeze announced the start of day, stood, stretched, and scanned her surroundings. That soft orange glow was still there, no larger, no smaller, in the same spot it had been when she went to sleep.

Stretching her arms before herself, the great long bow held in her upturned palms, Wind Sky sang him a dawn chant. Setting him on her carry pack, she pulled the small sack free, opened it, and ate First Meal, the multihead kernels that she had gathered.

After she finished wiping her hands on the flattened grass, she stuffed the small sack back into her carry pack, and saw that the sun was peering over the far horizon bringing the first faint warmth of the new day. Noting the slight environmental clues she needed, Wind Sky started toward the whatever, or who ever, it was, carry pack and quiver in place, great bow held in her left hand.

Standing on the next slight rise, she pulled his head down and fastened the bow string, took a arrow from her quiver, and strode toward her target. Wind Sky held him in her left hand, arrow nocked. In less than the blink of an eye something could be dead, perhaps two somethings.

To one side she could see the slight straight ripple in the tall grass that indicated the slow, stealthy approach of a hunting Grass Larpa. It had also been attracted to that spot.

Wind Sky increased her pace, watching both. Someone was in trouble, whether they realized it or not.

Nar'a'las stood in the small spot she had cleared, the Cherila Tree wood staff held in her right hand. It had the appearance of any other hiking staff, dark metal tip on the bottom, three short ribbons tied at the top: green, blue, purple. She had carried this staff for many seasons of training, the wood highly polished in those spots where her hand usually held it.

She was aware of those who approached and felt the concern of the one and the hunger of the other.

She waited. It was interesting, the concern of that one.

Soon, the great beast eased into the cleared spot that she had made in the tall grass, eyes fastened on its prey, paused, and prepared itself to attack. The Grass Larpa could easily outrun a horse.

They moved through the grass on short, muscular legs. The feet were wide with long fingers ending in short, dark claws. The Larpa's body was long and wide with a head that was also wide and anchored by the thick neck. The face was flat with prominent brow ridges. Its upper canines protruded over the lower jaw which could hinge back allowing those canines to sink deep into its prey. The canines and fore-paws held their victim while the long body curved forward to bring the rear legs into a tearing, shredding position. Most captives died within moments after being attacked.

She watched it.

The arrow ripped through the beast, dropping it where it stood, to twitch once and lie still.

Wind Sky hurtled into the cleared space, great

long bow held in her left hand, ignoring the dead Grass Larpa, to stare at this female.

Wind Sky frowned at this tall, slim young woman dressed in loose fitting garments of a faint purple color. "You almost died!"

Nar'a'las frowned back at this short, rather compact person wearing a jacket and trousers of a light brown color festooned with pockets, snaps, and straps. "No. I did not."

Wind Sky glared at her then stepped around the cleared space, staring at the ground, poking here and there at it with the toe of a boot. It didn't look like a burn or smell like one to her.

"Who are you?" both asked the other.

Nar'a'las laughed. Wind Sky glowered at her.

Wind Sky stepped over and slowly worked the arrow from the ground where it had buried its tip after shattering the Grass Larpa's chest. After carefully inspecting the shaft and the tip, she reached back over her shoulder and placed it in her quiver. She pointed at the clearing.

"I saw your, eh, light. What did you do?"

"Made myself comfortable. There is no danger to me in these grass lands."

"Wind Sky, archer/scout-guide." She frowned, then stated, "Traveling through The Plains of Singing Grass with only a stick is a not wise thing to do!"

"Nar'a'las." She smiled and the bare soil glowed soft yellow, a soft yellow that radiated warmth.

In a single leap, Wind Sky stood just inside the tall grass. The great bow was pulled back to its maximum, arrow pointed at this person. Wind Sky was as still as a statue.

"Fear me not, archer/scout-guide Wind Sky. It is a harmless thing." The yellow glow, the warmth was gone.

"Explain!"

Nar'a'las sat and set the staff across her lap. Then patted the bare soil with one hand. "Join me? There is no harm here. From me." She smiled at Wind Sky. "Ahhhhh, I used my, emmm, stick."

Wind Sky gave a quick nod and eased her pull. "We are nervous." She stepped carefully over and stood facing her, the bow and arrow still held in a ready position

"We?" Nar'a'las knew there was no-one else near.

Wind Sky nodded, sat, and set her bow and held arrow across her lap. "Him." She tapped one finger.

"Your bow?"

Wind Sky nodded.

"Tell me of the archer/scout-guide. This is new to me. Then, I will tell you of . . . Nar'a'las."

Adna'arl.

He woke.

His eyes popped open and stared up into clear blue sky. He had no idea of where he was.

Sitting up, he looked at his surroundings. He was sitting next to a number of wooden structures, all weatherbeaten to the same uniform grey color. Most of them were little more than piles of wood, whole and broken. From the look of the rubble, he knew that he had no idea of where he might be.

He stood and walked over for a closer look.

It appeared to have been a small place, perhaps twelve structures, or so, only one of which appeared marginally inhabitable. That one had a severe lean to one side.

This settlement (?) was set back from the edge of the wide bench of short grass upon which he and the shambles stood. Looking back and forth it appeared that this bench was well above the highest tide and was faced with a very wide and gently sloping beach of pale yellow sand.

In the distance, away from the beach and sea, he could see near vertical cliffs and the rugged faces of the peaks whose upper edges were shrouded in clouds.

Well, where ever he was, it was a strange place.

Then he looked down at his feet. They were further away than he remembered them to be. Waggling his hands in front of his face he realized that they were larger than he remembered. Sooooo, in some peculiar way he had grown taller, and he supposed, older.

He walked over, sat on the edge of the green bench, and stared out at the water stretching to the far horizons, and wondered, what had happened to him. It made no sense at all.

Honglar'a'at.

The pair stood in the broad, flat grass covered, isolated valley, The Land of The Unique Warriors, located in the northeast corner of An'darl, their backs to The Wild Sea. The drop behind them, three paces back, would plunge them into the great depth of that dark water.

Hy'pherian stood, apparently relaxed, arms by his sides. The large shield on his left arm, a dark-metal shield, made in the workshop of M'aga in the mountain enclosed Valley of Glar, was indeed dark, flat dark, no reflection dark, a black shadow cloaking that side of his body.

Stretching away from his body on his right side, his fingers lightly wrapped around the long hilt, was a dark-metal monster of a sword, thrice the length of a standard sword, the blade twice as wide and half the thickness. This thing was called The King of Swords. It was a two-handed great sword capable of chopping the head off a running horse clad in battle armor in a single swing. He thought that what they faced would be interesting but hard work.

His sister, Altai'dorionasha, stood near him, but not too near, leaving more than enough room between them to maneuver in the coming brawl. She stood much as he did, apparently relaxed. Her armor was several times lighter in weight than his, a thing of flowing scales and mesh, as shadow cloaked as his shield. The long thin O'azur leaned against her right shoulder, the ball end resting on the ground two foot lengths beyond her right boot toe tip. The upper end of her weapon was tipped with a flat blade that tapered to sharp point. The edges of the blade, one forearm in length glistened soft light back to the clear sky and the sun high overhead. The shaft, a soft brown color, if given only a fast glance, appeared to be dark wood covered with thick cording to provide a secure grip, whether wet or dry. However, upon closer inspection, one would find that the O'azur was crafted entirely from dark-metal. It had also been crafted in the workshop of M'aga as well as her armor.

The pair had spent hard seasons in learning their skills. He for six, she for five.

Now, on this spot, they were to be judged by those that had spent all those seasons training them, day and night. The Six stood on the tops of six high platforms situated in such a manner that one of The Six could always observe whatever happened.

Facing the pair, in various sized clusters, scattered across the open valley floor, were true monsters created by those who could. None of these creatures could escape this place for they were bound to it. But every one of them had only a single purpose: to rip, to tear, to kill, the pair watching them. The things strained for release.

Hy smiled at the things.

Altai frowned at him, a little. His smile was a smile of no humor. It was a promise of violence to be delivered as fast and as hard as possible. She shrugged. Oh well, she intended to do the same thing. She just didn't smile.

One of The Six looked down at the combatants and nodded.

He clapped his hands together. One loud clap.

And all were released.

It was a graduation ceremony that none had ever witnessed before, on a bright sunny day.

Warrior's Hand.

It was the only true plain on An'darl. The southern edge wrapped around the north side of Prime Shield and stretched out into three long lobes. These were the ever narrowing travel routes to the valley called Honglar'a'at in the northeast, to the Valley of Glar in the north, and to the towns, Iron Hammer and Two Swords in the northwest. Wagonways threaded their way to these places from their terminus at the northern edge of Prime Shield.

These three lobes were often called "fingers" by the folk who lived in the small encampments scattered widely across this plain of the blue-grey Haz Grass and scattered forest patches. Over time this plain was given the name it was called as warriors were known to often loose one or more digits from their hands over time.

Cereon, clad in the loose white garments favored

by the dwellers of the widely spaced the settlements in this plain, strolled from Inatal encampment on his way to Pa'a'un encampment through the thigh high grass. He rarely walked down one of the wagonways. Only the disturbance of the thigh high grass marked his passage. He was fulfilling his obligation to The Unseen, his guides in this most arcane of the arts. Each would peer seeing eyes at his ability, and if and when they were satisfied with his training, would pass him on to the next encampment. He grumbled softly to himself. It was something he had done from a very young age, mostly signifying nothing. He was eager to finish. This was the longest that he had ever concentrated on anything.

Cereon had spend five seasons doing this, traveling from encampment to encampment. Now he was almost done. He had almost become the figure of the great legends told out here in the plain, told and retold, in every encampment, "The One Who Was Not There."

The Tower of Iz'en'dar.

The pair stood on the small balcony, every house had one, and looked out at the sun rising above rank after rank of blue-grey mountains, most of them capped with a permanent layer of snow, all similar to the great mountain behind this town, and felt the cold air that flowed down toward the deep valley far below.

They had come to this place during their

fourteenth season as The Gift expressed itself. The town where they stood spread across the slope high on the mountain just below the edge of the mantel of permanent snow. Narrow walkways threaded in and around the buildings.

Any traveler who happened to look that high from the narrow valley floor would be hard pressed to recognize the houses as man-made structures. All were constructed from the blue-grey rock of the mountain where they stood. Their outlines were blurred from the sparse vegetation that grew up and around them. The structures were designed to shed all the snow that fell, in any form.

The pair had studied long and hard with the numerous teachers of this place. When they arrived to that narrow valley they had expected to find a great structure, a tower thrusting up from a town. Instead they found a mountain called "The Tower of Iz'en'dar" and a small community high above named "The Wisdom of Iz'en'dar," although, as they found out, it was often called "The Tower of Iz'en'dar" by the inhabitants.

The Gift had pulled them to this place.

And here, hard lesson after hard lesson, painful exercise after painful exercise, they had learned to control The Gift as it expressed itself in them, a very difficult thing to do.

The pair had been gifted with boundless curiosity and massive intellectual ability. Through the seasons they hard-learned focus and concentration. Had they not, they would have been doomed to leap from interest to interest, seeing much, learning little, merely a mental Flitter-talas of no consequence, a small creature that bounced from place to place and did little but take a quick sip of nectar and pass on for another elsewhere during its frantic existence.

Their final lessons had been the hardest to successfully control. Their teachers stressed, endlessly it felt to the pair, that with their concentration and focus, they must wear the facade of one who might be merely puzzled and perhaps a tiny bit curious. Otherwise the folk down there might become uncomfortable and dangerous.

But now, all the training, all the studies, all the exercises, the ability to truly use The Gift, were finished.

This was the day for them to say their farewells and take the long hike down and away.

The pair turned and walked back into the room, paneled in light wood, and took their place in the two wooden, straight-backed chairs that were the focus of the large semi-circle of similar chairs facing them, occupied by their teachers, who looked at them with satisfied smiles. The pair looked back with innocent, somewhat puzzled, expressions. Just as they had been taught.

The central figure cleared his throat.

"Equi-veronik, Bael'elyth, this is the last day. It may be the hardest. After eight seasons, learning to control, learning to understand The Gift, you are about to depart. You are leaving your family here and re-entering the lands below. Of all those who dwell out there, there are few, if any, capable of understanding what you are, who you are, or, are as capable of understanding as swiftly and thoroughly as you both do, twins in birth, twins in capability."

Tears wandered down the speaker's face as did tears on all those seated in the large semi-circle.

"Parents such as we have been do not run tears of fear at our loss, only those of regard for our daughter and our son in ability."

He stood, followed by the others.

"Tell us, what you will be about in your travels below?"

The pair stood and wiped their faces with their sleeves.

Bael'elyth cleared her throat. "All the volumes in the great collection spoke of those named as The Hidden Ones."

Equi-veronik nodded. "We shall spend some time seeking the true or the false of this."

"Be of great care, children," sighed the speaker. "For down below may look upon such an endeavor as a great threat to their mythological belief systems, a threat that can drive some of the folk toward great violence."

Then he frowned. Not at them, but at what he now had to tell them.

He waved one hand in a great arc. "Out there, in all the lands below there are those who would stand on the backs of all of the folk. These ones have created an artfully hidden order which we here now know to be named as The Dark Wind. These bent ones, those who have only their own self-regard in mind, serve a thing, a malignant entity, that they call The Great One."

The speaker sighed. "These foolish ones live in the lands, hidden, secretive, eager to be the ones to control all others. They are not of The Hidden Ones, merely those who skulk about. Be cautious, be very cautious. Things like they have become are very dangerous, not bothered by killing others. You must always appear to be much, much less than you are."

"Great focus," intoned Bael'elyth.

"Great concentration," stated Equi-veronik.

"Wearing a bland face," added Bael'elyth.

The teachers crowded around them, patting a shoulder or a back. Then they stepped aside and watched the most talented students they had from seasons beyond counting walk away.

The-Second-Twins-of-The-First strode down the hall, headed for the long, twisting trail to the valley below. They wore nondescript garb of faded brown and tan.

Here And There

Nine Ita Cluster.

The troop ran from the still hard packed sand of the wetway called The Tide's Gift and up the stairs carved into the low cliff of blue-black stone that encircled N'Farza. It was one of the continents without beaches.

They trotted into the gathering spot of their trading partners, which they called the Nine Ita Cluster, and jolted to a halt and stared at the fight.

A great black thing never before seen, surrounded by the warriors of Clan Par'ar'na wielding the long curved blades of the Tha'a'ea, surged around the gathering spot in their housing cluster. On all sides the troop could see shattered structures and battered and torn bodies.

"YAAAAAAAA!" Den'tza hurtled into the fray, shark-toothed weapon slashing a great tear in one of the many appendages supporting the monster. Something needed killing.

"YAAAAAAA!" screamed the troop, dropping everything they carried except weapons and shields, as they rushed forward. Following Den'tza.

"YAAAAAAAA!" The blood cry of mayhem

turned loose. Berserker fury released.

Inadat the Dower handed the gift box to a male of Clan Par'ar'na who was standing, barely, sagging against a tall tree, one hand holding a gore drenched curved blade, the other hand clenching his shoulder, blood oozing down his chest and through his fingers.

"Take this!" Inadat yanked the gore covered hand away and shoved the gift box into it. Quickly opening a small pouch at his side, the Dower scooped out a small quantity and tossed the red dust at the wound.

The warrior screamed, eyes flying wide.

"QUIET!" Inadat flicked a small pinch at the male's cheek and at the slash on his right thigh.

"It is stop bleed," explained The Dower. "Plenty pain but effective." He grimaced. He knew what it felt like. All members of the troop knew what it felt like.

Stop bleed was the dried fruit of the Yellow Flowering Red Sata Grass crushed into a fine powder. Every troop had a cultivated patch of this grass, carefully attended, and guarded, by the most senior females of the troop. They also prepared the precious powder.

Inadat snatched his weapon from the clasp on his shield and charged into the melee. "YAAAAAA!"

As the troop, lost in the blood lust of death battle, danced, slashed, ripped, and hacked at the monstrous creature, more warrior's charged into the gathering spot, warriors from Clan Dur'na, led by the runner sent for help.

Curved blades flashing in both hands, the warriors spun and leaped high in the air. Dark pieces, dark appendages, flew and tumbled around and into the ever increasing frenzy of the surrounding throng.

The thing screamed, a high-pitched whistle that numbed ears, and crashed into a heap, a twitching, trembling, slashed to ribbons, ichor drenched mass. Combatants leaped away in all directions.

Members of both clans clustered together to bandage and aid their wounded and to watch and wait for the battle crazed troop members, drenched in the monster's gore, to return to normalcy. They knew the crazed warriors very well.

As the troop members shuddered from their now felt wounds, opened pouches, and dusted themselves, teeth tightly clenched, the clan members of Par'ar'na made gifts to those of Clan Dur'na, who thanked them, nodded grateful, and trotted back into the denseness of the jungle forest taking their few dead with them.

The Voice of Clan Par'ar'na hobbled to where Den'tza stood, holding shield and shark-toothed weapon in his left hand, wiping the gore off himself with his right. He looked at The Troop Leader and saw the almost normalcy in the face of Den'tza..

Inadat snatched the gift box from the warrior holding it, stomped over the mess in the clearing, and offered it to The Voice, wondering at his expression.

"Not to be accepted," stated The Voice.

"Eeee ya," mumbled Den'tza. The troop began to gather behind him, wondering what they should do now.

The Voice pointed toward the steps. Males nodded and quickly snatched neatly wrapped bundles of the meat of the Dappled Ter, a grazer that roamed throughout the jungle forest of N'Farza, from shattered structures and ran to the entry stairs with them.

Troop members quickly joined them, securing the bundles to their carrying poles. It was a welcome, but unexpected, reward.

"Debt and more," intoned The Voice as he reached out and squeezed Den'tza's shoulder. "Debt and more."

Inadat walked away to stand in front of and to smile at the senior female of the clan. He handed her the Gift Box and frowned at the bloody hand print on it.

"Our females," he said, "who labored long and long, will have great sorrow and deep sadness if their gifts are not accepted and worn for all to see their great skill." He nodded.

She smiled, a very sly smile, and took the box.

"Some warrior is very clever." She turned and walked away to inspect her shattered home.

Inadat rejoined Den'tza and said softly, "The tides wait for none."

Den'tza reached over and squeezed the shoulder of The Voice, whirled away, and ran for the steps.

In moments, the troop was a long line running

north toward the bright spot in the distance. Down the hard packed sand of The Tide's Gift they ran.

Toward home.

In the far distance.

The Pool of The Dark Fates.

The waterfall dropped in a narrow silver stream from the high dark stone wall through the carefully constructed notch. As it fell it reached for the thick green growth far below.

Long before the water reached its goal it was transformed into multitudes of grey mist feathers that gently kissed the vertical side wall of this spot, coating rock and vegetation in a perpetual caress before some speckled the surface of the wide and deep pool with tiny kisses.

In the winter, this place was transformed into abstract shapes coated in glistening blue ice diamonds.

The notch funneling all this water was a small portion of the great stone wall whose ends were tightly anchored to the mountain side it self.

Behind this wall was a wide and deep pool channeling the mountain stream which filled the pool constantly, the excess spilling out and over into the space below.

Only creatures capable of scrambling on and over rocky slopes this high knew of this pool and could come to drink from it.

In the exact center of the pool stood a stone

platform whose top was close to the water's surface. Upon this gleaming white surface lay a sarcophagus of black marble.

The lid was carved, the sides decorated. Here on top lay a male wearing ornate armor, a great sword stretching the length of his body, from his hands crossed over his chest and holding the hilt, to his ankles, all carved from the black marble.

On this day, as the sun slipped above the nearby mountain ridge, striking rainbows in all that mist, the lid of the decorated coffin began to slowly slid toward one side, filling toppling over and resting at an angle, propped against the side wall.

Ever so slowly, he sat up, and then stood, holding the massive sword placed alongside him all those many seasons past.

His black armor glistened metallic shine in the sun as did his helmet.

Dark brown eyes peered from a dark, dark brown face as he turned his head and peered at his surrounding.

Hr crouched and leaped, limber and as sure as the watching mountain beast standing on the steep slope behind the pool. Standing on the edge of the wall next to the notch, he looked down, following the descent of the water toward the deep, deep pool below.

Pure Shadow stepped off.

It was the first step toward his goal, his far distant goal.

Honglar'a'at.

The pair sat on one side of the table eating the many course meal. They were ravenous but taking their time. There was no hurry. On the floor an ever widening puddle of grey ichor was forming and spreading. It was dripping from them, their armor, and their weapons. They would worry about being clean later. They were ravenous, focused on eating, satisfying the crying need. It had been hard work, very energy burning hard work.

Facing them across the table sat The Six, also feasting from the many varieties of food. They wore contented expressions on their faces and slight smiles. Their expressions and slight smiles had nothing to do with the banquet spread before them, not at all.

It had to do with the conversation they had held as they had walked through the churned earth of the great meadow and the scattered remains of all the true monsters that they had released.

Not one of The Six had known what would happen. And as they discussed everything that they had watched, they had come to the conclusion that they had done a great thing, that they had accomplished something beyond their expectations with that brother and sister.

The discussion had continued as softly murmured comments at the table, one to the other, as they watched that pair rapidly regain their health and vitality. This was a very special meal of specially prepared foods, just for that purpose.

One of The Six looked across the table and clapped his hands. A single loud clap.

The pair were clean.

Again.

The floor was clean.

Again.

The broad flat meadow was green and clean.

Again.

"We are finished," he announced. "That which we did set ourselves to accomplish has been done. These many seasons of lessons and chores and tasks are finished."

The Six stood and bowed to their students.

The pair surged to their feet and bowed deeply in return.

As all straightened up, The One of The Six, watched their faces, and asked, "What will you do? Now?"

The male looked at his sister.

"We think to visit The-First-Twins-Of-The First," she said. "It has been many seasons since we have seen any of the many from our home."

The One of The Six nodded and pointed at the wall behind them, at the door that not been there before.

"The way from here. It will bring you near the place where one finger of the plain called Warrior's Hand contains the wagonway you walked to reach this place." He pointed at the two packs. "Supplies for your travels."

He bowed and straightened up. "May you always be the ones who help those in need. Always remember this!" The pair needed to have that idea anchored deep in their minds. Just to keep them out of trouble, and to be aware that others, less able that they were, often needed the help that they were capable of delivering. Then he told them of a group that called themselves The Dark Wind, their beliefs and their goals.

The pair bowed, straightened up, grabbed their packs, opened the door, and stepped through.

As the door closed behind them another appeared in front of them.

They took three steps, opened it, and stepped outside.

They stood in a narrow meadow of Haz grass. It came less than halfway to their knees.

In front of them ran the wagonway. Far to the right of where they stood, it begin its twisting, torturous climb to the high pass, only open during warm times, over the top that led to the valley that they had just left.

To their left, the wagonway ran through this finger of the meadow that was slowly widening into the distance, the wagonway winding its way out of sight.

Altai looked behind them and only saw bare mountain rock.

She shrugged and walked to her brother's side. They strolled down the wagonway toward the open plain enjoying the pleasant warmth of the day and the leisure that they now had.

During the past seasons he had grown, not only in skills but in size. He was now a head, and then some, taller than she was and heavier and stronger.

Of course, she was taller and stronger as well but it wasn't as obvious.

Ea'na.

She sat on top of one of the many green stone boulders that were scattered along this stretch of narrow gravel beach and kicked her feet lazily in the warm water of The Friendly Sea at high tide and listened to the soft gurgle as gentle waves surged back and forth over the nearby rocks. It was a very relaxing activity.

Al'tana was dressed in her usual garb, trousers with a slight flare at the ankles, an over-blouse that draped to her waist. Her trousers were rolled up past her knees, her footwear placed up on the grass covered bench of land that bordered this spot. Her garments were made from the cloth that was woven from the soft green sea grass, Ua'an, that grew at the edge of the sea only in this small corner of northeast Shar'daine. The color of her clothes echoed the soft green of the shallows of The Friendly Sea.

She had spent four seasons living with the near-hermit singer Zal'ar'dun, whose dwelling was not far from where Al'tana sat. The singer's dwelling was one of the widely scattered dwellings within the short grass of Ea'na. This was a unique spot, the only habitat of the Yellow Many Stem, a flowering grass that ever bloomed.

Today, as she had done so many times in the past, she sang a soft song of loss to the sea and those who lived there. The perfume of the grass drifted on the soft breeze past her and out to sea.

And today, as on many of those past times, one of the Laterian floated in the green waters of the small cove, a cove deep enough to allow that great sea dweller to drift close and to stare at her with large blue-green eyes, to drift close enough to hear the soft song.

In times past, Al'tana would float in those waters, one arm thrown over the narrow neck of her visitor, and tell her one of the humorous tales told by those who lived among the blossoms of Ea'na. But not this time.

She and her brother had always been fascinated by, and attuned to, the sea, long before their fourteenth season. She remembered their many trips to the beaches of Nu'vern, splashing in the shallows and the tidal pools, watching the many sea beings, scooping up cupped hands of water containing the very small just for a closer look. Learning and learning.

The pair had spent much time visiting the fishing villages, talking with those who rode their Wooden Steeds, as they called them, out upon the deep waters to catch the things "that may be caught."

And finally, after a long time, the pair had been allowed to go with this one or that one on board their Wooden Steed, to observe the life of these folk, and to see, on rare occasions, the great dwellers of the many seas, who often swam close and watched their activities.

So, today, she had come to sit and enjoy the soft sounds of the sea as it tickled the shore and her feet, and to feel the warmth on her back.

But then, she had seen, on the far horizon, a bank of black clouds boiling up. And she had remembered.

She remembered this very spot and the happy inspection of the things in the shallows, laughing with her brother, four seasons past. A bright warm day.

Which suddenly changed.

A howling, rushing, midnight dark storm fell on them, crashing waves surged over them, and she was sucked out, toward the deep.

Her brother plunged after her, and somehow dragged her into the shallows and then up onto the bench.

As he laughed at her bedraggled appearance, reflecting back on the many times they had been drenched by sea waves, a wave taller than one of the Wooden Steeds, boiled over him.

And he was gone.

One of those who dwelled in Ea'na wrapped the screaming girl in warm covering and pulled her away from the shoreline and out into the flower covered fields and into her dwelling.

There the old one had sung soft calm to her and held her and told her, once she had calmed down, that she had the gift to learn the craft. Then the old one had fed her and had told Al'tana that she had been born to learn this, the first one to have ever come to Ea'na with the skill. Many seekers had come to find this knowledge. All had been turned away. The old one told her that she had feared that she would die before she could ever pass on all that she knew. But no longer. Al'tana was The Gift, her gift, a gifted one to teach. And she sang soft calm to her and held her tight for Zal'ar'dun had seen the soft glow of The Gift.

Al'tana had agreed as she felt she had no other reason to live. For four seasons all that Zal'ar'dun the Singer knew was passed on.

And now Al'tana was done.

She had come to this spot to think. And she had decided. She would return to Nu'vern and once again visit the fishing villages and the shores where she and her brother had long ago played.

Her song stopped. Al'tana leaned forward and told the Laterian what she was about to do.

The great one nodded her head, slowly drifted backward, and sank out of sight, into the deep.

Prime Shield. The Place of The Others.

His eyes popped open. He had just heard the inside bolt fastening his door slide back and thump against its catch. It was not possible.

He sat up, hit the glow globe with one hand, and pushed back into a sitting position in his bed, wondering whether he could leap to where his weapon leaned in a far corner and secure his safety before the attack.

The door to his room, one of the many plain and simply furnished rooms in The Place of The Others, slowly swung in and wide.

She stood in the hall and looked into the room, red eyes seeming to glow.

"May these ones enter?" she asked.

He nodded, and gulped. "Do."

The pair slipped silently into the room and stood next to the bed, red eyes scanning his face.

He swallowed loudly. "I thought that I had imagined you. The figments of a dying mind."

She reached out. He felt gentle fingers lightly touch the side of his face. They were quite warm.

"When the fiery eye of Relaer rises next to peer down and spread its warmth upon all surface dwellers, you will be as healthy as you have ever been."

"Who are you?" he mumbled.

"This one is Soft Touch, a One Who Saves." Her hand casually indicated the other. "This one is Final Touch, a One Who Does Not." Her voice was soft deep velvet, deeper than most of the Honglar. She touched her chest. "This one is what here calls a Healer."

He nodded. "Many thanks."

"You promised this one a forever debt."

"Umm."

"This one wishes to collect that forever debt."

He stared at her, at those red eyes that seemed to stare deep into his grey ones. He nodded, and rasped, "What do you wish?"

"Little. Much." She stepped back. "Be still."

Final Touch bent, a glittering short blade suddenly held in one hand. Her other hand clamped his head in a tight grip, holding his head immobile. He held his breath, eyes watching that sharp edge as she reached for his head and clipped a lock of hair from his head.

She stepped back, the blade disappearing into somewhere, and handed the lock of hair to Soft Touch, who tucked it into a pocket.

"This one," said Soft Touch, "would know your name, your true name."

He cleared his throat. "I am Rid'linar. It is my only name."

She nodded. "You must fare well, Rid'linar. There are dark, hidden evil folk who do not wish you well. They lurk in most of the lands. They already tried to end your life."

The pair turned and drifted silently from the room and down the hall. The door slowly closed. The bolt shot back, locking the door.

Rid'linar stared at the door and wondered what had happened. It was beyond his experience and his knowledge of the folk of The Seven Lands. But he was happy to be alive.

The Folly of Franbandan.

Sar'al, Zak'ke, and Viana made their camp in the fading light of day at the last camping spot on the tip of Nu'vern where it joined the wetway. Their Azkar guide had told them that it was safe to do so, then he faded back into The Forest of Sighs and was gone.

As the morning light flooded their surroundings, they ate, packed, and started out and onto the wetway, up the long stone ramp to the wagonway.

Sar'al smiled at the sight as it unfolded before them. It was an imposing sigh, just as she remembered from her seasons past journey back to Nu'vern.

Ban'da'ta Franbandan had brought into existence one of the greatest construction projects undertaken since many generations had last done so.

He had convinced all the members of The Trader-Merchant Affiliations of his time to provide the funds. The workshops of the Honglar had forged and crafted all the tools necessary for the project.

Franbandan had started his crews from the Shar'daine end of the long mountainous spine, cutting and forming great blocks of grey and blue banded stone from the mountain slopes as they proceeded.

His work force had carved their way high above the storm surges of the great seas, following the bends and twists of the mountain flanks, utilizing the stone they had removed to build retaining walls and supporting structures as well as the guard walls. They build wide camp spots and a wagonway broad enough to allow the immense wagons of the Trader-Merchant caravans to pass each other in opposite directions.

Every crevice and gap saw bridges erected across them.

In all, it took a full three seasons to reach the other end and the connection with Aydel's Track at the southern tip of Nu'vern. The builders left behind carefully stacked rows of unused blocks of stone, stacked in wide storage spaces.

It is said that all the Trader-Merchant Affiliation's outfits held great celebrations as this finally linked the three continents whose economies they were most involved with.

The three travelers spent the many days of their passage admiring the effort and construction of this wagonway and wondering why they hadn't met anyone traveling across this wetway. This and other topics had plenty of time for discussion. The Folly was the longest of all the wetways.

Finally, after many days travel, as the shadows of approaching evening were lengthening, the small group camped at the base of the long ramp that touched Shar'daine. It was an often utilized camp spot.

In the morning they rode into the lands of Clan Zalanal and The Silent Woods and dense forest silence that cloaked the southern end of Shar'daine.

Entering the gathering place of Grey Thicket village, they halted and quickly dismounted, weapons in hands.

Huts were splintered wood, the ground on all sides ripped and torn.

Zak'ke stepped to one side, shield and sword held ready.

Sar'al calmed her horse, lance clenched in her right hand.

Viana, blades in both hands, dashed into one of the many trails disappearing into the woods, calling back over her shoulder, "Wait there! Do nothing!"

Zak'ke kicked at the churned earth. "Battle, sister, great battle." He scanned the large opening and sniffed the air. "And death, and something most rank."

Sar'al watched him as he walked back and forth, and said to him, "Nothing passed us. Whatever the Azkar spoke of did not leave The Forest of Sighs."

Zak'ke began to walk slowly around the edge of the clearing, peering down each and every trail, searching for something to explain what had happened here.

Pushing aside a tangle of brush, he stared and gasped.

"WHAT!" Sar'al started in his direction.

"STAY!" He spun and jogged over to her.

"It was the Fast Rider's live stock, slashed and ripped into shreds. His body was not with them."

She stared at the surrounding forest. "There is no record of large hunting beasts living in The Silent Woods."

He nodded and indicated the torn soil. "It would

have been large, indeed."

They stood.

They waited.

They watched.

In the quiet of The Silent Woods.

Zak'ke hissed softly and indicated the glitter of blades approaching.

In a moment Viana strode into the opening accompanied by two others.

The Elder of Clan Zalanal and of the Tha'a'sa stepped close to Sar'al, dark eyes gazing into soft grey ones and waggled one hand. "Why have you come here, young Queen of Nu'vern?" It was a gesture from teacher to student.

Zak'ke jerked and stepped closer.

"We so chose to do so, We did." Sar'al indicated their surroundings with her left hand. "What happened here, Clan Elder?" She pointed with her lance. "Who is this?"

The one she pointed at stepped closer, a rather stocky man dressed in scale armor of a light brown color, a dull light brown that did not reflect light. A heavy mace hung from his thick and wide belt, a small round shield was strapped to his left forearm.

He bowed, a very formal bow, to Sar'al. And straightened up.

His eyes flickered to her and her brother.

"Ahhhhhhh, here stand the senior twins, the ones said to appear." He smiled at them. "Your hair tells me this."

He bowed again. "Warm greetings to House Noriyon Zacog. I am Arma'far Zalna'dei Beran Sacog, Head of House Beran Sacog." He stepped back. The twins stared at him. It was news. Nothing that they had heard, or learned, had mentioned a Royal House here in The Silent Woods.

The Elder sat and patted the ground with one hand.

"Sit! We will share tales. You will start, Sar'al who lived among us."

They sat, forming a small circle.

The Plains of Singing Grass.

Al'tana strolled along the edge of the slight bluff in the short grass that grew this close to the western edge of the sea. This was the third day, two days since she had left Ea'na. So far, it had been a pleasant walk.

Zal'ar'dun, the ancient singer had taught Al'tana all the craft that she knew, recognizing that this young woman had The Gift blossom within her.

Three days ago, Zal'ar'dun had prepared a traveling pack for Al'tana, kissed her on the forehead after handing the pack to her, and stretched herself out on the bare floor of their dwelling.

She smiled up at her startled pupil. "I have accomplished all there was and then some. You are my daughter, my only daughter in the craft, now and forever. Beware The Dark Wind, an evil secret folk!"

She crossed her ankles, then her arms across her chest. In a soft whisper she told Al'tana which flowers to pick and the exact pattern they must form in the opening of their dwelling.

Then she had smiled warmly at her now daughter, closed her eyes, and sank into The Other World.

Releasing that memory, Al'tana sat on the edge of the bluff and had something to eat. She knew all the edible things that could be gathered on the grass filled plains as well as along the shore line.

When she finished, she wiped her hands on the grass, then closed her eyes and allowed her breath and heart rate to slow down, and down. It was a resting technique, one of the many skills that Zar'ar'dun had taught her. In some few moments, she would stand and continue her stroll, as refreshed as if she had taken a short nap.

As she drifted inside, she could hear every grass stem creaking in the gentle breeze, the soft gurgle of water past small stones, the smell of small flowers, and the sound of footsteps approaching from her back.

Her eyes popped open. She sprang to her feet and spun around.

The tall male stopped, as startled as she was, an unstrung great long bow held in his left hand.

"Oh," he said. "Most sorry." He frowned at her and waggled his free hand at their surroundings. "This is not a safe place, that is not a safe thing to do, to sleep with no one to watch."

"Ummmm," she said.

"Dark Wind archer/scout-guide," he stated, looking expectant at her.

"Al'tana of Ea'na," she answered to his unspoken question.

"Eeeee ah nah. From there."

She nodded. "From there."

His eyes scanned their near surroundings. "Just wandering about?"

She shook her head. "Not wandering at all. I am going home. I am walking along the edge of the sea until I get there." She pointed in the direction that she was headed.

He crouched and stroked his hand through the short grass, thoughtfully, tenderly.

"The Silent Woods?"

"Nu'vern."

His eyes flew wide. Then he nodded to himself. She had the light skin, grey eyes, and pale hair of one of them.

"I will make this journey with you." He stood and resettled the pack on his back. "I have never been go-about to Nu'vern."

She shook her head. "There is no need for that."

He pointed at a spot out in the grass. "Do you see there, way out, that slight movement, contrary to the breeze ruffling the stalks?"

She stared, and finally, nodded.

"There prowls one of the Grass Larpa, a solitary predator of the plains." His eyes wandered over her. "Twice your weight. You would never know it was there until it pulled you down."

He smiled at her. "She and I will accompany you. It is a, ammmmmmm, obligation to do so."

"Obligation?"

He nodded. "Most so."

Al'tana looked to either side of him. They were alone.

"You and her?"

He stepped close and smiled, and held out his great long bow for her inspection. It gleamed a soft deep brown of artfully crafted wood. "She is a beauty!"

Al'tana studied his face for long moments. Then nodded. "I will accept your company archer/scout-guide. You and she may leave me whenever you wish."

She turned and began her stroll along the edge of the sea.

As he hurried to walk by her side, she said, "Tell me of the archer/scout-guide folk. None of your kind ever ventured into the Ea'na."

The Silent Woods.

Sar'al spoke of all that had happened since the three of them had stood on top of The Tower of The Soaring Dragon and wondered how they would ever stop the Azkar horde from overrunning everything.

"Ah huh, ah huh," grunted the Elder. "So, that is

how The Gift expressed itself, Sar'al. You are able to speak to The Ancient One herself."

"Who?"

"Your older than old tales are confused. That one is not one of The Jewels. The Jewels have been lost to us since the ever many long ago. The Ancient One is almost before everything."

"Oh, my."

Zak'ke gave Sar'al a slight nudge. He didn't think that "oh my" was a proper response for a Queen to make.

The Elder waggled her hand at him and frowned.

"Now," said the Elder, "this is my tale." She frowned darkly at Viana. "And you will be calm!" The Tha'a'da could be impulsive at times. She related her story.

The Discussion Circle had reformed after the appropriate waiting time of two days to discuss the report by the fast rider. Talk had worked its way half around the circle when "it" appeared in the middle of the open space. The monster attacked the fast rider and all things associated with him.

The circle scattered into the forest, sending calls for warriors.

In quick moments the gathering spot was a'swarm with warriors from the four clans attacking the black monster, from all sides, short stabbing spears at work.

The Elder looked at Sar'al. "By the time some of

your kind had arrived," she nodded at Arma'far, "the thing had been wounded into death but many had been injured, some died."

She reached out and patted Sar'al on one shoulder. "We agree with your request for many arrows and short bows."

The Elder turned to Viana. "Listen you carefully."

Viana sucked in a breath and slowly exhaled.

"That monster was Mishra, the dark beast."

Viana bowed her head. "An ancient tale." It was going to be another Elder tale.

"Ah huh, ah huh," grunted the Elder. "Not ancient. A tale of things to come err we fail to prepare. Go now! You have a duty!"

Viana bounded to her feet, eyes jumping around the open space. Then she ran to her horses and pack string, and spun around.

"Queen sister," she called. "I must go!" She leaped onto her horse, checked that the spare mount and pack string was properly attached and headed from the gathering spot on the north trail to the wagonway.

"I will find you . . ." came her voice back to them as she disappeared from sight.

Sar'al frowned at the Elder.

"Young Queen, Viana is the Spirit of her clans, those of the Avelerain Tha'a'da." She patted Sar'al's shoulder. "They do things differently up there."

The Elder nodded. "Now we must speak of your

kingdom, young one. You have been given the title, Queen of The Seven Lands, true?"

"Our birth and the deaths of Our Father and the three Mothers in The Great Fire did place that upon my shoulders."

"Ah huh, ah huh. Who beyond the tillers and the fishers agreed to this?"

Zak'ke leaned forward. "The Azkar, The Hidden Ones of The Forest of Sighs."

"Ummm ha! So, it does begin, it does." She looked from Zak'ke to Sar'al. And nodded. A very old legend was coming to pass.

"So and so. The four clans of the Avelerain Tha'a'sa who bow their heads to none, bow their heads to you now. The Silent Woods will answer your call."

The Elder stood. "For now we are done. We have families to console and clans to make ready."

She strolled into the forest.

Ranagaz.

He sat.

A great figure wrapped in shadow in a great dark space.

He sat, slumped and relaxed in a large chair.

It might have been a throne, that chair. But it wasn't. It was just a large chair. He had no need of a throne.

He knew who he was. Thrones were symbols of power. Totally unnecessary.

He was power. He was the power that was, so far, unseen and little felt.

He had been aware of them for ever so many thousands of seasons, spreading and changing. Before he had come and settled here, they had been given something, something that made those changes. It could be a problem.

He had felt its effect appear, every once in awhile, making, to his way of thinking, minor changes.

Now, all of a sudden, it had blossomed into something new, unexpected. And he had reacted, much too hastily. That had been a mistake. It would not do to have them become aware of his presence, not yet! There were a small number of beings whose intentions he could not yet understand clearly.

He sighed. At least he had trapped those others. They wouldn't be able to help these few.

He would just wait. He might not be able watch them, but they had an effect on others and that would point those useful tools, The Dark Wind, to them. He laughed about that. He had created them, in a manner of speaking. They were so expendable. But they could watch and report and even kill a few of them. Those who belonged to that organization were gaining that what they were so anxious to have and sought: power and wealth. It made them ever so much more dedicated to do those things that he wanted done.

However, he could send things as well to assist matters. It was an easy thing to do, for him.

After all, there could only be one Ruler of The Seven Lands. And whether they, or the other folk, understood that, or wanted that, it would make no difference. That Ruler sat here, in this large chair.

He smiled. His presence on the surface wasn't required. Yet!

Sooooooooooo. He sent things.

The Great Blue.

Clerian'tra stood to one side and listened as Den'tza and Inadat told Vechannal The One Who Spoke For All, Kranz the Limber, and all the assembled members of The Troop of Many Fingers, everything that had occurred during their meat-hunt to N'Farza. The other Troop Leaders had gathered here to hear as well.

Inadat described the monstrous thing in greater detail than Den'tza could as Inadat had more time to examine it before rushing into the melee.

Den'tza told Vachannal that he already had a shield group placed at the point where The Tide's Gift touched Farza whenever the tide exposed that wetway.

"This was a hidden beast of N'Farza?" asked Vachannal.

"Neh, neh!" Den'tza stomped his foot.

He crossed his arms over his chest. "As far as memory passes into the ever lost, neither the Troops of Farza nor the clans of N'Farza speak of such as that." He glared at Vachannal. "The clans of N'Farza know their lands as well as the troops of Farza know their's."

As Den'tza and the others sat to discuss other matters, Clerian'tra slipped from the gathering and strolled in the direction of Three Drinks Green.

House Beron Sacog.

Sar'al sat at one of the many windows in her guest rooms and stared out at the dark waters of The Dismal Sea. It was the deep blackness that gave that sea its name.

She sighed. Again.

How could she, someone given an impressive title but no training, one who had no idea of who or what really lived in the many lands much less how they lived, presume to call herself, The Queen of The Seven Lands? Or even to dare take on the obligations and duties that the title demanded, the obligations and duties that she saw her father and mothers engaged in but little understood, then. Now she was beginning to understand about that, a little.

She watched one of the wind floaters coast along the edge of the bluff not far from where she sat and asked herself, who are your subjects, Queen? The tillers and fishers of whom she knew very little? The hidden creatures of The Forest of Sighs that she could barely understand? The four clans of the Tha'a'sa where she had spent much of her young life? One of The Ten Royal Houses?

The four clans were the only ones that she truly knew and understood. And this was only because her father had hidden her among them for many seasons, living and learning their culture and customs.

She took a sip from her goblet of juice. And sighed again. And frowned out the window, feeling quite displeased at it all.

He stepped from the blackness of one corner of her room.

"Such a dark expression." He laughed. "Is it proper for a Queen to glower anger at some harmless wind floater?"

Sar'al jerked and spun in her chair and smiled at her twin, a weak and strained but relieved smile. "Shadow?"

He hurried over and knelt next to her chair. "What?"

She took another sip. "I was just thinking."

He nodded. "Those thoughts must have been bad." He cast a puzzled look in her direction.

She sighed. "Worse than that." She grabbed one of his hands and squeezed it. Hard.

"Ouch!" He laughed. "You have to be careful, My Queen, to not crush the hands of the people you wish to sway."

She looked sheepish, but released his hand. And sighed, again, heavier.

He smiled at her, ignoring that sigh, as he waggled the offended appendage at her. "It is true! Your grip must come from hefting that great lance everyplace." He stood and leaned against the wall next to the window. And grinned slyly down at her. "We should acquire some fair-faced youth bedecked in gaudy clothes to walk, one step back, one step to the right, to tote that thing around. The Royal Lance Bearer. Tad dah!"

Sar'al laughed, a real laugh, at the image he was suggesting.

"Much better," he said. "Now, what is the problem?"

She carefully told him all the things she had been pondering. "So, brother mine, that is what the problem is. We are ill-prepared, most ill-prepared." She stood and thumped his chest with both fists. "What is the great power wielded by this, The Queen of The Seven Lands?" She waved her arms. "We can call The Ancient One to come to me. And what does she do when called? She tells Us that We have no Armed Mass to defend Our people! She tells Us that We have to travel out into The Seven Lands and become their Queen! She tells Us only that . . . it is a learning experience, appropriate for a Queen!"

She jerked away and twisted back to stare out the window, and grumbled, "We should have hit her with Our lance."

He laughed. "Certainly can hear the Royal pronoun for one who doubts their place as Queen! But it probably wouldn't have been a very good idea to strike her. I doubt that it would have any affect or have done any good either." And spun her around by the shoulders.

"Attire yourself in your most Royal best, sister self. We have a most serious meeting to attend. And I suspect, most weighty matters to discuss. We have been resting for enough." It was time for her to be a Queen.

He grinned into the dark sister Royal frown she gave him. "Shall I carry your lance?"

The Plains of Singing Grass.

Nar'a'las and Wind Sky had been wandering through the tall yellow grass in a northwesterly direction, more north than west, and were now approaching the mouth of the wetway that led to An'darl.

During the time they had walked, Wind Sky had been telling Nar'a'las about the life of an archer/scout-guide, their upbringing and their activities and about doing go-about. She had been doing most of the talking.

Nar'a'las, so far, had quite reticent about her life after her fourteenth season.

They walked up the moderate rise and looked out across the grass at the entrance to the wagonway that led to An'darl.

Just there, they could see a young woman dressed in black, halting her horses and pack string.

Blocking her passage, standing between her and the entrance to the wetway, stood three Grass Larpa. They spread into a line that began to slowly advance toward her.

By the time that the feet of the figure dressed in black had hit the hard packed soil of the wagonway, blades glittering in both of her hands, Wind Sky had strung her bow and had drawn it to its furthest extent, long arrow in place.

The woman stepped in front of her horse, weapons held out to her sides, and waited for the attack.

The arrow smashed into the skull of the central beast, dropping it where it stood. Two crackling flashes of light threw the other two tumbling limply back into the tall grass at the wagonway's edge.

The woman spun and stared up the moderate rise at the two figures standing there. Then she saluted them with her blades, stuck both of them on her back, leapt to the back of the lead horse, and raced toward the wetway, spare mount and pack string galloping behind her.

"One in a hurry," observed Wind Sky as she returned the second arrow to her quiver. "What did you do?"

Nar'a'las shrugged. "Very little. That young woman was one of the Avelerain, I believe."

"True speak?"

Nar'a'las nodded. "Quite! Black clothes and those long blades."

Wind Sky unstrung her bow and pointed at the staff held by Nar'a'las. "Very little?"

"Quite! We couldn't let those beasts kill and eat

her, ah ummmm, could we?"

"No. But their behavior was most unusual. They are solitary beasts. They do not hunt in packs." She wondered what was wrong with them, to behave so strangely.

Nar'a'las nodded. "So, which way? Archer/scout-guide?"

Wind Sky pointed, to the west and to the south.

The pair headed that way, their pace somewhat faster than they had been using up to this point.

Warrior's Hand.

Viana had walked her horses and pack string through the main gate of Prime Shield and the great white paved open space that was surrounded by the towering structures that represented the center of Honglar culture. None of the folk hurrying here and there paid any attention to her. She was, after all, one of those folk from the forested areas.

Yet Viana felt it. Eyes were watching her, eyes wishing her harm. But try as she might, she hadn't been able to spot them. They were very hidden lurkers, it seemed.

Compared to the Honglar, Viana was tall, but not as tall of those of Nu'vern. All of the Honglar were short, wide, barrel chested. Their heads appeared, to her, to be rather large for their torsos. She knew that the folk varied widely throughout the seven lands, but the Honglar were probably the shortest and thickest of all the folk.

Once she had entered the open grass land that was the Warrior's Hand, she had kept her livestock trotting at a good pace, one that they could maintain for long distances without having to stop too frequently to rest. She was headed along the wagonway that would take her toward the western and northwestern towns of the Honglar that were the gateways to the wetways. All along this route she knew that there would be plenty of food and water for her livestock.

The widely spread encampments of those who lived in this grass land were barely visible from the wagonway. Now and then she passed short wagon caravans of the Trader-Merchant outfits that were passing in either direction.

She nodded at them in passing and thought that their season of activity was finally starting, albeit somewhat late. She smiled to herself. But then the Trader-Merchant outfits kept their ideas of when and where to go to themselves.

As she headed for her destination she wondered who that pair had been, back there in Shar'daine, killing those hunting beasts. One must have been one of those folk that used those great long bows. All the Avelerain had heard accounts of that weapon. But she had never heard of anyone, in any of the Seven Lands, that could do what that other person did. She would question the Elders heavily about that!

The Fa'a'darl Trail.

He had slipped silent as a night wraith past the sleeping folk of the Trader-Merchant encampment just above the great river delta and then across the wetway.

It was early morning, not yet dawn, as he walked through the gateway into Two Swords and then slipped east and out of town and onto The Fa'a'darl Trail.

This was an ancient trail, once utilized to connect this area to the main town, Prime Shield, long before any of the wagonways were constructed and when the towns of An'darl were just small clusters of dwellings.

Now, to any eyes but his, there was no longer a visible trail, not a trace.

But he followed it, knowing that it would slip into the distant mountain range and then pass into other lands through the crooked and narrow valleys once occupied by bands of The Wild Folk. He didn't know whether any of them were still in existence or not.

If they were still there, it was of little concern.

Nothing was of concern except that of getting to where he must be. Nothing was of any concern to Dark Shadow, one of The Baine'lar.

Happenings

The Wild Fields.

Wind Sky and Nar'alas had arrived and had spent a day talking with Cloud Spirit in the small Hall of Meeting of the archer/scout-guides. Wind Sky told him about the peculiar behavior of the Grass Larpa. She didn't speak of what she had seen other that her actions. Nar'a'las nodded at Wind Sky and told Cloud Spirit the rest. He nodded, and waited for an explanation. She didn't give him one. He stood, thanked them for the information and told Wind Sky what he thought would be a good thing to do. She nodded.

Cloud Spirit wondered who Wind Sky's friend was, or rather, what she was? He had never heard of such ability as they had talked about.

The pair walked from the Hall of Meeting and across the settlement along one of the many routes restricted to foot traffic. Nar'a'las looked at the blocky structures that lined either side of the way. Everything, it seemed, was constructed from large grey stone blocks. A few, much wider ways allowed horse traffic and small carts within the Stonehold.

Wind Sky was headed for her dwelling. As they

walked she told Nar'a'las that the archer/scout-guides did not take orders from Cloud Spirit even though he was the most senior of them. All the archer/scout-guides reported everything to him that they saw. If there was a real need, Cloud Spirit would gather the most senior from each Stonehold to discuss it. Every one of the archer/scout-guides were folk who had a strong independent streak as well a great familiarity with the great grass spaces of Shar'daine. They knew all the plants and animals out there. They also visited other lands as they wished and knew them as well. Of course, all the folk of The Wild Fields were quite independent although they did pay attention to Cloud Spirit when he spoke to them.

Wind Sky turned and led Nar'a'las into a building and then up into one of the high watch towers of the Stonehold just to show her something.

Wind Sky pointed toward the north after greeting the two standing watch.

"Look closely. See those grooves coming this way from the direction of the wetway."

Nar'a'las leaned on the railing and stared in the direction Wind Sky was pointing. Finally she nodded. "What are they?"

"The Builder's Way. All the grey stone for the eight Stoneholds came from a great quarry in An'darl. Every block was hauled on platforms and over time, as the many, many blocks were brought here, that traffic cut deep gouges in the grass plains. Many seasons past those trails were deeper with sharper edges. Now the remnants are soft rounded and have less depth. They are hard to see from the ground, but from up here we can see how much time and effort went into the building of our villages. However, if you stand in one you can see the groove stretching away in two directions."

She waved one hand. "Looking out from here we can connect to those long ago seasons and all the folk that labored so long and so hard."

She headed them down. As they stepped out onto the paved road, she pointed at a structure just across from the tower. "My dwelling."

She led Nar'a'las over and through the front door after rubbing a strange mark off it and pointed. "You may sleep in that room. Feel free to stay as long as you wish. It will be a number of sleeps before I start go-about." She smiled. "You may accompany me, if you wish."

Stepping into another room, she spoke back over her shoulder. "I will fix a meal."

Mart'den.

The continent's mountain ranges all plunged steep flanks into the surrounding seas. There were no beaches, no benches, no coves, no handy place for anyone to land with one exception. That exception was the place where the wetway met the great river delta in the territory of Clan Amenji, The Guardians of Mart'den.

Viana led her horses and pack string in an easy

walk from the wetway and onto the wagonway that curved to the east around the out thrusting brow of the mountain range plunging into the sea to the west.

The wagonway, cut into the steep flank up slope from the An'unl'dur, the wide river that coursed from the high county far in the north to build the river's delta adjacent to the wetway's northern connection to the continent. The wagonway curved to the east and north around the end of the mountain range to end at the large and only camp spot for outsiders. The camp was adjacent to the wide intersection of the river and a side stream pouring into it from the northwest canyons. These northwest canyons and valleys were the territory of Clan Fa'dinji.

This camp spot was large enough to hold, comfortably, four of the largest Trader-Merchant caravans and their display booths. The large camp spot was the only one allowed on Mart'den by the seven clans of the Tha'a'da Avelerain. No-one was allowed to wander any further inland. Few outlanders, as the Tha'a'da labeled all the other folk of the Seven Lands, had ever seen the interior of their continent. An exception was made for the archer/scout-guides if they chose to travel this way. Viana had never met one of them.

As soon as one of these caravans was seen settling themselves in this spot, the word spread rapidly up the main drainage and side streams and canyons to all the scattered villages. Various members of the clans would drift down to visit and to trade, if they wished to do so.

Viana nodded to the Trader-Merchant staff just setting up their booths as she passed through the camp spot. She followed the narrow trail from there up a side stream to a wide spot of shallow water and gravel where she crossed to the other side. From here one branch of the trail meandered eastward and then northward along the edge where mountain flank met valley floor.

Leaving the territory of Clan Amenji behind, she followed the eastern trail into the territory of Clan Tuarji and camped near one of their villages. In the cool dawn she proceeded up the wide valley and into a village on the edge of the lake of Clan Czenji.

Here she rested for two days in the dwelling of her first sister, Viu'ja, who had mated with a tall male of Clan Czenji. Viana enjoyed the soft breeze that floated over the lake and around the dwellings of the settlement. All the Seven Clans were interlinked as females found mates-of-choice in clans other than their own. Clan members visited back and forth at whim, often leaving gifts. At First Meal of the first day, Viana had given her first sister the spare mount. It was considered as a Fine Gift by her sister and others who had come to visit. The horses of Nu'vern were often called "Pretty Horses" by the Tha'a'da. Most of the large beasts in this mountainous land tended to be quite stocky and short-legged.

When Viana, after a day's steady riding, passed into the territory of Clan Veronji, she smiled. Soon she reached the end of the horse trail at the village Kar'antil'anza, The Village By The Great Rift, a wide and long lake at the junction of the large river and a large side stream pouring into the wide valley and filling a great depression. She was home and the sun was setting.

Viana dismounted, told her mother that she was keeping the horse she had been riding but that her mother could distribute the pack string and all the supplies as she felt was appropriate.

The next day Viana spent resting and relating various aspects of her journey from Nu'vern to her family.

It was late at night when she told The Elder of the events with the Azkar and at The Decision Circle of the Tha'a'sa Clan Zalanal. The Elder nodded. Over the next three days The Elders of the Seven Clans would gather here and then decide what must be done.

The Ruins of Huroma.

It was said by some that Huroma came from beyond the sky. Others argued that the bottomless pit at this place was the place from which she came, climbing up into the lands from a place beyond knowing, she and her cohort, Nachts.

And so, as was the usual case with quasi-theological arguments whose beginnings were lost in time before remembering, it was never resolved, but had become mostly a traditional debate rather than a cause for armed conflict.

The Adherents of Huroma, very early in the spread and differentiation of the folk, in a burst of understanding, perhaps due to The Gift, perhaps due to something else, scattered into everywhere becoming members of all the groups and cultures. The Adherents, however, maintained the reason for which they had done this.

They kept mental notes of their local happenings and histories, eventually writing down these memories when writing and alphabets finally came into existence. All these materials were sent, in a never-ending stream, to the encampment that had settled around the bottomless pit. This gathering of knowledge became, in their minds, the largest and the most complete library in The Seven Lands. The gathering, the protecting, the maintaining of a record system, and the housing of everything in appropriate structures became the core activity of the Adherents of Huroma living in this place.

Over the countless seasons a small group within the larger had taken on The Core of Understanding. They had begun to see, as they read and analyzed and cataloged the materials, a very subtle thing occurring mainly within one of the populations. They called this happening The Gift, for it seemed to them that it was a gift.

They began to watch for this gift to occur and as it did they began to see a recurring tale also emerge. From this they came to realize that someone, or something, was appearing, now and then, that all called The Ancient One.

This entity predated the appearance of Huroma and Nachts although nothing was ever found to show a relationship between the three. This puzzle remained a puzzle down through the seasons.

Now and then, over the countless seasons, it would happen. One of The Adherents of Huroma would express The Gift. Those few, from the moment that happened, would wear the flaming robes of The Hand of Huroma. This fairly rare occurrence would only occur within that small group, The Core of Understanding. All members of The Core felt that this occurrence appeared to have some relationship to their understanding and study of bits and pieces of arcane knowledge scattered throughout all the materials gathered together. Those few who had The Gift were considered as selected, known to all the Adherents, but never spoken of as such to outsiders, as The Touched of Huroma.

One of these now sat in a small room puzzling over a small communication from one of the Adherents that lived among the archer/scout-guides. This note told of a tale passed on to the Adherent by another who had heard of an event by a archer/scout-guide on go-about while accompanied by one who had most unusual abilities, abilities never before written about.

Verin'yashi returned the document to its container, which sat in on the small table, stood and walked over to the window, her robes reflecting a soft amber glow onto the nearby wall. She leaned on the sill and stared out over the grassy plain toward the far distant western horizon deep in thought. Verin was one of The Touched although her expression of The Gift had been from a difference source than the study of documents.

Perhaps she ought to take a stroll over there and visit with the folk of The Wild Fields and see if she could find and speak with this young woman of unusual abilities. It would be interesting.

House Beran Sacog.

Arma'far smiled at them as they entered the room and settled in the chairs that he had placed in a cluster for comfortable conversation. Soooo, he thought, nodding to himself, from their attire, their weapons, and their expressions, they are being Royally formal.

He leaned back in his chair and nodded, to them this time.

"Warm greetings to House Nuriyon Zacog, the ruling line, the First Royal House, from me and all the members of House Beran Sacog, the Second Royal House."

He watched their faces carefully. Ummm, he thought, wonderfully blank.

Clearing this throat, he continued.

"This house, this rather small and rather self-isolating house, The Second Royal House, knows more of our true history than most. Our true history, and I wish to repeat that, our true history, started in the very long ago many past seasons, much longer in the past that the oft told and accepted tale that has been passed down by our lineages." He smiled at them. "We, the house members, are also somewhat shorter and stockier than most of Nu'vern." He shrugged. "Comes from isolation, I suppose."

He nodded again and smiled just a wee bit as he saw their curiosity replacing the formality on their faces.

"The current tale begins with the often talked about Kand'ald'dentar The Mighty." Arma'far held up one hand to stop the comments he saw forming. "Our house has always been focused on the true history of our lineages and the meaning of that history to the affairs of The Seven Lands. We, somewhat like those ever-collectors of information, The Adherents of Huroma, know much. But we understand more."

He reached over, picked up a large container of the clear yellow Ceba Berry juice and filled three cups, handed each of the twins one, and took a sip from his own cup.

"Know this then. That tale, that carefully crafted tale about Kand'ald'dentar, was created by the Adherents of Huroma for purposes only they know. But! It . . . is . . . not . . . true! Our lineage, and branch-lineages, reach much further back than that."

He took another sip and set his cup back on the nearby small table. Now they were paying attention. Good!

"It was the Adherents of Huroma that created that name, The Gift, to signify certain capabilities that our lineages and branch-lineages develop every now and then, not just in the recent past five kings." He leaned forward, staring intently.

"Your father was a very clever man. He married the first daughter from each of the three other Royal Houses that were showing those capabilities. He married Salanda of House Cueron Tacog, your mother, whose House greatly affected the tillers, The Stewards of the Soil. He married Runsda of House Melta Nacog, whose House greatly affected those who work the seas, and Oanna of House Oalen Hacog, who affected those who became the Trader-Merchant." He grabbed up his cup and took a deep swallow. "Those three wives came from The Third, The Fourth, and The Fifth of the Royal Houses." And laughed.

"That is a surprise is it not?"

The twins slowly nodded, looked at each other and then back at him.

"You and all your siblings are the beneficiaries of the merging of those capabilities of the three houses with those of your house." He shrugged. "Whether this turns out to be a good thing or a not so good thing is yet to be seen." He sighed. "That is the burden all of you are carrying, like it or not." He waved one hand broadly.

"Seventeen siblings scattered throughout The Seven Lands doing who knows what, learning who knows what, is certainly something to think about and to ponder, especially for one named as Queen."

He stood and bowed to them.

"I bow to you, two young folk marked to lead all

the Houses and to carry such a heavy burden." He looked at Sar'al. "To be so marked and called The Queen of The Seven Lands is an even heavier burden. In our very long history a number of kings have failed under much less of a burden. This House will do all it is capable of doing to assist you."

He shrugged and down heavily into his chair.

"Our Queen, do realize this, and do plan and behave accordingly." He pointed toward the north. "There are many folk out there, some of whom have been named The Hidden Ones for they are so. There are others, ummmmm, let's call them "Beings" for the lack of a better term, who might meddle in our affairs. Seventeen siblings of unknown capabilities may, ah eh, prompt meddling in unexpected ways, good or bad."

Arma'far leaned his head back against his chair and closed his eyes. He hoped that what he had told them would make a difference. He certainly hoped so. This new Queen needed all the help that she could get. It wasn't much, but hopefully, it will start them thinking.

"This is all of what I wished to say to you, and nothing more. I wished to, ummmm, further your education, a small amount, and to urge you to do these things. Tred carefully! Question everything! Do not accept all that is assumed to be true! In the morning do proceed on your journey, if you wish. We will see that your pack string has all the supplies that your beasts can carry."

His eyes popped open. He stood.

"A meal awaits. Shall we eat?"

Warrior's Hand.

Cereon left the last of the encampments on his circuit of learning. He had finished all that had been set before him. Those who taught him had done all that they could do. He felt really good, at finally being done, at finally being able to do what all that training was supposed to allow him to do. As far as he could tell, it did.

For no particular reason other than pure relaxation he was, this time, walking along the wagonway that led to the northeast beyond the last of the encampments. As he strolled along he left no sign of his passage in the bare soil he walked on. He cast no shadow in the bright light of the middle of a warm day.

Then he stopped and stared.

Walking toward him were two very tall and very robust folk, a male and a female, taller than anyone that he had ever met. They were talking softly to each other and seemed to be enjoying all that they saw.

He stared harder at them. Neither the armor that they wore nor the weapons they carried were anything Cereon had ever seen or had heard described. They must be, he decided, members of some of that small number of unknown folk who lived far beyond the mountains of the northeast, often spoken of as a wild place. But, it seemed to him, that they did look vaguely familiar.

He stood and waited for them to pass him by,

puzzling over that. He hadn't heard of a group of folk that looked like that pair.

Altai'dorionasha halted her brother and shifted the O'azur, which she had been carrying canted back over her right shoulder, to her right side. She had been enjoying the walk and had just realized how good she really felt. And she could tell that her brother felt the same way.

"Ahhhhmmm?" Hy'pherian had been enjoying the casual walk, just as she had suspected, and the warmth of the day and their soft conversation. He didn't remember that this grassy plain had been so pleasant when they had walked this way those many seasons past, being pulled to somewhere unknown, being filled with apprehension and worry of that unknown.

"Look you there," she murmured ever so softly. "Twenty paces ahead of us right in the center of the wagonway." She slipped her left hand from his right hand and stepped one pace away.

His eyes drifted around and back and forth.

"Well," he mumbled. "What do you think that might be?"

"None of The Six ever spoke of such a thing," she whispered.

"Ahhhmmmm," he mumbled, and smiled, a pure mischievous smile. "Shall we catch it?"

"We could."

"Let's." He shrugged. "But don't hurt it." He

wondered what it could be.

The Wild Fields.

They had been resting and taking it easy for three days. Wind Sky had been preparing all the meals, explaining as she worked what the various ingredients and seasonings were to Nar'a'las. Many of the archer/scout-guides enjoyed cooking fine meals when they were home. It came from all the time they spent camping and eating very plain foods while they were on go-about.

Wind Sky had returned from the workshop of the Master Craftsman, the one that had built her bow, with her bow cleaned, polished, and carefully checked for any sort of damage, however slight, two new bow strings, the extra bow string in her pocket.

"He is beautiful again," she purred as they were finishing First Meal.

When they were done, she washed, dried, and placed the dishes and utensils away.

"Eh erm," murmured Nar'a'las, watching Wind Sky load her carry pack with many small packages.

Wind Sky looked up and at her. "What?"

"Would you come with me to those who taught me. It would much easier for you to see and talk with them than for me to try and explain what I can do?"

Wind Sky stood and stared out a window at a passing cloud. Then she spun around and nodded.

"I am ready for go-about. Where?"

Nar'a'las stood, took her staff from where it

leaned in a corner, and said, "An'darl. Deep in one of the many narrow canyons, a hidden canyon."

Wind Sky walked to the outside door and opened it and made a small design on it. "My dwelling is packed and ready. I am packed and ready." She shrugged on her carry pack and then settled her loaded quiver in its place.

Nar'a'las smiled at her. "Quite! As are we."

They walked along the narrow pavement, out the gate, and headed for the wetway to the north, Wind Sky guiding.

The Plains of Singing Grass.

She had been walking at a steady pace, not too fast, not too slow, for a number of days, and had finally crossed the north-south wagonway. It would take as many days again before she reached The Wild Fields.

It had been, and was, a pleasant walk, one that she was enjoying greatly. She topped one of the many rises in the great plain, stopped, and looked at the vista around her. There was a special beauty to all that swaying grass, moving in the very pleasant soft breeze that carried a cooling touch.

She started down the gentle slope, noticing the subtle movement in the chest tall grass directly before her. As she curved around it, that faint rustle changed direction and came toward her. So she stopped and waited.

The great predator poked its head from the grass, ears flat back against its skull, and stared at her, yellow eyes watching carefully.

Verin'yashi held out her right hand, palm down, bent loosely at the wrist, and gently touched it on the nose.

Its ears rose. It soft rumbled deep in its throat.

"Er er er er," replied the red robed figure as she stepped closer and scratched the narrow space between those large yellow eyes. "Walk with me awhile."

She started toward her goal again, the great beast gliding silently by her side.

Three Drinks Green.

She stood near the beach and stared toward the south, toward the vague grey-green shadow mostly hidden in the perpetual fog mists that swirled around N'Farza. She was wondering what it was, exactly, that the troop had helped tear into shreds.

Behind her she could hear the normal sounds of the troop, The Troop of The Fierce Continence, going about their early morning business. She had eaten First Meal with the female Elders and talked with them about their patch of Yellow Flowering Red Sata grass.

Now she stood watching the tide beginning to ebb and expose The Tide's Gift, the wetway connecting Farza and N'Farza, and smelled the sea-salt of the gentle surf caressing the slowly being exposed sand.

Clerian'tra waved to the troop and headed down the wetway. Some of the troop, those watching her, began to talk excitedly. She seemed to be moving rapidly even though it appeared that she was just strolling. In moments, she was no more than a rapidly receding speck. Then the discussion shifted into speculation as to what she might be, exactly. They had never seen anyone do what she had just done.

Prime Shield.

He pushed open the great door of Origin Hall and walked down the short hall, sword hanging from his belt. He had yet to replace his shield. This was the place that he had been sent to carry his messages and speak with the correct folk.

As he walked, he winced at the sight of the thin gouge in the polished wood floor. In the central space he stopped in front of the Senior Day Staff.

"Rid'linar, Fast Rider of Nu'vern. I have an audience."

The Senior Day Staff nodded, consulted a paper, and indicated a wide side corridor. "This way." Rid'linar was led to the eighth door on the left side.

The Senior Day Staff rapped on the door twice with a short silver rod and pushed it open, gesturing for the Fast Rider to go in.

The door closed behind Rid'linar as he stepped inside the room.

It was a small square room furnished with a large desk, two chairs on one side, one chair on the other. He was surprised. He had assumed that the room would be much more, ah, ornate.

The two chairs were occupied. On the left as Rid'linar looked at them was The Senior of The Work, the one in charge of all manufacturing throughout the Lands of the Honglar. The other chair was occupied by The Senior of The Thought, in charge of all the designers of weaponry and armor manufactured in the workshops of the Honglar.

"Sit," rumbled The Work, indicating the only chair available.

The Thought nodded.

Rid'linar sat and cleared his throat.

Then he told the pair all that his documents had contained. It was a skill of the Fast Riders to read and memorize any documents they were transporting, just in case of loss. Now that ability was being utilized.

The Thought nodded when Rid'linar finished.

The Work frowned.

Then the two leaned close together and had a long and softly murmured conversation.

They straightened up and looked at Rid'linar.

The Thought nodded. "We will prepare drawings of four designs that we feel would be appropriate for your needs. It will less than a hand of days." He held up four fingers.

The Work leaned forward. "Only one of those designs will be made. You will chose which. It will take part of a small hand's of days to make the quantity asked for. You will see that a Trader-Merchant caravan is ready to transport all to Nu'Vern."

The two stood.

"Come back in less than a hand of days to make your selection," said The Thought.

The pair walked out a side door and left Rid'linar sitting there.

Rid'linar stood and, deep in thought, slowly walked back down the corridor and from Origin Hall.

Once he was back in The Place of The Others he lay on his bed and stared at the ceiling.

He was a Fast Rider, one that carried messages here and there. How was he supposed to know which design would be best? He had never had to deal with the Trader-Merchant outfits either.

He sighed and wondered what was going to happen to him when he and those weapons arrived in Nu'vern. He sighed heavily. Well, he had a small part of a hand's of days to worry about that and to hope that the new Queen wouldn't have him beaten too badly. No one had any idea how she would react to anything, she was so new a Queen.

Warrior's Hand.

The pair walked along the wagonway toward the whatever it was that they had noticed.

He was strolling just a little to one side of the center of the dirt wagonway while she was walking closer to the far edge. Neither was staring directly at it. But both was being quite wary and cautious as they approached the whatever it was. Of course, none of that showed. They both looked to be just strolling along, unconcerned about anything.

As they came even with it, she spun, dropped to one knee, and swept the ball end of the O'asur parallel to the surface. She felt the soft hit and heard something thump to the surface of the wagonway. Red dust spurted out on all sides of the thing.

Hy stepped on it and felt something under his boot squirm. Reaching up and back, he yanked The King of Swords free, slithering soft metallic hiss as it left its scabbard, from his back and set the tip of the point next to the side of his boot, the one holding the thing in place.

Then he looked at his sister and shrugged.

"Now what, Altai? Think that this might be one of those sneaky ones that we were warned about?"

She stood and brushed her knee clean and walked over. And shrugged back at him.

"Perhaps I could coat it with wagonway dust. Maybe that would give us some idea of what it is."

"You pair of prazga rap'dat'on'za!" snarled someone. "Let me up!"

She stared, knelt, and ran one hand over it.

"Cereon, is this thing you?"

Her brother laughed. "Well, it certainly sounded to me like the vocabulary of The-Son-and-Youngest-of-The-Second." He looked at her. "Maybe it is a mimic beast?"

A young man appeared, glowering up at them and the large foot and sword tip resting on his stomach.

"Daz tak! Get off!"

Hy'pherian stepped away, frowning down at him. "That really you?" He swung the great sword up and over a shoulder and into its resting place on his back.

Altai'dorionasha glowered at the short figure, now standing, busily brushing red dirt from as far back around himself as he could reach.

Then she laughed. "Well, it seems that whatever has happened to you, Cereon, it certainly hasn't improved your vocabulary."

Hy'pherian pointed. "Perhaps we could all sit in that, ummmm, clean grass and talk."

Cereon snarled at them and stomped from the wagonway into the grass and dropped to sit and glare at them as the pair walked over and joined him.

"Nothing can see me," he grumbled as he brushed the foot print from his mid-section. "How could you?"

The Scatter of Boulders.

The pair stood at the base of it and looked up the long slope of brown ashy talus. They were far to the east of Prime Shield. Just behind them was the large area covered with great brown boulders in an open pattern. The boulders were many times the size of them. Nothing that they had read explained how this area had come into existence or why it was the way it was.

In front of them, rising high, very high with deep grooves, were the eroded supporting walls of the plateau called Thanato's Field. They had been told by everyone that they had spoken with that one might climb up there without too much trouble. But, they all said, none have ever returned from such a climb. Those that resided "in that place" delivered death with a word or a gentle tap with the scepter that they carried, so it was said.

The two of them had talked with the Night Staff from Origin Hall in Prime Shield and heard various stories about what had happened to the Fast Rider from Nu'vern. The only thing that all the stories agreed on were that the Fast Rider had been healed and the description of the folk that were responsible and what few words that they had said. Nothing explained why they would be wandering around in An'darl.

Then they had talked with the caretakers at The Place of The Others and had heard just a little bit more. This little bit more clearly described the strange pair much as The Night Staff had done.

Eventually, after having spend considerable time in various libraries, large and small, they had come to the conclusion that up there, on that forbidding plateau, they would find an answer. It was a place of one of The Hidden Ones as far as they could determine.

Bael'slyth nudged her brother.

"Think we will survive?"

Equi-veronick shrugged. "We do look innocent."

The twins started up the incline. It was longer than they had thought or what it looked like when standing down on the plain, in The Scatter of Boulders, looking up. It took them the better part of a day to trudge to the top.

Then they stepped back down until they could not see the plateau floor, scraped a flatter spot near one edge. This would be their camping spot. If attacked they planned to leap over the edge and slide on their feet, down the extremely steep side of the great talus slope, moving much faster than anyone could run after them.

The Plains of Singing Grass.

The Royal twins left as soon as First Meal was finished.

They thanked Arma'far for his hospitality and for all the supplies now neatly stored on their pack animals. Then they headed westward, following his directions along a series of trails inside The Silent Woods. Finally they exited the forest and out into The Plains of Singing Grass and started along the mostly overgrown horse trial that followed the very edge of The Silent Woods. At the junction of this trail with the wagonway they had been instructed to turn north and then left at the first horse trail they came upon. This trail would bring them to The Wild Fields, the land of the archer/scout-guides.

They walked their horses and pack string at a gentle pace. It was going to take them a number of days before they arrived at their destination. There was no reason to hurry.

As they approached the junction, four dark clothed figures rose from the grass where they had been sitting and stood on the trail, waiting for the horse party to approach.

"They are Tha'a'sa," stated Sar'al, noting their clothes and weapons.

"Ummmm," replied Zak'ke. She ought to know.

They stopped their horses and dismounted close to the small group.

"Warm greetings," said Sar'al.

The four stepped closer, holding their short bows in their left hand, a round shield strapped to the forearm. At their waists hung quivers of arrows. On their backs they had each slung a large case of short, stabbing spears.

One of the males nodded to her.

"Warm greetings, Our Queen. The Elder chose each." He waved a hand at the other three. "She has placed a great Uoda on us. We are to be with you in all places."

Zak'ke looked at Sar'a and frowned.

She leaned close to him and whispered, "Uoda means that they have been given the right and the obligation to keep me from all harm. This is a thing that I can not refuse. If I did, they would never be able to return to their lands and homes. It is a thing that The Elders can do."

Sar'al turned to the four and bowed to them. "It is a great honor."

The four smiled at her.

The one who had spoken to her thumped his chest.

"Dirtan, Clan Zaland. He looks at you."

Dirtan pointed.

"Filion, Clan Pel'na. She looks at you. A'rona, Clan A'a'tar. He looks at you. Pa'zat, Clan Mu'antar.

She looks at you."

Dirtan smiled. "You ride. We walk. Easy."

Sar'al nodded and mounted her horse and waited for Zak'ke to join her. Then she led her small party in an easy walk toward the north.

The tall grass on either side of the wagonway rustled soft song to them in the light breeze.

The Silent Woods.

They had walked a good distance and had stopped not far inside the forest.

Dark Wind pointed. "The horse trail goes that way."

Al'tana nodded and pointed. "I am walking along the edge of the sea."

He stepped to her side.

They walked for some time in the silence of their surroundings. Then he cleared his throat.

"What?"

He pointed upward. "The light is passing." Then he pointed to a small patch of grass on a level spot. "Camp?"

"Yes." While he did that, fix their camp spot, she stood on the edge of the land and looked out at the dark sea. The land plunged steeply downward with no beach. Not far off shore, she could just see the great shape of one of the Laterian floating, back barely above the water.

Al'tana turned back and walked to their camping spot, and dropped her pack. Sitting next to it, she fished out a small sack of edibles she had collected as they had strolled along. She held it out to Dark Wind who shared some of the dried foods he carried. It seemed to her that the archer/scout-guides were rather quiet companions. And comfortable to be around.

It was a silent meal surrounded by the peace of the forest. Soon it was dark.

Dark Wind set his bow on top of his carry pack, quiver next to it, laid down, curled around them, one hand on his bow, and fell asleep.

She lay on her back and watched those stars visible through the foliage overhead until she fell asleep.

The Plains Of Singing Grass.

Wind Sky led them toward the north.

She had decided that Nar'a'las ought to stand inside one of the Builder's Ways and experience it. Then she would understand what Wind Sky had told her about the building of the Stoneholds.

They had been walking all day and were finally approaching the southern end of the side by side deep grooves.

Nar'a'las stopped and pointed to the west. "What is that, way over there, that white line?"

Wind Sky looked and laughed. "That is Bar'ta's Wall."

"And?" prompted Nar'a'las as she sat in the deep grass and waited.

Wind Sky sat next to her, holding her great bow

across her lap.

"Many long seasons ago," began Wind Sky, "Trinalin Bar'ta constructed that wall. It is said that he had special skills. The wall is tall and smooth, so smooth that none can climb it. It is said that the wall itself repels all who would try."

"And?"

Wind Sky pointed. "Just there, there is a bulge in the wall. It bumps this way because it curves around the opening to Zaz'za'gaz Cavern. The wall is anchored at each end by the cliffs. The wall seals that cavern away from the rest of Shar'daine."

"And?"

Wind Sky patted some of the grass next to her, flattened when they had sat. "It is said that in the cavern there are things, beings, folk of great skills, great powers that Bar'ta believed should be held away."

"What kind of great skills and powers?"

Wind Sky shrugged. "It has never been said."

"Ummmmm ehhh." Nar'a'las frowned, for just a moment. Perhaps she would go take a look. After their current journey was done. She stood.

Wind Sky stood and led them into The Builder's Way.

"This will lead us right to the wetway," she explained.

Q'an'a Ya'Kar.

She strode up the stairs of N'Farza and into the central gathering spot of Q'an'a Ya'kar village, "Those

Who Trade With Crazed Warriors," and stopped and stared.

On all sides of the clearing Clerian'tra could see numbers of dwellings that had been repaired or were still being repaired. So the story had not been embellished in the telling.

The Senior Female walked from her dwelling to speak with their visitor.

"Warm greetings," said Clerian'tra.

The Elder nodded. "Warm greetings." Her eyes wandered over the flowing robes and the symbols that circled around the cuffs of the wide sleeves and the hem of the light yellow garb.

"A light skin from Nu'Vern, not one of The Crazed Warriors."

Clerian'tra smiled. "I was visiting them." She touched the runes on her sleeve. "They named me as Bar'Farza, one who may walk and visit anywhere in their lands."

"Er ah ah," mumbled The Elder.

Clerian'tra handed her a small gift box. "I wish to visit these lands, if you do so agree." She bowed her head.

The Elder took the gift box, looked inside, and then into Clerian'tra's eyes as Clerian'tra looked up. "It may be done." She gestured for Clerian'tra to follow her.

Zaz'za'gaz Cavern.

She stood, hands on hips, glaring at him as he

strolled up the pavement and up the long ornate stone stairs to stand in front of her, smiling happily.

"Where have you been!" It was a growl and a demand.

He leaned forward and gave her a kiss.

Leaning back, just a little, he answered, eyes twinkling. "Outside. Looking around. Visiting."

She swung a fist. He easily caught it.

"Ah umh ta!" he grunted. "You should have come with me. Do you good to get outside, now and then."

He stepped away and sat on the edge of the high platform and dangled his legs in the open space. He grinned up at her and patted the polished marble surface next to himself. "Come and sit. Please?" He stared out at all the quiet dwellings.

"Zarlar," she growled. But she sat next to him and dangled her legs next to his.

He slipped his arm around her and sighed.

"Hinali, you know that none of the folk, or anything else out there, would have any idea that I, or we, could do that. That wall is quite useful. It keeps them from causing us any bother."

He pointed at the bright spot far above their heads, the mouth of the cavern. And laughed. "It is a frightfully long way to fall." He rapped the platform with a knuckle. "A rather hard surface to go splat upon."

"Soooooooooo?" she murmured.

"Umm ah ha?"

"What did you learn?" she hissed.

He turned his head and grinned at her.

"Insufferable," she grumbled.

He pointed in a southern direction.

"That bunch of tillers and fishers have produced seventeen children, all from one family unit."

"Soooooooo?"

He nudged her gently. "Remember The Ancient One?"

"Yesssssssss . . . "

"That seventeen are all developing skills, quite unique skills. In most cases, if not all, these skills are well beyond anything ever seen before, eeeee, by the folk up there, um oh, on the surface. She put a strange capability into them, especially one family line, many, many, many seasons past."

"Like what? Skills?"

"Dun know," he mumbled. Then he shrugged. "They are scattered all over the lands." He laughed.

"What?"

"One of them has taken on the title of *Queen of The Seven Lands*."

"WHAT!"

"Settle, Hinali, settle. She has just started. I really doubt anything will happen, or begin to happen, unless it looks like she will succeed."

She gently tapped her teeth together, one long fingernail trapped between them. Then she leaned against him.

"We could send a Sinit to watch her and to tell us what she is about. None of those folk could see it." She straightened up and bumped his shoulder with her's. "After all, they believe that wall has us penned up down there. Do you know where this *Queen* is?"

He kicked his heels against the wall. "She is riding up the trail to visit that bunch living in the place they call The Wild Fields."

He pointed upward at a slight angle. "Not far from here. Just about there."

"Do it."

He hugged her. "Done."

The Vale of Treliana.

They had rested at The Place of The Others for one day and had then journeyed on, traveling due east of Prime Shield along the edge of a long mountain chain that edged the coast. The pair had been walking. Nar'alas had thought it was the best thing to do. Although she hadn't told Wind Sky that.

Now they stood at the end of one of the many narrow draws in the mountain flanks.

Wind Sky scanned their surroundings and the blank slope directly in front of them and looked at her companion, a very puzzled look. "Here?"

Nar'a'las nodded. "Quite!" She held out her arm. "Take my hand, close your eyes, and walk by my side. I will guide you into The Vale of Treliana where I spent six seasons studying."

Wind Sky grabbed the offered wrist with her

right hand, her left hand clenching her long bow tightly, and closed her eyes.

"We are ready."

"Quite! It is only ten steps. I will count them. When I say ten, you may open your eyes. But only then."

Nar'a'las gave Wind Sky a gentle tug forward and began the slow count.

"One . . . two . . . three . . . "

It felt to Wind Sky as if they were moving quite rapidly.

" . . . eight . . . nine . . . TEN!"

Wind Sky felt sudden warmth on her skin, saw bright light through her clenched tight eyelids, and heard children laughing.

Her eyes flew open.

She gasped and stared at them.

"You are not children!"

The eight diminutive figures laughed at the comment. One stepped forward and smiled warmly at her. She was shorter than Wind Sky. "Most true." Her eyes looked deep. "Wind Sky. Be at ease. You and he are welcome as friends."

Then she turned and looked up at Nar'a'las.

"So soon you return?"

"Just for some short time," replied Nar'a'las. "Wind Sky wished to understand and I thought it best if she could speak to you, Treliana."

Treliana smiled. "I see. Of no concern. This Wind Sky is an honorable one." She reached out and took

Wind Sky's free hand. "Walk with me. In a little we will have a light meal."

She started them down a path lined with round blue paving stones.

"Nar'a'las is unique," she began. "For one of her kind." She waved her free hand at their surroundings. "We felt her standing outside six seasons past, crying. She didn't know how to enter. Then."

As they walked along, Wind Sky studied her diminutive companion. She was small like a child but proportioned like an adult. Everything about her seemed delicate and fragile. But somehow Wind Sky felt that there was a deep underlying strength in these ethereal appearing small folk.

"May I hold him?" asked Treliana as she stopped. "Your long bow."

Wind Sky nodded. Then she set the bow in the outheld small hand. She smiled to see such a long bow stretching to either side of this small folk.

"He is truly beautiful," whispered Treliana as she carefully inspected him.

Wind Sky smiled. She thought so.

Treliana looked up. "You are friends with Nar'a'las, you and him?" Her crystal clear eyes watched Wind Sky's face carefully.

Wild Sky frowned. She hadn't really thought about anything like that. Then she smiled broadly. "We are, we are that. Friends!"

Treliana beamed at her. "May I give him a gift, friend to friend, for I am also a friend to Nar'a'las?"

Wind Sky nodded and wondered what sort of gift Treliana could give him. He already had a new bow string and she had a spare one in her pocket.

Treliana slowly ran her hand over the smooth wood with the deep color of night. "Straighter, truer, farther," she intoned. "Now, Brave Heart," she whispered to the bow, "you and Wind Sky may do great things."

She handed the long bow back to Wind Sky and smiled as the archer/scout-guide took him in her hand and frowned as she inspected him for some small change or damage.

Treliana pointed at a small table near the path.

"Shall we have a light meal? As we eat I will speak of what Nar'a'las brought you here to understand."

Warrior's Hand.

Cereon looked at them, carefully.

"You both seem much taller, larger than I thought you would get."

They both smiled at him.

"We trained for many seasons," said Hy'perian. He hadn't thought about that. Nor had he really noticed it until it was mentioned.

"I suspect that it also had to do with the types of food we ate," explained Altai'dorionasha.

"Those who trained us, The Six," added her brother, "told us that all the foods that we ate were special and would add to our abilities." He nodded.

"Until we meet with more of the folk we won't be sure about that, but I believe we may be somewhat taller than most."

Altai'dorionasha smiled at Cereon. "We were trained to see faster, to see minute changes, to see the very subtle."

Hy'perian grinned at Cereon. "You appeared to us like the ghost of a ghost of a ghost, just the tiniest hint."

"So," she added, "we decided to catch it, just to see what it was. Tell us, how did you learn to do that?"

Cereon leaned back on his elbows and began to describe the many seasons he had spent passing from encampment to encampment and how, just a few days past, he had completed his own training.

When he finished, she said, "We thought to walk down to Nu'vern and visit the First-Twins-Of-The-First and find out what all our siblings are doing. Come with us?"

Cereon stared at them for long moments, then he nodded. "Sounds as good as anything. I hadn't really thought about what I was going to do next. No hurry?"

Altai'dorionasha stood. "As slow as you wish. Many seasons have passed. A some more days will mean little."

The trio started down the wagonway, Cereon walking between them. They were just strolling along. In no hurry.

He began to tell them some of the tales he had heard in the encampments.

Learning

The Plains of Singing Grass.

The small group had finally arrived at the junction of the horse trail heading west with the wagonway heading north-south.

They paused while Sar'al opened The Traveler's Guide and checked one of the maps. She nodded and headed up the horse trail. The map indicated that the trail headed in a northwesterly direction toward their destination, The Wild Fields.

As they had been traveling toward The Wild Fields, Zak'ke had been carefully watching his twin. He had been doing that ever so carefully and wondering about what he thought he saw and then deciding that it was true. She had changed.

Ever since her, their, discussion with the Head of the Second Royal House, Beron Sacog, and their acquiring of her four Tha'a'sa guards, she had changed. He now saw it in the way she rode. He heard it in her voice. She sat straighter in her saddle, her shoulders no longer slumped.

Sar'al had not only accepted the role of Queen of The Seven Lands, she had become The Queen. In very subtle ways, she moved, talked, and presented herself as The Queen. Ah ehm er, he thought, keeping his expression safe from her casual glance, she has finally taken up the challenge set to her by The Ancient One.

He almost laughed, but didn't. He didn't feel it would be a good idea to explain what he had been thinking.

Life was certainly going to be getting ever more interesting from now on. It was something to look forward to. He looked further away from her and smiled, not wishing to attract her attention, not at this moment.

While they were following the directions given to them by Arma'far, Sar'al was also following his advice: question everything, including the directions that they had been given.

A short way up the trial, she decided it was time to make camp not too far off the trail. So they did.

Once they were settled and eating Late Meal, Zak'ke pointed across the horse trail at the tangled mass of vegetation that bordered the other side of the trail.

"What do you think all that is?" He began to chew on some of the dried food stuffs.

Sar'al unfolded a map, one of the maps attached to The Traveler's Guide. "It is called Bane's Thicket." She pointed. "Eventually we should be able to see something called The Well of The Lost poking up above all that growth."

"Umh." Zak'ke swallowed. "Think that anything lives in there?"

Pa'zat shook her head. "None enter there. None

exit there."

Zak'ke nodded. "You would have to cut your way in there, every step of the way."

He looked at the four Tha'a'sa. "It only grows on one side of the road. Why doesn't it spread?"

The four shrugged.

Sar'al folded the map and closed the book. "The Guides only gives place names but no history or other explanation for them. Maybe those who live in The Wild Fields will know."

Zak'ke smiled and shrugged. "Um well, then it is just a number of day's camping before we learn anything."

He rolled up in his sleeping gear and fell asleep. Shortly afterwards, the rest did the same thing.

The Wild Fields.

She walked through the gateway, red robes bouncing amber glow reflected sunlight from the morning sun on all the walls.

She was observed by one of those who wished to remain unknown. He thought that one of those that followed Huroma coming here was a bothersome thing. But he also felt that, at the moment, it would be best to do nothing. Neither the hidden observer, nor the woman, nor the small party headed this way saw the Sinit watching everything.

The Grass Larpa had been thanked for her company. The pair had separated before they could be seen from the high walls. Neither thought that it would be a good idea to cause some unneeded excitement among the dwellers of this Stonehold.

She strolled down the wide central street and walked into The Great Hall.

Cloud Spirit looked up from the document that he was reading, set it on a small table, stood, and bowed.

"Warm greetings, um, to The Hand of Huroma."

He filled a cup with Darlu Berry juice from a container on his small desk and offered it to her.

Verin'yashi bowed her head and took the offered cup.

"Warm greetings, Cloud Spirit." She took a sip and smiled at him. "Ahhh, Darlu Berry."

He waited for her to sit, then sat. And looked at her, a slight frown creasing his brow.

"It is almost never," he said, "that one of those of Huroma venture travel so far."

She nodded and emptied her cup.

He reached over and refilled it. "Why have you come here?"

"The folk of The Wild Fields are known to be direct folk." She smiled warmly.

After refilling his own cup, he leaned back in his chair, holding it in one hand. "That we are." And took a sip.

"I have come to visit with one of your's and an, ah eh, unusual visitor."

"Eh? Who?"

"Archer/scout-guide Wind Sky."

He nodded and took another sip. "We talked, we three. It was a strange story. But!" He held up his free hand. "They both claimed it to be so." He shrugged. "Wind Sky's traveling companion does seem to have unusual, most unusual, um oh, skills."

"Does this companion have a name?"

He nodded and emptied his cup, setting it back on the small table. "That one gave her name as Nar'a'las. From her physical appearance she appeared to be from Nu'vern as do you."

Verin'yashi laughed, then clamped a hand over her mouth, then took it away as Cloud Spirit frowned at her.

"A laugh of surprise," she explained, eyes sparkling. "A great surprise."

"Some secret thing?"

She shook her head. "Not at all. Nar'a'las is the Last-Daughter-of-The-Second as I am called the First-Daughter-of-The-Third. She is my near-sister. I have no idea as to what she has been doing or learning. I parted from Nu'vern before she did."

Cloud Spirit stood. "Wind Sky and, eh, Nar'a'las went to her dwelling. It is not far from here. May I guide you there?"

Verin'yashi stood and smiled at him. "Most kind. Would you tell me of the archer/scout-guide as we walk?"

"Of course."

Setting their cups on the table, they headed out the door.

He led her down a small side street that followed the outer edge of the Stonehold and talked with her as they walked along. Then he pointed.

"There, that dwelling directly opposite the entrance to the Watch Tower."

They stopped in front of the door.

Cloud Spirit shrugged. "She went on go-about."

"How do you know?"

He pointed at a rune marked on the upper panel of the door. "That design tells all that she is out there, somewhere."

Verin'yashi sighed. "For how long?"

He shook his head. "Until she returns. The archer/scout-guides go where they will, as they will, for as long as they will. They return when they are ready to do so."

Verin'yashi chewed gently on one corner of her mouth. "Would you suggest to them when you see them, or just Wind Sky, that it would be a, uma, good thing if they came to visit me?"

He nodded. "I will so speak to Wind Sky when next I visit with her, and her companion if she is still with Wind Sky. Perhaps she will do that." He shrugged. "They all do as they please. Erm, most of the time."

She bowed to him. "Then I give this to you." She handed him a ring with a flame jewel set into it.

He took it and ran a finger over the jewel.

"If you should have such a need, speak my name, and I will come." She bowed deeply to him. "But, for now, I think that I will take a leisurely stroll back."

She spun away and headed for the gateway.

Cloud Spirit ran his hand back over his hair and wondered what all that was about. And how could she so casually speak of leisurely strolling through and across all those stretches of grass-covered plain, with prowling Grass Larpa wandering about, by herself. Unarmed.

Prime Shield.

Ran'dyal, now Second of The Trader-Merchant outfit located here, looked out his window, the window of his new office on the top floor of The Trader-Merchant structure. Of course, the structure only had two stories, but still, it was on the "top floor."

Outside, the shadows were lengthening as he watched various members of the staff wandering toward the main gate and their homes.

He closed The Assignment Book, slipped it into the middle drawer of his desk and smiled to himself.

Things were certainly looking better. New office, new position, new and improved income, new status, new prestige.

Only he knew why, at least as far as the Trader-Merchant outfit was concerned.

He was acquiring more contracts for moving goods than his predecessor. His caravans and their booths were pulling in more income than his predecessor's.

It was all due to his organization.

The Dark Wind members helped each other in

whatever manner they could. Some of them already held positions where that help was extremely beneficial.

And it had happened in such a short time!

Even he was amazed.

He wandered down the stairs and then toward his favorite restaurant. He still went there even though his new status meant that he could frequent some of the "other places."

As he strolled along he thought that if things continue to progress and grow as they were doing, it wouldn't be too many seasons before they, his organization, would be ready to begin to take control. Now they should begin to move into new areas to spread their influence.

That was such a pleasant thought that he smiled broadly.

Thanato's Field.

His eyes popped open.

He stared up at the night, a dark night, a clear, no cloud sky dark night strewn with myriads of bright stars. Someone had gently nudged his shoulder.

He turned his head. His sister slumbered on.

He looked the other way. Someone knelt next to him.

"Ummmm?"

The shadow bent forward, a gentle deep voice spoke to him.

"This One is Fair Death. Those who dwell in all the lands below do not venture up here to tempt death.

This One would know why you do."

"May I sit up?"

"One does as One does." The shadow settled back.

Equi-veronik sat up. He could see the faint metallic glint of the thing that his visitor held in one hand. It had a faint yellow glow.

"My sister and I have no desire to tempt death. We, in our travels, have heard tales of a Hidden Folk that were told to live up here. We heard of one who healed a badly injured Fast Rider in the Origin Hall of the Honglar in their town, Prime Shield."

"It was so done."

Equi-veronik cleared his throat. "My sister and I wished to speak with that One who did that, eh ah, to verify the truth of what we were told. Ummmm eh, if it is permissible, eeee, acceptable, ahhhh, to do that."

The figure stood.

Now that his eyes were more dark-adapted, it seemed to Equi-veronik that his visitor wore a loose jacket and billowing trousers of silver and white. These garments now seemed to have a soft sheen that created a soft cloud of faint light around him.

"The brother and the sister will come with this One."

"We will do that," said Bael'elyth as she stood. Their conversation had woken her.

The pair followed their guide, that is how they saw him, up the slope and onto the flat space that was called Thanato's Field. Fair Death led them along a narrow trail that curved around a tall conical mound and toward another mound which they could just see in the dim light of late night. A faint mist drifted over and around everything.

When they reached the edge of the great mound, also quite conical in form, they halted. Fair Death pointed up.

"Up there and in! That One, Soft Touch, is there. This One may not enter that space."

He waited for them to start up the trail leading to the top, watching them carefully, clenching the silver and gold scepter in one hand.

As the pair started up, Bael'elyth leaned close and murmured to her brother, "So far all appears calm."

He took her hand in his. "He didn't kill us," he whispered.

At the crest, at the top, they stopped, and stared, at it.

There was nothing up here other than a great black circle that capped the entire mound.

"Eh er," she mumbled.

"Just step in?" he asked.

"Seems so."

In unison they did. They took one step.

And gasped.

They were standing inside a vast hall, on the floor of that vast hall. High overhead they could see the domed ceiling. Soft light flooded the space from unseen sources.

Directly in front of them, standing near the far

wall, were two gigantic stone statues. The female was wearing flowing robes. The man was dressed in a short jacket and trousers.

Someone standing just in front of the great art works waggled a hand at them.

Equi-veronik tugged her into motion.

The twins stopped a respectful distance from the still figure and waited.

Her garb, made from a strange cloth of silver and white, seemed to radiant a soft sheen, a cloud of light around her, obscuring details. But what could be seen was that she wore a loose jacket and billowing trousers. Her skin tones were a dense grey almost black, made all the more dramatic by the contrast between that and her costume. Red eyes bored into their eyes. Her lips were as red her eyes.

"This one is Soft Touch, a One Who Saves. Why are you here?"

Bael'elyth told her of their search and their conversations with various others, including Fair Death.

"Seekers for truth are rare among all those folk out there." She waggled one hand at what the pair assumed were all the lands outside.

"Come with this One." She walked toward a dark spot in a far wall.

As they came close it became apparent that it was an opening to a tunnel. It was a very long tunnel.

After some time they entered another great chamber similar to the one that they had left.

Here the giant statues were seated in chairs that

would have been quite comfortable if made from the usual materials.

A long stone bench faced the seated pair.

Soft Touch led them to it and sat down, indicating that they should do the same. She waggled her hand toward the great space around them.

"Here do these Ones dwell, here in The Heart of Darkness. Here, seated before The Mother and The Father, you will hear the truth. Listen carefully."

Then she told them.

Long before memory is capable of knowing, they became. They looked around and saw an empty world and decided that it should not be so.

The Mother Of Us All looked around and said, "I see three empty domains. I see The Domain of The Wet. I see the Domain of The Dry. I see the Domain of The Open. It should not be so."

And it changed.

Creatures, all of life in all of its forms, appeared in the three domains.

The Father Of Us All watched what she had done and said, "I see The Three Domains filling and filling without end. It should not be so."

And so, life in all of its forms has an end so others may have a beginning.

The Mother Of Us All and The Father OF Us All had two daughters. They gave to each daughter one aspect of all living things.

The Lady of Life is a reflection of their mother. This daughter gave to her favored ones the gift of healing and of health. They could use this gift on others, if they were called or chose to do so.

The Lady of Death is a reflection of her father. This daughter gave to her favored ones the gift of death. If necessary or to defend, this gift could be given to others.

The favored ones, when they are outside, always travel in pairs, Life and Death together, a reflection of all living things, a beginning and an end.

Soft Touch stood, stepped forward, and turned to face them.

"This is our truth. Come! It is time for a meal."

Prime Shield.

The three decided to spend a few days in the central town of The Honglar, resting and gathering supplies for the long walk to Nu'vern.

Given their training they didn't mind the rather simple lodgings they had in The Place of The Others.

It was mid-morning and they were strolling around the central part of town looking at the various large buildings that surrounded it.

Hy'perian nudged Cereon gently.

"Huh?" He looked up at him.

"I was curious about your ability," Hy said.

"Oh? What?"

"Could we learn something like that, to not be seen, or, even just a little bit blurred?"

His sister laughed. "A great idea, Hy!"

"Ummmmm eh ah," mumbled Cereon.

Altai'dorionasha winked at her brother.

Hy'perian nodded. "Much nicer than some of his responses." He smiled at Cereon.

Cereon jerked to a halt and glared up at them, eyes darting from face to face. Those two were quite a lot taller than he was. Of course, he was much shorter than most folk.

"Piz a'pik ta!" he suggested.

"See, Altai," laughed Hy.

"Welllllllll, Cereon," she purred. "Possible?"

"Gupa," grumbled Cereon. He shrugged. "I did hear an interesting tale about learning, ummmmm, other kinds of skills."

"And?" she prompted.

Cereon sighed, it was a long put-upon sigh. He pointed. "We can get something to eat over there."

They followed him to a small stall set up in the narrow space between two of the large structures.

As they finished the items that they had bought, Cereon said, "I was told of a place not too far from and west of The Silent Woods where we might ask about things like that.

"And?" Hy'perian asked softly.

Cereon frowned at him, just a little. The three of them had spend lots of time together before their fourteenth season gently poking at each other and becoming fast friends.

"I was told that it was a dangerous place to visit." He scuffed one boot on the pavement.

Altai nodded. "Does this dangerous place have

a name?"

"The Ghost Stones," mumbled Cereon.

"Hy?"

He smiled. "Cereon is pretty ghostly all by himself. Let's go visit that place." It sounded like a good idea to him.

Altai nodded. "It is on our way." She looked at Cereon. "And we will be very, very careful when we get there. Do you have any idea of who lives there?"

Cereon shook his head.

They hurried back to their rooms to pack everything for traveling at first light next day.

As they packed, Altai told Cereon of The Dark Wind and that she felt that they had been being watched. But she hadn't been able to tell who was doing that.

The Heart of All.

The twins had a great archery field constructed shortly after the Trader-Merchant caravan had delivered great numbers of short bows and half a wagon of bundles of arrows.

That Trader-Merchant caravan would shortly be headed from Nu'vern with their wagons filled with dried foods of the fields and the seas, some of which would be delivered to the Tha'a'sa, the rest for markets elsewhere as the fee for services.

Half of the Armed Mass that the twins had assembled were practicing their archery skills.

In an adjacent field the other half were banging

with renewed enthusiasm at each other with wooden practice weapons. Another Trader-Merchant caravan had delivered a large number of long swords with a gentle curve and large triangular shields. Those judged sufficiently skilled by the trainers would be allowed to have real weapons and shields. The rest would practice on.

Rau'ke and Cant'al, acting King and Queen, had held several long conversations with Rid'linar. During these they had assured him that he had done very well. The Fast Rider had been worried that his choices would be refused and that he would be given some lessor assignment than that of Fast Rider. It had taken some time for the twins to convince him that he must stop worrying. They had been left in charge after all and if they were satisfied with what he had done then that would be the end of that discussion.

Now the three of them stood before the open gateway and discussed what his next assignment was.

They handed him a rather thick report. He was to deliver this to Sar'al and Zak'ke wherever they might be. They knew this would be difficult as no-one knew what that pair were doing. But Fast Riders had highly developed tracking skills. That massive report contained information that dealt with all the matters in Nu'vern and the development of the Armed Mass.

They watched Rid'linar trot his horse down Aydel's Track, leaded the string of pack animals and spare mounts. He was well supplied for a long journey. He was also armed with one of the new swords and shields.

Two Swords.

The triplets had just frighten their Teachers in The Hall of Learning in the Adept's building. They hadn't intended to do that. It had been their Teachers' fault, in a manner of speaking.

The Teachers had launched a Beast of Horrible Thought at them. It was unexpected and had never been seen before by the three students. They had reacted instantly with their merged thought and energies.

That concentrated energy, released by the triplets, erased the monster as the wind disperses smoke. They had also cracked the ceiling of the great hall and made numerous holes in the far wall. Where the Beast had stood there was a large scorched and smoldering patch on the floor. Given that the floor in the hall was dark grey stone, this was something to stare at. The flames were green.

"Good focus, Verd," stated Cer'alda, smiling up at her brother. They had all grown quite a bit during their training but he was now taller than either of his sisters by a good head-and-a-half. She wrinkled her nose. The smoke from the burning spot where the monster had been was quite unpleasant.

"Lovely swipe," added Caevelos. "Nice touch, Verd." She sent a gust of wind to clear the hall of smoke. Cer'alda nodded her thanks.

Verdorion-elvershair grinned at them. He threw an arm around their shoulders and gave them a gentle hug. He was standing between them.

"Very smooth," he said to them. Then he murmured every so softly, "But they don't look all that happy about it to me." He coughed. The odor from the burning floor had tickled the back of his throat. He looked at the green flames. They went out.

"Ummm, we did hurt the hall," observed Caevelos.

"A little," added Cer'alda.

Verd nodded, and sighed. "Let's go hear how bad a report we get, this time."

The three walked slowly over to where the Teachers were gathered, whispering among themselves.

"Not good," mumbled Cer'alda, looking at all that whispering. The others nodded agreement.

The three stopped the proper distance from the Teachers and bowed deeply, three times, looking very proper, very, very student proper. Then they stood, hands at their sides and waited to hear how they should have done this or that better.

Kran'alka, The Voice of The Teachers, stepped forward and bowed three times to each of them, and straightened up, and looked at them, his face a perfect blank.

"Oh gooba," whispered Caevelos.

Kran'alka stepped close and rapped each one of them on the forehead with a sharp knuckle and stepped back.

"Three students of one mind," he intoned, now looking very stern, black eyes searching each face. Then he smiled, shocking the trio. They had never seen him smile at anything that they had ever done, nor ever at them.

Cer'alda wobbled, just a tiny bit.

Verd stood straighter.

Caevelos hissed softly.

"We are finished, we have finished," stated The Voice. "Every skill we know, you have mastered. Every aspect, every twist, every alteration, everything!"

His smile broadened. "We are very proud." He nodded at them. "We will watch. If you should be in need, of that we have great doubts of it ever happening, we will aid. But first, a cautionary tale." He began to explain, slowly and carefully.

Finally, he waggled one hand. "Your packs and your staffs are just over there. Where will you go now?"

"Home," stated Verd, looking from sister to sister, who nodded agreement.

"Fair journey, students, fair journey. And be mindful, very mindful of all that I have just spoken upon."

The Vale of Treliana.

Treliana smiled at Sky Wind as soon as their meal was finished.

"This narrow valley," she waved her hand at their surroundings, "is one of the hidden places in the lands. We wish it to be so, and so it is. We care little of what all of them, outside, chose to do. We have never, before Nar'a'las, had a student from out there."

Treliana patted one of Wind Sky's hands gently and smiled broadly, exposing long canine teeth. "As you can see, as you now know, we are different." She laughed. "Besides our stature."

She pointed at others, sitting here and there on the grass, eating a meal.

"We all have skills . . . abilities which none of those outside have." She smiled. "Until we took in that one sitting next to you."

Treliana reached over and touched the staff leaning against their table.

"She made this hiking staff from the wood of the Cherila Tree." She pointed. "Those tall fuzzy trees you see way over there against the mountain slopes. It was her first chore."

Treliana held the staff and waggled it causing the streamers to flutter.

"Nar'a'las has passed through three levels of training. That is what those ribbons indicate."

Carefully placing the staff against the table, Treliana turned slightly to face Wind Sky.

"We would like our only student to study and complete the fourth level, the hardest level." She held up a finger. "But!"

Nar'a'las made a soft sound.

Treliana nodded and touched Wind Sky's hand.

"But. You must help her."

Wind Sky looked from Treliana to Nar'a'las and back again, frowning, puzzled at her suggestion. "I am an archer/scout-guide," she stated firmly. "We do not know how to do things like that!"

Treliana laughed, high tinkling laughter.

"Of course not!" she said, smiling broadly at her.

"Eh ah?"

"There is a certain gem stone that is required. It is found only in certain places. I would like you, friend of Nar'a'las, to help her get this thing."

"Oh." Wind Sky nodded.

Nar'a'as stared at Treliana. She had never mentioned anything like this before.

Treliana smiled at her. "Each thing comes in its own time."

Then she turned to Wind Sky. "You two must go a long distance from here. Your journey will take you north of that rarely visited Valley of Glar wherein resides the Master Smith, M'aga. Far beyond that place there is a small valley deep in tall mountains, tall, snow covered mountains. In this small valley there is a mine cut deep into one of those mountain slopes. That valley is the home of a surly folk who name themselves Czat'akar. They are the miners. There is a gem there that Nar'a'las must have. She now knows what it looks like."

Treliana stood. "Come! I will take you to a place to rest and prepare."

As they rested, Wind Sky began to tell Nar'a'las about growing up, knowing from the time that she was handed her first bow that she would become an archer.

Like all the children when they were first handed their first bow she was unable to draw it back. But she told herself that she would do that and that she would do that before anyone else could.

That bow never left her hand. She carried it everywhere.

And every day she pulled. And every day that the archers practiced she watched them and asked questions. What they did they made look easy.

And every day she pulled.

She began to run up and down the stairs of one of the watch towers.

Within a season she was given a new bow.

And every day she pulled.

She began to visit the workshops of the Craftsmen and the Master Craftsmen just to watch. Then she began to ask questions and to learn.

Over time, she had long conversations about materials and designs. She learned about the attributes of this material or that material as it related to the function of a bow and to the bow's ability.

As the seasons passed, the bows she was given became stronger and stronger.

She spent time, every day, standing on the roof of her family dwelling, bow pulled to its maximum, standing rigid, holding that stance, holding, holding, holding.

Seasons passed. She practiced and practiced. And she learned more and more about the subtleties of bow construction.

By the time that she was selected to join the archer/scout-guide ranks, she knew exactly how she wanted her bow to be built and had convinced one of the great Master Craftsmen to built it that way. He told her that it would take some many days to do that. He smiled at her, Wind Sky's design was "different."

Wind Sky looked over at Nar'a'las, they had been stretched out comfortably on the floor, Wind Sky's great long bow lying by her side.

"Even with his size, he is the strongest of all of those carried by the archers. No other bow was made as he was." She grinned. "I am shorter than most of the others but he reaches further that they can."

She sat up and laughed. "The Master Craftsman promised to never build another like him."

The Plains of Singing Grass.

The Sinit lay in the grass close to the horse trail and watched them approach and pass by. Nothing noticed its presence, neither the riders nor the walkers nor the horses, ridden or led.

Zak'ke pulled his horse up and along the side of Sar'al's. "Much further?"

She pointed as they approached the intersection with another horse trail coming from the east.

"Those large hills are topped by the towns of the folk who dwell in The Wild Fields. We can camp near the intersection and enter the main town in early light."

He laughed. "It will be good to sleep on something other than the ground. Are we being Royal then?"

Sar'al nodded.

Lu'yat'far'a Ya-Kar.

She had strolled along the trail, passing through the lands of the Dur'na, who nodded at her, noting the ornament pinned on her robe, and watched her pass into the lands of the N'dara.

She had spent two days, resting and talking with the Elders of N'dara in their village, called "Those Who Look Across The Great Blue."

One edge of their village was bordered by the sharp edge of the steep cliffs of N'Farza that plunged down into The Great Sea, a sea of a deep blue color.

The Elders had been told by runners from the Par'a'na, who had slipped through the dense jungle/forest unseen by their visitor of the light skin that the Farza had accepted as a special one.

The Elders were too polite to ask this visitor what she wanted or why she was here, but their many conversations circled around and around these unspoken questions.

And, as they talked, Clerian'tra said a little of this and a little of that until the Elders relaxed.

On the second day, the Elders had pointed toward the south and told her that "up there" were the lands of the Bindulin.

If she walked along that trail, the one just there, she would come to stairs carved into the black rock. It would lead her "up there."

Then they cautioned her. The Bindulin were a rather reclusive folk for being Tha'a'ea. But, they felt, that the clan "up there" would honor the message of the ornament that she wore.

She bowed and thanked them for their wise words.

The next morning she started along the correct trail and wondered what "up there" meant.

The Silent Woods.

Al'tana and Dark Wind were strolling along the top of a low bluff in the grassy border between forest and bluff edge.

They had been surprised to find a small cluster of buildings scattered around a point of land surrounded by The Silent Woods.

They had been equally surprised when a rather stocky male dressed in scale armor of a light brown color, a dull light brown that did not reflect light, approached them. A heavy mace hung from his thick and wide belt, a small round shield was strapped to his left forearm.

They carefully watched him come closer.

Al'tana wondered whether he was going to attack them for entering his dwelling complex.

Dark Wind studied his approach. If he reached for that mace, the archer knew that he could jump back, pull an arrow from his quiver, and kill him in the blink of an eye.

The stocky man nodded to himself and stopped.

"I am Arma'far Zalna'dei Beran Sacog," he announced. "I am The Head of House Beran Sacog.

Might I know your names? Please?"

"Dark Wind, archer/scout-guide."

"Al'tana, Last-Daughter-Of-The-Third, House Noriyon Zacog. Warm greetings." She was surprised. None of the mothers or her father had told of one of The Royal Houses being located here in The Silent Woods.

"Ah erm," said Arma'far. "One of the seventeen." He bowed to them. "May I offer the hospitality of my house?"

Al'tana bowed to him. "Most kind."

He led them to one of the buildings and explained, as he escorted them into a room with comfortable chairs and a large window overlooking The Dismal Sea, that there had been a rather bad event some many days past and that the house members were still quite nervous and cautious upon seeing strangers.

Al'tana and Dark Wind spent two days resting and visiting before returning to their journey south.

Arma'far had seen that they had all the supplies that they wished to carry and wished them a safe journey and an invitation to visit again. As they walked away, he wondered how The Queen was doing and what this sibling had learned, and what she was doing just walking along the water's edge.

Some distance along, as they walked around a rather sharp bend in the coastline, Al'tana stopped and pointed.

"That is The Folly of Franbandan, as it is called. He constructed the wagonway along that mountainous spine that connects Shar'daine and Nu'vern."

Dark Wind stared at it. "I have heard that tale but have never heard a good description of it, nor have I ever seen it. I will have much to talk about when I return to The Wild Fields."

Al'tana laughed. "As will I when we reach the lands of my folk."

Kar'antil'anya.

Viana had sat with The Elders of The Seven Clans to talk and to discuss what The Elders felt ought to be done. They sat in the Decision Circle in Viana's home town and talked for three days. Viana practiced patience as the discussion circled around and around.

Viana was called The Spirit of the Tha'a'da, The Seven Clans that lived in Mart'den. She was the one who could call all the clans into action if she decided that such a thing was necessary.

After the three days of discussion, The Elders had finally decided. They had all agreed that too little was known and too much was guessed as to what various myths might indicate.

But, finally, it had been decided.

Viana would rest for two day. Then she would ride south and speak with Sar'al and Zak'ke.

Then, finally, it had been decided.

For now they would called Sar'al "The Queen of The Seven Lands." But, they would decide whether such a title was to be permanent or merely some short-term temporary label.

If Viana had disagreed with anything they had

decided and said so, she could have stated that something else would be done. And it would have been done. But there would have been much grumbling and the casting of dark looks in her direction. Regardless, they would have done as she said. But Elders were Elders and had much accumulated experience and knowledge. So, Viana had agreed.

Viana distributed gifts to The Elders, gifts from Clan Veronji who had hosted the gathering and from Viana who had called the gathering. The Elders left, headed back to their own clans to discuss with their clan members what had been decided.

The Clan Veronji Elder hugged her and then wandered down the pathway to her dwelling, saying back over her shoulders, "Rest well, Viana. Carry our decision to those twins. All will wait until you return before any other action will be discussed or taken." She raised one arm in the air and said back over her shoulder, "As you well know."

Viana's mother had prepared a special great meal and invited all from their village who wished to come, to visit and talk with her daughter.

It lasted into the night.

The Plains of Singing Grass.

One day's walking east from The Wild Fields she made camp, flattening a spot in the grass.

As she ate Last Meal, the Grass Larpa that had traveled with her before pushed through the grass and sprawled next to her.

Verin'yashi laughed softly.

"I would offer you some of this but I doubt that dried grass kernels would be very appetizing to you."

The great beast made deep rumbling sounds.

When Verin'yashi finished her meal, she wiped her hands on the grass and reached out to scratch behind one fur covered ear.

"You must speak to them. They will have to stop, they must stop, this wrong behavior. Those that have already threatened travelers are dead. Many more will die if they do not listen."

The massive predator flowed to her feet, turned her head, and licked Verin'yashi on the forehead. Then she slipped silently into the grass.

She stared at the spot where the Grass Larpa had slipped away and wondered whether she would be able to change the dark touch that seemed to have settled over the Grass Larpa.

Lying back she stared up at the stars beginning to appear and thought that it was time that The Adherents did more than study information. They had to discover who or what was responsible for this.

Two Swords.

Viana had ridden to this northwest town of An'darl, settled herself and her horse at The Place of The Others and began making the rounds of those that would have horses for sale.

By the end of the day she had acquired a spare mount. Next day she would begin to check a few establishments for pack animals.

During her conversations with the horse traders some of them had told her about three pale skins who were also looking for good animals. Others told her that the three had been in Two Swords for eight seasons or so. She also pondered the feeling of awareness of someone carefully hidden watching her. She wondered who those hidden watchers could be. But they were very well hidden. She couldn't identify them.

As she fell asleep in her bed, an overly soft bed to her, Viana wondered who those three were. They must be from Nu'vern. Perhaps they were some of Sar'al's siblings, she had so many. Maybe she would see them on the wagonway as she rode toward Sar'al and Zak'ke.

She could feel the spark of her clan-sister pulling her.

This and That

Zar'za'gaz Cavern.

They sat at a table in a large room and ate a small meal. They ate the meal, not for the nourishment but for the experience. The meal was mainly fruits from the lands above.

The room had three walls and was open on the fourth side. Stretching across the great space below they could see the sprawl of numerous dwellings, some more fanciful than others. All very quiet.

Zarlar smiled across the table at her.

"I have been thinking," he said.

She frowned at him.

He laughed.

"It is just a little thing," he offered.

"What?" she snapped.

He pointed up and at a slight angle.

"The Queen will be visiting the folk that dwell in The Wild Fields. The Sinit saw them pass through the gateway." He smiled. "She now has four of the Tha'a'sa with her. They appear to be her guards. Heavily armed." He shrugged. "Probably a good idea."

Hinali nodded. "The result of the dark one's rash decision it appears. Do you think that she knows of those cretins that call themselves *The Dark Wind*?"

Zarlar laughed and took a bite out of a large red fruit. He chewed thoughtfully and swallowed.

"Probably not," he said. "The Sinit also saw one of the folk that wear those flaming red robes, The Touched of Huroma, leaving the same town the day before. She had been visiting. The Sinit had been lurking around there waiting for the Queen to appear on the trail. It also reported one other, trying to stay a hidden observer."

He leaned back and stared into her eyes.

"What?" she asked.

"I think that the one in the flaming red robes was one of the Queen's many siblings."

"Ah."

He nodded. And moved the small knife next to his plate back and forth.

She hissed at him.

"Yes," he agreed. "I think one of us ought to have a small talk with that one."

He smiled.

"You go," she grumbled. Then reached over and patted the back of one of his hands, gently and firmly, acknowledging that she knew that he really wanted to do that.

The Valley of Glar.

The pair had followed the narrow twisting passage northward, in and around the mountains, and had finally entered the small round valley ringed by towering snow-capped peaks.

In the center of the valley there was a rather haphazard collection of structures more or less centered around one much larger structure. All the buildings were constructed with dark stone quarried from the nearby mountain sides. The structures all had steep sloping roofs sheathed in stone.

That larger structure had a number of chimneys poking high, many showing the heat shimmer of active forges at work. In addition, there were a number of platforms with short walls set here and there on the largest, higher sections of the roof. This was the workshop of the Master Smith, M'aga, who was noted for his one-of-a-kind creations. He made those only for the ones that he felt worthy of having them.

M'aga paid little attention to the authorities who resided in Prime Shield. He rarely ventured beyond this valley. Those authorities tended to leave him at his work. After all, there were very few Master Smiths and it would not do to alienate any of them. These few artisans of such advanced talent were given great latitude to do whatever they pleased, but, now and then, they were asked for a favor. They were asked very carefully.

M'aga had tossed the last Messenger, who felt that he could demand whatever it was that he felt was necessary, out his front door. Fortunately for the thrownee, the door had been swung open at the time. Then after not too gently booting that Messenger in the side, M'aga had suggested in a loud bellowing voice that it would be very healthy for that one to not return to this valley. EVER!

This very small settlement, unlike the three main towns of The Honglar, did not have a Place of The Others. None of the small settlements did. Nar'a'las and Wind Sky had stopped the first individual they met, asked, and were given directions to a small inn that offered accommodations to the infrequent traveler that came this way.

Once inside their room, Nar'a'las suggested, "Let's rest for two days and see if we can find anyone who can give us information about the valley where the Czat'akar live."

Wind Sky set her carry pack on one of the beds and nodded.

"We have come a distance. Two days rest would be good." She smiled. "Perhaps M'aga will talk with me. I have been thinking of a change in arrow design."

Early the next morning, they wandered through the twisting streets and stopped in front of the main door to M'aga's workshop. Nar'a'las had decided to come along just in case M'aga became violent. She had heard that tale.

Wind Sky gently knocked on the door and waited.

Eventually the door was swung in. He stood there, a much wider, thicker, and taller than normal Honglar, wearing a heavy and very work-worn leather apron.

"WHAT?" he growled in their general direction.

"Wind Sky archer/scout-guide." She bowed, straightened up, and added, "I have been thinking of a change in arrow design and wished to speak of this with a Master Smith. If it is permissible to do so?"

M'aga frowned down at them and grumbled in her direction, "An archer who designs?"

She held out her bow. "I designed him in consultation with one of our most Senior Master Craftsmen."

M'aga carefully took the bow and held it close to his face and began to very carefully, very slowly, examine it, humming to himself softly.

Finally, he nodded, and handed it back to Wind Sky, and smiled, a little.

"Very clever, very clever," he rumbled. "Come in, come in." He stepped back. "Let us discuss this arrow design you are, eh ah um, thinking about."

They followed him inside, past several great work benches, all cluttered with bits and pieces of things, oddly shaped parts, of designs that M'aga was working on, and to a table covered with sheets of drawings and sketches.

M'aga shoved everything to one side, snatched some clean drawing materials from a nearby shelf, and handed Wind Sky a drawing instrument as he smoothed the clean paper on the bench top. "SHOW ME!"

The Plains of Singing Grass.

They had just strolled south along the

wagonway, taking it easy. It was pleasant and quite peaceful, listening to the soft song of the breeze stroking across the grass that stretched out of sight in all directions.

They had, so far, not met any other travelers other than the few Trader-Merchant caravans which had passed them, coming and going from where ever they had been or were headed.

The trio camped not far off the wagonway in the grass. All in all, this had been a very enjoyable trip, headed for the place that Cereon had heard about.

Cereon grumbled, now and then, about something or other.

But this behavior didn't bother either Altai'dorionasha or Hy'perian. They were used to it. It was just Cereon being Cereon. Besides, in between the grumble spurts, he had kept them entertained. It seemed the Cereon had learned a vast number of tales from his time in the encampments scattered throughout Warrior's Hand.

After a number of days, they had passed a junction where a horse trail led toward the west from the wagonway and were now walking along an area where a peculiar heavy thicket grew right up to the edge of the wagonway.

"Oh gooba!" Cereon jerked to a halt and vanished.

"Ummmmm," said Altai.

Two Grass Larpa had slipped from the grass and stood blocking their way south. Their yellow eyes were watching the two that they could see.

"Ah eh," said Hy, yanking the great King of Swords from his back. "I will take the one on the left."

Altai swirled her O'azur from her shoulder into a ready position and focused upon the Larpa on the right.

The Larpas slipped on soft paws, claws glittering in the sunlight, slowly creeping toward them.

"Not good," grumbled Cereon. "There is another one approaching from behind us."

"If that one charges, let me know," ordered Altai. "Say when it is about ten paces away."

"How about twenty paces?" mumbled Cereon.

"Good enough," agreed Altai.

"I wonder if they are edible," mused Hy'perian. "After all, they will be three piles of carved meat in a moment."

Cereon sizzled.

"Eh! Eh!" Altai stared. Another Grass Larpa had just slipped from the grass. It looked to her to be somewhat larger that the two approaching them.

"Eeeeee mmmmm," agreed Hy. "It is going to get messy."

The third one charged.

It batted one of the others on the hind quarters, sending it tumbling into the other one.

Then it reared up and screamed and stalked forward, the fur on its back bristling.

The two staggered to their feet and slunk into the grass.

"Gis tak!" snapped Cereon. "That one behind us just ran into the grass with its tail tucked in."

The last one, stared at them, turned and walked casually into the grass.

"A territorial dispute?" suggested Hy.

"How about we just stand here awhile and see whether they return," suggested Cereon, reappearing.

"We can do that." Hy'perian swung the great weapon back onto his back.

"Shall we eat while we wait?" he asked.

The Forest of Sighs.

Al'tana and Dark Wind made camp in the spot at the base of the long ramp that led from the wetway of Franbandan's Folly to Nu'vern.

They could see Aydel's Track bending in a great curve as it trended deep into the Forest of Sighs.

"A great work," said Dark Wind, pointing at the wide wagonway carved into the spine of the wetway that they had just crossed. It was truly an amazing sight to see.

Al'tana nodded and began to open some of the small food sacks. As they sat, eating Last Meal, she pointed at the wagonway in the woods. "If we go that way it will be a number of days to reach my home. But the way that I am going, along the coastline, will be somewhat longer. There are still portions of the old horse trail in existence so it won't be all that hard a walk."

Dark Wind nodded. "A very dense forest. It will

be pleasant to merely walk along its edge."

As the light dimmed, they settled themselves, watched the stars appear, and then fell asleep.

The Plains of Singing Grass.

Verin'yashi had passed through the junction of the horse trail where it met the wagonway and was now walking through the grass with a steady stride, her robes casting soft amber all around her as she passed up one of the higher rises.

As she reached the top she saw a man standing there. He smiled at her.

She stopped and looked at him. He must have been sitting and waiting, she thought, as she hadn't seen him a moment before. But how would anyone know where to sit and wait for her to appear in all these vast grasslands?

She smiled back. Perhaps he would explain.

"I am Zarlar," he said, bowing to her. "May we talk?"

She nodded and watched him approach.

He stopped a polite distance away. "I have never met one of The Touched of Huroma before."

Her eyebrows rose, she frowned.

"Oh," he gasped. "I do apologize. I probably shouldn't have said that." He knew that it was a secret, that label. A great round patch of grass flattened around them as he waved one hand.

"Shall we?" He sat and looked expectant at her.

She sat, facing him, the sun at her back.

"What do we have to speak about? Zarlar?"

He leaned forward, forearms resting on his crossed legs.

"Your, ummmm, conversation with your furry companion would have had no effect on her kind's behavior, none at all."

"Oh?"

He nodded. "Those predators hadn't made a rational choice to change their behaviors, not at all."

She rested her hands on her knees, eyes scanning his face. "Explain."

He waggled one hand. "All of them, save the one you talked with, had been, errr, influenced by a rather, errr, narrow-minded entity seeking to disrupt, errr, things."

Leaning back, a little, he smiled. "But that is no longer the way it is. I, errr, put things back the way that they had been. Oh! With one small change."

"One . . . small . . . change?"

"Ummmmm so. Your fuzzy companion is now a, oh, some might say, Queen of The Grass Larpa, ummmm, now. They will do whatever she tells them to do." He shrugged. "Had to be done."

She nodded slowly. "And you did this?"

He smiled.

"Who is this . . . other entity? And who, or what, are you?"

Zarlar slowly shook his head. "I think, for now, that we won't talk about that. But, I do think that The Core of Understanding ought to look into and ask that of your records. I do believe that you might find the answers to those questions there. The one I mentioned is hidden, very hidden, and being that, he is hard to find. He is doing mischief for his own benefit, as he sees it."

He sighed. "And it seems that he has found folk, here and there, who will follow him, those who wish to prosper and advance themselves and have no qualms about doing harm to others in order to gain that advancement."

He frowned and plucked a grass stem loose and began to chew on one end. "He has to be found and dragged, or lured, out of his hiding hole before anyone can do anything about him. Of course, he might decide to pop out on his own. But! And this is a warning. If he chooses to do that before all your folk are prepared, he could do damage, long lasting damage."

He stood and shrugged. "Have to wait and to see." He grinned. "But he will be quite unhappy about losing his touch over the Grass Larpa."

He took one step.

She stared, stood, and searched the area. He was gone.

Now she would have to hurry.

She did. And as she did she thought about that visitor and that what he had related must have something to do with the First Twins, somehow.

The Wild Fields.

Cloud Spirit met them in one of the small

meeting halls. A runner had come to his dwelling telling him of the strange group that had entered the Stonehold seeking him.

He stood near a window and watched them enter the hall. The runner had been correct. This was a strange group. In front walked two young folk, brother and sister twins, from their faces. She was dressed in ornate clothes. He appeared to be a warrior of some sort and wore a warrior's garb, mostly soft brown and grey. Cloud wasn't sure what she was, but she wore jewelry in her hair and carried a long lance that was heavily decorated. The warrior wore a strange gold circlet.

Behind them walked four warriors dressed in dark clothes He assumed from their garb and physical appearance, that they were from one of the dense forest regions.

He smiled at them.

"Warm greetings," he said. "Cloud Spirit, archer/scout-guide."

He gestured at the chairs and waited for them to settle themselves before he sat. Then he watched them and waited.

The young woman stood and bowed. As she straightened up, her grey eyes fastened on his.

"Sar'al Rada'doa Noriyon Zacog, named The Queen of The Seven Lands by custom, heritage, and right. There is a great danger looming that threatens all the folk of the lands." She indicated the four seated behind her. "This danger has already killed one of my Fast Riders and a number of their folk, the Tha'a'sa."

She sat, her spine straight. It didn't touch the gently sloping cushion of her chair's back.

Cloud Spirit nodded and filled three cups, stood, and handed one to each of the pair.

"Darlu Berry juice. Two of the Stoneholds have fields of the vine and produce the juice." He took a sip. "Would it be permissible to give some to your, eh um, associates as well?"

Sar'al nodded.

Cloud Spirit filled four cups and handed them to the four guards, he assumed that they were guards of some sort. Then he returned to his seat, took another sip, and wondered what to do next. He had heard vague rumors that the folk down in Nu'vern had a governmental structure called Royalty but other than that he knew little and he certainly had never met any of them before. They had been content to remain in their land, raising crops and fishing, and trading those commodities to the rest of the lands.

Of course, he knew some of the stories that dealt with the Nu'vern history and origin myths as they were told. But now, here they sat. So, time to come straight to the point.

"Why are you here?" he asked her.

"We were told, We were, by The Ancient One, that for all the folk to survive We must gather most, if not all, under our rule. We have traveled far to ask you to do this for We do believe what The Ancient One told Us. We will need your help if We are to defend all the folk from this great threat which is even now beginning to stir." She thought making a slight change in what The Ancient One had told might be more convincing.

Cloud Spirit stood, picked up the large pitcher and walked around refilling cups. Then he walked over to a small table, set the pitcher down, and stared out the window and stood deep in thought.

Finally he turned back and nodded at his guests.

"Perhaps I should tell you of our history, the history of The Wild Fields. You must understand our customs, our values, the way we look out and see the lands. And then, young Queen, you will see the problem that you face here."

He dropped into his chair and began.

The High Land of Short Trees.

Clerian'tra stood and peered up the stairs carved into the towering cliff of dark stone. It seemed to her that the narrow passage upward stopped some distance above.

She shrugged and started to climb the stairs. They didn't stop. It was a square landing with another narrow notch of stairs climbing to the left.

Up she went, to another landing with stairs heading in a different direction.

And so it went, landing after landing, stairwell after stairwell, until, finally, she stepped out and onto flat ground.

As she looked around, it appeared to her that this end of N'Farza was a high plateau mostly covered with a forest of peculiar trees, short, thick leaved trees, none of which she had seen anywhere else as she had traveled to get to this place.

A figure dressed in black stepped from the deep shadow of these woods and walked up to her.

"I be Na'anat, Clan Bidulin."

"Clerian'tra." She bowed. "Warm greetings."

Na'anat stared at the ornament that Clerian'tra wore. Then she nodded. "We have heard of the pale skin named Bar'Farza by the Crazed Warriors. Warm greetings, favored one."

Na'anat waggled one hand toward a narrow opening in the forest.

"Our village is just there, not far."

Na'anat led her to and then along the narrow and twisting path until they finally, not too far, stepped out into a large open space.

Dwellings were scattered, apparently in no pattern, around the opening.

Rising from the middle of the clearing was a short, square structure constructed of dark stone blocks.

The two most senior females stood, walked over and greeted Na'anat. They stepped up to Clerian'tra and reached out, running their hands over her robe, fingering the material.

"Eeee ah um," said one. "The cloth of the Crazed Warriors."

"Um hum!" stated the other. She turned, beckoned and led them to a small space outlined by small, square dark stone blocks set into the soil. A number of other villagers sat there and watched this pale skin approach.

When all had sat, The Elder waved a hand. All began to pass bowls of prepared food from individual to individual, each taking some in turn. Soon, all were eating and talking, now and then asking Clerian'tra a gentle question.

Clerian'tra recognized the process and answered accordingly. Finally, she indicated the stone structure.

"No where," she said, "on N'Farza have I seen such as that."

"Um hum!" The Elder nodded at her. "There is no other such on N'Farza. That is The Deep Tower."

"Deep?" Clerian'tra frowned, just a bit. This was a strange thing.

The Elder nodded.

"If I may ask," said Clerian'tra very softly. "What is down there?"

Smiles broke out all around the gathered clan members. A few laughed, a gentle laugh.

"Your kind," stated The Elder.

"My . . . kind?"

"Um hum! Pale skins."

The Plains of Singing Grass.

The three of them had found suitable mounts and adequate pack animals, gathered the necessary supplies, and had headed toward home.

After days of preparation and travel and two days resting in The Place Of The Others in Prime Shield, they had finally crossed over the wetway into

Shar'daine, headed south.

Now, riding three abreast, their horses at a slow amble, they were practicing various small effects that they had learned. Some of these effects were just for the fun of doing them. They were in no hurry.

They particularly enjoyed the small flash of bright light or the small dark humming cloud of Bat'za flitters.

But, in a rather short time, they had tired of doing these tricks and were mostly riding in silence and looking at the vast grass plain on all sides of the wagonway.

Eventually Cer'alda noticed far overhead a small group of wind drifters, circling around and around, apparently headed in the same direction as the trio.

Cer'alda frowned and cleared her throat loudly, a rasping throat clearing sound.

"Oh, oh," mumbled Verdorion-elvershair. He recognized that sound. It meant that his sister was bothered by something and would shortly decide that they all ought to do something about that.

Caevelos leaned forward to look past her brother at her sister. He was riding between them. She hissed, "What?" And frowned. She had recognized that throat clearing sound as well. And her sister's facial expression.

Cer'alda shot a frown past Verd. "Don't be nasty, Cae! I do not think that those things up there are wind drifters at all! They have the wrong wing shape. And they are headed toward us."

Verd halted his horse and jumped down, turned and looked to me what those things were that were approaching them so fast. "Eh huh. Sharp eyes, Cer, very sharp."

His sisters dismounted and stepped over to stand by his sides.

Cer'alda nudged him. "I would like to keep one of them whole so we can see exactly what they might be."

He nodded. They were certainly not wind drifters. The things had formed a long line and were now hurtling in a steep dive toward them.

The trio merged.

There was a loud explosion.

One carcass thumped nearby causing a large puff of wagonway dust to blow into the air. A few bits and pieces of the rest fluttered down around them, all that remained of the flock.

Verd walked over and nudged the body with his boot tip

"Larger than they looked." He bend and twisted the round head at the end of the long neck so she could look at its face. "Lots of pointy teeth, lots and lots of them." He looked the question at his sisters as he released it.

"No," said Caevelos.

Cer'alda kicked the body. "Those were spell created things." Of the three, she had developed the ability to recognize such things well beyond the others capability.

Verd straightened up and stretched. "Wonder what is happening now? I do not believe that they are still testing us."

His sister walked back and remounted her horse. "Not from the Teachers!"

"Let's go faster," suggested Caevelos as she mounted her horse.

Cer'alda watched him mount his horse.

"Let's," he agreed.

The Place Where Akar Dwelled.

They had traveled through the ever twisting narrow and steep sided canyon for days walking alongside the rock filled gouge that in a warmer part of the season this far north would be a rushing stream filled to the brim with frigid water.

As they camped on their second day, Wind Sky told Nar'a'las that the Master Smith M'aga was going to make two quivers full of the new arrows that they had designed together. He had told her that they would be ready by the time that they returned from their trip.

Camping for them in this environment was not uncomfortable. Nar'a'las cast a circle of warmth around them at all times.

Finally, after more days than anyone had told them this trip would take, they entered a wide spot with numbers of buildings built against one mountain slope. They were all constructed from the local stone. Each structure had very narrow windows, with doors having a low lintel.

They had arrived at their destination. This wide spot in the narrow canyon was *The Place Where Akar Dwelled*. Here lived the Czat'akar, the ones who mined the mountain across the way from their village.

As they had been passing along the narrow passage leading to this spot, Nar'a'las had finally asked Wind Sky, "Aren't you damaging him using him for a walking staff?"

Wind Sky shook her head and laughed softly. She swung her great bow up so Nar'a'las could examine the tip.

The bow extended past the point where the bowstring would be attached and ended in a cap of dark metal. The color of the cap matched the color of the bow.

"Ahhmm, I see." Nar'a'las smiled at her companion.

Now, as they stood looking at the small village, Wind Sky reached down and hooked the bow string to that lower attachment. She held the bow and the bow string in her left hand, the string hanging loosely down over her hand. In one swift motion, Wind Sky could grab the free end, bend his head down, and attach it.

Nar'a'las headed them toward one of the larger structures.

"It would be nice if they were not too unfriendly," she said.

Grey Stone Quarry.

They stood at the base of what appeared to have

been a grey stone stairway carved for the use of giants. The step's width shortened as each step progressed upward, forming a great pyramidal shape. At the very top of the quarry there was a black square. The twins had learned that this black square was the mouth of a tunnel that pushed deep into the mountain range.

To reach the top they would have to walk to the ocean side of the lowest ledge and then make their way up the unbroken slope that bordered the immense excavation.

The ledges were the end product of the cutting and shaping of the grey stone blocks once used for construction. Many of these blocks had been hauled for the erection of the Stoneholds of The Wild Fields.

The twins' research had convinced them that another of The Hidden Ones dwelled deep inside this end of the mountain range.

They had come here after spending many days living in the below ground home of those who called their dwelling, The Heart of Darkness.

Soft Touch, a One Who Saves, had been their host and their guide and instructor. Eventually she had handed them over to Final Touch, her companion wherever she traveled on the surface, a companion who could kill anything with but a gentle tap of the short silver and gold scepter that everyone with this training carried. She had continued their education until the pair were finished.

Soft Touch and Final Touch had joined them to Gentle Smile, a female, a One Who Saves, and her companion, Dark Night, a male, a One Who Does Not, in a ceremony in the Hall of The Parents Of Us All, before the statues of The Father and The Mother. At the end of the ceremony the twins were told that they were now marked by The Heart of Darkness.

As marked ones, they were now able to return as often as they wished. Soft Touch then told the twins that as they were seekers of truth, which they had told her they were, and which she saw in them, a very rare thing, that Gentle Smile and Dark Night would now travel with them.

"Seekers of truth are to be treasured and guarded," she told them as they all stood at the top of the long slope of brown ashy talus.

"I know your true name, Equi-veronik. I know your true name Bael'elyth," said Soft Touch. "As do Gentle Smile and Dark Night. It is now a thing between us." She nodded at them. "You must fare well."

Soft Touch spun on her heels and strolled back into the dimness that shrouded the plateau behind them, accompanied by Final Touch. Even then, on a bright sunny day, it was rather dim and mist covered.

Equi-veronik scanned the great quarry and looked at the others, then pointed at what he hoped would actually be a route up to that tunnel.

"Shall we go?" he asked.

"One does as One does," replied Gentle Smile, softly. Her red eyes seemed to glow in the sunlight as did the eyes of Dark Night.

Bael'elyth nodded and started toward that edge

of the first grey stone ledge, wondering what they would find this time.

Prime Shield.

Ran'dyal, The First Voice of The Dark Wind, quickly scanned the faces of those seated around the large table. The individuals seated there were The Whispers of The Dark Wind. They were those that controlled the Fists in their assigned territory.

He nodded at them and cleared his throat and waited for the various side conversations to dwindle away.

"We," stated Ran'dyal, "have ever so slowly, ever so carefully, built our organization. Now we are ready!"

Heads nodded. Some smiled.

"We," he continued, "have been very careful, very, very careful, and now we are ready!"

"We have sent our, ah, representatives with every Trader-Merchant caravan, folk trained to be persuasive, who think as we do. Now we have members in the three important lands, An'darl, Shar'daine, and Nu'vern. Many of you, and them, have garnered rewards, and positions where decisions are made. We, our organization, are moving into control, little by little, yet far faster than had been anticipated."

Ran'dyal stood and nodded at each of them. Then he explained what he thought their first "real action" ought to be.

When he had finished, he sat and waited, ever so

patiently, while the discussions rattling around the table to wash over him. Soft talk and loud argument flowed and roared around the table, soft talk and loud argument about those that had rebuffed their representatives. Those that did that were an impediment that ought to be removed.

Finally, once silence had once again fallen in the room and settled around the table, he tapped the hilt of his dagger on the table and agreed with them what their first action was to be.

The Plains of Singing Grass.

Rid'linar had pushed his horses as hard as would be healthy for them. He had taken a string of three extra mounts with him when he left Nu'Vern, and had changed horses frequently.

He had spent a short time in The Silent Woods talking with the Elder of the Tha'a'sa about whatever had happened there. Then she had pointed out the horse marks that Sar'al and Zak'ke's horses had made, the few marks still visible.

Then he had hurtled up the wagonway.

At the intersection of the horse trail leading to the northwest, he had stopped and carefully inspected all the marks on the wagonway and the horse trail. Finally, he had found The Queen's horse shoe marks and headed that way.

He passed the area of the dense thick growth, stopped, and carefully searched the intersection of the two horse trails.

He trotted his horses toward The Wild Fields and the main Stonehold. As he headed toward his destination he noted that other horses had come through that intersection from the east. From what he could see it appeared that these horses were in a great hurry to get to The Wild Fields. He sped up.

The Wild Fields.

After tying her livestock to whatever was handy, she stomped through the door of the building she had been directed to.

He looked up from something that he had been reading, set the document aside, and took a sip from his mug.

"Ummm eh?" he said. She must be one of the Avelerian, he thought, dark clothes, two weapons strapped to her back. From the dust and travel stains on her garb, she must have been traveling hard.

"I seek The Queen!" she snapped. "I was told that she was here!"

He nodded, and said, softly, "Cloud Spirit, senior archer/scout-guide."

She nodded back. "Viana Tiveon Tru'ert, Clan Veronji, Tha'a'da."

Cloud stood, and smiled. "Eh, the young woman with the many color hair." He smiled. "I was just about to be on my way to, ummm, visit with her. May I lead you there?"

Viana stepped back. "Do!"

He guided her across the Stonehold and out the

far gateway, leaving her horses where she had tethered them.

"We are going to the Testing Ground. All gather there to watch and judge the age groups ability with the bow. Some few will be offered the opportunity to join the archers this day."

As they walked along, he explained what that meant to the eight Stoneholds.

Entering the Testing Ground, Cloud pointed at a tall platform. "She will be up there with the Judges. The, ummm, Queen wished to speak to all gathered here to request them to allow herself to be their Queen, eh, after the judging was completed."

He shrugged. "I told her that the folk here are very independent."

They climbed the long staircase and stepped out onto the viewing platform.

"Viana! Welcome!"

Viana was grabbed and hugged. "My Queen," she gasped.

Zak'ke stood near and laughed. "How fare the Tha'a'da?"

Sar'al released her and stepped back.

Viana bowed, and said as she straightened up, "The seven Clans of the Tha'a'da greet their Queen." She would talk about what that meant when they were in a less public space.

Zak'ke looked at her expression and grinned. "We will discuss this later, I suspect."

Viana nodded.

Sar'al looked at Cloud Spirit. He pointed. "They are finished and will gather close to hear what you wish to say."

Sar'al nodded and walked to the spot Cloud indicated. Zak'ke joined her and handed her the lance. He had been standing to one side holding it while she had engaged the judges in conversation between their judging of the archers.

The crowds gathered quickly and waited, peering up at her, wondering what that one had to say to them.

Cloud Spirit had spread the word to all the Stoneholds that is was important to hear what she had to say. So they were curious about that. It had never happened before.

Sar'al spoke to them, her voice carrying clearly to one and all. She was using a minor skill of her gift. Her father had insisted that she learn this as it would come to good use, sooner or later. It was one of the few things that she had been taught.

She spoke of The Ancient One and of all the things that she had experienced, and what that meant to all the folk of all the lands.

"Now, two of the lands accept Us as The Queen of The Seven Lands. The land of Nu'vern and the land of Mart'den. Of Shar'daine, the four clans of the Tha'a'sa of The Silent Woods. Now We shall ask another to speak to you."

Holding the lance tightly, she paused, taking a slow calming breath, then began the chant used once before. The soft words took wing, glittering gold and black against the deep blue sky, the call flew, the request of Priestess to Priestess. *Come,* said the call, *come to our aid.*

The crowds gasped a collective gasp as they saw those words appear.

The call flew outward and outward and outward until it eventually drifted into her chamber, rousing her from her deep slumber. As she stood and yawned and stretched, she wondered why that one had called to her, again. She smiled. That young Queen was getting better at it. She was beginning to learn her "gift."

The small figure strode from The Beyond, slipped through The Inbetween, and out into the Audience Hall of the Crystal Palace, a rather short female of delicate features and form, dressed in soft robes of a deep blue color.

The Crystal Palace was perched on the peak of one of the highest mountains on the Continent An'darl. It gleamed with and refracted the always bright sunlight into multicolored bands on the floors, walls and ceilings.

The ever present cloud layer of this mountain range was held away from the palace by a great circle barrier, cast by the one who now stood here, admiring the beauty and elegance of the structure she had brought into being here on this mountain top many long ago.

In this form she appeared much like the rest of

the population, except for her eyes. The slanting, large oval eyes, filled with the azure of the sky above, were the eyes of her true form.

A young woman suddenly appeared on the viewing platform, dressed in robes of a unfamiliar cut and design, colored a deep blue, startling everyone but Sar'al, Zak'ke, and Viana.

"Young Queen, why did you call?"

Sar'al pointed at the gathering below. "We wish to convince them to join with Us, as did eleven clans of the Avelerain Tha'a'da and Tha'a'sa, as did the Azkar, as did five of The Royal Houses."

"Soooooo," hissed The Ancient One, "you have been busy."

"As you suggested We should be," Sar'al stated cooly

A tired figure thumped up the stairs and onto the viewing platform, interrupting their conversation.

"My Queen," he called, hurrying to her side, dropping to one knee.

"Fast Rider Rid'linar?" Where did he get that strange sword and shield?

He lurched to his feet, bowed stiffly, and thrust a thick report at her, one he had hastily dragged from his traveling pouch.

"This is written and sent by Rau'ke and Cant'al who labor mightily to see that all you wished to be is to be!"

She took the thick document and peered at it. "And it says?"

"That the Armed Mass of Nu'vern is being trained and made ready. All the details are here."

Sar'al smiled, a Royal smile, at The Ancient One. "This answers one of the questions you asked before."

"Why did you call?" repeated The Ancient One.

"Cloud Spirit tells Us that the folk of The Wild Fields are very independent. We felt, We did, that if you would show them who you are that they might then understand all that We have said to them and agree to do what We suggest, to allow them to accept Us as their Queen."

"A clever thing to be asked by one so young." The woman nodded and clothed herself in a wide, whirling column of dense fog which quickly hid her from sight. "It seems," said the voice from inside, "that you are learning and becoming."

Sar'al frowned at the fog, turned and watched the folk below, and took a few careful steps to the side. She could hear deep within all that swirling fog the rasp of talons on the wooden planks of the platform. What was The Ancient One now inferring?

The fog began to collapse and spill down toward those gathered below, dissipating before it reached them. The judges stepped back, and back again, making room, watching carefully. Down below archers, bows in hand, peered upward and waited for some sign from Cloud Spirit to defend those up above.

Immense wings stretched and stretched, wider and wider, glistening iridescent azure points of light. Then the great head was slowly lowered on the end of the long neck as she stared down at those gathered around the viewing stand.

"I came because the Queen called!" boomed the gentle voice to all below. "I have come a long way. Pay attention to what she has told you. Great danger builds for all the lands and all must make themselves ready to face it and defeat it. This young Queen has embarked on a hard, and a dangerous, and a frustrating chore, the saving of all her people. She will require many, many to join her in order to succeed." She smiled, long pointed teeth glittering in the sunlight. "Think of it as a learning experience, appropriate for a Queen and all the folk gathered here." She turned her head and smiled at Sar'al.

And was gone.

"Learning experience," huffed Sar'al. She turned back to the crowd. "We wait your decision, mighty archers, as well as all of the folk of the Stoneholds."

"It will take two days," murmured Cloud Spirit to her.

"In two days," she stated in her carrying voice and watched them begin to disperse, animated conversations breaking out as all headed back to their respective Stoneholds. And grumbled darkly, "Learning experience . . . "

The Ghost Stones.

The trio strode toward their destination, a strange structure constructed of stone. As they walked closer, it appeared to them that it was circular. Not far beyond it they could sea the sea stretching to the horizon. To their left there were two large earthen mounds.

"This the place?" asked Hy'pherian. It certainly looked strange.

"Think so," replied Cereon. "It does fit the description that I was given."

Altai'dorionasha looked around. "Wonder where the folk are? I don't see any dwellings."

It lifted above the blue-green stone structure, seeming to come up from its center, and drifted slowly toward them on large feather covered wings.

The body was long and thin, covered with round scales that glistened dark brown. The body floated, long and thin, coiling back and forth as the creature came their way.

Two long legs hung loosely just in front of the wings. They ended in bird-like feet, three toes in front, one behind, all ending in long black talons.

The head on the end of the thin neck was more like a long muzzled dog than anything else they could think of.

The edges of the wing feathers gleamed soft gold.

It dwarfed the trio, and hissed at them, stopped close, peering at them from three empty eye sockets.

"I am The Guardian of The Folded Lands. Did you come here to help or to hinder?"

They stared at The Guardian. Two were visible, one was not.

Altai'dorionasha cleared her throat.

"We," she said, "have heard a tale that here in this place one might learn new skills. Is that true?"

The Guardian hissed, short snorts of hissing. It was laughter.

"True!"

Altai'dorionasha took a step to the side. "What new skills might we learn?"

"None!" The Guardian drifted closer.

"Oh!" Altai bowed. "Then we will go about our journey."

"Unlessssss," hissed The Guardian.

"Ummm?" said Hy.

"Help is needed."

She looked at her brother, leaning just a bit his way, being careful not to nudge Cereon who she assumed still stood between them. There was a slight smudge to the space there.

"The One of The Six," she murmured to Hy, "said to us, May you always be there to help those in need."

He nodded and looked at the great creature floating just before them. "How may we help you?"

The Guardian settled close to the ground, forelegs just touching the grass.

"Many long seasons ago, a vile creature of darkness who wishes to rule all, attacked as I slept, ripping out my eyes. That one placed terrible creatures in the Folded Lands to guard them so I may not see all that I should."

"Emmmm?" mumbled Altai.

"One looks toward the sea and sees two large mounds and a great stone ring. Each is an entrance to one of The Folded Lands. Each has one of my eyes. The help you offer is to recover them in any manner you might wish."

"How does one enter those places?" asked Hy.

"Enter from the most southern. But understand this! Once started there will be no return until all three of my eyes have been recovered."

"Ummmm," mumbled Hy, frowning at the idea of being trapped inside these Folded Lands.

"Let's," said Altai.

The Guardian snorted. "Three eyes! Three gifts! One gift to each in this small party. Agreed?"

"I do," stated Hy.

"Of course," added Altai.

"Piz gak," growled Cereon, as he appeared. "Agreed!" He was beginning to think that his training had neglected to tell him of the beings that might be able to see him.

The trio headed toward the most southern of the three structures.

Standing in front of the opening in the southern end of the southern structure, Altai pointed.

"They are aligned. This is a single complex."

Cereon peered at the darkness in front of them, and grumbled softly. "You two will keep me alive, won't you?"

Altai smiled at him. "To the best of our ability.

Shall we start?"

Hy stepped in, tugging Cereon along, who grumbled softly. Again.

The Folded Lands

The Eye of Foreboding.

"Eh ah," said Altai'dorionasha as she rested her O'azur on her right shoulder. "Not exactly what I expected to see."

Hy'pherian laughed. "My thought as well."

Stretching before them, twisting to the right around the end of a low mound covered in bright green grass, was a broad paved wagonway unlike any they had seen before.

It was a bright yellow.

Cereon knelt and scratched at one of the rectangular paving stones with a finger nail. "Stone, hard stone." He stood and looked from side to side and then back at the dark opening they had just stepped through. Placing one hand on that dark spot, he grunted.

"Ak pak!" he growled. "Solid stone. That Guardian spoke true. No going back!"

"Then," suggested Altai, "let us see what is around that turn just ahead."

"But slowly," grumbled Cereon. "The Guardian told of terrible creatures in here."

"Most careful," stated Hy, strolling alongside his

sister as they started forward.

In a very short time they had walked around the bend, a very sharp right-hand turn, and stopped to stare at the vista opening up before them.

The strange wagonway stretched arrow straight ahead of them, rising and falling over the slight undulations of the land. On either side of the wagonway there were vast agricultural fields planted in crops that were different than anything that they had ever seen grown in Nu'vern.

The field on their left had a crop that was planted in row after row stretching away from the wagonway. The tall stems were taller than Hy'pherian. The single stem was thick and had a few thin leaves poking from it here and there. Some sort of fruit was growing in the junction of leaf and stem. This field made a soft rustling sound as a faint breeze drifted through it.

The field on the other side was a mass of flowers, bright red flowers. The tops of the flowers would come to mid-calf on Hy'pherian. Each was a single blossom on a single stem surrounded by a thick cluster of dark green foliage.

The flowers swayed gently as the breeze passed by.

Hy smiled at his sister. "Well, Altai, I've a feeling that we're are not in Shar'daine any more."

They started strolling down the wagonway, slowly as Cereon had suggested, and watched the strange fields for the tillers of those fields and admired the clear blue sky overhead.

After they had walked for some distance, Altai said, "There are no creature noises coming from those fields, nothing but the rustle of the growth."

"Where are the tillers of these fields?" mumbled Cereon. "We ought to see one or two at work."

Altai nodded. "A different land this is," she suggested.

They walked on, each wondering about this land and where the inhabitants might be. From what little that they had been told by The Guardian this place didn't seem to match its words.

Topping the fifth crest, Hy pointed. "Down there, in that wide flat, at that intersection, there appears to be a number of signs, perhaps direction markers."

They hurried down the gentle slope. It had been, so far, an easy and pleasant walk, but all were beginning to feel a little bored and just a little apprehensive. Where were the monsters that were supposed to be here?

They stopped to read the small signs.

One pointed to their left: *Chin Village* 🖎.

One pointed to their right: 🖙 *Green Az.*

The third apparently indicated straight ahead, or so they assumed: ≜ *Wild.*

"I prefer Chin Village," said Cereon. "First. Perhaps the inhabitants there can give us some information."

Hy looked at his sister.

"Let's," she said. "Perhaps we will be able to

sleep comfortable instead of camping in these fields."

They headed left and walked up the long slope and out onto flat land the stretched into the distance. And in that distance something sparkled.

As the sun was sagging toward the horizon they could see roof tops. They came in many colors and shapes. Ornaments on the peaks sparkled.

"They seem to like bright colors," said Altai.

Hy laughed.

And, eventually as they must do, they arrived close enough to clearly see the village.

It appeared that all the structures were facing three sides of a large paved square. The wagonway entered the square from the fourth side, everything paved with identical yellow, rectangular stones.

As they approached the village proper they passed a badly damaged structure of weather-beaten wood residing near the edge of the wagonway. It appeared to be mostly collapsed.

"Different," observed Hy.

They strolled into the square and stopped, waiting to see what would happen now.

The inhabitants were lined up in rows, staring at them. They were shorter than Cereon. Their clothes, like their houses, were a riot of colors. Many of them wore elaborate hats, often with one of those single-stemmed red flowers poked into the headband of the hat.

After the trio stood quietly watching and waiting, an elderly male stepped forward and announced in rolling tones , "Welcome to Chin Village.

Are you here to help or to hinder?"

Hy'pherian stepped forward, two steps, and bowed. "We are here to help as The Guardian asked."

In the gathering throng, as more and more of the villagers had joined those already here, numerous conversations erupted.

A few of those in the gathering, overcome by curiosity, approached the trio and began to run gentle fingers over their garb.

The elderly male stepped very close to Hy and made shooing motions with his hands, scattering the curious into the ever gathering crowd now edging closer and closer to their visitors from three sides.

"Help?" he asked.

Hy nodded. "We came to retrieve The Guardian's eye."

Sudden silence surrounded them.

"Can any of you tell us which way to go?"

This question started the conversations going again. Eventually a sort of a consensus was arrived at.

The elderly man nodded and it became quiet again.

He pointed at the way they had come.

"Green Az, The Great City, that is the place to ask that question." He smiled and pointed at a large flat grassy spot that was next to the junction of the yellow wagonway and the town square. "You may stay there. Our only inn would be too small for such tall folk. Dark approaches. May we share a meal with you?"

Cereon smiled at him, then bowed. "An honor."

Altai stared at Cereon. Perhaps he had learned some manners during his seasons of training.

All through the meal, the three talked with the village's appointed spokesman. He told them that it would take some days to walk to Green Az. They had heard of the dark horrors that were keeping The Guardian's eye but that was all that they knew. However, they felt that much more could be learned in Green Az.

Then the folk began to gather everything and head back to their homes.

"One last question," said Cereon.

"Of course," replied the eldest. "What?"

"What is that structure back there?" Cereon pointed. "The one with all the weathered wood."

The spokesman shrugged. "We really have no idea. A few seasons ago, it fell from the sky and crashed right there. We searched but there was nobody in it." He smiled. "But we do try to keep the children from playing there. It is rather badly damaged."

He stood. "In early light we will bring a meal and some supplies for you before you leave." He walked away.

Just after the sun had slipped above the horizon, a number of the villagers brought platters of steaming food and a number of carefully wrapped parcels for their journey.

And soon, the trio headed back the way that they had come.

Some of the villagers walked a short way with

them, then stopped and called, "Good travels," at their backs.

With the sun shining down, they walked down into the depression, checked the signs, and strolled up the slope toward whatever Green Az might be.

Finally, late in the day, they camped on a grassy patch next to the wagonway, deciding that it might not be a good idea to camp inside someone's field.

Two days later, having eaten all the food the villagers had given them, they saw, as they topped a low hill, a large town looming up in the distance. It appeared that it favored the color green. The roofs and what they could see of other surfaces reaching above the tall outer wall surrounding the place were all shades of green.

They increased their pace and were soon standing in front of the tall wooden gate, a deep brown construction of thick planks.

Hy'pherian pushed on it. "Locked."

Altai thumped on it with the round base of her O'azur.

It made a loud booming sound.

"Guess that they will know that we are here," mumbled Cereon.

They waited. For some time.

Altai was about to thump the gate harder, when it happened.

High over head, a small hatch was thrown open and a head poked out.

"What do you want?" demanded a wild-haired

man in a high pitched squeaky voice.

"To come inside," replied Hy.

"Come back tomorrow!" The head jerked back and the hatch slammed shut.

Cereon turned from inspecting the surface of the gate. "I think that I could climb up there and get inside, through that hatch."

"Wait." Altai began a rhythmic thumping on the gate with the base of her O'azur.

Eventually the hatch popped open. The same head popped out.

"STOP THAT!"

"We want to come inside and talk with someone who can answer our questions," she called.

"We are helping The Guardian," added Hy.

"Well," snapped the man, "why didn't you say so!"

He jerked back, the hatch slammed shut.

Three puzzled faces looked at each other.

Then the great gate began to slowly, silently swing in, until it stood wide open. The yellow wagonway continued inside, running deep toward the interior. Large structures soared on all sides, all colored green.

"Welcome to Green Az," said the wire-haired man. "Follow me! I will take you to The Voice of Green Az. You may ask your questions there." He peered back out the gate. "Only you three?"

"Eh huh," grumbled Cereon. "Just us three."

They followed their guide along the wide way

past a number of side ways. Many folk were hurrying in every direction, passing through the intersections. They all smiled at their visitors and appeared to be quite relaxed.

Hy watched them and wondered why. If there was somewhere out there a number of black things guarding The Guardian's eye, it didn't seem as if these folk were disturbed by that at all.

Everyone that they passed were dressed in a variety of colors and costumes, almost as vibrant as the folk of Chin Village.

They walked deep into the town until their guide stopped and pointed. The structure had broad stairs across the front and a number of stone columns holding up a short roof over the entry platform.

"Up there," said their guide. "Follow the corridor until you get to the main chamber. Then ask your questions."

He spun and hurried away, apparently toward the main gate.

Cereon started up the wide stairs. "A strange folk," he rumbled, mostly to himself.

Hy and Altai hurried after him.

The corridor was wide, stone columns lined the sides, set against the walls, spaced in even intervals. The floor was paved with smooth, highly polished dark green stone. They could see their reflections in its surface as they walked along.

Far ahead they could see a wide gold door in the wall that terminated the corridor.

Altai swung her O'azur around and held it by the middle next to her side.

"Uh?" asked Hy.

"Just cautious. Cereon is correct. A strange folk."

Hy nodded.

When they reached the door, Cereon said, "If you don't mind." And disappeared.

Altai laughed and pulled the door open.

They walked in.

The door closed behind them with a dull thump.

A figure, dressed all in green, sat in a gold throne on a high dias, and stared at them.

"I," he intoned in deep rolling tones, "am Az. Why . . . are . . . you . . . here?"

Hy and Altai bowed, deeply.

"We," stated Hy, as he straightened up, "are helping The Guardian. Do you know where we might find those that have the eye?"

"Deep in the Wild do they lurk, foul, vile things. Neither Chin Village nor Green Az have the arms to take the eye back. Can two warriors do this?"

Hy smiled. "We intend to do that. Where is this place and where are the creatures that hold the eye?"

"At the intersection you will see the sign pointing to Wild. Follow it. Small place of few dwellings will you meet first. Hidden there is a box containing a key. Take the key. This container is guarded by the foul and vile."

Altai took a step forward. "After we have the key and the eye, how do we leave these lands?"

"Bring all that you find to this very chamber. The

door will open." He leaned back and watched them.

They bowed, turned, and headed back the way that they had come.

As they walked down the stairs, Cereon appeared.

"He didn't say how many of these foul and vile things that there are," he grumbled. "This is becoming a very long camping trip, a very strange camping trip."

Several days later, they once again stood in the intersection. The folk of Green Az had handed them small packets of food as they had walked back toward the gate.

Cereon kicked the sign labeled "Wild."

"If we had known that was the place we could have saved a whole lot of walking."

Hy nodded.

"We wouldn't have known about the key," suggested Altai. "Nor how to leave these lands."

"Purgle," mumbled Cereon, pulling the sign back to vertical.

They walked on. At the top of the slope they could see the wagonway disappearing into a thick forest.

It took all day to reach that spot.

"Shall we camp here?" asked Altai.

"Let's," replied Hy, dumping his pack next to the pavement.

They set up camp, ate a Final Meal, and sat and talked.

As the gloom crept into darkness, Hy stood and

grabbed his great sword. "I will take first watch." He strolled off, but not far.

"I will take second," mumbled Cereon.

Altai thanked him, stretched out, and fell asleep.

In the morning, they sat eating First Meal and watching those woods carefully. It was a silent place. Nothing in there was making a sound. It had been that way all night as well.

Finally ready, they started in.

After some time, Hy'pherian said to Cereon. "How about you go ahead, a long way ahead. No one will see you. If, or when, you see anything, uh eh, dangerous, just head back and let us know. That will give us time to get ready."

Cereon grumbled, just a small grumble, and hurried ahead of them.

And on they trudged, a casual stroll, watching both sides as they did.

Finally they were walking in dimming light as dusk settled on the forest.

Hy and Altai had been discussing whether they ought to just walk all night and forget camping inside these dense woods, when Cereon suddenly appeared, breathing heavily.

The pair stopped and waited for him to catch his breath.

"What?" asked Hy.

"Not far from here, the wagonway curves sharply to the right. Just around that turn there is a small cluster of ill cared for dwellings." He sucked in a deep breath.

"I didn't see many that looked like villagers but there were a number, I didn't count, of black creatures, not as short as me, not as tall as Hy, clumping around and around a central structure like they were guarding it."

"Weapons?" asked Hy.

"Looked like thick clubs of some sort."

Hy looked at Altai.

"Let's," she said. "Cereon can watch our backs."

They began to hurry.

Down the wagonway, around the curve, to the edge of the village, such as it was.

"Quite small," observed Altai, pulling her O'azur from her right shoulder.

Cereon pointed. "Just there, that building."

Hy laughed. "Be gone, Cereon. Be careful." He began to walk slowly into the small village, The Sword of Kings held in his right hand.

He walked close to the left hand edge of the narrow passage between the buildings, his sister on the right hand side. There was room to maneuver between them.

As they approached the structure that Cereon had pointed out, they stopped and Hy yelled, "HEY! GO AWAY!"

"Doubt that they will," he murmured, watching to see what those things would do. In the dusk he was a large shadow in the shadows draping the side of the buildings.

His sister had faded into the shadows as well.

The black creatures began to move in their direction making soft coughing noises, pointed teeth glittering in what little light there was.

Altai stepped toward the center of the space, O'azur held in a ready position.

Hopping, lurching, the horde charged.

And ran into a swirling blur of razor sharp, forearm long blade. The first rank dissolved into bits and pieces blowing to all sides.

Hy stepped silently past them, turned and swung, a sweeping horizontal cut. Body halves fell where they stood.

Then mob and opponents blurred together in a blast of carnage and death. The horde banged into each other as they pushed into the narrow space, bumping and jostling to get at those they were eager to kill.

Cereon stepped closer and stared at his near-sister and near-brother. All around them there were bodies, twisting and thrashing as they died, body parts, and mounds of unidentifiable stuff.

It was hard to believe that those two could move that fast and do what they were doing.

Hy was smashing things with his shield and chopping others down as easily as the three of them used to do when they were young, wacking flower heads off stems with long wooden sticks.

Then the noise was gone. In the silence he could heard the pair breathing, loud but not very hard.

Cereon hurried forward, finding it difficult to not

step in what he preferred not to look at.

He was visible. "Are you two really safe? Ahhhhh, safe to be around?" He sounded worried. He was.

Hy wiped the monstrous blade clean on something, then swung it up and over his shoulder to its place on his back.

He grinned at Cereon. "Shall we see what is inside?"

Stepping to the door, he shoved, and stepped forward, banging his forehead.

"OUCH!"

"Hy?" Altai hurried over, frowning.

"Locked," he said. "Step away." Altai hastily yanked Cereon back. Hy snatched down the sword and swung.

Wood fragments flew up, out, and inside.

"Now it is open." Hy kicked his way through the rubble and walked inside.

A table occupied the center of the room. It was the only piece of furniture. On it sat a small chest with four thick candles anchored to the table top with wax. The candles provided all the illumination that the room had.

Altai stepped close, handed the O'azur to Cereon. "Hold this, please?"

He did, grumbling about the stuff still dripping from it.

She reached out and gently lifted the lid with one finger until it fell open. Inside she could see a golden key lying on the bottom. It was the only thing in the chest. She reached in and ever so carefully picked it up. Then she peered at it and dropped it into a pocket which she fastened shut.

"So far, not a problem." She took her weapon back. "We better find someplace to stay until the sun rises."

They wandered around the village until they found the place where the yellow wagonway exited out the other side and followed it into the surrounding forest.

Early the next morning they were up and moving.

Even Cereon, noted by all the other siblings when they were young, to be a very late sleeper, was up at the first touch of dawn.

Each of them was anxious to be done and to be finished with whatever lurked ahead guarding the stolen Guardian's eye.

They didn't hurry but their pace along the yellow wagonway was faster than they had been walking before.

And sooner, much sooner than they had thought it would be, they exited the dense forest and stepped into the edge of a great meadow.

Right in the center of all that grass they could see an ornate chest. Between them and the chest stood a thong of the dark creatures.

In the early light they could see that these things legs were shaped more like a birds than anything else.

Hy nodded to himself. That explained the strange way they moved.

"Same weapons," he observed, backing up into the opening. He wanted to have dense forest on either side. The smaller the frontal space the better.

Altai did the same thing.

Cereon," she said, looking around, "where ever you are, stay back!"

The pair stood ready, weapons set, and watched the creatures coming their way with that strange hopping lurching gait.

Hy'pherian stared over the tops of their heads. That chest was sliding in a diagonal away from the central spot.

Altai grunted. "That is very strange!"

She spun, chopping the legs from the front rank as they approached her. To her side she could see bodies tumbling in two parts as Hy slashed horizontally, the Sword of Kings slashing through the mass almost as if they weren't there.

In the sunlight, green fluid splashed in all directions as arms, legs, heads, bodies were sliced away.

Hy and Altai stepped back to clear ground as the mob slipped and lurched over the carnage, snarling coughing at their prey.

Hy and Altai lunged forward and the piles grew larger and higher.

In their concentration on the task at hand they had lost sight of the strange chest slithering through the grass.

Then it was quiet.

The pair stood and waited, scanning the meadow for any more of the things.

Finally, satisfied there were no more, they stepped through the mess and out into the clean grass. Wiping their weapons clean on the grass they looked around for the chest.

Hy leaped to one side.

The chest was sliding in his direction.

"Careful!" snapped Cereon, appearing, bent over, hauling the chest by one handle toward them.

He stopped in front of them. "I was going to hide it if more of those things came from somewhere."

Cereon examined the chest.

"Doesn't seem to have a lock. Shall I look inside?"

Hy nodded.

"Let's," said Altai.

"Eh huh," gasped Cereon as he did.

A large crystal sphere, nestled in soft blue padding, was all that the chest contained.

"Doesn't look like an eye to me," he grumbled.

"Must be it," said Hy.

Altai nodded. "Let's stay in the Chin Village and rest up."

Hy laughed, bent over and picked up the chest and tucked it under one arm. "I'll carry it."

They headed back toward the intersection, Cereon mumbling vague complaints about having to walk through the wide band of remains and about why they had been told to get a key that wasn't required.

A number of days later, rested, and clean from their stay in Chin Village, Altai thumped the base of her O'azur on the great wooden gate.

The hatch high above banged open and the same head popped out. "Oh, its you!" And disappeared, slamming the hatch shut.

"Didn't seem to be very happy to see us," mumbled Cereon.

"Strange folk," suggested Hy.

The gate swung wide and the same male stepped forward, eyeing the chest under Hy'pherian's arm.

"Follow me!" he snapped, and hurried them along the wagonway, the gate slamming closed behind them.

Some time later, the trio found themselves in the same great hall, facing the same figure, dressed all in green, seated in the golden throne on the high dias.

"You are returned," he observed, "with a new member."

Hy nodded and set the chest on the floor.

"We have the eye and the key," he stated.

Slowly raising one arm, the figure pointed at one of the walls. A door slowly appeared.

"There is the passage to the next of The Folded Lands." He smiled at them. "We are impressed. May you remain as fortunate."

Hy smiled back. "Do we take the eye with us?"

"Oh, no need for that. The eye has already returned."

Cereon knelt and opened the chest. Only the blue padding remained. "Gooba," he mumbled as he stood.

They headed for the door which was slowly swinging wide.

On the other side they could see green grass, bright sunlight, and a wagonway passing between two low mounds.

Hy laughed and waved them to follow as he strode for the opening.

They did.

They heard the door slam shut behind them.

The Eye of Memory.

"Eh ah," said Altai'dorionasha as she rested her O'azur on her right shoulder. "Not exactly what I expected to see."

Hy'pherian laughed.

Stretching before them, twisting to the right around the end of a low mound covered in bright green grass, was a broad paved wagonway like the one that they had seen before, with one exception.

It was a bright red.

Cereon knelt and scratched at one of the rectangular paving stones with a finger nail. "Stone, hard stone. Just like the yellow one."

"Eh," said Altai, "let us see what is around that turn just ahead."

"But slowly," grumbled Cereon. "The Guardian told of terrible creatures in here. Maybe this time they will be waiting for us"

"Most careful," stated Hy, strolling alongside his sister as they started forward.

In a very short time they had walked around the bend, a very sharp right-hand turn, and stopped to stare at the vista opening up before them.

The strange wagonway stretched arrow straight ahead of them, rising and falling over the slight undulations of the land. On either side of the wagonway they were vast agricultural fields planted in crops that were different than anything that they had seen grown in Nu'vern.

The field on their left had a crop that was planted in row after row stretching away from the wagonway. The short stems would only come to the knees on Hy'pherian. The single stem was thick and had a few thin leaves poking from it here and there. Some sort of fruit was growing in the junction of leaf and stem. This field made a soft rustling sound as a faint breeze drifted through.

The field on the other side was a mass of flowers, bright purple flowers. The tops of the flowers would come to Hy'pherian's ankles. Each was a single blossom on a single stem surrounded by a thick cluster of dark blue foliage.

The flowers swayed gently as the breeze passed by.

Hy smiled at his sister. "It seems these lands follow a similar pattern."

They started strolling down the wagonway, slowly as Cereon had suggested, and watched the strange fields for the tillers of those fields and admired the clear blue sky overhead.

After they had walked for some distance, Altai said, "There are no creature noises coming from those fields either, nothing but the rustle of the growth."

"Where are the tillers of these fields?" mumbled Cereon. "We ought to see one or two at work. Someone has to take care of these fields. I wonder where they live?"

Altai nodded. "A different land this still is."

They walked on, each wondering about this land and where the inhabitants might be. From what they had been told by The Guardian this place didn't seem to match its words, again.

Topping the fifth crest, Hy pointed. "Down there, in that wide flat, at that intersection like that other one, there appears to be a number of signs, probably more direction markers."

They hurried down the gentle slope. It had been, so far, an easy and pleasant walk, but all were beginning to feel a little bored and just a little apprehensive. Where were the monsters that were supposed to be here? And why were these lands so identical?

They stopped to read the small signs.

One pointed to their left: *Undil Village* ☜.

Two pointed to their right: ☞ *Purple Az.*

☞ *Tammest*

(danger).

The third apparently indicated straight ahead, as it had in the previous land: ≙ *Unruly.*

"I prefer Undil Village," said Cereon. "Perhaps these folk will give us some food and a camping space as did that other village."

Hy looked at his sister.

"Let's," she said. "Perhaps we will be able to sleep comfortable again." She laughed at the strangeness of this place

They headed left and walked up the long slope and out onto flat land the stretched into the distance. And in that distance something sparkled.

As the sun was sagging toward the horizon they could see roof tops. They came in many colors and shapes. Ornaments on the peaks sparkled.

"They seem to like bright colors," said Altai. "Also."

Hy laughed. "Just like Chin Village, it seems."

And, eventually as they must do, they arrived close enough to clearly see the village.

It appeared that all the structures were facing three sides of a large paved square. The wagonway entered the square from the fourth side. Red square. Red wagonway.

They strolled into the square and stopped, waiting to see what would happen now.

The inhabitants were lined up in rows, staring at them. They were about as tall as Cereon. Their clothes, like their houses, were a riot of colors. Many of them wore elaborate hats, often with one of those single-stemmed purple flowers poked into the headband of the hat.

After the trio stood quietly watching and waiting, an elderly male stepped forward and announced in rolling tones, "Welcome to Undil Village. Are you here to help or to hinder?"

Hy'pherian stepped forward, two steps, and bowed. "We are here to help as The Guardian asked." Well, he thought, the same questions as before so one gives the same answers as before.

In the gathering throng, more and more of the villagers had joined those already here, numerous conversations erupted.

A few, overcome by curiosity, approached the trio and began to run gentle fingers over their garb.

The elderly male stepped very close to Hy and made shooing motions with his hands, scattering the curious into the ever gathering crowd now edging closer and closer to their visitors from three sides.

"Help?" he asked.

Hy nodded. "We came to retrieve The Guardian's eye."

Sudden silence surrounded them.

"Can any of you tell us which way to go?" He assumed that it would be same as before, but that he might as well ask, it might be different.

This question started the conversations going again. Eventually a sort of a consensus was arrived at.

Just like before.

The elderly man nodded and it became quiet again.

He pointed at the way they had come.

"Purple Az, The Great City, that is the place to ask that question." He smiled and pointed at a large flat grassy spot that was next to the junction of the red wagonway and the town square. "You may stay there. Our only inn would be too small for such tall folk. Dark approaches. May we share a meal with you?"

Cereon smiled at him, then bowed. "An honor." He thought that he had better do the same thing as before. Maybe if he didn't things would change for the worse.

All through the meal, the three talked with the village's appointed spokesman. He told them that it would take some days to walk to Purple Az. They had heard of the dark horrors that were keeping The Guardian's eye but that was all that they knew. However, they felt that much more could be learned in Purple Az.

Then the folk began to gather everything and head back to their homes.

"One last question," said Cereon.

"Of course," replied the eldest. "What?"

"Why does the sign indicating the direction of Tammest have a warning written under it?"

The spokesman frowned darkly. "I have never been there but I will tell all I know of that place."

He cleared his throat and did.

"That is the town of the Slynara and these are the things you must know." Then he slowly related the tale that he had heard.

Slynara offspring have colorless eyes until their tenth season. At the celebration of their tenth season, The Select One has them drink a potion so secret that it is never written down but passed from Select to Select as part of their oral tradition. Depending upon what eye color then begins to show, the offspring become a member of one of the several caste-guild organizations.

If you dare to venture to there, you might befriend one of the Hakar, The Defenders. It is said that the Hakar have been known to slip into a new state of being which the Slynara call *Timder*, "The State of Being To Protect Another." The chosen are named *Kararane*, "The One To Willing Die For." *Another* is their label for all non-Slynara.

The Hakar female eye color can be red, green, or orange; the males are black, brown or grey.

Their mythology states that The Great Protector, Andercal, directed them to tear apart any of *The Another* that would dare enter their territory. But after many, many seasons they have become merely disinterested in the few that dare to visit unless the traveler breaks one of their taboos.

Andercal, the daughter of Azril, is called The Right Hand of Azril. Her brother, Razonar, is called The Left Hand of Andercal. Why this is so, is unknown, at least to outsiders.

Some of the Hakar are chosen to become Warriors of Andercal. Those chosen are given special equipment and trained endlessly in enhanced skills. This organization has four orders based on the Slynara primary colors: The Order of The Blue, The Order of The Green; The Order of The Red; and, The Order of The White.

He stood and said, "Now you know all that I do. In early light we will bring a meal and some supplies for you before you leave." He walked away.

Just after the sun had slipped above the horizon, a number of the villagers brought platters of steaming food and a number of carefully wrapped parcels for their journey.

And soon, the trio headed back the way that they had come.

Some of the villagers walked a short way with them, then stopped and called, "Good travels," at their backs.

With the sun shining down, they walked down into the depression, checked the signs, and strolled up the slope toward whatever Purple Az might be, but they all thought that they knew what it would be.

Finally, late in the day, they camped on a grassy patch next to the wagonway, deciding that it might not be a good idea to camp inside someone's field, whether they ever saw anyone working those fields or not.

Two days later, having eaten all the food the villagers had given them, they saw, as they topped a low hill, a large town looming up in the distance. It appeared that it favored purple. The roofs and what they could see of other surfaces reaching above the tall outer wall surrounding the place were all purples of varying shades.

They increased their pace and were soon standing in front of the tall wooden gate, a pale grey construction of thick planks.

Hy'pherian pushed on it. "Locked. Again."

Altai thumped on it with the round base of her O'azur.

It made a loud booming sound.

"Guess that they will know that we are here," mumbled Cereon. He was beginning to think this quest was feeling rather dumb.

They waited. For some time.

Altai was about to thump the gate harder, when it happened.

High over head, a small hatch was thrown open and a head poked out.

"What do you want?" demanded a wild-haired female in a high pitched raspy voice.

"To come inside," replied Hy.

"Come back tomorrow!" The head jerked back and the hatch slammed shut.

Cereon turned from inspecting the surface of the gate. "Not again," he grumbled.

Altai began a rhythmic thumping on the gate with the base of her O'azur.

Eventually the hatch popped open. The same head popped out.

"STOP THAT!"

"We want to come inside and talk with someone who can answer our questions," she called.

"We are helping The Guardian," added Hy.

"Well," snapped the female, "why didn't you say so!"

She jerked back, the hatch slammed shut.

Cereon grumbled loudly.

Then the great gate began to slowly, silently swing in, until it stood wide open. The red wagonway continued inside, running deep toward the interior. Large structures soared on all sides, all colored purple.

"Welcome to Purple Az," said the wire-haired female. "Follow me! I will take you to The Voice of Purple Az. You may ask your questions there." She peered back out the gate. "Only you three?"

"Eh huh," said Cereon. "Just us three." He frowned at Hy who was grinning broadly.

They followed their guide along the wide way past a number of side ways. Many folk were hurrying in every direction, passing through the intersections. They all smiled at their visitors and appeared to be quite relaxed.

Hy watched them and wondered why again if there was somewhere a number of black things guarding The Guardian's eye, it didn't seem as if these folk were disturbed by that at all. This was getting stranger and stranger.

Everyone that they passed were dressed in a variety of colors and costumes, almost as vibrant as the folk of Undil Village.

They walked deep into the town until their guide stopped and pointed. The structure had broad stairs across the front and a number of stone columns holding up a short roof over the entry platform.

"Up there," said their guide. "Follow the corridor until you get to the main chamber. Then ask your questions."

He spun and hurried away, apparently toward the main gate.

Cereon started up the wide stairs.

Hy and Altai hurried after him.

The corridor was wide, stone columns lined the sides, set against the walls, spaced in even intervals. The floor was paved with smooth, highly polished dark purple stone.

Far ahead they could see a wide silver door in the wall that terminated the corridor.

Altai swumg her O'azur around and held it by the middle next to her side.

"Uh?" asked Hy.

"Just cautious. Cereon is correct. A strange folk, even if it all appears to be similar."

Hy nodded.

When they reached the door, Cereon said, "If you don't mind, again." And disappeared.

Altai laughed and pulled the door open.

They walked in.

The door closed behind them with a dull thump.

A figure, dressed all in purple, sat in a silver

throne on a high dias, and stared at them.

"I," he intoned in deep rolling tones, "am Az. Why . . . are . . . you . . . here?"

Hy and Altai bowed, deeply.

"We," stated Hy, as he straightened up, "are helping The Guardian. Do you know where we might find those that have the eye?" He suspected he knew what the response was going to be.

"Deep in Unruly do they lurk, foul, vile things. Neither Undil Village or Purple Az have the arms to take the eye back. Can two warriors do this?"

Hy smiled. "We intend to do that."

"At the intersection you will see the sign. Follow it. A small place of few dwellings will you meet first. Hidden there is a box containing a key. Take the key. This container is guarded by the foul and vile."

Altai took a step forward. "After we have the key and the eye, how do we leave these lands?"

"Bring all that you find to this very chamber. The door will open." He leaned back and watched them.

They bowed, turned, and headed back the way that they had come.

As they walked down the stairs, Cereon appeared.

"He didn't say how many of these foul and vile things that there are, just like the Green Az," he grumbled. "This is becoming a longer and longer camping trip. And strange, very strange."

Several days later, they once again stood in the intersection.

Cereon kicked the sign labeled *Unruly*.

"Maybe the next time we can skip the side trip to whatever Az it is."

Hy nodded. But he felt that maybe they had to do the same thing again. He suggested this to Cereon.

"Purgle," mumbled Cereon, pulling the sign back to vertical. He pointed. "Let's go visit them. It will be different."

Hy looked at his sister.

She shrugged and nodded. "Let's."

Not far from the intersection in the direction toward Purple Az a wagonway headed due south toward Tammest. In the distance it appeared to terminate at the nearby high ridge.

They hurried that way and saw that it entered a tunnel.

Cereon grunted as they stepped inside tunnel, "Different."

They strolled along and around a very sharp bend to the left, then to the right. Far ahead they could see light.

"Careful and cautious," warned Hy. "We do not know these folk and they do not know us."

Cereon nodded. He figured that the warning from Hy was mainly aimed at him.

They stepped from the tunnel's mouth into a large, well laid-out town. Folk were hurrying here and there. They ignored the trio.

The ways running between the structures were

paved with cobble stones of blue, red, green, and white, in no apparent order or arrangement. Most of the buildings that they could see were octagonal in shape capped with domes of blue, softly polished blue stone. The walls of these structures were constructed of alternating rows of grey and green stone. The doors and windows were all trimmed in bright yellow.

The inhabitants that they could see all had a gliding gait that seemed to skin over the uneven surface beneath their feet.

Cereon whispered to the others, "I see a few dressed in red armor, a couple in blue. Those must be their warriors."

"I wonder if they have some kind of inn for outsiders." Altai was looking at various of the buildings for some sign that would indicate something like that.

A male dressed in white armor came around a nearby corner, saw them, and hurried toward them. He was wearing scale armor and carrying a shield. A long sword hung from his belt.

"Why come you here to Tammest?" he asked them, dark grey eyes watching them carefully.

"We are helping The Guardian," said Hy. "My companion," he indicated Cereon, "saw the sign at the intersection and wished to visit."

The warrior turned to Cereon, who was a full head shorter. "Why does a non-warrior, geh, wish to visit Tammest?"

"Curiosity," replied Cereon.

The dark grey eyes searched their faces and

indicated Hy and Altai. "Be these close product?" he asked Cereon.

Cereon frowned. "Close product?"

"Much in faces suggest this."

"Ahhh em," said Cereon. "We all have the same father but they have one mother and I have another."

"Zzzzzzzzz," hissed the warrior. He pointed. "Do these warriors behave?"

Cereon nodded violently. "Absolutely! Always!"

The warrior pointed with his free hand at one of the ways. "Follow! A place of comfort, comfort for us." He shrugged.

They followed him down the pavement.

After a turn to the right and then a turn to the left, they were led into a building.

A male bustled up to them, coming from somewhere deeper in the building.

"An'others," stated the warrior. "Room! Food!"

The inn keeper stared at them from clear blue eyes and nodded. "Come."

He led them down a hall and opened a door. It was a large room with three beds and a small wash room.

"Here," he said. "Food later."

"May we wander around your town?" asked Hy.

The male pointed at the beds and then their weapons and shields. "Leave!"

Hy nodded.

The male left, closing the door to the room.

"Shall we look around?" Hy dumped his shield

and the great sword on one of the beds.

Altai nodded and set her O'azur on another. "I suspect that it is safe. Ummm, given what we have seen so far."

"Let's," urged Cereon. He thought exploring a new town was a really good idea. Besides, it would be nice to do something other than just repeating everything that they had already done once before.

They headed out to see what they could see.

Then they wandered, back and forth, here and there, and were ignored by the inhabitants.

Hy was enjoying the walk and memorizing the way back to their lodging at the same time.

They walked around a corner and were halfway to the next intersection when Altai stopped and spun around.

"Cereon, are you there?" She couldn't see him.

"No games!" she hissed.

"Back!" said Hy.

They hurried back to the corner and looked up and down all the streets.

Altai sighed. "Not again!"

Cereon had always done things like this when they were younger. If something attracted his attention, he would head that way, forgetting who he was with, or where they were going, just assuming that he would shortly be rejoined with them. Hy and Altai had pulled him from these misadventures, more than once

Hy nodded and grinned. "Might as well head back and hope that someone will guide him back to the correct place. Unless we hear loud shouting coming from some place."

He led her in the correct direction and sighed. Cereon still seemed to have that bad habit of wandering off as something attracted his attention.

Cereon had been walking slower than the others and saw them turn the corner up ahead. No worry, he thought, he could easily catch up. Then he saw two females wearing trousers and over-blouses of a soft grey that seemed to flow around them in interesting ways.

The pair entered the building across the way. Through the open door he could hear happy laughter.

He walked across the street. It would only take a moment or two to see what was going on in there.

Strolling casually across the cobble stones, he climbed the stairs, and walked inside, into a large room where a number of females were standing, sitting, holding happy conversations. Some of them were wearing armor of the four colors he remembered that their warriors wore. Must be more of those Warriors of Andercal, he thought.

One of the females rose from the couch where she had been talking with another wearing red armor and headed his way.

Oh gooba, he thought, she moves just like Hy and Altai. She must be a trained warrior of some kind. Maybe she will just tell him to leave. He didn't think that turning and running would be a good idea. Yet!

She stopped in front of him.

He noted than she was a head taller than himself and that she was wearing some of that same grey, more or less, clinging garb.

She was slender and had the smooth movements of a feral predator, a very healthy predator, which caused her garments to make a soft whisper. Her soft brown hair was tied back from her left ear with a bright green ribbon the echoed the deep emerald of her eyes. Her soft smile exposed the tips of her upper poison canines, protruding over her lower lips, stark white against soft red lips.

Her stare was direct and searching.

"You have a pleasant appearance," she observed.

He thought of disappearing but didn't. It might break some sort of local taboo or other. Then all three of them would be in trouble. So, he smiled at her. Instead.

"What want you here in a Hakar House?" she demanded.

"Oh maka," he gulped. He certainly had stepped into the wrong place.

"Er?" She waited.

"I heard happy laughter and wanted to see, that's all," he mumbled. And hoped that response would be good enough.

She stepped closer, reached out, and ran a rather warm hand over his cheek.

"EEE um nar," she murmured to him. "I be Slinal."

"Cereon," he gasped. His cheek tingled. What did she do to him?

Numbers of the others crowded around them, staring at him, smiling at her.

Well, he thought, at least no-one looks angry.

"Timder," she whispered. "Timder . . . Timder."

She stepped very close and bent her head until their foreheads touched. "Kararane," she sighed. "Slinal kararane Cereon."

"Me?" he squeaked. Oh no! Not to him! He had just remembered what they had been told by the spokesman in Undil Village about the Slynara.

She stepped back and smiled broadly at him, upper canines protruding over her lower lip.

Now what was he supposed to? He didn't think that he could possibly outrun her, even if she couldn't see him. His footsteps would be heard, running. He sighed heavily.

"Do you have purple gems?" asked Slinal.

"Me? Purple gems?"

"Yush." She nodded.

"Eh, um, what are purple gems?"

"To purchase my armor, shield, and weapon."

Cereon gulped and vigorously shook his head.

"Me? No, I have none of those gems. I don't even know where to get them." She'll just have to find someone else, he thought.

She laughed, a soft, deep in the throat laugh. "A small quest. I will guide, Kararane."

"A small quest?" he mumbled. "For purple gems?" That didn't sound good. Not to him. Questing got folk killed. "You will guide? Me?"

She smiled at him. "Yush." It was the thing to do.

He sighed, resigned to whatever it was. "Can you guide me back to the place where I am staying. I will need to discuss this with my, erm, companions."

He shrugged. Maybe Hy and Altai could talk her out of whatever she had in mind.

"Yush. All know where," stated Slinal, heading for the door.

As they walked along, she pointed which way to turn at each intersection.

He asked her, "Please explain Timder and Kararane, I am a little vague on the details. It is rather, em, new to me."

Smiling broadly at him, she said that she would do that.

"Timder is a rare thing for the Hakar, a special bond of great importance, of great meaning. It comes suddenly, unbidden. I now have a great feeling to protect the pretty Cereon named Kararane, the One Willing To Die For, the one more important than all! Kararane must take care of their Timder in all things, at all times."

Cereon nodded slowly. "And that is why I have to get purple gems, do that quest?" And how does one take care of their Timder?

She smiled warmly at him.

He sighed and wondered what Hy and Altai were going to say about all that.

Slinal halted and pointed at a door. "Lodgings."

Cereon opened the door and led her across the

room, down the hall to the room that they had been given. The inn keeper goggled at them.

They stepped into the room.

Altai bounced to her feet from the bed where she had been sitting, waiting. "CEREON!" *Now what has he done?*

Hy spun from the window he had been staring out. "Who is this?"

Cereon sighed, heavily. He pointed at them. "Hy'pherian, Altai'dorionasha. Just call them Hy and Altai."

"Hy, Altai," repeated Slinal.

"This is Slinal," Cereon stated. "She is my, ummmmm, guardian, or something."

"What did you do?" snapped Altai. *This time,* she added to herself.

"Nothing," he mumbled. "She did it, whatever it is." He frowned at Altai. After all, it wasn't his fault. All he had wanted to do was to see what all that laughter was about.

"Timder," stated Slinal.

"Maybe," added Cereon, "she can explain all that, and purple gems, and the quest." He dropped into one of the chairs and stared at the floor past the tips of his boots.

Slinal did, slowly and carefully.

Altai sat down, staring at Cereon. When they were young, he was always getting tangled in something but this was something she didn't think they could him get disentangled from. Not this time.

Hy leaned against the wall and grinned at Cereon. "Welcome, Slinal. Let me explain why we are here in The Folded Lands."

Just as he finished, the inn keeper thumped upon their door and announced loudly, "FOOD!"

He gasped when he saw Slinal walk from the room with them. While they ate the meal, he watched them. Then he hurried off to arrange for two rooms. He had recognized that she was Hakar and that it would not do to upset her.

When the four were finished with their meal, he led them down a different hall and opened two doors. He urged Hy and Altai into one and Cereon and Slinal into the other.

"Ah, eh," murmured Altai.

Hy laughed.

The next morning, early, the four of them headed for the far gate, guided by Slinal. Hy and Altai were armed again. Slinal told them to do so.

Far across the town, Slinal halted them and pointed at a structure with a door trimmed in dark gold.

"The pretty Cereon must enter and talk with Lurin else there will be no binding. He must do this successfully by himself!"

She pointed at the benches on either side of the door. "We us will here wait."

Slinal made shooing motions with her hands at Cereon, walked over and sat down. Hy and Altai joined her. Altai turned to Hy and whispered, "The pretty

Cereon?"

He shrugged.

Cereon stared at them, gulped, turned, walked over, and opened the door, and stepped inside.

She sat in a brown wooden chair with a high back and flat arms, and watched him with large golden eyes.

He took two steps and stopped, wondered what he was supposed to do in here and closed the door.

She licked her lips, exposing her poisonous fangs.

"Closer," she purred. "I would see what Slinal feels for!"

He carefully stepped closer

Lurin straightened up and peered into his eyes. And frowned. "So young. A mere nineteen seasons."

Then she jerked. "With a special skill! Show me this thing!"

Cereon disappeared. Her comments hadn't sounded every reassuring to him.

"How very interesting," she said. "You cannot open that door or leave by any other way, nor are you able to harm me."

He appeared.

She flowed to her feet and stepped up to him, standing very close, golden robes soft rustling.

Cereon swallowed loudly. Now what?

"I will be hugged tightly," she stated firmly.

Carefully, cautiously, he leaned forward, swung his arms around, and did as ordered.

She tilted her head back and murmured, "That is very friendly. Kiss me!" Her smile was broad, upper canines showing over her lower lip. "Don't mind my fangs, I am still kissable."

Exhaling loudly Cereon did as she asked.

Lurin sighed, and rubbed her hand over his chest. Then she reached into somewhere and handed him a golden pendant.

"Take this. It is part of what you require. Leave me now, it will not do for us to get excited."

She stepped back, and back, and settled into her chair, eyes never leaving his face.

Shoving the pendant into a deep trouser pocket, Cereon spun, leaped for the door and yanked it open.

The trio sitting, waiting on the bench, jerked, and watched as he sailed through the open doorway, cleared the steps, and landed with a heavy thump on the pavement.

They stood and stared at him.

Slinal smiled and pointed the way that they had been heading. "The book store is not far."

Hy looked at Altai.

She shrugged and wondered why they needed to visit a book store.

They had not walked far when Slinal stopped, spun, and headed for the door of a building.

"Armak's Books," she announced, grabbing one of Cereon's wrists and pulling him along. "Come, Pretty One."

Hy and Altai followed, casting puzzled looks at

each other.

A male dressed in dark grey with white trim turned from a stack of books on the counter and faced them.

Slinal patted Cereon on a shoulder. "This male requires one of the books."

Armak smiled at Cereon and headed into the book stacks, returning shortly with a thin volume bound in light tan leather. "Pay later," he said as he handed it to Cereon.

Cereon turned the book around until he could read the title, then stared at Slinal, who smiled at him.

Hy looked over Cereon's shoulder and stifled his laughter.

Altai nudged him in the side.

"The Care and Feeding of The Hakar," he whispered.

Cereon stuffed the book into a side pocket. "I will read it later," he mumbled.

Outside the shop, Slinal held out her hand. "Lurin's gift," she stated. "If you received it!"

"Oh." Cereon handed her the pendant.

She grinned at him and laughed happily. "Pendant and book. It is done. One to one, never to be parted."

She nudged him into motion in the appropriate direction.

Cereon sighed. And wondered how and why this was happening to him. He hadn't done anything.

Some distance down the way and around a

corner, they stood in front of a wide gate constructed of thick Hag Tree wood, noted for its strength and durability. On either side of the gate, high walls stretched and curved around this side of the town. A narrow roof covered the gateway.

The gate slowly swung open. As it did they could see a narrow path curving and disappearing into a steep-walled canyon.

"QUESTING!" called Slinal to the watch-guard high overhead.

Hy and Altai walked in front of the others as they headed into the ever-twisting path. Soon they were alone, feeling very alone. They could no longer see any portion of the town behind them nor anything other than the trail ahead of them, steep canyon walls on either side.

Hy and Altai heard the great sigh and grumble from Cereon, stopped, and turned.

"What?" asked Altai, frowning, just a little..

"I was just thinking. When we were small, as the Last-Son-Of-The-Second, I always felt that I should hide. There were so many of us and you two were my only real friends."

He looked from Altai to Hy, who nodded.

"I think," he said, "that is why The Gift took me to where I could learn how to really do that."

Hy stared at him.

"Eh heh," said Altai. "A rather deep thought."

She held up one hand, palm side out toward him. "But! I think that you have thought of something we have not. Hy and I never thought about that. We have always enjoyed the rough and tough play."

Hy frowned, then nodded. "Cereon, you are amazing." He thumped him on a shoulder. "I would wager that none of the others have thought of that either."

"Of course," suggested Altai, "I doubt that The-First-Twins-Of-The First had any thought of what would happen to them. Our Father dragged them away at an early age."

They started up the trail again wrapped in thoughts considering what Cereon had just suggested and wondered what all the others had become.

The trail wandered back and forth, snaking its way ever upward, and passed a gaping hole on the left side in the steep slope.

Slinal stopped there and pointed at it.

Cereon turned and frowned at it. "In there? Really?"

She nodded. He sighed.

They started into the dark ever expanding space, walking carefully. Ahead of them they could see a faint light.

Then they entered it, a large cavern. Great stalactites and stalagmites had grown together to form thick pillars throughout the great room. A steady dripping echoed around the space told them that this cave was still active. It wasn't totally dark as some faint light came from somewhere overhead.

They stood and peered around the great space,

squinting into the gloom and shadow draped far walls. Then they heard it, a soft voice whispering from somewhere.

"Free me. Free me, please? Before those things come back and eat me. Alive!"

Hy turned and pointed.

Altai nodded and stepped silently that way.

As she approached the spot from which the soft voice had come, she could see a gentle red glow. She called the others to come.

They gathered around and wondered what they had found.

From inside the small sphere, her wings folded and bent, she stared at them, great purple eyes pleading for help. Her wings were sparkling multi-colors. She was holding a tattered and torn gown of Blue Ahn Worm Silk closed.

"Ah ummm," Hy stared at the small glowing globe. "Give it a little tap, Altai."

"A Winter Sprite," observed Slinal.

Altai gently tapped the sphere with the base of her O'azur. The sphere rang like a tiny bell.

"I am Teema," gasped the tiny prisoner.

"Eh." Altai banged it harder. The globe chimed louder.

The Winter Sprite screamed at her, "Freeeeee me!"

Altai sucked in a breath and slammed her O'azur across the top of the sphere.

The sphere puffed into pink dust and Teema shot

into the air smiling happily at them to be finally free. She wrapped the tatters of her gown around her, attempting to be modest. Her wings beat a rainbow of colors as she hovered in front of them. She grinned at them. "Am I not lovely?"

Then she scanned their surroundings. "If you can find the gold coin will you give it to me? Please?"

Hy started in one direction, Altai another, Cereon and Slinal in a third.

Near one of the small pools filled by water dripping from somewhere overhead Cereon stared at a large patch covered in deep blue flat paving stones.

"Strange," he mumbled to himself as his eyes began a careful search as he walked ever so carefully back and forth. Kneeling, he began to search again, running one hand back and forth over the stones, the soft light making it hard to see the imperfections in the stone.

Slinal stood back and out of the way, watching carefully. She decided this was not a time to ask him questions.

As Cereon kept running his hands back and forth the stones begin to glow a soft blue. "Purba" he mumbled. As he continued his exploration in the faint blue light he found an imperfection near the center of the paved area. Crawling over to that spot, he began to run his fingers over the slight depression in the otherwise smooth surface and poked one finger into a hole that he felt. Waggling his finger around he suddenly felt something smooth. Carefully Cereon edged this object out of the hole and onto the paved surface. Picking it up, he held the thin disc close to his eyes.

"It is a gold button," he grumbled, standing and brushing his knees clean with the other hand. "Certainly doesn't look like a coin, but it must be what she wants."

Hurrying over to the tiny figure hovered over her destroyed prison, Cereon held out his find. "This what you want?"

Teema clutched it in one hand. "Yesssssss!"

A rainbow of color flashed around her, wrapping her in a cocoon that began to swell and grow. Suddenly, in a soft puff, the colors sparkled away, Teema stood before him looking very pleased and happy to be her proper size again. She was a full head shorter than Cereon. She stretched and yawned. "It is good to be warrior size again." Then she frowned at him. "Now if we can just retrieve my armor and my weapon."

As she lifted up and floated past him he could feel soft lips caress his face.

Cereon spun around to stare at her. "Any idea where we ought to look?"

Teema drifted into the cavern "Over this way, somewhere."

At the far side they gathered together. Two chests sat on the floor next to the wall. One was quite large, the other quite small.

Teema settled to the floor and gave the largest of the chest's lid a great heave and grunted, "Locked. Or something."

Hy cleared his throat as he strolled up to the chest and waved them back as he yanked his great sword from his back. Then he looked at Teema. "Any idea what will happen when I, eh, open them?"

She shrugged.

"Ummmm, maybe all should be a little further back." Hy watched and when he was satisfied that they were safe, he spun and brought the sword down in a great glancing overhand strike to the top of the large chest. Wood splinters sailed in all directions as a number of objects tumbled into a heap in the wreckage.

Teema zipped past and snatched up everything and started to shake them vigorously. She quickly slipped her white and silver armor on, adjusted her belt and hung her long blade from it.

Hy turned and smashed the small chest, bent and fished from the debris a shining object, straightened up and handed it to her.

She laughed happily as she slipped it on one wrist. "Now we are complete, we are," she sighed.

"Ah goobat!" Cereon stared at her. "Let's head outside."

Teema violently shook her head. "The way in is not the way out. This way!" She lifted into the air and began to drift across the cavern to stop and wait for them to arrive.

Cereon followed Hy and Altai, grumbling various and sundry deep mumbles, and wondered why things always seem to keep getting so complicated.

A set of stairs corkscrewed upward around a wide central pillar of white marble. Far above a spot of light shone down. Little could be seen other than the steps curving around and around, higher and higher. The steps were bowed in the center from many, many feet climbing up and down them for seasons and seasons.

Cereon sighed heavily and cast a glance at Slinal who nodded encouragement. "UP!" he growled.

And up they went.

Long before they reached the top, the floor below had disappeared into the darkness below.

But, finally, they stood on flat ground.

Cereon sucked in deep breathes while the rest, apparently not winded at all, waited patiently for him to recover. Teema hovered nearby.

Up here, the sun was shining, the grass was green and thick. The open space stretched to all sides but appeared to be a plateau. In the distance there was a large mound.

As Cereon straightened up, Teema drifted close, smiled warmly at him and pointed. "Welllll, Bold One, here we are in a nice big, soft meadow. Let's go over there and do nice things to each other."

Slinal's fist flashed past the tip of Teema's nose as she snarled, "Hakar do like not brazen anythings. So be you are warned, poota brain!"

Cereon hastily shoved himself between them. "STOP!" And wondered what *poota* meant.

He thrust his outstretched arm, index finger pointing, between the two glowering faces, and said, "Enough of that! Let's go over there and look at that brown mound!"

He stomped past them, grumbling loudly, stopped, and shot dark glower at Hy and Altai. "What is so funny?"

Altai clapped one hand over her mouth, snorted, and yanked it away, replying sweetly, "We just never realized that you were so attractive." She grinned at her brother. "Hy?"

He managed to have better control than his sister.

Cereon jabbed his finger at the far side of the plateau. "I am going to look at that mound way over there," he snapped, stomping off, his feet making soft thumps.

In a moment the other four hurried after the still loudly grumbling Cereon, just to see whatever he was so intent at looking at.

Halfway there, he looked at it and mumbled, mostly to himself, "Certainly looks large."

Finally, he stood not too far away. "Really large."

The mound shuddered and began to rise, higher and higher. A large head, longer than Cereon was tall, emerged on the end of a long neck, and lowered itself down to peer at him from one yellow eye, a forearm wide. The beast hissed soft smoke at him.

Cereon angrily waved the smoke away and backed up, a little.

"Who are you?" they both asked each other.

"I am Cereon."

"Zmarzarl," rasped the great beast. "Why are you here?"

Hy walked up to Cereon's side and looked at the great eye, now watching him, and cleared his throat. "We are helping The Guardian." He pointed to his sister. Then at Cereon. "He is also searching for purple gems."

"Oft!" Zmarzarl twisted her head and stared at Slinal. "Andercal banished me to this spot because she felt that my two, urp, vices as she called them, golden objects and fair young maidens, were not appreciated by all the folk in these lands. Are you a fair young maiden? The appropriate response is: yes Zmarzarl, no Zmarzarl." The beast snickered blue flames and gurgled, "And I do appreciate brevity from others."

Slinal stepped up beside Cereon, and smiled up at it. "Most of course."

The monster hiccuped and looked pleased, grumbled happy in her chest. "Welllllll, not exactly the answer that I requested, but close enough. You look fair and young enough for me." And laughed. "Kickle, kickle, kickle." Turning her head, moving it closer, she flicked out an lengthily forked tongue and quickly slid it here and there on Slinal. Then she smiled slyly, and asked, "Would you like to join me for dinner? You can be the first course?"

Cereon growled softly up at the great beast and snarled, "Behave!" And jerked, surprised that he would do such a thing.

Zmarzarl snapped her head back and glared down at him, hissing loudly. "INGRATE! Don't you realize that fair young maidens have a certain subtle taste to one such as I, the one with such a cultivated taste. It is probably the subcutaneous fat layer below their skins, which males do not have." She stared down her snout at Cereon, then at Slinal, and tried to look abused, and mumbled, all soft rumble, "How about just a small taste? Just a little nip? Someplace that won't show except to very close and intimate friends?"

Cereon sighed and glared up at her. "No!" He sighed. "Just behave. Please?" He had decided that she wasn't really going to do anything too bad to them. At least he hoped so.

"I am extremely well behaved, for one such as I am." She rolled both eyes at Slinal.

"Well," she grumped at Slinal, "you are probably not very nice, for a fair young maiden! I will shrink down to a mere lump at this rate, starving away, ever soooooooo slowly!"

Then Zmarzarl belched purple smoke in all directions and whispered," All right, Tender Parts, how about giving me some small golden gift? If you do, I shall return the favor."

Altai, standing a bit back with the others, nudged Teema, "Give her that button."

Murmuring under her breath, the Winter Sprite floated close and held out the gold button. "Here. Take it."

Two dark, very sharp talons reached out and delicately took the small disc from her fingers.

"Much nicer," she rumbled. "For this, I shall help you. Stand back!"

As soon as they did, Zmarzarl began to carve a wide groove through the grass sod with one talon on the paw not holding the gold button and peeled back the grass. Then digging in the soft soil underneath, she slowly pulled a leather sack free and dropped it in the grass in front of Cereon. "Purple gems for those in need."

Then she curled up and slowly sank and took on the appearance of a large brown mound again.

Cereon picked up the leather sack, took a peek inside, and looked at Slinal. "How do we get down from here?"

Laughing gaily, Teema floated up to him. "I will take each one down. Ready?"

"Huh?"

Wrapping her arms around him, she lifted up, drifted to the edge, and sailed in a lazy spiral down to the trail far below. They all could hear Cereon yelling as he disappeared from sight.

As she dumped the last one on the trail, Teema lifted above their heads and smiled down at Cereon. "Perhaps I will meet you and your over-weight Hakar somewhere." She shot into the air and was soon nothing but a speck of flashing colors disappearing into the distant mountain haze.

Slinal pointed down the trail. "Back to Tammest.

The lovely Cereon can now buy my armor, shield, and weapon." She stepped close to him and kissed him on the cheek, and gave his arm a sharp tug.

The trail back to town seemed to be shorter than when they had come.

Cereon thought that it was because they were going downhill at a more rapid pace than when they came up.

As they passed through the gate, Slinal pointed to a side way, "Maka's Place of Adventure."

They followed her as she hurried along, each wondering what they were up to this time.

Slinal opened the door in the tall building and led them in.

The large room had a single desk set against the far wall next to the only hall.

The ceiling was way up there, painted a soft purple. Large lamps hung on long rods flooding the room with light.

A large painting of many panels covered one wall. Some of the scenes depicted weary adventurers, often accompanied by Slynara in armor, engaged in activities fantastic or grotesque. Other panels showed laughing but heavily battered survivors holding something high over their heads. The upper edge of the painting was open sky and The Great Protector, Andercal, looked down, watching everything.

On stands equally spaced around the room hung suits of armor of various designs and colors, shining and dull.

Cereon watched Slinal as she began to slowly circle the room carefully examining each suit, often running a finger over them. Finally, she stopped, turned and smiled at Maka who hastened over to speak with her in low tones.

After a short discussion Maka smiled broadly, patted her on the shoulder, and led her down the hall, returning shortly, to stand and peer from face to face with a expectant expression of his face.

Cereon stepped forward and handed him the leather sack, hoping that they were enough purple gems to cover the cost. He wasn't eager to go through another search. What they did had seemed rather easy but even so, not another search. It would probably be worse, much worse. "Here. She also requires a shield and a weapon."

"Most of course," gushed Maka. "Most, of course!"

Walking rapidly to one of the walls he began to open large doors, revealing all manner of weapons and shapes of shields, in as many colors as the armor on display.

Hy and Altai wandered over to inspect the weapons, a professional curiosity of a sort.

They were deep in a conversation when they heard Cereon gasp loudly. Hy spun around, hand jumping to his weapon.

Cereon was staring across the room as Slinal strolled into the main room. She was wearing a suit of armor, a dull bronze color, that looked as if it was made of sea creature scales.

Smiling happily, she strode past Cereon, trailing one hand over his chest as she passed, to join Hy and Altai in front of the shield and weapon displays.

She quickly selected a rectangular shield and a long blade whose upper edge was serrated with sharp teeth. The blade and sheath she hung on her belt before turning to face Maka and Cereon.

"Most ready now," she announced and then stepped quickly to Cereon's side.

Then she beckoned Maka over, reached into the leather sack he was holding and extracted a single purple gem.

"For your book," she said to Cereon and headed for the outside door.

Not all that much later, after paying the book seller, the four were at the intersection looking up the wagonway that led toward Unruly.

Cereon was mumbling quietly to himself. Slinal had walked by his side since they had left Tammest and he was still wondering how she could walk that close and not make a sound, other than the soft hiss of scales sliding over scales. He had heard no footsteps, no thump or rattle from either her shield or the weapon hanging from her belt.

Hy gestured toward their destination. "It will be the same as before, I suspect. But we will still be careful cautious."

Altai nodded and followed him as he started along the wagonway.

They walked on. At the top of the slope they could see the wagonway disappearing into thick forest.

It took all day to reach that spot. The same as before.

"Shall we camp here?" asked Altai. "Again."

"Let's," replied Hy, dumping his pack next to the pavement.

They set up camp, ate Final Meal, and sat and talked.

As the gloom crept into darkness, Hy stood and grabbed his great sword. "I will take first watch." He strolled off, but not far.

"I will take second," said Cereon.

Slinal thumped his shoulder. "No, I will."

Altai thanked her, stretched out, and fell asleep. Cereon soon followed her example.

In the morning, they sat, eating First Meal and watching those woods carefully. It was a silent place. Nothing in there was making a sound. It had been that way all night as well.

Finally ready, they started in.

After some time, Hy'pherian said, again, to Cereon. "How about you go ahead, like last time, a long way ahead. No one will see you. If, or when, you see anything, uh eh, dangerous, just head back and let us know. That will give us time to get ready."

Cereon grumbled, just a small grumble, and hurried ahead of them, vanishing from sight.

Altai reached over and halted Slinal as she started to follow him. "Not! It is his skill. Not your's."

And on the three trudged, a casual stroll, watching both sides as they did.

Finally, they were walking in dimming light as dusk settled on the forest.

Hy and Altai had been discussing whether they ought to just walk all night when Cereon appeared, breathing heavily. He had run back to them, again.

They stopped and waited for him to catch his breath.

"What?" asked Hy.

"Not far from here, the wagonway curves sharply to the right. Just like the last time. It is around that turn, a small cluster of ill cared for dwellings." He sucked in a deep breath. Then he frowned and grumbled, "Big surprise!"

"I didn't see many that looked like villagers but there were a number, I didn't count, of black creatures, not as short as me, not as tall as Hy, clumping around and around a central structure like they were guarding it. Just like the last time."

"Weapons?" asked Hy.

"Looked like longer clubs of some sort. They appear better armed."

Hy looked at Altai.

"Let's," she said. "Cereon can watch our backs. Again."

They began to hurry.

Down the wagonway, around the curve, to the edge of the village, such as it was.

"Another one, quite small," observed Altai,

pulling her O'azur from her right shoulder.

Cereon pointed. "Just there, that building. Same thing."

Hy laughed. "Be gone, Cereon. Be careful." He began to walk slowly into the small village, The Sword of Kings held in his right hand.

He walked close to the left hand edge of the narrow passage between the buildings, his sister on the right hand side while Slinal walked a short distance back in the middle of the wagonway. There was room to maneuver between them.

As they approached the structure that Cereon had pointed out, they stopped and Hy yelled, "HEY! GO AWAY!"

"Doubt that they will either," he murmured, watching to see what those things would do. In the dusk he was a large shadow in the shadows draping the side of the buildings.

His sister had faded into the shadows as well.

Slinal stood still as still, long blade held ready and out from her side.

The black creatures began to move in their direction making soft coughing noises, pointed teeth glistening in what little light that there was.

Altai stepped toward the center of the space, O'azur held in a ready position.

Hopping, lurching, the horde charged her.

And ran into a swirling blur of razor sharp, forearm long blade. The first rank dissolved into bits and pieces blowing to all sides.

Hy stepped silently past them, turned and swung, a sweeping horizontal cut. Body halves fell where they stood. Slinal slid forward past Altai, her blade a blur.

Then mob and opponents merged in a splash of carnage and death. The horde banged into each other as they pushed into the narrow space, bumping and jostling to get at those they are eager to kill.

Cereon stepped closer and stared at his near-sister and near-brother and Slinal. All around them there were bodies, twisting and thrashing as they died, body parts, and mounds of unidentifiable stuff.

It was hard to believe that the three could move that fast. He stared at Slinal who appeared to be dancing through the black things, gore splashing in all directions.

Hy was smashing things with his shield and chopping others down.

Then the noise was gone. In the silence Cereon could heard the pair breathing, loud but not very hard. Slinal appeared quite relaxed as she wiped stuff from her shield and weapon on the things laying all around her. She wasn't breathing hard either

Cereon, now visible, hurried forward, finding it hard not to step in what he preferred not to look at. He quickly checked Slinal for injuries, or something. She smiled at him and his concern. It was proper behavior for him to do that.

Hy wiped his monstrous blade clean on something, then swung it up and over his shoulder to its place on his back.

He grinned at Cereon. "Shall we see what is inside?"

Stepping to the door, he shoved, and stepped forward, banging his forehead.

"OUCH! Not again!" He laughed. "Forgot."

"Hy?" Altai hurried over, frowning.

"Locked," he said. "Step away." Altai hastily yanked Cereon and Slinal back. Hy snatched down the sword and swung.

Wood fragments flew up, out, and inside.

"Now it is open," said Hy as he kicked his way inside.

As before, a table occupied the center of the room. It was the only piece of furniture. On it sat a small chest with four thick candles anchored to the table top with wax. The candles provided all the illumination the room had. It was the same as the last time.

Altai stepped close, handed the O'azur to Cereon. "Hold this, please?"

He did, grumbling about the stuff still dripping from it, and wondered why she couldn't clean that thing first.

She reached out and gently lifted the lid with one finger until it fell open. Inside she could see a silver key lying on the bottom. It was the only thing in the chest. She reached in and ever so carefully picked it up, peered at it and dropped it into a pocket which she fastened shut. Now she had two keys.

"So far, not a problem." She took her weapon

back. "We better find someplace to stay until the sun rises."

They wandered around the village until they could find the place where the red wagonway exited and followed it into the surrounding forest until they found a place to camp.

Early the next morning they were up and moving.

Slinal had nudged Cereon awake.

They didn't hurry but their pace along the red wagonway was faster than they had normally been walking.

And soon, they exited the dense forest and stepped out into a great meadow.

"Again," grumbled Cereon.

Right in the center of all that grass they could see an ornate chest. Between them and the chest stood a thong of the dark creatures similar to those that they had met last night.

"Same weapons as the others," Hy observed, backing up. He wanted to have dense forest on either side. The smaller the frontal space the better. "Same meadow, same chest, same everything. Almost."

Altai backed up as did Slinal.

Cereon vanished.

The three stood ready, weapons set, and watched the creatures coming their way with that strange hopping lurching gait.

Hy'pherian stared over the tops of their heads as the front ranks approached and stepped back. "Nothing happening with that chest."

Altai spun, chopping the legs from the front rank as they approached. To her side she could see bodies tumbling in two parts as Hy slashed horizontally, the Sword of Kings slashing through the mass almost as if they weren't there. Somewhere close by creatures were tumbling as their limbs and heads were chopped free by the whirling dancing blur that was Slinal.

In the sunlight, green fluid splashed in all directions as arms, legs, heads, bodies were sliced away.

Hy and Altai stepped further back into the clear ground as the mob slipped and lurched over the carnage, snarling coughing at their prey. Slinal bounced past the black creatures and spun around, slashing the rear rank to ribbons.

Hy and Altai stepped forward, weapons flashing, and the piles grew large and higher, the space between the three of them turning into a butcher shop, one of the butchers being Slinal as she worked toward them.

Then it was quiet.

The three stood and waited, scanning the meadow for any more of the things.

Finally, satisfied there were no more, they stepped through the wide patch of gore and out into the clean grass. Wiping their weapons clean on the grass they headed for the chest.

Cereon bent and examined the chest.

"Doesn't seem to have a lock either. Shall I look inside?"

Hy nodded.

"Let's," said Altai.

"Eh huh," gasped Cereon as he opened it.

A large crystal sphere, nestled in soft blue padding, was all that the chest contained.

"Doesn't look like an eye to me," he grumbled. "Again."

"Must be it," said Hy. "Again."

Altai nodded at them. "Let's stay in the Undil Village and rest up. It was pleasant the last time. And we can get clean! Again."

Hy laughed, bent over and picked up the chest, tucking it under one arm. "I'll carry it."

They headed back toward the intersection, Cereon mumbling vague complaints about having to walk through the wide band of the remains. Slinal patted one of his shoulders. She had wiped her gloves clean first. It wouldn't do to dirty him.

A number of days later, rested, and clean from their stay in Undil Village, Altai thumped the base of her O'azur on the great wooden gate.

The hatch high above banged open and the same head popped out. "Oh, its you!" And disappeared, slamming the hatch shut.

"Didn't seem to be very happy to see us, either," mumbled Cereon. "Something is very wrong with these folk."

"Strange folk," suggested Hy. "Strange lands."

The gate swung wide and same female stepped forward, eyeing the chest under Hy'pherian's arm.

"Follow me!" she snapped, and hurried them

along the wagonway, the gate slamming closed behind them.

Some time later, the four found themselves in the same great hall, facing the same figure, dressed all in purple, seated in the silver throne on the high dias.

"You are returned," he observed, "with new members."

Hy nodded and set the chest on the floor.

"We have the eye and the key," he stated, being careful to say the exact same thing as the last time.

Slowly raising one arm, the figure pointed at one of the walls. A door slowly appeared.

"There is the passage to the last of The Folded Lands." He smiled at them. "We are impressed. May you remain as fortunate."

They headed for the door which was slowly swinging wide.

Once the other side they could see, as before, green grass, bright sunlight, and a wagonway passing between two low mounds.

Hy laughed and waved them to follow as he strode ahead.

Behind them the door slammed shut.

The Eye of Perception.

"Eh ah," said Altai'dorionasha as she rested her O'azur on her right shoulder. "Not exactly what I expected to see. For the third time. These lands were put together by someone with very little imagination."

Hy'pherian laughed.

Stretching before them, twisting to the right around the end of a low mound covered in bright green grass, was a broad paved wagonway similar to those they had already seen twice before.

This one was a bright blue.

In a very short time they had walked around the bend, a very sharp right-hand turn, and stopped to stare at the all too familiar vista opening up before them.

The wagonway stretched arrow straight ahead of them, rising and falling over the slight undulations of the land. On either side of the wagonway they were the usual vast agricultural fields planted in crops.

The field on their left had a crop that was planted in row after row stretching away from the wagonway. The tall stems were taller than Hy'pherian. The single stem was thick, twisted in a corkscrew fashion, and had a leaves poking from it in all directions. Some sort of fruit was grew at the ends of the stem. This field made a clattering sound as a faint breeze drifted through.

The field on the other side was a mass of flowers. The tops of the flowers would come to mid-chest on Hy'pherian. Each was a single white blossom on a single stem surrounded by a thick cluster of dark orange foliage.

The flowers swayed in the breeze.

They started strolling down the wagonway, slowly as Cereon had suggested, and watched the strange fields for the tillers of those fields and admired the clear blue sky overhead.

They walked on, each wondering, once again,

about this land.

Topping the fifth crest, Hy pointed. "Down there, the same thing, the usual direction markers."

They hurried down the gentle slope to see what the signs said this time.

They stopped and looked at them.

One pointed to their left: *Bedo Village* ☜.

One pointed to their right: ☞ *Blue Az*.

The third indicated straight ahead, telling them:

△ *Awful*.

"I prefer Bedo Village," said Cercon.

Hy looked at his sister.

"Let's," she said. "If the pattern holds we will be able to sleep comfortable instead of camping in these fields. And get more supplies!"

They headed left and walked up the long slope and out onto flat land the stretched into the distance. And in that distance something sparkled.

As the sun was sagging toward the horizon they could see roof tops. They came in many colors and shapes. Ornaments on the peaks sparkled.

"They also seem to like bright colors," observed Altai.

Hy laughed.

And, eventually as they must do, they arrived close enough to clearly see the village.

As before, all the structures were facing three sides of a large paved square. The wagonway entered the square from the fourth side, everything the same blue paving blocks.

They strolled into the square and stopped, waiting, as they knew they should.

The inhabitants were lined up in rows, staring at them. They were shorter than Cereon. Their clothes, like their houses, were a riot of colors. Many of them wore elaborate hats, often with one of those single-stemmed white flowers poked into the headband of the hat.

After the four stood quietly watching and waiting, an elderly male stepped forward and announced in rolling tones , "Welcome to Bedo Village. Are you here to help or to hinder?"

Hy'pherian stepped forward, two steps, and bowed, and repeated the standard response. "We are here to help as The Guardian asked." He had decided that it was all part of some sort of strange ritual.

In the gathering throng, more and more of the villagers had joined those already here, numerous conversations erupted.

A few of those, overcome by curiosity, approached the four and began to run gentle fingers over their garb.

The elderly male stepped very close to Hy and made shooing motions with his hands, scattering the curious into the ever gathering crowd now edging closer and closer to their visitors from three sides.

"Help?" he asked.

Hy nodded. "We came to retrieve The Guardian's eye."

Sudden silence surrounded them.

The spokesman pointed at the way they had come.

"Blue Az, The Great City, that is the place to ask that question." He smiled and pointed at a large flat grassy spot that was next to the junction of the blue wagonway and the town square. "You may stay there. Our only inn would be too small for such tall folk. Dark approaches. May we share a meal with you?"

Cereon smiled at him, then bowed. "An honor. And could we get some water to clean ourselves with."

All through the meal, three talked with the village's appointed spokesman. Slinal sat close to Cereon and listened. The spokesman told them that it would take some days to walk to Blue Az. They had heard of the dark horrors that were keeping The Guardian's eye but that was all that they knew. However, they felt that much more could be learned in Blue Az.

Then the folk began to gather everything and head back to their homes. A number returned carrying large basins and containers of steaming water.

The spokesman stood. "In early light we will bring a meal and some supplies for you before you leave." He walked away.

Just after the sun had slipped above the horizon, on the next day, a number of the villagers brought platters of steaming food and a number of carefully wrapped parcels for their journey.

And soon, the four headed back the way that

they had come.

Some of the villagers walked a short way with them, then stopped and called, "Good travels," at their backs.

With the sun shining down, they walked into the depression, checked the signs, and strolled up the slope toward Blue Az. They had decided that they should go through the usual routine.

Finally, late in the day, they camped on a grassy patch next to the wagonway, once again, not camping inside someone's field.

Two days later, having eaten all the food the villagers had given them, they saw, as they topped a low hill, a large town looming up in the distance. It appeared that this time the town favored blue. The roofs and what they could see of other surfaces reaching above the tall outer wall surrounding the place were all blues of varying shades.

They increased their pace and were soon standing in front of the tall wooden gate, a deep brown construction of thick planks.

Hy'pherian pushed on it. "Locked." He laughed. "No surprise!"

Altai thumped on it with the round base of her O'azur.

It made a loud booming sound.

"Here we go again," mumbled Cereon. Slinal gave him a nudge with her shoulder.

They waited. For some time.

Altai was about to thump the gate harder, when

it happened.

High over head, a small hatch was thrown open and a head poked out.

"What do you want?" demanded a wild-haired man in a high pitched squeaky voice.

"We want to come inside and talk with someone who can answer our questions," she called.

"We are helping The Guardian," added Hy. He had decided to skip a part of the process, such as it was.

"Well," snapped the man, "why didn't you say so!"

He jerked back, the hatch slammed shut.

Then the great gate began to slowly, silently swing in, until it stood wide open. The blue wagonway continued inside, running deep toward the interior. Large structures soared on all sides, all colored blue.

"Welcome to Blue Az," said the wire-haired man. "Follow me! I will take you to The Voice of Blue Az. You may ask your questions there." He peered back out the gate. "Only you four?"

"Eh huh," grunted Cereon. "Looks like these folk like blue."

They followed their guide along the wide way past a number of side ways. Many folk were hurrying in every direction, passing through the intersections. They all smiled at their visitors and appeared to be quite relaxed.

Everyone that they passed were dressed in a variety of colors and costumes, almost as vibrant as the folk of Bedo Village.

They walked deep into the town when their guide stopped and pointed. The structure had broad stairs across the front and a number of stone columns holding up a short roof over the entry platform.

"Up there," said their guide. "Follow the corridor until you get to the main chamber. Then ask your questions."

He spun and hurried away, apparently toward the main gate.

Cereon started up the wide stairs, grumbling softly, Slinal right by his side.

Hy and Altai hurried after them.

The corridor was wide, stone columns lined the sides, set against the walls, spaced in even intervals. The floor was paved with smooth, highly polished dark blue stone.

Far ahead they could see a wide copper door in the wall that terminated the corridor.

Altai swung her O'azur around and held it by the middle next to her side.

When they reached the door, Cereon said, "If you don't mind, again." And disappeared.

Altai laughed and pulled the door open.

They walked in.

The door closed behind them with a dull thump.

A figure, dressed all in blue, sat in a copper throne on a high dias, and stared at them.

"I," he intoned in deep, rolling tones, "am Az. Why . . . are . . . you . . . here?"

Hy and Altai bowed, deeply. Slinal just stood

and watched. Hakar did not bow to anything.

"We," stated Hy, as he straightened up, "are helping The Guardian. Do you know where we might find those that have the eye?"

"Deep in Awful do they lurk, foul, vile things. Neither Bedo Village nor Blue Az have the arms to take the eye back. Can three warriors do this?"

Hy smiled. "We intend to do that. Where is this place and where are the creatures that hold the eye in it?" He was following what appeared to be the ritual in these lands, or perhaps just a strange ritual of their quest.

"At the intersection you will see the sign. Follow it. Small place of few dwellings will you meet first. Hidden there is a box containing a key. The key will unlock the container holding the eye. This container is guarded by the foul and vile. Bring all that you find to this very chamber. The door will open." He leaned back and watched them.

They bowed, turned, and headed back the way that they had come.

As they walked down the stairs, Cereon appeared.

"He didn't say how many of these foul and vile things that there are, once again" he grumbled. "This is like a bad, recurring dream!"

Several days later, they once again stood in the intersection.

Cereon kicked the sign labeled *Awful*. Just

because he felt like it. Then he pulled the sign back to vertical.

They walked on. At the top of the slope they could see the wagonway disappearing into a thick forest.

It took all day to reach that spot.

"Shall we camp here?" asked Altai. "One last time?"

"Let's," replied Hy, dumping his pack next to the pavement. "For the last time."

They set up camp, ate Last Meal, and sat and talked.

As the gloom crept into darkness, Hy stood and grabbed his great sword. "I will take first watch." He strolled off, but not too far.

"I will take next," said Slinal.

Altai stretched out, and fell asleep. Shortly joined by Cereon.

In the morning, they sat eating First Meal and watching those woods carefully. It was a silent place. Nothing in there was making a sound. It had been that way all night as well. Cereon had popped awake with the rest. He was ready to be done with this quest and The Folded Lands.

Finally, they started in.

After some time, Hy'pherian said to Cereon. "How about you go ahead, a long way ahead, one more time."

Cereon grumbled, just a small grumble, just because he felt like it, and hurried ahead of them.

And on they trudged, a casual stroll, watching both sides as they did.

Finally they were walking in the very dim light of dusk.

Hy and Altai had been discussing various topics that they liked to talk about when Cereon appeared, breathing heavily. Slinal had just walked along listening to the pair talk.

They stopped and waited for him to catch his breath.

"What?" asked Hy. "Or again?"

"Not far from here, the wagonway curves sharply to the right. Just around that turn there is a small cluster of ill cared for dwellings." He sucked in a deep breath. "Just like the last two times."

"Weapons?" asked Hy.

"Looked like long staves of some sort. This time."

Hy looked at Altai.

"Let's," she said. "Cereon can watch our backs like he usually does."

They began to hurry.

Down the wagonway, around the curve, to the edge of the village, such as it was.

"Another small one," observed Altai, pulling her O'azur from her right shoulder.

Cereon pointed. "Just there, that building. Same, same, same!"

Hy laughed. "Be gone, Cereon. Be careful." He began to walk slowly into the small village, The Sword of Kings held in his right hand.

He walked close to the left hand edge of the narrow passage between the buildings, his sister on the right hand side. Slinal stood in the middle, back just a little. There was room to maneuver between them.

As they approached the structure that Cereon had pointed out, they stopped and Hy yelled, "HEY! GO AWAY!"

In the dusk he was a large shadow in the shadows draping the side of the buildings.

His sister had faded into the shadows as well.

The black creatures began to move in their direction making soft coughing noises, pointed teeth glinting in what little light that there was.

Altai stepped toward the center of the space, O'azur held in a ready position.

Hopping, lurching the horde charged, making loud grunting noises.

And ran into a swirling blur of razor sharp, forearm long blade. The first rank dissolved into bits and pieces blowing to all sides.

Hy stepped silently past them, turned and swung, a sweeping horizontal cut. Body halves fell where they stood.

Slinal danced forward past Altai on warrior's feet and whirled, blade flashing.

And once again, mob and opponents blurred together in a blast of carnage and death. The horde banged into each other as they pushed into the narrow space, bumping and jostling to get at those they were eager to kill.

Hy was smashing things with his shield and chopping others.

Then the noise was gone.

Cereon hurried forward, finding it hard not to step in what he preferred not to look at.

Hy wiped the monstrous blade clean on something, then swung it up and over his shoulder to its place on his back.

He grinned at Cereon. "Shall we see what is inside? Probably locked," he said. "Step away." Altai hastily yanked Cereon and Slinal back. Hy snatched down the sword and swung.

Wood fragments flew up, out, and inside.

"Now it is open." Hy laughed, kicked his way inside.

A table occupied the center of the room. It was the only piece of furniture. On it sat a small chest with four thick candles anchored to the table top with wax. The candles provided all the illumination the room had. Just like the previous two times.

Altai stepped close, handed the O'azur to Cereon. "Hold this, please?"

He did, grumbling about the stuff still dripping from it. It seemed to him that it was worse than before. Couldn't she ever clean this thing before handing it to someone?

She reached out and gently lifted the lid with one finger until it fell open. Inside she could see a bronze key lying on the bottom. It was the only thing in the chest. She reached in and ever so carefully picked it up. Then she peered at it and dropped it into the pocket holding the other two.

She took her staff back. "We better find someplace to stay until the sun rises."

They wandered around the village until they found the place where the blue wagonway exited and followed it into the surrounding forest where they picked out the same camping spot that they had used before.

Early the next morning they were up and moving.

Slinal had to violently shake Cereon awake this time.

As they prepared, each of them felt anxious to be done and to be finished with whatever lurked ahead guarding The stolen Guardian's eye. It was time to finish what felt to them like an endless process.

They didn't hurry, but their pace along the blue wagonway was fast.

And soon, they exited the dense forest and stepped out into a great meadow.

Right in the center of all that grass they could see an ornate chest. Between them and the chest stood a thong of the dark creatures like those they had met last night.

Hy nodded to himself. "Same weapons as back there," he observed, backing up. Once again he wanted to have dense forest on either side. The smaller the frontal space the better.

Altai did the same thing.

Slinal waited in the middle and slightly back.

"Cereon," said Altai, "where ever you are, stay back, one more time."

The pair stood ready, weapons set, and watched the creatures coming their way with that strange hopping lurching gait they all had seemed to have.

Altai spun, chopping the legs from the front rank as they approached her. To her side she could see bodies tumbling in two parts as Hy slashed horizontally, the Sword of Kings slashing through the mass almost as if they weren't there. Slinal danced forward slashing a swath clear as she did. As she entered clear ground, she spun back and chopped her way into the rear ranks.

In the sunlight, green fluid splashed in all directions as arms, legs, heads, bodies were sliced away.

Hy and Altai stepped back onto the clear ground as the mob slipped and lurched over the carnage snarling coughing at their prey. Slinal bounced forward, following the mob, and began to clear huge swaths toward Hy and Altai before the creatures in front realized it was happening.

Hy and Altai surged forward and the piles grew larger and higher. Slinal continued to sweep away everything she could reach.

Then it was quiet.

The pair stood and waited, scanning the meadow for any more of the things. Slinal looked around. The meadow was empty of those things.

Finally, satisfied, Hy and Altai stepped through the piles of gore and out into the clean grass. Wiping their weapons clean on the grass they looked at the chest.

Cereon was already examining it. Slinal stood close to him.

"Doesn't seem to have a lock. Shall I look inside?"

Hy nodded.

"Let's," said Altai.

"Eh huh," gasped Cereon as he did. "Same, same, same," he grumbled.

A large crystal sphere, nestled in soft blue padding, was all that the chest contained.

Altai nodded. "Let's stay in the Bedo Village and rest up and get clean again."

Hy laughed, bent over and picked up the chest and tucked it under one arm. "I'll carry it."

They headed back toward the intersection, Cereon mumbling vague complaints about having to walk through the wide band of the remains.

A number of days later, rested, and clean from their stay in Bedo Village, Altai thumped the base of her O'azur heavily on the great wooden gate, putting small round dents into the wood.

The hatch high above banged open and the same head popped out. "Oh, its you!" And disappeared, slamming the hatch shut.

"Still don't seem to be very happy to see us," mumbled Cereon. "And who could they be expecting?"

"Strange folk," suggested Hy. "Strange lands. Be glad to leave."

The gate swung wide and the same male stepped forward, eyeing the chest under Hy'pherian's arm.

"Follow me!" he snapped, and hurried them along the wagonway, the gate slamming closed behind them.

Some time later, the four found themselves in the same great hall, facing the same figure, dressed all in blue, seated in the copper throne on the high dias.

"You are returned," he observed, "with new members."

Hy nodded and set the chest on the floor.

"We have the eye and the key," he stated formally.

Slowly raising one arm, the figure pointed at one of the walls. A door slowly appeared.

"There is the passage." He smiled at them. "We are impressed. May you remain as fortunate."

They headed for the door which was slowly swinging wide.

On the other side they could see tall grass waving in a soft breeze, and bright sunlight.

Hy laughed and waved them to follow as he strode for the opening.

They did.

They heard the door slam shut behind them.

Gem of a Quest

The Valley of Gems.

Nar'a'las and Wind Sky walked through the narrow spot that restricted passage from The Place Where Akar Dwelled into the this valley.

Down there they had found lodgings in an inn which had also functioned as a place that sold all the things needed by the folk dwelling in the village. The lodgings, such as it had been, had been a single small room with a large bed and little else. Anything else was provided elsewhere in the inn, either down the short hall or in the main room that served as the village gathering spot, a place to obtain a meal, a store to buy things, and any other function that the local folk deemed appropriate.

One of those appropriate functions had been various of the local folk sitting and talking with Nar'a'las and Wind Sky. After two days of wandering discussion the pair had learned that the local mine was temporary lacking the gem stones of the type that Nar'a'las had described, at least the miners hoped that this was so. They told her that what she was searching for was very, very, very rare and that they hadn't found one of those in the past two seasons. But the local miners were hard at work driving their tunnels in new directions that all felt would punch into a new vein.

The chief miner suggested that they go up to The Valley of Gems, as those folk "up canyon" called it, and talk with them. Perhaps they had what she was looking for. They were also Czat'akar and relatives, of a sort, to the folk in this village, and miners as well. From everything that he had heard, their mine might have found what she wanted. Then he cautioned her to be careful, they were known to be very hard bargainers.

As the pair emerged into this upper valley and walked along the trail that was little more than an infrequently used wild animal trail, they could see far ahead a cluster of structures which they both assumed was the village of the miners that they sought.

It turned out to be a shorter walk that it had first appeared to be. And here, as at the previous village, they found an inn of the same sort and obtained a room, equally as sparse as the previous one had been.

They dumped their packs and moved to the central room to sit at one of the two small tables, to eat a simple meal, talk quietly, and wait.

By the time they finished the plain dessert and were sipping some hot beverage of a type never before encountered, a heavily built man walked into the room from outside, stared at them, and approached their table.

Nar'a'las indicated the other chair at their table. "Join us?"

He nodded and dropped heavily into the chair

which creaked alarmingly.

"Rarely see other folk here," he rumbled.

Nar'a'las explained why they were here, in this village.

"Oooom dik dik!" he grumbled, shoving thick forearms onto the table as he leaned forward and stared at her.

"Problem?" she asked in a soft voice.

He nodded. And told them.

Their mine works, he pointed directly across from the village, high on that mountain slope, had been expanding three new shafts, following the edges of the deposit. From all indications they fully expected to hit a very large concentration of the deposit that contained the gems within which, once a season or two, the type of gem she was seeking was found.

They had sent the last shipment of gems "down valley" and had fully expected to finish the new works in two hands of days.

But then, two things happened. His frown darkened as many more wrinkles formed on his brow.

The first thing had been when the leftmost shaft had suddenly punched into a vast cavern. Once they had brought sufficient lamps to peer into it they could begin to see exactly how vast it really was, the far wall a vague grey. Standing in the hole that they had made they could see numerous small tunnels leading elsewhere in the curving walls. Then "things" came from those tunnels, long things with many legs.

They fled and watched carefully. The creatures

stopped at the edge of the hole in the wall, apparently unwilling to leave the cavern.

The next day, as they started out to work in their mine, a great winged thing had dropped from the sky and hovered between them and their mine works. They had never seen anything like that, ever!

It swooped down and snatched the miner closest to the works and carried him off. But it soon reappeared. The miner did not.

Day after day, anytime anyone attempted to cross from the village to the mine they were threatened by the beast. So now, everyone sat and stared across the narrow valley and wondered how they were going to survive if they could no longer mine.

One miner tried to sneak over there late at night. They heard his screams, and that was that!

"Eeee eh," sighed Nar'a'las.

Wind Sky stood and headed for the outside door.

Outside, she quickly bent his head and fastened the bow string. Then she slowly walked toward the distant mine, watching the sky. Slow step by slow step she advanced, and then she saw it, a dark speck high above, rapidly growing larger and larger as it descended, coming directly at her.

She pulled an arrow from her quiver, nocked it, and waited, judging distance and speed until it was time.

In one smooth motion she pulled and released.

The arrow blurred away, flashing from the bow faster than Wind Sky had ever experienced before. Then she remembered what Treliana had said as she spoke her gift to him. *Straighter, truer, farther.* She had called him "Brave Heart."

She heard the arrow thump loudly as it struck. Dark feathers blew in a cloud from either side of the thing's body as the arrow blasted through. The feathers floated slowly down and scattered in the gentle up slope breeze of the canyon. The body dropped like a stone, smashed into the rocky canyon floor, bounced once, and lay still.

Nar'a'las, standing behind Wind Sky, stepped up to her side. "Shall we see what sort of thing that was?"

Wind Sky smiled at her and stroked the side of her bow. "He even amazed me." She laughed happily and started toward the large carcass not too far away. Nar'a'las walked with her, staff in hand.

As they stopped and stared at it, loud footsteps came thudding over the rocky terrain from the village. It was the man that had spoken to them.

What ever the creature was, it was large. The body was covered in black feathers while the wings appeared to be tough black skin. The head was round, most unusual for a flier of the sort that could been seen in any of the lands. Unlike those fliers this thing had rows of pointed teeth.

Wind Sky inspected the large hole that the arrow had punched through its chest. Then she stretched out the wings and paced from wing tip to wing tip. "Almost my height twice," she observed.

Nar'a'las poked the thing with her staff. "Dark vile creation," she stated.

"Creation?" gasped the village spokesman.

"Quite!," she replied. "Something does not want the miners is know what ever is in that great cavern."

She straightened up from her inspection and turned to him. "Can someone guide Wind Sky and me to this cavern that you found?"

Nar'a'las scanned the general area. "Perhaps early day next? After First Meal?"

The miner nodded. "I will ask Taknar to do that. He is one of our best."

Nar'a'las smiled at him and started back to the inn. "We will also need some supplies, eh, food. I suspect that we will be some days in there."

He hurried after her, checking the sky every other step.

"I see nothing," stated Wind Sky.

The pair spent that afternoon filling their carry packs as the inn keeper brought them small, carefully wrapped packages of food. When they finished that chore, Wind Sky carefully examined her bow and then every arrow that she carried.

"We are ready," she told Nar'a'las.

"As am I," came the reply.

Early the next morning after First Meal, they followed Taknar across the valley, up the slope to the mouth of the mine works. Wind Sky watched for another of those things, but none appeared.

The pair followed their guide as he led them

deeper and deeper, through a number of intersections and turns in the tunnel system.

As they walked Taknar pointed out the low grade gems still in the matrix, telling them that these would be harvested after all the high grade materials were taken. It was just an economic factor in their dealings with the merchants in the large towns.

Finally they stood in the opening to the cavern.

Taknar pointed at the small tunnels in the side walls that they could see in the faint light coming from somewhere inside the cavern. "Them things come from therein."

"Return to your home, Taknar," said Nar'a'las as she cast light into the cavern. "We will be fine."

Wind Sky, arrow nocked and ready, carefully stepped into the vast space, now illuminated as bright as day outside the mines.

Taknar stared at them, at the light, stammered something to them, and hurried away, wondering if any of the others would believe him when he told them about what had just happened.

Nar'a'las looked around the large cavity. "Let us walk around the outer edge first and get some idea of how large this great space is."

Wind Sky nodded. They started a slow walk along the wall of the cavern.

As they walked they would pass, every so often, one of the small tunnels going somewhere. These holes were only about hip high on Wind Sky. At each one that they passed, they bent over and listened. And every time they could hear faint rustling sounds from deep inside.

And, finally, after a very long walk, they were back at the spot that they had started from.

Nar'a'las waved her free hand at the cavern. "No obvious exit other than this hole. I suspect that those smallish tunnels all lead somewhere but I am not of a mind to crawl into one of them just to see."

Wind Sky shook her head. "Nor I." She pointed. "Search the floor?"

Nar'a'las nodded and started them on a path that would bisect the more or less circular cavern.

When they reached the middle, they stopped and stared.

Right there, more or less in the center of the cavern, there was a heap of grey-green stone blocks. A few remnants of brightly painted wood protruded from the rubble.

"Wait here." Nar'a'las started to walk around the great debris pile, checking carefully, poking here and there with her staff.

"Interesting and peculiar," she said as she walked up from her slow circuit. "I could feel strange magic in there!" She turned to face the pile.

"I would like to try something." She looked at Wind Sky. "I think that it will be safe, although you might like to take a step or two back."

She waited, watched that Wind Sky did do that, arrow nocked, ready to shoot anything.

Nar'a'las spun back to face the mound and

nodded.

Soft crackling blue light spread from her staff, washed over the jumble, and faded away.

"It must have been a great tower," suggested Nar'a'las. "Back! Back!"

She pushed Wind Sky backward and backward until they were far enough away, or so Nar'a'las hoped.

A mist, a grey mist, was shimmering with some internal light and oozing upward from the pile. Slowly, ever so slowly, it rose, and defined a tower, the image of the tower than once stood there.

High overhead, thick swirling clouds formed, crackling, hissing. Slowly, ever so slowly, the tower took form and shape and solid reality. A narrow staircase blurred into shape, leading from the door, head high above the base, almost to their feet.

"Um eh um." Nar'a'las turned and looked at Wind Sky. "Shall we see what is inside?"

Wind Sky smiled and hurried up to her. "A strange place, a tower inside a cavern."

They walked up the staircase and through the unlocked door, into a mostly empty room, a large circular, mostly empty room.

The walls of the room were constructed of tightly fitted, grey stone. The floor, paved with black tiles that had a slightly pebbled texture, glistened softly in the soft light from overhead.

The corpse lay in the center of the floor, a desiccated long dead body.

Nar'a'las knelt next to the remains and begin to

search through the remnants of the faded green jacket. From one surviving jacket pocket she extracted a many faceted green jewel. The hilt, only the hilt, of some weapon was still thrust under a wide leather belt. He clenched in bony fingers a small scroll, badly burned around the edges.

Dropping the jewel into one of her pockets she carefully eased the scroll from the hand, and ever more carefully unrolled it, amazed that it still would do that.

Clearing her throat, she read it to Wind Sky.

"To who ever, or what ever, might find and read this, Greetings and Farewell from Mazarnato. It was a fatal mistake to come to this place, as I now realize as I write this. We, my Hakar and I, accompanied by one of the Warrior Class Winter Sprites, somehow entered this place from another place. We are being assaulted by swarms of long creatures pouring from their tunnels. The Winter Sprite named them Rock Rills. It will not be long . . . "

Nar'a'las straightened up from her search and pointed at the opening in the high ceiling where the staircase curving up the wall entered the next floor.

Wind Sky nodded and started up, followed by Nar'a'las.

"Most strange," said Nar'a'las as they climbed. "The very gem stone that we were seeking was in his jacket pocket. Why would a folk traveling with one of The Hakar and a Winter Sprite have such a thing? And where are their bodies?"

Wind Sky shrugged. "Hakar and Winter Sprite are unknown folk to me."

Nar'a'las laughed. "I only know of them because Treliana spoke in some detail of those folk. She knew of the Winter Sprite but nothing of their lands. The Hakar are a most different folk. They are supposed to be fierce warriors and can bond in some way unknown to outsiders. It must be that was what Mazarnato had done. Why they would travel with a Winter Sprite is a mystery as well."

"Where do these Hakar folk dwell?"

"Treliana told of The Ghost Stones far to the south and west in Shar'daine."

"Mazarnato told the Rock Rill creatures to be terribly vicious." Wind Sky frowned and wondered whether those beasts could now enter the tower and follow them.

They stepped from the stairs into a room very different that the one they had left below. "Nothing other than a strange creature has ever been seen near The Ghost Stones," said Wind Sky.

The walls and ceiling of this room sparkled and scattered light in bright shafts from the radiance that poured from a large white globe hanging suspended over a round stone altar. Blue winged flitters buzzed around the globe, chittering and squeaking to one another. Against a far wall there was a large bed, a chair, and a small table.

The large bed was neatly made, the green thick top cover tucked in. Each of the carved bed posts was topped with a grotesque creature that seemed to peer at them from red jewel eyes.

The table shifted slightly from side to side on small padded feet. It acted as if it wished to flee but was uncertain of which way to go.

The chair smiled at them and crooned, "Boo boop a doo doo."

"Nar'a'las?" Wind Sky had nocked an arrow and drawn her bow back to its furthest extension.

"Strange, strange, strange." She pointed at another staircase winding its way up the walls to the next floor. "Up there. This is not a good place to stay."

They hurried up the stairs looking down frequently to check on the behavior of the bizarre furniture, and in a rush stepped onto the next floor.

"Ahhhhhh, zak zak!" gasped Wind Sky. She reached up and put the arrow back into her quiver.

"Twisted!" Nar'a'las snarled as she spun, checking what she saw. "Twisted magic!"

The space they had stepped into was open. A warm summer breeze drifted soft caress across the bare stone floor, swept clean by frequent winds. The floor was cut and polished grey-orange Frazac Marble only found in the Zzar Quarry whose location has been long lost to memory. Folk tales often suggested that the quarry was once guarded by twisted creatures from the deep down below.

The sky room was a great circle edged by a waist high wall constructed of tightly fitted grey stone blocks that had been polished to a near mirror surface.

Nar'a'las walked to one edge and peered over. "A long way down, most like a high mountain ridge."

Wind Sky stepped to her side as Nar'a'las pointed.

The far distance horizon was edged by a glittering sea with a nearby spot glowing, shifting through a flickered series of ever changing color.

"There lies some town," Nar'a'las stated, then she sighed. "There must be someplace where these two spots are connected else how did Mazarnato and his companions find this tower and cavern."

She turned away from the view and pointed. "That thing is vile!"

In the exact center of floor stood a massive throne of wood and stone with grinning skulls edging the high back. A soft purple fog oozed from it to be blown away by the gentle breeze.

She carefully walked over to inspect this thing. Then she bent and stared at the floor next to it. There was a small door outlined by a thin crack. It had a small opening at one edge with a strange name carved near the small opening, *NIFNAC*.

Straightening up, she looked over at Wind Sky. "The door here appears to require a key. Sooooooo, there must be one here."

Once again she began to inspect the throne. The seat cushion was thick, plush sides pressing against the sides of the seat. Then she noticed a narrow gap between the cushion and the seat back.

Carefully, cautiously, bending forward, she slipped her fingers into the narrow space and began to slide them back and forth. In one corner she felt a small, cool to the touch object. Fishing it free, she held it up to the light. It was a red key.

Beckoning Wind Sky close she pointed at the door in the floor and the key hole. Wind Sky nodded.

Nar'a'las knelt next to the door and shoved the key in the assumed key hole and gave the key a twist, first one way, then the other. They heard the tinkling sound of ice falling into a tall glass and a loud *CLICK*. She yanked the key free.

The door began to swing upward as they both scrambled to get out of the way. Then it fell with a heavy thud on the floor. Both peered over the edge at the wooden steps leading into the darkness below.

Nar'a'las laughed, shrugged, and started down, Wind Sky close behind her.

The moment their heads were clear of the opening the door slammed shut.

Nar'alas sighed loudly. "This is ever more twisted. I wonder why Mazarnato and his group did not come this way?"

"Perhaps they were unable? Perhaps this tower

thing kept them down below and called The Rock Rills?"

"Eh ah," grumbled Nar'a'las at her. "An ugly thought."

As they stepped on what were the bottom steps the chamber filled with soft yellow light, similar to that Wind Sky had seen Nar'a'las create so many days past.

"Not me!" hissed Nar'a'las.

The chamber was quite small as compared to the floor that they had just left. The walls and ceiling were constructed from powder blue stone, the floor covered with thick carpeting. Unlike all the other floors, this space was square. In the center of each wall there was a closed door, one red, one blue, one white, one red.

Nar'a'las laughed and smiled at Wind Sky. "Pick a color, any color."

Wind Sky nodded, looked at her choices and walked over to rap one knuckle on the blue door.

Nar'a'las shrugged and stepped to her side.

"Together," she said, clenching Wind Sky's free hand tightly.

Wind Sky kicked the door open and they stepped through.

Into thick blue fog.

"RIDDLE ME A RIDDLE!" demanded a booming voice from somewhere.

Wind Sky nudged Nar'a'las, who nodded, and stated loudly, "What is tall and not tall, here and not here!"

"A tricky riddle with no answer," rumbled the

voice.

"Not so!" snapped Nar'a'las. "You now owe me!"

The voice sizzled loudly, and grumbled at her, "DONE! If you tell me the answer."

Nar'a'las hissed back at it, "The tower!"

The blue fog exploded.

The pair tumbled wildly across the ground and wound up sprawled flat on their backs.

"Arrrrrr, ne'ak ta'ga marzzzz-PATA!" growled Wind Sky as she checked herself for injuries.

"I agree with whatever that means," grumbled Nar'a'las, sitting up. "But we seem to be no longer in that tower. Does anything here look familiar to you?"

Wind Sky lurched to a sitting position and slowly checked him and then his arrows for damage, finished, she looked at their surroundings and shook her head. "Unknown."

They were sitting in a small meadow, somewhere.

Nar'a'las stood and began to brush grass pieces from her garb. Wind Sky stepped closer, setting an arrow in place on her great long bow.

"Be we a'done dare we to there be?" asked a gravely voice from the thick patch of brush.

Wind Sky shrugged. "Unknown dialect."

"Do be," suggested Nar'a'las.

A tall male, dressed entirely in dark brown leather apparel, carefully stepped from the brush to the edge of the meadow.

Now they both noticed that there was a very narrow trail of a sort heading that way.

"Be these," he waggled one hand at them, "Wilanar?"

Nar'a'las shook her head and watched him almost as carefully as Wind Sky was doing.

"Eyah," he mumbled at them, wiggling his fingers in a complicated pattern. "Most not," he observed, his eyes wandering over their faces and forms.

"Wilanar not be, most be Tempter Beasts."

"Ah eh," mumbled Nar'a'las to herself. "What be Wilanar?" she asked him.

The male jabbed one finger at the ground. "Youghy beasts!" He frowned at them. "Be great aspar to burst from nowhere and thunk bek a'so, bodar, bodar, bodar." He waved his hand up and down to demonstrate their arrival then wiggled his fingers in that same strange pattern. "Be must do sturdy beasts."

"Where be we?" demanded Nar'a'las.

"Far'a'Near be err." He waved one arm at their surroundings.

Wind Sky shook her head.

"Be one err Far'a'Near, ehhh, who can tell us where we be?" Nar'a'las watched him carefully.

"We took a wrong turn," added Wind Sky.

He gurgled a wet chuckle and pointed at the trail. "Be a'me?"

Nar'alas nodded and headed toward him as he turned and started down the trail. Wind Sky followed, watching everything carefully, arrow nocked, bow ready.

As he walked ahead of them, he wiggled his fingers in that strange pattern again.

Once they were out of the brush the trail widened allowing Nar'a'las to hurry up and walk alongside this male. She nudged him and pointed at his fingers, "Eh?"

"Taken a'me do." He grinned at her and increased his pace.

Nar'a'las waited, then walked next to Wind Sky. She bent her head and whispered very softly to her companion, "I think that he believes that all that finger twitching is a charm of some sort to control us with." She laughed equally softly, "Some folk are in for new ideas." That laugh offered something unwanted.

Wind Sky paused, halting Nar'a'las and carefully whispered back, "How are we going to get home?" And watched her companion's face carefully.

"I have been thinking about leaving." She held out her free arm. "Hold tight."

Wind Sky clamped her fingers around the offered wrist and did as she had been told. It felt to Nar'a'las as if someone had clapped a metal band around her wrist. Until this moment, she hadn't realized how strong Wind Sky's arms and hands had to be to handle her great long bow as easily as she appeared to do.

They vanished.

The chamber appeared to be the same small one

that they had recently been in. The walls and ceiling were constructed from powder blue stone, the floor covered with thick carpeting. Unlike all the other floors, this space was square. In the center of each wall there was a closed door, one red, one blue, one white, one red.

Nar'a'las snarled. "This time I pick a color, any color."

Wind Sky nodded, and waited.

Nar'a'las shrugged, stepped over and kicked the red door open. "I am really getting irritated," she grumbled. "Someone, something, is interfering with us.

"Together," she said, clenching Wind Sky's free hand tightly.

They stepped through.

Into thick red fog.

"RIDDLE ME A RIDDLE!" demanded a booming voice from somewhere.

Wind Sky nudged Nar'a'las, who nodded, and stated loudly, "STOP THE NONSENSE!"

"A tricky riddle with no answer," rumbled the voice.

"Not a riddle!" snapped Nar'a'las. "I want an answer!"

The voice sizzled loudly, and grumbled at her, "DONE! What is your question?"

Nar'a'las hissed back at it, "How do we leave this tower!"

The red fog swirled around them violently.

"If you kept that key, just go up the stairs and

leave."

The fog solidified and shoved them out of the room. The door slammed shut.

Nar'a'las spun and stomped up the wooden stairs. At the top she cast a soft yellow glow, and jabbed the red key into the keyhole.

The door, or hatch, flew open and slammed back against the floor above.

"Up here," she called to Wind Sky as she stepped through. "HURRY!"

Wind Sky rushed up the stairs and stepped out onto the platform.

The sky room was the same great circle edged by a waist high wall constructed of tightly fitted grey stone blocks polished to a near mirror surface that they had seen before.

Nar'a'las walked to one edge and peered over. "Still a long way down, still most like a high mountain ridge."

Wind Sky hastened to her side as Nar'a'las pointed.

The far distance horizon was edged by glittering sea with a nearby spot glowing, shifting through a flickered series of ever changing color.

"There lies some town," Nar'a'las stated and sighed. "There must be someplace there were these two spots are connected else how did Mazarnato and his companions find this tower and cavern. Time to find out!"

She held out her arm again. "Hold tight, ammm,

but not quite as tight as before, we are about to visit that town, way over there."

And they were there.

Wind Sky released her grip and stared at her companion, who shrugged and looked at the town, and said, "Now all we need to do is find someone who can, or will show us the way out of here." She sighed. "And if they won't, then we will just have do this again."

She smiled at Wind Sky. "Takes a lot of energy to do that. And I am getting quite tired. Quite!"

Nar'a'las lurched heavily to one side. "Really tired. We need an inn . . . "

Folk were hurrying here and there. They ignored the pair.

The ways running between the structures were paved with cobble stones of blue, red, green, and white, in no apparent order or arrangement. Most of the buildings that they could see were octagonal in shape capped with domes of blue, softly polished blue stone. The walls of these structures were constructed of alternating rows of grey and green stone. The doors and windows were all trimmed in bright yellow.

The inhabitants that they could see all had a gliding gait that seemed to skin over the uneven surface beneath their feet.

A female dressed in red armor with an ornate design in light yellow across her breast plate came around a nearby corner, slowed up, stared at them, and then hurried toward them. She was carrying a shield. A long sword hung from her belt.

"Why come you here to Tammest?" she demanded, dark green eyes watching them carefully. She stared at Nar'a'las who was beginning to wobble back and forth. "Have you brought illness here?"

"No!" Wind Sky shook her head violently. "She is just very, very tired, and requires rest, quickly."

The warrior pointed with her free hand at one of the ways. "Follow! A place of comfort, comfort for us." She shrugged.

They followed her down the pavement, Wind Sky still tightly holding Nar'a'las by her free hand.

After a turn to the right and then a turn to the left, they were led into a building.

A male bustled up to them, coming from somewhere deeper in the building.

"An'others," stated the warrior. "Room! Food!"

The inn keeper stared at them from clear blue eyes and nodded. "Come."

He led them down a hall and opened a door. It was a large room with two beds and a small wash room.

"Here," he said. "Food later." He backed from the room.

As the door closed, Nar'a'las stumbled forward and sprawled on one of the beds and was instantly asleep.

Wind Sky yanked a covering from the other bed and tucked it around the inert form. Then she nodded to herself and slipped silently from the room and headed outside using her bow as a walking stick, a very tall walking stick.

As she strolled along the way, no one so much as glanced at her.

Wind Sky knew that she would have no problem finding her way back to that inn in spite of the lack of road markers here. Archer/scout-guides always built a mental map of their travel where ever they went. It was a learned and often practiced skill, now second nature to her.

So she wandered along looking at this or that building and observing the folk who lived here.

She had never heard any description that matched this place and was curious as to how this could be. The scout-guides had drawn and ever updated their maps for all the lands and yet here she was in one of which they had no knowledge. So her curiosity was high as she continued building an image of the place and its folk. When she returned to the Wild Fields she would have all that she knew turned into a map.

She was strolling along over the cobble way on the far side of the town when someone called out to her.

"YOU THERE! COME HERE!"

She turned and stared. The caller stood in an open doorway that was trimmed in soft gold. That female beckoned her over.

Wind Sky stepped to the base of the few stairs that led up and looked at this person wearing the flowing yellow robes and wondered what she wanted.

The female watched the archer/scout-guide with large golden eyes. She licked her lips, exposing her poisonous fangs.

"Closer," she purred. "I would see what has come to us!"

Wind Sky took a step forward and stopped.

"I am Lurin," announced the female. "I wish to know why you, armmmmm, two are here. We do not feel easy having one such as your, arrrmm, companion among us."

"Wind Sky, archer/scout-guide," she stated as she stopped on the top step, turned, and sat down. She patted the space next to herself.

"Sit here. It is a strange, strange tale."

Lurin nodded and sat next to her. "Strange is not a thing unknown to us. Tell me your tale."

Wind Sky did, starting with what Treliana had asked her to do.

Late in the day, Wind Sky walked into the inn. Nar'a'las sat a table having Last Meal. Wind Sky pulled out a chair, sat, and looked across the table at her companion.

"It is quite good," stated Nar'a'las, indicating the several serving bowls on the table.

The inn keeper hurried over with another dish, utensils, and several additional bowls of food. He set everything just so and hurried away. Wind Sky nodded. The several foods all smelled quite good.

After some time had passed with each enjoying their meal, Nar'a'las smiled. "Welllllll, what did you find out? I assumed that you were out looking at things."

Wind Sky swallowed, took a sip from her mug,

and nodded.

"I had a long talk with Lurin. She must be the leader, or spokeswoman, or something like that. She didn't talk about that."

"Ehm er." Nar'a'las took another helping from one of the bowls.

"Here is Tammest," stated Wind Sky, "the town where the Slynara live. She told me that they, mostly, do not want magic folk here." She took another sip and waggled one hand loosely. "This town, all the lands around it, and us, are in The Folded Lands."

She stared into Nar'a'las' eyes. "There are no maps or information in the many files in our Record House of such lands, no matter how many seasons old the map or information is. Nothing!"

She poked the table top with one of her utensils. "Do you know where we are?"

Nar'a'las shook her head. Then she smiled at her friend. "But, we can leave."

They had enjoyed the dessert and were in the process of finishing the last few crumbs when the inn keeper rushed into the room, wild-eyed.

"You must leave!" he gasped. "Now! This instant! Hurry, hurry, HURRY!"

Two pair of eyes stared at him.

"Why?" asked Nar'a'las.

Wind Sky stood and bent her bow's head down and fastened the bow string to him, turned and watched the outer door.

The inn keeper sucked in a deep breath and

exhaled loudly. "Lurin has called all to a great ingather. All The Warriors of Andercal are assembling in full battle gear. Every color!"

"Ermmm," mumbled Wind Sky. She looked at Nar'a'las. "I gave her the scroll we found, the one written by Mazarnato."

Nar'a'las shrugged and stood. "We will gather our gear and leave," she told the inn keeper. "It will take but a moment."

The pair hurried to their room to do what little packing they had to do. Then they hurried outside.

Nar'a'las held out her free arm and looked startled when Wind Sky didn't instantly grab her wrist.

"What?"

"We must go to where M'aga lives first. I have to get my new arrows."

Nar'a'las waggled her arm. "Then that is where we shall go."

Wind Sky clamped her free hand around the offered wrist.

The inn keeper gasped and ran up the cobblestone way toward the ingather.

That pair of females had just disappeared.

The Valley of Glar.

They stood in front of the large structure that had a number of chimneys poking high, many showing the heat shimmer of active forges at work. It was the workshop of the Master Smith, M'aga.

Wind Sky gently knocked on the door and

waited.

Eventually the door was swung in. He stood there, a much wider, thicker, and taller than normal Honglar, wearing a heavy and very work-worn leather apron.

"WHAT?" he growled in their general direction, then smiled at Wind Sky. "It has been some many days, archer," he rumbled at her. "Thought that you might have gotten lost." He chuckled deep in his throat. Everyone knew that archer/scout-guides never got lost.

Stepping back, he waved them down a long hall and into one of his workshops and led them to a long bench along a far wall. Two large bundles of arrows, neatly wrapped, sat there.

M'aga picked up a loose arrow and handed it to Wind Sky to inspect.

"Both bundles are like this. I am going to keep this one, hang it on my wall."

Wind Sky hooked her bow over one shoulder and began to inspect the arrow. Then, she looked up at M'aga, eyes glistening. "Beautiful," she murmured, then smiled at him. "Endless thanks, Master Smith."

M'aga jerked and stared at her. No one had ever told him something like that before.

"How may I reply you," she asked.

He laughed, laughed hard and loud enough to rattle tools on the walls. Then he hugged her in a great bear hug, bow and all.

Releasing her, he smiling broadly. "It was, is, my pleasure to make those for you, archer. You are a rare one, you are. Feel free to visit here any time that you wish." Then he frowned, a rather gentle frown for him, and said. "Of course I do expect a report from you on how well they work!"

Wind Sky beamed up at him and stated firmly, "It will be done!"

Nar'a'las cleared her throat.

Wind Sky nodded. "We have to leave now, Master Smith M'aga. We are anxious to finish our, amm, journey."

M'aga made shooing gestures with his hands. "Safe journey, Wind Sky, safe journey."

He led them to the outer door and watched them step into a clear patch of ground.

Wind Sky grabbed Nar'a'las by her wrist.

They were gone.

M'aga closed the door, mumbling to himself, "Interesting folk," and headed back to the project that he had been working on, wondering who the archer's companion was.

The Vale of Treliana.

They stood at the end of one of the many narrow draws in the mountain flanks.

Nar'a'las held out her arm. "Take my hand, close your eyes, and walk by my side. I will guide you in."

Wind Sky grabbed Nar'a'las' hand with her right hand, her left hand clenching her long bow tightly.

"We are ready."

"Quite! It is only ten steps. I will count them.

When I say ten, you may open your eyes. But only then."

Nar'a'las gave Wind Sky a gentle tug forward and began the slow count.

"One . . . two . . . three . . . "

It felt to Wind Sky as if they were moving quite rapidly.

" . . . eight . . . nine . . . TEN!"

Wind Sky felt sudden warmth on her skin, saw bright light through her clenched tight eyelids, and heard what sounded like children laughing, although she knew better.

Her eyes flew open.

The eight diminutive figures laughed, the sound of tinkling bells. One stepped forward and smiled warmly at her. Her eyes looked deep. "Wind Sky, welcome here again."

Then she turned and looked up at Nar'a'las.

"So you return succesful?"

Both of them nodded.

"Quite," said Nar'a'las as she reached into a deep pocket and retrieved the gem stone which she handed to Treliana.

"I am very tired," said Nar'a'las. "We have moved twice today. After I rest we have a great lot to tell before I do anything else. Wind Sky can tell the most of it." She turned and headed for her rooms.

Treliana peered up at the archer/scout-guide.

"It was strange, very strange," stated Wind Sky to the unasked question.

Treliana nodded and led her along one of the paths lined with blue stones. "We will sit, be comfortable, and you will tell all about that strange."

Finally, Wind Sky was done with her narrative. She had described and related all that she and Nar'a'las had seen and done.

Treliana stared at her.

"What?" Wind Sky wondered whether they had done something that they shouldn't have.

"You are much more than you had seemed to be or what I had thought you to be."

"Emmmm?"

Treliana laughed, the soft sound of crystal bells chiming. "It is good Nar'a'las has such a friend. We are very pleased. Will you wait the days for Nar'a'las to finish her training?"

Wind Sky nodded and smiled at her. "I have some training to do as well. Is there a place for archery practice here?"

Treliana pointed. "From here to that mountain slope." She waggled one hand at the distant slope. Four archery targets appeared. "Will that do?"

"Most so. Will your folk know to not walk between here and there?"

Treliana smiled. "For as long as you desire." She stood. "Now I must see to Nar'a'las."

Wind Sky spent the next hand of days destroying targets as she adjusted to the flight pattern of her new arrows.

The silence of the valley was broken by the

steady thump, thump, thump, thump, as she shot again and again.

Far up the valley, in the training spot where Nar'a'las was learning her new skills, things flashed multi-colors, hissed, and rumbled.

Now, satisfied that her new arrows would do exactly as she wished, Wind Sky was relaxing at one of the tables in the early light of day just finishing First Meal after having sung to her great long bow a particularly nice morning chant. She was happy. She had only lost a few arrows from damage. Now she watched Nar'a'las walking along the path headed her way, the gem fastened in its gold mounting on the top of her staff was sparkling colors in the sun bright shafts pouring into the valley between the tall mountain peaks.

Wind Sky smiled at her as she sat at the table.

"I am done," she told Wind Sky.

Wind Sky nodded. "We are ready."

Nar'a'las tapped the top of the table with one finger and began to eat the meal that appeared. Between bites, she said, "I wish to go home and see what has happened since I left. Will you come?"

Wind Sky took a last swallow from her mug and set it down. "Most so. I have never walked down to Nu'vern."

Treliana strolled from somewhere and joined them at the table.

"Traveling on?" she asked them.

"Quite," replied Nar'a'las.

Treliana patted one of Wind Sky's hand. "Wind Sky told me of all the events you two had during your gem quest. We," she gestured at the valley, "feel a, umm ummm ah, twisting out there in the lands. It is most bothering. Be very careful."

Nar'a'las bowed her head and said, all soft voice, "We will." She looked up and smiled at Treliana. "We will, my friend and I."

She stood. Wind Sky stepped around the table to her side and grabbed Nar'a'las' wrist.

They vanished. She could only travel out, never in.

Treliana nodded to herself and sent word that all in the valley were to gather to make plans.

Shadow Dancers

The Black Tunnel.

The twins, Equi-veronik and Bael'elyth, peered into the tunnel and started walking. Gentle Smile and Dark Night followed them, right on their heels.

As the twins walked slowly, carefully into the fading light from the entrance it became apparent to them that there was, far ahead, a spot of faint light.

In the darkness the twins began to walk slower and slower, carefully sliding their feet with each step, seeking to find any obstacle before they tripped over it, wondering what would be there, way down there.

Their companions stepped to either side of them and slipped an arm over one of their's.

"These Ones see better in here than do you surface dwellers," said the deep voice that Bael'elyth recognized as Gentle Smile as Bael'elyth felt her arm given a gentle squeeze. "Just walk naturally. Dark Night and This One will guide you."

"It is so," added Dark Night, holding Equi-veronik's outside arm. His voice was deeper than that of Gentle Smile. "There is a figure waiting ahead for us."

"Two," added Gentle Smile. "It does appear, it

does, that our Seekers have found that which they sought."

"Eh er," murmured Bael'elyth.

"Nothing that we read said anything about what type of folk would be in here," stated Equi to their companions, "only that there were folk living deep in here."

"Of no concern," stated Dark Night. His scepter began to glow, a faint golden light, a vague thing almost not seen in the black of the tunnel. "Few would tempt death."

As they approached the spot of illumination, it was apparent that the tunnel opened into a wide and round space where two dark figures stood facing in their direction.

A number of large boulders sat in a cluster in the center of the space just behind those waiting figures.

The four stepped into the chamber, stopped, waited, and looked at the pair.

They were tall with thin arms and legs. Their heads were also thin and somewhat elongated in shapes. The lower canines protruded just a small amount above the lower lip. Their eyes were large ovals with a pale grey iris so large as to almost fill the front of the eye.

"We do be the Zarnarz," said one, "we do be. Among ourselves we are Zarn. Why would some such as we do see before us prowl so deep? Why would some such as we do see stand with those red-eyed ones? It is a puzzle thought, it is."

The speaker sat on one of the large round grey boulders with a slight concavity on its top and indicated the other boulders. "Be there! To Jina dar," he thumped his chest, "end this puzzle thought!"

Jina dar crossed one long leg over the other and draped his crossed wrists over the top leg and looked expectantly at them. It was obvious that his hands and feet had very long digits, each ending in dark red, pointed talons.

He waited. Patiently.

The small group sat on the boulder chairs.

Equi cleared his throat and began to explain why they had come and what little they had learned from searching old documents and maps, some of these belonging to those that had cut the great quarry into the mountain slope just below the tunnel's mouth.

He finished and wondered what reaction they were going to get. It was hard to read the very blank expressions he saw.

Jina dar stood and gently touched the other on the shoulder. "We do be Jina dar, Nartra S'Mas-ka, and Nima zar, Nartra Ar'Sas-ba, Bonded Ones, Warriors of Janizar, The Blue Guild of Ar'sas The Cold Death." He pointed at them. "What do such be?"

Bael looked at them, very carefully. The one that had spoken to them had skin that was a dark green while the other one was a light brown. The dark green one had a delicate pattern of lighter color on both arms and chest.

"I am," she said, "Bael'elyth." She touched her twin's shoulder. "He is Equi-veronik, my brother twin." Reaching sideways she touched her companion's shoulder, "She is Gentle Smile," and indicated the fourth member of their group, "and he is Dark Night. They are, eh ummm, Bonded Ones of The Heart of Darkness."

Equi was watching the pair of Zarnarz carefully, but not staring, as he felt that might be an impolite thing to do. He realized that their skin was covered with small scales.

Nima zar said something all guttural hiss to Jina dar.

He bobbled his head, patted his chest, and pointed to the far side of the chamber. "Seekers seek!"

Equi took his sister's hand and started them that way, followed by the rest. How did this pair know that?

Bael nudged him and whispered, "Think we will survive?"

He shrugged and whispered back, "Gentle Smile and Dark Night don't look worried." Then he realized that he had never seen any expression on the faces of those two.

They walked across the chamber in the direction Jina dar had pointed and stopped at the blank wall. It was the same as all the other walls of the chamber, rock studded with small projections in a loose scatter.

Jina dar stepped past the twins and patted a

number of the projections in a blur of hand movements.

The wall, a large section of the wall, silently slid back and then to one side.

Jina dar stepped through the opening, turned and clicked the claws on his thumb and forefinger of one hand at them.

The rest hurried inside the large and long tunnel.

The wall slipped back into place and appeared unbroken once again.

Jina dar waggled one hand at them and hurried down the tunnel, Nima zar at his side. Neither appeared concerned that the four were walking behind them.

Bael murmured to Equi, "It appears that we have guides."

He nodded. "It is to hope so."

Gentle Smile and Dark Night strolled along behind the twins, gliding silently along, their garb making soft sighing sounds.

The tunnel appeared to stretch far, far ahead, dwindling to a faint point. It had a slight down slope.

The twins searched the walls and ceiling but where or how the dim light was produced they could see no signs of fixtures or any other thing that could explain it.

The group walked along in silence, more or less silence, making soft sounds from foot steps and garb. Up ahead they could hear the soft guttural hiss of conversation.

"They appear to be dark adapted," whispered

Bael.

Equi nodded. "There was nothing in all those things we read that spoke to that." He looked from side to side. "Perhaps these are a subterranean folk."

"Seems like," she whispered back.

On they walked.

"A far distance," observed Equi as they approached the end of the tunnel.

Jina dar's hand flew across the wall in another complicated pattern of hand slaps. A large section of the wall did the same thing as before.

They all hurried in, the opening closed.

The cavern stretched to all sides with large openings running off in all directions. Mound shaped structures stood in a confusing array across the floor, all colored a soft grey.

The inhabitants went about their business with only side glances at the small group, apparently unconcerned with these strangers in their midst.

Jina dar clicked his claws and headed into the tangle of passages between the buildings. He and Nima zar led them deeper and deeper into the tangle of dwellings, shops, and places of activity hidden in the recesses of the larger structures.

Suddenly the party stepped into a large open space. In the exact center stood a tall conical building.

Jina dar beckoned them to the only opening that they could see and gestured for them to go inside.

Bael looked up and pointed. Over the entrance,

cut into the rock, were three lines of text they could read that alternated with lines of what must be the local script. The lines that they could read stated:

To call on the Goddess Zmarmarzl is to gain
    life.
To fight to the death is the way of life.
To be strong in the Bond-Mate Quest is to honor
    The Choice.

                    Thus spoke Quetlz dar The Wise.

Equi, still holding Bael's hand tightly, stepped carefully inside and down a short hall toward the light ahead, followed by Gentle Smile and Dark Night. The guide pair stayed outside.

"Ah eh," mumbled Equi.

They walked into a large room whose walls, ceiling and floor were various shades of soft green. Large boulders of dark grey stone with slight concavities on their tops formed a small circle.

On two of these boulders sat an elderly pair of Zarnarz.

"I am Sha dar," the male said, "and this is Sha zar. We are Bonded-Ones." He pointed at the twins. "You must be The Seekers."

He bobbled his head at them and smiled, black pointed teeth gleaming in the soft light. "Not all the Zarn are as fluent in surface dweller tongue as we are."

He pointed at the other boulders. "Sit. All. You

tell me of you. I will tell you of Us."

The four sat.

Equi cleared his throat and began, starting with their search in various archives and libraries and then a little of their time in The Heart of Darkness, very little.

Sha dar bobbled his head. "It has come to our ears of the red-eyed ones. Most welcome to you, Gentle Smile and Dark Night."

He crossed one leg over the other and draped his wrists, one over the other, on his upper leg.

"We the Zarnarz are often called Shadow Dancers by the surface dwellers. It is a skill we have." He looked from face to face. "You are in Drakar Zarta, one of our two large places. We have other much smaller places."

Then he began to explain what he thought they should know.

It was their ancient belief that the Goddess Zmarmarzl had brought the Zarnarz into existence just after there were surface dwellers. Thus she and her children were among the first to walk across the many lands.

As the surface dwellers began to spread, Kranzanaknar The Terrible created the guilds that are collectively called The Warriors of Jenizar and the folk began to dig deep from the sight of those strange surface folk.

The guilds each have unique skills, he explained.

The Blue Guild of Ar'Sas The Cold Death has a

skill restricted to their female warriors. They have links to winged beings that teach them unusual forms of what surface dwellers would call magic. It is said that those of this guild are as strange as the creatures that their females know.

The Green Guild of S'Mas The Bloody has warriors that are noted as being more aggressive and ferocious that any other. Often the males are looked upon as somewhat less desirable as Bond-Mates.

The White Guild of Ka'Zat The Terror of The Moon has warriors that immobilize others through the sheer terror and strength of their attack. Females of this guild are sought after as Bond-Mates.

The Red Guild of A'an'Ka'za The Few of Jan'zar are those few that have survived The Pit of Sza'az. It is said that the red guild color reflects the terror of passing through The Pit, a unique rite that few attempt. Females of this guild have strange and rare knowledge. All that survive The Pit have their skin color changed to a red color, unique to only them.

The normal skin color of all males is dark green, dark brown, or dark grey. For all females it is light green, light brown, or light grey.

All Zarnarz are born into one of four Nartra: S'Mas, Ar'Sas, Ka'Zat, and A'an'Ka'za, the naming process is much too complicated to explain to non-Zarnarz. Males and females can become Bonded-Ones, but never within the same Nartra. Bonded is forever. Bonded-Ones are led by the female.

Sha dar smiled at them. "This is all very confusing yet very clear. To us." He gently touched the shoulder of Sha zar and bobbled his head.

She smiled at the four. "Share a meal and a sleep here. We have other to speak of after."

In the morning, after First Meal, the twins assumed that it was morning, they all gathered in the same room and sat on the same boulders.

Sha dar looked from face to face and indicated the twins. "Us did speak of us. Speak of . . . " He jabbed a long finger at them.

Bael nudged Equi. "All," she murmured.

He nodded and looked at their hosts. Wiping his hand across his lower face, he paused, and started.

"I am Equi-veronik." He gently patted her shoulder. "She is Bael'elyth."

Bael nodded to their hosts.

"We," continued Equi, "are formally called The-Second-Twins-of-The-First. Our Father had three wives."

Then he began to tell what he knew of their history, the history of the Ten Royal Houses, and what they called "The Gift."

The two Zarnarz sat still as still, listening carefully to everything he was relating. Gentle Smile and Dark Night listened intently as well. Much of what Equi was relating was new to them as well.

It took a long time, but finally he was done. During his long presentation, small tables and then mugs and containers of refreshment had been brought in and set next to each of the small group. For Equi it was a surprise. He filled his mug and took a long drink. It was refreshing.

"There are seventeen of us," he said. "We have no idea of what the others have studied or where they might be. Each of us, I assume, has followed where ever The Gift guided them. In our own travels we haven't met any of the others. In time, we will return to our home and then, maybe, we will find out, er uh, assuming that any of the others have returned as well."

Sha zar said something softly to Sha dar who bobbled his head.

"The Folk of The Dark," he began, "pass from shadow to shadow, silent as a night flier. We see and hear many things that others are not able to see or to hear."

Sha dar leaned toward the four, eyes searching each face. He jabbed a talon at Equi and than at Bael.

"Hidden from almost all that dwell in the lands of the light there is a thing of great malevolence. It is a thing that came to these lands many seasons after all the kinds began. It has a, zzzzzz, desire to bring great bad to the surface of all the lands. This thing knows of you and your other, zzzzzz, Nartra siblings. It wishes all to be no more." He hissed. "That thing has found followers among the surface dwellers. These hide among their others to do dark behaviors. We have heard them call themselves The Dark Wind."

Sha dar stood and gestured for Equi and Bael to stand. As did Sha zar.

Each stepped forward and close to one of the twins.

Sha dar grabbed one of Equi's arms and shoved his sleeve up to his elbow. Sha zar did the same thing to Bael.

In one swift motion, the Zarnarz cut a small design on each of the twins forearms with the talon on a forefinger, then they spit something on the wound.

Dark Night surged to his feet and stepped, soft gliding steps toward the Zarnarz, scepter gleaming soft yellow in the gentle light of the room.

"No," said Gentle Smile, a soft deep voiced command, that halted Dark Night instantly. She slipped around him and looked at the wounds, then at the Zarnarz.

"Explain." She stood, hands folded over each other, as she watched them back away from the red eyes focused on them.

Equi and Bael wiped their arms of the sides of their trousers. They had felt only a quick pain and then nothing. They stared at their arms, at the green design. There was no scab, no blood, no sign that they had been cut, other than that mark.

"Please do," said Bael.

Sha dar bobbled his head.

"You wear a mark that sings to all Zarnarz that The Seekers are one of us." He held out his own arm, showing a similar but different design. "It sighs this mark that the, zzzzzzz, twin siblings Nartra are of all Zarnarz."

He bobbled his head as did Sha zar.

"Until the last egg hatches, The Shadow Dancers," he smiled, pointed teeth glittering black, "will protect The Seekers Nartra and others who see as we see."

Dark Night slipped his scepter back into his belt. The soft yellow glow faded away.

"An honor," said Equi.

"Indeed," agreed Bael.

"The decision, the marking, the, zzzzzzz, never done before," stated Sha dar, gently patting Sha zar on a shoulder, "is now known by all Zarnarz. Many eyes will see you."

He pointed at the door to the room as two figures entered.

"Jina dar and Nima zar will guide."

Surprise! And Surprise!

N'Farza Plateau.

Clerian'tra had spent one hand of days talking with the Elders of Clan Binulin Tha'a'ea on N'Farza. Their conversation had wandered in the usual indirect manner of the Tha'a'ea until Clerian'tra was satisfied that she had learned all that she was going to learn about The Deep Tower and the "pale skins," as Clan Bunilin called the dwellers in that place.

Now, she stood in the entrance of The Deep Tower, her small carry pack full of supplies offered to her by the Elders. Peering into the dim space, she could see that the stone structure surrounded a wooden one which supported wooden stairs that were headed down into the gloom below the floor.

She turned and smiled at the Elders, standing and watching her, then spun back and walked over to the stairs and carefully started down. All the Elders had told the fact that those who lived down these stairs had been there for many, many seasons. She thought about that as she stepped ever so carefully down and around, down and around. What sort of Nu'vern folk would live in a hole in the ground? If they were indeed from Nu'vern.

Nothing that she had heard about the history of

Nu'vern said anything about some of them coming to N'Farza. So who were these "pale skins" down there?

She laughed softly to herself. She would soon find the answers to those questions. She supposed.

As she stepped lower and lower, the area below become slowly brighter. She could see more detail. There was a great patch of water, a deep blue color from light reflected from the bottom, that light apparently coming from a wide gap in one wall. Slight waves coursed through that gap and made faint splashing sounds as they bounced off something.

She stepped out onto a small platform as the stairs stopped descending. From here there was a walkway headed for the far wall. Looking up she could see that this portion was suspended from thick chains anchored to a ceiling that was not far above her head.

When she arrived at the end of the walkway, she could see a long, straight stair that was anchored to the wall. Peering over the railing, she could see that it ended on a surface which would bring her close to the water.

Down she went, stepping ever so carefully. The view down these stairs dazzled the eyes. So she looked elsewhere, one hand trailing along the outside railing.

Finally, she stepped off the last step onto a rock surface. Far across the water she could just see in the soft light a long dock with a number of Wooden Steeds of a peculiar design tied alongside. She smiled to herself, at least that is what the fisher folk of Nu'vern called them. She shrugged. Soon, she assumed, she would learn what a long ago separated folk would call them.

From here she could see that the far cavern wall rose up and then curved out in a great arch, hiding them from sight from above. Perhaps, she thought, these folk had chosen that spot deliberately for that very reason.

She turned and headed along the path leading from the base of stairs toward the far wall. It felt good to be walking on a flat surface.

As she slowly strolled, she could begin to see that there were numbers of structures along the far wall. Some appeared to her to be dwellings, some were large enough to be warehouses, or some such thing. The surge of the water and its soft sounds was quite pleasant on the rock lined edge. She could smell the sea and feel the moisture of it in the air.

She headed for one of the assumed dwellings intending to knock on the door. The door opened and a tall, broad shouldered male stepped out, closed the door, and watched her approach. When she was close enough to see details, she saw that he was wearing sandals, trousers that flared widely from knee to ankle, a loose shirt, his garb made from material of a light green color. Hanging from his waist belt was a heavy sword that tapered from a rather narrow shaft at the hilt to a very broad flared tip. That tip had an upturned and sharp point.

He nodded to her.

"Most surely Nu'Vern," he said.

She nodded back.

His face was heavily weathered with deep wrinkles radiating from the corners of his eyes. In spite of the bronze color of his skin, he was obviously of Nu'vern as well.

"Us am," he stated, "Tenil'an, Head, The Tenth Royal House, Aaden Dacog. Who be ya?"

She stopped, smiled a soft smile at him, and wondered at his dialect. It was archaic Nu'vern.

"I am Clerian'tra, The-First-Daughter-of-The-Second, Noriyon Zacog."

One corner of his mouth twitched, grey eyes twinkled.

"One of tha seventeen, eyah. We'en do hear'd of that."

He crossed corded arms over his chest. "Why'n come ya a'here?"

She pointed upward.

"Clan Binulin, Tha'a'ea, told of pale skins living down here. I came to see." She shrugged one shoulder. "None spoke of The Tenth House."

"So tis! None do speak of The Tenth Royal House!"

She stepped closer.

"The Tenth House disappeared many, many seasons past. So it is told," she said.

He nodded at her and pointed at a table set with four chairs, cloaked in shadow, next to the dwelling, walked over and sat.

She joined him.

"We'en do be'en commercial sea folk, we'en do be'en."

She indicated the cavern with one hand and the bright spot in the far wall and looked the question at him.

He nodded. "Us'en t'will share tales, us'en t'will."

Another male, dressed in the same garb as Tenil'an walked up, set two thick mugs and a tall container on the table, and walked away. Tenil'an filled both mugs, shoved one across the table at her, picked up the other and took a sip. Then he nodded for her to start as he leaned back, mug cradled in his hand.

Clerian'tra did.

She told of her wander into Farza and of the folk that lived there. Then how she had been given the status of Bar'Farza and what that meant to those folk and indicated the various runes that decorated her own garb.

Then she spoke of her visits with the various clans of the Tha'a'ea of N'Farza, and finally finding, in a manner of speaking, the entrance to this place, up there, on the top of the cavern.

When she was done, Tenil'an leaned forward, took another sip, refilled his mug and added a small amount to her's, and stared at her.

"Eh ah?" she said.

He leaned back, holding his mug and laughed. Then he waggled his free hand at her.

"Naght be mere laughter a'surprise," he

explained.

He took a swallow from his mug, leaned forward and banged it down on the table top.

"We'en here be'en a'hearing tales of the many siblings and a'mumbling of The Gift. Course we'en do be'en familiar wit our history and, eha, the famblies. Inna this place we'en do be'en a'livin many seasons, many, many seasons. So much heard be'en thought childern story tales." He grinned at her.

"A King with several Queens do be'en bound for to haven many childern. A'natural thing. But all childern coming wit The Gift be'en most, er na, unusual, praps even strange. But here you do be'en a'sittin." He sighed. "As to thisa House, the tellen of it passes thisa way."

He told her that The Tenth Royal House was small, it had always been very small. Long many seasons past they had lived in the south-eastern village of Zualin of Nu'vern. In those long many seasons past, The House had seen the rise of The Merchant-Traders and their rapidly expanding monopoly on the transportation of goods in the lands.

The House Head had discussed this with all the house members and the decision was made to develop an alternative to The Merchant-Traders by moving goods by sea, routes that could not be controlled.

After long discussions with those that built The Wooden Steeds for the fisher folk, a new design was arrived at and construction begun on a number that could carry goods, have spacious living quarters, and would have the ability to travel great distances on the many seas surrounding the lands.

He laughed at her expression and continued his tale.

It was on the first voyage, the five Cargo Steeds occupied by the entire population of The Tenth Royal House, who planned to live aboard permanently rather than on land, that it happened.

The flotilla ran into a great storm, a great unexpected storm. Actually it ran into them as they were crossing the southern edge of N'Farza. They had come this way as the many wetways blocked sailing the interior seas of the lands from land to land. They had noted the sea cavern on the southern edge of N'Farza as something to be looked into. The storm interrupted that endeavor.

In order to save themselves and their Cargo Steeds they had sailed with the storm which drove them steadily west. After time not counted, the storm subsided and left them, isolated far from any sight of land bobbing on a flat smooth sea, still sailing slowly toward the west. The five Heads gathered on the first vessel to plan and ponder what they ought to do.

In the midst of a long and heated discussion, a member sitting on the tallest mast head hollered down and pointed toward the west at a long line of clouds.

The Heads agreed, it did appear most like the clouds that occurred and marked the seaward edge of coastal lands. Having no better option they continued to sail in that direction, hoping that it was really land, otherwise they faced a slow death as supplies and water were exhausted.

Tenil'an leaned forward and slid thick forearms onto the table top.

"T'were a'new land, a new, totally unknown to our lands, with a'new, totally unknown population." Waggling his head from side to side, he said, "Suffice it, we'ne do be'en the first strangers these folk ever a'seen with goods of the never before a'seen."

Refilling his mug, he took a long swallow. "Now we'en do'a'trade there and back, one trip a season."

Running a finger back and forth on the table top, he looked at her. "Those folk fish they waters but believed, until we'en do appear'en, there do be'en none lands other!"

He jabbed one forefinger at her and frowned. "Tis secret! Tis secret them do want!"

Clerina'tra nodded. "And kept," she agreed. She took a sip and smiled a soft smile at him, "I wish to visit these folk and their land."

Tenil'an jerked.

"I will be safe," she stated.

"Most long a'journey."

She shrugged.

Lurching to his feet, he pointed across the water.

"Sea Foam and her sisters do leave a'now. Hurry! Us'en do speak wit the Cargo Steed Heads."

He hurried her down the wide pavement toward the wharfs where they could see that the final stages of preparation were in progress. Tenil'an wondered why one of The First Royal House would want to do what she wanted to do.

One Step Forward

The Wild Fields.

Sar'al and Zak'ke had been wandering aimlessly around the Stonehold for two hands of days, waiting for the folk here to come to a decision. It was taking much longer than the two days that they had been led to believe it would take. During their wanders the pair had come to the conclusion that this Stonehold was the central one of the eight Stoneholds, that is, it appeared to be where major decisions were made, in its meeting halls where such discussions were held.

As they had strolled here and there, Sar'al had been thinking of the seasons that she had spent among the four clans of The'a'sa learning their customs, values, and culture as taught by The Elders.

It had been, for her, a much less complicated time than how she now had to live and behave. The peculiarities of her heritage and family felt to her, at times like this, strange, very strange. When she had lived among the Tha'a'sa her life had been orderly and she had clearly known what she was capable of doing. Now, here she was, a Queen-in-training, without any training at all. She sighed heavily, causing Zak'ke to cast a wondering glance at her.

She smiled at him. And nodded.

He smiled back. It had been a very Royal nod from a Queen.

Now the pair were heading down the wide way through the center of the Stonehold when a messenger caught up to them. He had been running from place to place, searching for them. Viana and the four Tha'a'sa had remained in their quarters.

Stopping in front of them, he bowed an awkward deep bow, sucking in great breaths at the same time.

"Rain Storm, archer/scout-guide," he announced, identifying himself to them. "Cloud Spirit asks The Queen and her Warrior to attend a gathering. Eh, if you please." He bowed again, a clumsy gesture that the folk of The Wild Fields were unaccustomed to doing.

Sar'al smiled at him. "Lead on, archer."

He spun and strolled rapidly away. But not too rapidly. He didn't want to leave them behind.

After some time the three entered the small Hall of Gathering.

Sar'al recognized Cloud Spirit but none of the others standing in a loose cluster talking softly among themselves. Viana and the four Tha'a'sa were there sitting in chairs, having been called from their quarters by Cloud.

Cloud Spirit gestured the group to their chairs. The cluster settled themselves and sat quietly, watching the pair take the chairs indicated by Cloud Spirit.

Then Cloud strode to the front of the room and faced them.

He nodded at the twins and waved one hand.

"Sar'al Queen, these are the most senior of the archer/scout-guides, representing their Stoneholds, two from each. They have come here, little by little, to bring the decision of their Stonehold, the decision you requested them to consider."

He paused and sucked in a deep breath, his eyes fastened upon her's.

"Be you most aware that each Stonehold arrived at their decision totally independently of any of the others. It is our way." He smiled a soft smile. "I told you that we are an independent folk."

Cloud reached behind himself, dragged a chair close, and sat.

"Before I speak of their decision, there is something you must hear and become aware of, something that we have just learned."

He glowered at something, sighed, and then relaxed. One arm lifted and pointed at a dark corner.

"Here is Early Dawn, archer/scout-guide" he said as a tall female stepped forward. "She brought to me the most unpleasant, eeee eh, information. Three archers, three that she found, had been killed. It is unheard of for we have walked the lands for seasons beyond counting, free and unbothered as all the folk of all the lands know of us and our values."

He leaned forward, hands on his knees.

"Early Dawn brought a tale of a gathering of a group, naming themselves The Dark Wind. They are the ones responsible for this dark, vile deed. Why? Because we are known for our independence, a thing that this organization cannot abide."

He looked into Sar'al's frown.

"How do we know this to be so?" He pointed at a side door. Early Dawn walked over, opened the door and walked through. And returned, leading a very battered male, dressed entirely in black, into the Gathering Hall. A thin cord was tied around his neck, one end wrapped around her right hand.

She jerked the cord, halting him.

"This thing was found," she said, "bending over Fair Wind. He attacked me, apparently believing that I couldn't draw my bow in time." Her free hand snapped back and forward, now holding a long blade. "This thing was unaware, as is true for most folk, that all archers carry one of these in an out of the way place." In one smooth motion, her hand flashed behind herself and returned, empty.

She jerked the cord again. He gasped.

"This thing told me of their group, unwillingly. A bow string is a very persuasive thing." She looked at Sar'al, eyes staring into eyes.

"The Dark Wind fears what you, Fair Queen, are trying to do and any others that might agree. They wish you dead! They wish all that might agree with you, dead! They hide in plain sight and plan murder and disorder because they believe that they should be the ones who tell all others how to live. We now know who this thing's friends are, and where they dwell, who are soon to be dead friends."

Early Dawn spun on her heels and hauled him

from the room, slamming the door shut.

Cloud Spirit stood.

"All the seniors met and discussed what Early Dawn had learned and, ah um, discussed this with the thing she caught. Now all archer/scout-guides will travel in pairs." He nodded at those seated. "All here brought to me what their Stoneholds have decided."

He nodded slowly.

"Small time past, we had already become aware of a strangeness settling in the lands, and made our own preparations. Now, it does appear, that the strangeness is of a greater concern that we had supposed it to be."

He bowed stiffly to Zak'ke and then to Sar'al.

As he straightened up, he said to them, "We, the folk of The Wild Fields, retain our independent ways. Always!" He watched Sar'al struggle to hold her expression and her emotions under control.

Cloud Spirit smiled at the pair.

"Zak'ke Warrior, Sar'al Queen, we accept! Warm greetings to this, our now Queen. What would you have us do?"

Those gathered in the room turned in their chairs to watch her as she stood. Viana nodded.

"Do!" She bowed to them, a very formal bow. "Thank you, it is my honor. Do?" She smiled at them. "Nothing other than be yourselves. My home is preparing. The hidden ones of Nu'vern are preparing. The Tha'a'sa and the Tha'a'da are preparing. I wish you to do the same. Prepare!"

She nodded at them. "Being Queen is as new to

me as it is you. I would hear anything you wish to say as to the best way to approach the other folk in the lands as well as what to do about the Dark Wind and anything else one might suggest."

Zak'ke nudged her gently. "I do have a suggestion or two." He stood and smiled at the gathering.

Home Again.

The Heart of All.

Nar'a'las and Wind Sky were there, standing next to the high wall, just to one side of the gates. The gates stood wide.

Nar'a'las smiled at Wind Sky.

"Now we shall just stroll inside as if we walked up the wagonway without, I hope, causing any commotion."

The pair strolled through the gateway, walked into the large open space of the entrance plaza, and stopped. The watcher in the tower above the gate stared down at them and wondered why he hadn't seen them approach along the wagonway leading to the gate.

Ahead of them, to their left, there were a long row of archers practicing, shooting at targets set at the full distance that their short bows were capable of hitting.

Wind Sky pointed at a tall male.

"That is an archer/scout-guide teaching them. How did he get here? And why?"

To their right there was a great mob of folk, battering at each other in a vast melee.

"Eh umm," mumbled Nar'a'las. "It appears that

things have changed greatly since I left. Quite!"

From a nearby doorway, a pair stepped out, and hurried in the direction of Nar'a'las and Wind Sky.

"Nar'a'las!" stated the male as they hurried up. "Home at last."

"Quite!" She smiled at both of them.

"Rau'ke, Cant'al," Nar'a'las said, just so Wind Sky would know their names. "This is Wind Sky, my friend."

"Most welcome," said Rau'ke.

"Where are The First Twins?" asked Nar'a'las.

Cant'al shrugged. "The last message that we had said they were in The Wild Fields talking with the folk there."

Wind Sky pointed. "I will speak with that one." She hurried toward the tall archer/scout-guide.

Nar'a'las indicated the two groups. "What is this all about?"

"Sar'al," said Rau'ke, "ordered us to build it. The Armed Mass, she called it. Then the twins left. She told us to run things until she and Zak'ke returned."

He shrugged. "So we have been doing that."

Nar'a'las bowed to them

"What?" gasped Rau'ke.

"Warm greetings, King and Queen."

Rau'ke's face flushed, then he asked her, "Do you know why we are doing all this?"

She shrugged. "A little. Perhaps. We should speak of this in a more, err um, private place." She smiled. "Wind Sky and I will require lodgings." Then she yawned widely. "And I need to rest some."

Cant'al nodded. "Come with me. I will see to that."

As the two of them walked toward the building, Rau'ke sighed heavily. There had been something bothering in the tone of voice that Nar'a'las had used.

She strolled up to the tall male and looked up.

"Wind Sky," she stated. "Stonehold Anda."

He turned from the one that he was instructing.

"Dark Wind," he replied. "Stonehold Onda."

The bulk of the archer/scout-guides did not know many of those from the other Stoneholds as they mostly associated with those they grew up with. It was considered good manners to name the Stonehold from which one came so that the other could properly identify them.

Dark Wind nodded. Stonehold Anda was the main Stonehold and he had heard some interesting tales about an archer/scout-guide from there.

He smiled at her.

"May one see him?"

Wind Sky nodded and held out her great long bow.

He gently lifted the long bow from her hands, held it close to his eyes, and carefully inspected it. Finally, after some time, he handed it back to her.

"He has an interesting design."

She smiled at him. "Master Smith M'aga did so say also."

He stared at her. "You traveled to Glar?"

She nodded. "Most so."

Dark Wind pointed at a far distant target. "Small contest?"

She grinned up at him. "You will lose."

"Ah ah na," he stated, frowning slightly at her.

Wind Sky bent his head and attached the bow string, nocked an arrow. Dark Wind waited for her to go first. As he had made the challenge it was correct that she do so.

He stared at her strange looking arrow, turned, and watched the distant target.

"Three?" he asked. Then he gasped.

Wind Sky's arrow flashed across the distance and punched a great hole in the center of the target.

"Gaz a pok!" he gasped. How could she do that?

Wind Sky fired twice more. The distant target burst, materials filling the air around it. The top half tumbled backward and fell to the grass.

"Archer Wind Sky!" he snapped. "What kind of arrow is that?"

Wind Sky reached back, pulled one free, and handed it to him. "M'aga and I designed them."

After carefully inspecting it, he asked softly, "May I?"

She nodded.

He took careful aim at the target adjacent to the destroyed one, and fired.

The arrow plunged into the ground far short of the target.

"Ahhhhh nak pa!"

Wind Sky reached out and lightly touched his bow and said very softly, "She is not strong enough for them."

He looked down at the shorter Wind Sky. "May I try him?"

She nodded and held him out.

"Very careful, Dark Wind," she cautioned.

He grunted, took one of his arrows, nocked it, and pulled. At the full extension, his arms began to quiver. He fired. The arrow snapped away. And sailed over the top of the target.

Handing the bow back to her, he said, "Never met a bow that strong. Ever." He stared at her. "Tales told of a young archer who practiced endlessly. You?"

She smiled and stroked her bow with soft touch. "He is very special, he is."

He laughed. "Archer Wind Sky, I believe that you are a rare pair. Most so!"

They walked to the distant targets to retrieve their arrows, inspecting each one for damage as they did.

Dark Wind laughed and indicated the long row of archers that were supposed to be practicing, now staring at the pair.

"Would you help train?" he asked.

Wind Sky grinned at him. "Most certainly so!"

As they walked toward their students, three horse riders passed through the gate and halted in the open space.

One pointed.

"If I remember correctly, The Royal Stables are around that way."

They headed that way, their horses at a walk.

Another pointed at all the action in the two practice fields. "That is new."

In the stables, they dismounted, gathered their belongings from their mounts, and left the mounts in the able hands of the stable staff who cared for mounts and riders alike.

The trio walked from the stables and back and around to the large paved plaza in front of the gateway.

Verdorion-elvershair pointed at the long row of archers practicing and the great mob attacking each other with gay abandon. He laughed. "Things have certainly changed. Let's head into the main building and visit with The First Twins."

His sisters nodded and headed that way.

As they approached the main door, it swung open and a tall, slim female wearing trousers and a loose jacket over a blouse of soft shimmering material, everything in shades of light purple, stepped out.

"Nar'a'las," gasped Verd. "Is that you?"

She laughed at his open-mouthed amazement. "Quite!" Her eyes flowed over them, then walked closer and stopped, to stare and stare. "Ummm ah eh, the triplets have returned with interesting skills, it feels."

Cer'alda stared back at her. "A spell caster? You?"

"Quite!" She nodded at her. "Similar, but different. When you wish we shall speak of this."

Nar'a'las walked past them, long staff in her right hand, the jewel tip reflecting colored shafts of light as it refracted the bright sunlight, ribbons fluttering.

"Cer?" Verd stared at his sister.

Cer'alda turned toward the others.

"It feels to me that our younger sister has learned a great amount of unique skills. Her Gift is to be a spell caster, a very powerful spell caster."

She frowned slightly. "I wonder where she learned all that."

Caevelas watched Nar'a'las stop and talk with a female archer who was somewhat shorter. The pair left the training line, strolling slowly away, talking.

"Inside?" she asked.

"Let's." Verd threw an arm around each sister And headed them for the door. "Wonder if anyone else has returned. And do either of you have any idea who those two with the great long bows are? Certainly not from here."

"Not!" said Caevelas.

Cer'alda shook her head at her sister's tone of voice. "Just have to ask the twins."

Once again they didn't make it to the door. It swung open and a pair of twins walked out. They stopped and stared.

Cant'al laughed happily.

"It appears," said Rau'ke as they approached the triplets, "that the offspring of The Second are coming home.

Verd smiled at him. "We were just going inside

to talk with The First Twins and ask them about all that." He waved one hand at the activities.

"You can't," said Rau'ke.

"They are not here," added Cant'al.

"Eh ah?"

Rau'ke grinned at three confused expressions, then he cleared his throat.

"Cant'al and I are acting Queen and King, as ordered by Sar'al. All that out there is what she wanted done." He nodded. "So it is done."

"Fast Rider, Rid'linar," he continued, "has recently returned from The Wild Lands. The Queen and Zak'ke are there attempting to convince that folk to accept her as their Queen."

"She intends," explained Cant'al, "to unite all the folk of all the lands under her, eh um, banner. She has been told that she must do this else a great evil will fall over the lands."

Verd looked at his sisters. They nodded.

Then all three bowed to Rau'ke.

"At your command," they said in unison.

Rau'ke sighed. "Could we not do that. We are good at organizing and all that. But not the Royalty aspect." He shrugged. "Sar'al spoke of very little other than what you can see." He looked from face to face. "Any thoughts or whatever would be helpful."

Cant'al waved her hand at the archers. "Both Nar'a'las and Al'tana walked through the gateway accompanied by one of the archer/scout-guides. They are helping train."

Verd looked around. "Al'tana is here? By herself? Where? Those two are archer/scout-guides?"

"She went to visit Palana Village and the fisher folk there, as she did many seasons past. Most so. They are archer/scout-guides."

Cant'al spoke softly to them. "Do not ask her about Neverishan. He died in a sudden storm not long after The Gift called them away."

"Ohhhhh," sighed Caevelas. She had always enjoyed his company when they were younger and all still living in Nu'vern.

Cant'al patted her arm.

"All the rooms have been kept ready the many seasons, waiting for your return and all the others." She smiled. "You know the way. Just tell anyone you meet what you would wish. You are probably hungry." She pointed. "Nar'a'las and her friend are headed this way. I suspect that they are going to have Mid Meal. Everything stops at this time."

She and Rau'ke headed back inside to get the meal organized. Both felt that it was good to see their siblings beginning to return home. It had been many seasons since they had scattered into the lands.

They were part way through Mid Meal when a loud voice came from the hall just before the door opened and they walked in.

Verdorion-elvershair swallowed and laughed loudly.

"I would recognize that voice, and comments,

anywhere. Join us, Cereon."

"And Altai and Hy," added Caevelas.

"Who is that?" asked Cer'alda. "Do join us."

The four took chairs at the table and began to pass around serving bowls.

Cereon frowned at Verd and Cer'alda. "This is Slinal. She is, ah um eh, with me."

"A long story?" asked Verd, dumping an large quantity on his platter before handing the bowl on, reaching for the next one.

Rau'ke looked at Hy and his sister.

"Certainly grew," he observed.

Cant'al jabbed him with her elbow.

"Well they did," he whispered to her. "Big!"

But, after some time, the meal was over.

They all headed outside to enjoy the pleasant weather and to find a more comfortable place to sit and to talk.

Each of the siblings took turns relating how they trained and what they had been doing before they finally reached home.

Wind Sky, Dark Wind, and Slinal listened carefully. Slinal cast apprehensive glances at Nar'a'las. The Slynara had a low opinion of magic using folk and she wasn't too sure about the triplets.

When all the tales were done, Nar'a'las turned and said, "Show us, Cereon." Her eyes watched him carefully as he stood.

And disappeared.

"Ahhh," she sighed. And smiled at him as he

reappeared. "What did The Guardian gift you?"

"Nothing," he mumbled. "I asked it for her."

Slinal leaned against him and smiled, and explained, "The same as Altai and Hy. Stronger armor, faster, sharper weapons."

"And?" prompted Verd.

Cereon sighed and held out his right hand. A short, dark blade appeared. Then disappeared.

"The Guardian seemed to think that I ought to have a weapon of some sort, for some reason."

"A short sharp," stated Slinal.

"Perhaps," suggested Rau'ke, "you three warriors might, ummm, help train those of our Armed Mass?"

Hy smiled. "Of course."

Altai nodded.

Slinal looked at Cereon who gave a quick nod.

"Good practice for all," she stated, smiling at the thought. It would be good exercise.

Ever Onward

The Sky Mountains.

He had just finished his twenty-fifth season celebration and decided to climb in the great cloud-capped mountain range far to the north of The Valley of Glar, some distance from The Valley of Tall Trees.

Alaine'an'dar was the oldest male offspring of House Zilin Aacog, the Seventh Royal House, located in The Valley of Tall Trees. On formal occasions he was addressed as Alaine'an'dar Tan'dei Zilin Aacog.

Alaine, as his several siblings called him, was broad-shouldered, tall, and fair-skinned. As he carefully worked his way upward, his dark-grey eyes searched the slopes for the best route. His features were regular and rather ordinary, but somewhat battered. Climbing accidents many seasons past had been the cause of the slight bend in the upper portion of his nose, the scar next to the side of his mouth that caused him to have a rather crooked smile, and the several scar tracks cris-crossing the left forearm, marks normally hidden by garments with long sleeves.

But now, having learned the hard way, he was one of the best, if not the best mountain climber in the House.

The place he had chosen was considered as a place not to climb. A few climbers from elsewhere, before this day, had tried. None of them had returned.

As the eldest male sibling he knew that if he had mentioned where he was headed he would have been told that it was prohibited. And as such he would not have been able to climb here. So, he had started in one direction and then eventually turned in another.

He grinned as he found a very good route headed up. And beside, he thought, it was much better to explain things afterward that beg for permission before.

But as he worked his way steadily toward the hovering cloud layer, he could not explain exactly why he had felt such a strong urge to make this climb. It was not something that he would be able to explain as the storm of parental anger, or dark glares from incredulous younger siblings, washed over him upon his return, all demanding to know "why."

As the one-of-these-days Head of The House he was not supposed to be doing things like this, things that others would think are too dangerous, especially for rather strange reasons.

However, strange reason or not, here he was, walking on the rather gentle slope just below the lower edge of the thick cloud layer that always capped this range, walking carefully along the contour of this peculiar slope headed toward a distant lighter spot in the grey-white denseness overhead.

The Ruins of Huroma.

Verin'yashi stood on one of the balconies of the spire and peered down at the small group approaching the small village and ancient temple that clustered around the base.

She smiled to herself as she walked inside and started down the long spiral staircase. She had recognized The First-Twins riding slowly through the tall grass, followed by a small party of guards. At least she assumed that is what they were.

By the time she stepped from the door to the interior of the spire, red robes casting soft amber glow in the bright sun, the party had entered the small plaza of the village. The Twins stood next to their mounts, holding the reins. Ummmmm, Verin thought, four Tha'a'sa and two archer/scout-guides.

"Warm greetings, My Queen, and, First Warrior, ah um, First Blade. It has been many seasons."

She gestured at one of the buildings. "Food? Refreshments? The mounts will be taken care of." She led them into the small hall, seated them around a large table and saw that all had a large, filled mug of a refreshment suitable for the end of a long journey from The Wild Fields.

Then she sat and waited.

When a proper time had passed, Sar'al looked at her near-sister and smiled.

"Cloud Spirit spoke to us of your visit. You have been here for many seasons."

"Most so," sighed Verin. She set both hands on

the table, folded them together, and spoke softly to Sar'al.

"The Gift expressed itself as I trained and studied. Within The Adherents of Huroma I am, now, one of the few called The Touched of Huroma."

She loosened her fingers and held up one hand, palm out. "That name is never spoken outside of our members, near-sister. It is a secret of meaningful things."

Sar'al nodded. "None here will ever so state!"

Verin smiled at her. "Most Royally stated." She gestured. Younger members brought bowls of food, plates, utensils, and quickly set the table, and hurried away.

"While we eat," stated Verin as she took several servings from one of the bowls, "tell me why you have come here?"

Sar'al did. She spoke of all that had happened, starting with them standing on top of The Tower of The Soaring Dragon, her visit from The Ancient One, and finally, the decision of The Wild Fields, and what she had learned there.

"Viana, once again, rides to her folk, to speak of The Dark Wind." Her eyes watched Verin's. "Have you knowledge of those vile ones?"

Verin nodded and related her conversation with the strange male named Zarlar.

"In all our vast collection there is no mention of this Zarlar. His ease of doing, errr, things speaks to me of great powers." She smiled. "I did as he suggested.

And other things. This Dark Wind group finds the morally-weak and those with avarice for position and power." She waved her hand. "Even here there were a few." She sighed. "They are no more. They were an abomination!"

Verin placed a finger over her lips, then said, "Our records are vast, but orderly. I will sent others of my abilities to Nu'vern and the various folk of Shar'daine to ferret out these lurkers."

She waggled one hand. The air crackled around them.

"Now, none may hear what we speak." She sat silent for long moments, then sighed. "I can tell you the name of the monster that wishes you to fail, Queen of The Seven Lands."

She took a long swallow from her mug.

"This being is named Ranagaz. Where he came from is unknown. He arrived after the folk had appeared and spread and developed. The Dark Wind is a recent group of folk who believe that he will reward them once all are subjected to his control. He is what The Ancient One warned you about and why you are traveling the lands to become The Queen of The Seven Lands in fact. This is all that I know about that."

She leaned back in her chair and looked around the table at the others and waved one hand gently.

"Out here, in the lands beyond Nu'vern, there are folk who have abilities that can be loosely described as magic, an alien concept for those of Nu'vern, but not for the one who carries The Lance of Power." She smiled at Sar'al.

"I have some of that. Certainly Ranagaz and Zarlar do. There are probably others of whom we do not know. Yet! Although I did hear an interesting tale from Cloud Spirit."

Her eyes fastened on Sar'al's. "The Chosen of Huroma will do all in their power to help all the folk." She pointed at her. "Near-sister Queen, I wish to travel with you."

Hanalera.

The Cargo Steed, Sea Foam, costed gently up to and against the long wharf, shortly joined by her sisters. Workers on the wharf caught the thick ropes and quickly wrapped them around anchor points. Sliding a wide gangplank to the deck, a number of them walked aboard to greet The Head of this vessel and to began the discussion about the unloading of the cargo from all five vessels.

As soon as all five were ready, workers began to unload and carry the cargo to the assigned warehouse where The Cargo Steed Caravan Head would meet with interested merchants to wheel and deal.

The Head turned to Clerian'tra and gestured at the town and the visible coastline.

"Here'en do'en be'en Hanalera as this great land haft be'en named."

She nodded and smiled at him.

He frowned at her. "We'en do'en be agreed never a'pass beyond err warehouses."

She stepped onto the gangplank and turned to face him. "I will be safe." Spinning away, she strolled up and onto the wharf. She turned one last time and waved at him. "I will find my own way back. Do not stay here waiting for me. I do not believe that the folk here will see me as part of your crews, or hold you responsible for my walking around."

Slipping between the hurrying dock workers she ambled toward town, loose yellow robes gently billowing around her. The Head stared, open mouthed at her, and wondered if this was going to affect their trading.

Passing through the gate she strolled down one side of the curving roadway that started, or ended, at the land connection of the wharf where the Cargo Steeds were tied. It seemed to her that the folk here were, in appearance and attire, not all that different than the folk of the other lands. She nodded to herself. That was something to think about.

The buildings, however, were different, in shape and form, than anything she had yet seen. And in spite of what she had been told during their voyage to this land, none of the inhabitants seemed to pay any attention to her.

As she strolled along, it became apparent that this was a sizable town, every road curving off in some direction or other. It seemed that the local culture did not favor straight lines. The bulk of the structures were single story buildings with gently curving roofs covered with materials of soft red, blue, or green squares.

She headed as directly as she could, as the ever bending ways allowed, away from the wharf area and toward the distant conical hills she could see poking up beyond the buildings.

As she passed from the town into the open farming area, she could see the wagonway gently curving in a great arc to her right toward a lower spot in those hills.

This must be a peaceful place, she thought, as she wandered along. There were no town walls or massive gateways.

The Wild Fields.

They were there.

Standing in The Great Hall.

Startling one and all. Almost.

Verin'yashi looked at the various expressions and smiled at Sar'al as she indicated one of the folk.

"He called. I gave him a ring."

She stared at the four still kneeling next to the mess on the floor that they had been in the process of cleaning up. Then at the two bodies lying next to a wall.

"Cloud?" she asked.

Cloud Spirit walked over and bowed to them.

"Warm Greetings to the Hand of Huroma and to my Queen."

Straightening up, he smiled at Sar'al. "I hadn't expected this at all."

"We were traveling together," explained Verin. She pointed at the mess and the bodies. "What?"

Cloud Spirit beckoned the group to an undisturbed part of the hall, gestured to the chairs, and sat.

Then he explained.

He had been sitting at his desk in The Great Hall, alone, reading some reports just recently handed to him by four archer/scout-guides that had just come back from their go-about. The outer door had opened and two figures dressed all in black had entered the empty hall.

Cloud Spirit stood and stepped from behind his desk. "Ummmmmmm?"

The pair walked closer, stopped, and stared at him.

"You are Cloud Spirit?" asked one.

"The Leader of the archer/scout-guides?" asked the other.

Cloud shrugged. "True. And not true."

"Explain!" hissed one.

A pair of obvious trouble, Cloud thought. "I am Cloud Spirit. No one is The Leader of the archer/scout-guides. They are, as are all those of The Wild Fields, a very independent folk. What do you want?"

The pair stepped way from each other, short knives appearing in their hands.

"To finish that which our disappeared acquaintances hadn't finished!"

Cloud took a few steps backward. "Who . . . are . . . you?"

"The Dark Wind," they snarled as they rushed at

him.

Cloud's hand flew behind himself and back as he stepped into them and swung.

He sighed and looked at his small audience.

"There are a great number of them assaulting the Stoneholds, emmmm, outside the walls. Here at Stonehold Anda they have been able to do little." He shrugged.

"Other than to die. I think that those two," he nodded at the bodies, "thought to eliminate me and then lead their, eh, associates inside through an open gate."

He stood. "They appear to have been badly informed but are a problem, none the less. I have heard nothing from the other Stoneholds, yet."

Cloud waved one hand.

"We can't go after them with just bows or the knives that we carry and they can't enter. The Stoneholds are well provisioned and can sit and kill any of them that wander into bow range. But we do have fields and crops to attend. They are now mostly staying far enough back from the walls to stay alive and are apparently believing that they can wait us out." He shrugged. "We have sufficient supplies stored in every Stonehold to wait for two seasons."

Verin'yashi nodded.

"Take us up one of your towers. I need to see."

Cloud nodded and led them from The Great Hall toward the closest watch tower.

As they walked, he grumbled, mostly to himself,

"That floor is going to be permanently stained." Up the stairs they went. At the top he smiled at the four archers watching, and leaned on one of the railings and pointed. "There they are."

Verin peered down at the deep grass and then at the various spots indicated by the watch tower archers.

"Just beyond reach," said Light Sky. "Now."

Verin's robes reflected amber glow in the sunlight as she placed both hands on the railing and stared outward at The Plains of Singing Grass. In a moment she turned and smiled at Cloud Spirit.

"Soon," she waved one hand outward, "your problem will cease to exist. Watch carefully! What you will see will be occurring at every one of your Stoneholds."

Everyone stared and then they could see them.

Faint disturbances in the grass were approaching from all directions, converging on the Stonehold.

"You sent Swift Wind and Bright Sky to accompany The Queen and her party. Shall we leave them here? When we leave?"

Cloud frowned at her. "Leave?"

"Most so." She nodded. "Those of The Dark Wind down there are about to find that The Plains of Singing Grass are a very inhospitable place to be. For them."

She looked at Sar'al.

"Shall we proceed? There is nothing out there to, eeee uh, worry about. Now."

Sar'al ducked her head and started down the

stairs.

The small group walked along the narrow way toward the main gate accompanied by Cloud Spirit.

"Swift Wind and Bright Sky will remain with The Queen's party," he stated as the gate swung open.

Sar'al bowed to him. "Most welcome."

He bowed back. "My Queen."

Thunder Mountain Range.

The Thunder Mountain Range was one of the vast northern mountain ranges of An'Darl. The north side of this range rose steeply from the depths of The Wild Sea. The lower reaches on that side were stark jagged black rock, swept clean of soil and vegetation by the great storms that assailed the range as they roared across the deep water.

The mountain range was pierced by two steep gorges whose bottoms plunged deep below the water where the fingers of The Wild Sea reached far inland.

The small party, heavily bundled against the weather, stood on the eastern slope of one of these fingers, *Thall Thrust*, the straight "finger." They all stared at the mouth of the large cavern across the small flat bench from where they stood. That cavern was the reason that they had trudged this deep into the forbidding mountain range.

Equi-veronik and his twin sister, Bael'elyth, had spent a number of days visiting various libraries and the ancient collections, doing research. Standing here, a very many days travel from the more settled portions of

An'darl, was the result of that research.

Their companions, Gentle Smile and Dark Night, waited patiently, standing close to the twins as the wind roaring from the open sea and buffeted them.

Bael indicted the dark interior facing them. "Shall we?"

Equi nodded.

They started over the bench and into the opening, and far enough back to be out of the wind howling past the cavern's mouth.

It was a relief to be finally out of the violence of "summer" in these mountains.

Equi pulled off his thick gloves, stuffed them into the large side pockets of his outer jacket, reached inside and pulled from a pocket a folded piece of material and opened it.

They gathered around as he did.

It was a carefully made drawing, copied and annotated from a number of documents that they had found.

The drawing indicated that somewhere deep inside this cavern was the dwelling of The Mountain Thrall, one of The Hidden Ones.

From all that they had read they only knew that name and this location and a single warning that stated that no one ever came to this place. It was a mystery, one that the twins wished to solve.

"Ummmmm," said Bael as she knelt and began to unwrap a heavily wrapped bundle that she had been carrying slung over one shoulder. These were the torches, prepared and wrapped long before they had started on this journey. From what they knew of the size of this cavern, they had more than enough to completely explore the stygian depths as indicated in one of the several documents they had found and studied.

If their search found nothing here, then they would head away and begin the search for the next name on their list of Hidden Ones.

Setting aside two of the torches, she wrapped the rest, stood and slung the bundle by its carrying strap from one shoulder.

Equi took one torch and handed the other to her.

He smiled at her. "Ready?" In moments he had both torches aflame. He pointed. "Straight to the back wall. Then we will decide which way to turn."

The twins started forward followed by the others whose red eyes seemed to glow in the reflected torch light.

At the back wall the pair carefully examined the wall that stretched away into the darkness as it reached upward and outward over their heads. Far behind them they could the dim light of the mouth of the cavern. The maps and the documents that they had studied had indicated that the cavern was large but not how large. Now they knew.

Equi held his torch high and wandered back and forth peering at the floor. Then he stopped and pointed.

"That way. This back wall appears to bend further back on this side."

He started that way, stopped, and peered at the floor.

"Look!"

They did. It was an obvious well-worn path on the cavern floor coming and going somewhere. It was hard to determine its age or when it was last used. It appeared that none of the weather outside ever reached this far back.

"Eh am ah," mumbled Equi as he started to follow the path deeper into the cavern. "This may be very ancient history."

"Perhaps." Bael followed him, carefully searching all the floor that she could see in their torch light.

As they walked along the passageway, it slowly began to narrow.

Soon it was no wider than would allow two folk to walk side by side without brushing against the side walls.

"Well!" stated Equi as he stopped to stare.

Just at the edge of his cone of torch light they all saw it. The end of the passageway.

The artificial end of the passageway.

A wall filled it.

Every large block in the wall was cut to exactly the same size, shaped so carefully that the joints between the dark grey blocks were nothing by mere lines. The stone face of the blocks were as smooth as a craftsman's job done in woodwork.

Set exactly in the center of the wall was a grey

wooden door of wide vertical planks. These were as smooth as the stone, shining with a soft polished sheen.

Equi stepped close, and pulled, then pushed.

"Locked?"

He turned to his companions.

"Shall we knock?"

Prime Shield.

Ran'dyal, now Second In Command of The Trader-Merchant outfit stationed here, and The First Voice of The Dark Wind, stared at the individual sitting in his office.

An'tarna, allegedly here to discuss some business as far as a lessor clerk who had ushered him into this office knew, was actually here to notify Ran'dyal what he had learned. An'tarna was one of The Whispers of The Dark Wind, those who were in control of the various Fists of The Dark Wind, each of whom had been given a piece of territory to develop.

"What?" gasped Ran'dyal. He was having a hard time understanding what his long time friend An'tarna was telling him.

"Ran," insisted An'tarna, "it is true!"

The pair had know each other for many seasons, long before Ran'dyal had begun to recruit and organize The Dark Wind.

"Pel'dan," repeated An'tarna, "sent his Fist into Shar'daine. They intended to do damage, to make a point. That is what he stated. Pel'dan said that he was no longer receiving messages from his field folk."

An'tarna leaned closer to his friend.

"That entire Fist is gone. No-one is willing to cross that wetway to investigate. Not right now. An entire Fist disappearing into those grass lands has all my folk, very, very nervous."

Ran'dyal nodded.

"The next caravan," he stated, "heading that way will have your folk going with it. No one will pay attention to the caravan unless they stop and set up booths, or until they reach their destination. Your members can talk with any of the local folk they meet. Maybe someone will know something."

He nibbled on the end of the writing tool that he held. "I have never heard of any group traveling through those grass plains that disappeared. Never!"

An'tarna stood and nodded.

"Tell me when. The Fist will be ready!"

The Ghost Stones.

Lurin strode through the tall grass, loose golden garments soft sighing with her movements. She slipped between two of the massive supports and stepped into the large circular open space and over to the immense being floating just above the ground in the exact center of this round structure.

She stopped and stared up into the three great eyes watching her, each a dark color, each a different dark color. Her large golden eyes watched them carefully.

"Pleasant greetings, Lurin, Favored of Andercal,"

it rumbled softly.

"There is something that you must do," she stated, sitting comfortably on the ground.

"Must . . . do . . . ?"

"Here is the why of it," she said, patting the ground next to her. The Guardian floated closer, then settled near.

She carefully explained all that had occurred with the several visitors, all of them from the outside of The Folded Lands. Then she opened the scroll and read out loud what had been written by Mazarnato. She carefully explained that she understood the need of the warrior pair to travel through The Folded Lands, the pair and the one other that The Guardian had sent. Then she told of the events that the non-warrior had brought to be. Then, after describing the archer and her magic using companion, who appeared later, she related everything that she had since learned.

"Now," she stated, "this is what you will do."

The Guardian lifted into the air and stared down at her.

"Will . . . do . . . ?"

The Silent Woods.

She raced through the dense forest, hurtling along one of the several trails.

Finally she charged into Grey Thicket village of Clan Zalanal and into the hut of The Elder, to stand, sucking in deep breaths, sweat glistening on her skin.

The Elder looked up from where she was sitting

and patted the mat covered floor in front of her.

"Uh huh, uh huh," she grunted. "Sit, sit, and tell me why one of Clan Pel'na has run to here, so hard."

The messenger thudded into a sitting position in front of The Elder, her breath already slowing down.

"Dinala, Clan Pel'na. She looks at you," she stated most formally.

"Uh huh, uh huh. I see you." The Elder filled a mug from a handy jug and handed it to her. And waited.

Dinala slowly drank the juice, nodded thanks, and set the mug to one side.

"Some days past," she began, "loud crackling sounds, very loud sounds, were heard. The sounds came from south of the south mound of The Ghost Stones, north of the edge of The Silent Woods, on the great flat whose edge touches The Great Sea. I was one of those that watched and wondered. As I, and the others, watched, the entire area was covered by a dense cloud cover, a very dense and deep fog bank!"

She stared at The Elder, her eyes going round as round could be.

"In this spot," she said, "where once there was tall grass dancing in the gentle caress of the wind, there is a new town, a walled town. It became visible when that cloud cover rose, when that fog bank was blow away."

She stared at the floor, fingers picking at the mat.

"It must have something to do with The Ghost Stones," she murmured. "It settled itself there, where no town has ever been. It was felt that all the clans of the Tha'a'sa must be aware of this strange."

"Uh huh, uh huh." Slowly The Elder stood. "We will gather and you will speak to all of this thing."

Adna'arl.

He was halfway around the soaring mountain range that ringed the interior of the land on his walk, planning on stopping at another of those ruined structural areas.

This one was very much like the first one he had seen. Piles of weather beaten wood turned grey and fuzzy from the passage of many seasons.

The wide bench he was strolling along encircled the entire land mass.

Having nothing better to do, he had walked around and around that mountain barrier, trekking past the unchanging and unbroken walls to the interior. He had finally stopped counting the number of times he had done this. His many passings had made a trail where none had been before. The long, never ending trek did keep him in good physical shape. On all the trips he had yet to meet anything other than the small dwellers of the place that scurried through the high grass or prowled the wide beaches searching for things to eat.

He, like them, always seemed to find something edible, sea creatures floundering on the beach, bushes and shrubs covered with berries and fruit.

Jerking to a halt, he stared, and stared, and

stared.

There was a narrow opening in the barrier to the interior, an opening that had not been there ever before. He knew this to be true. After all, during his many circumnavigations he had memorized the place. He recognized everything that he had seen, over and over again. And this had not been here before.

He shrugged and walked into it. It was something new.

"Eh!" he gasped.

There was a door facing him. It was set in a high wall that blocked the way. The wall rose up and into the cloud layer high overhead. There was no way around that wall.

"Strange," he muttered to himself. "Very strange."

Then he jumped back. The door was swinging wide.

A rather husky male, dressed entirely in brown colored garments, stood in the opening and smiled at him.

"Won't you come in?" he asked pleasantly. "We think that it is time for us to meet you." He laughed. "Or for you to meet us!"

He stepped back, waved one hand in a wide gesture of invitation.

The Heart of All.

The watcher standing on the top platform of The Tower of The Soaring Dragon stared at the edge of The

Forest of Sighs. Something was moving out there, right where Aydel's Track entered the dense woods. He leaned on the top of the short wall and squinted.

He jerked back and spun around to lean over the back wall and bellow at those standing down there, on either side of the gate.

"FOLK APPROACHING!"

Someone ran into a nearby building to carry the message. Moments later, two folk ran from the outside door of the building to join those at the gate.

The messenger hurried back to his place next to the gate.

The twins, Rau'ke and Cant'al, acting King and Queen of Nu'vern, stood and waited. Warriors, now named, somewhat unimaginably, Bows and Swords, ran from the two practice fields of The Armed Mass and formed in ranks behind the pair. Just in case.

Soon, all those standing there could begin to make out details as the small group walked up the wagonway and strode through a sunny patch.

One of them seemed to glow amber fire as she strolled along. It appeared to have something to do with the robes she wore.

The five finally walked through the gateway and stopped to face the crowd watching them.

The one in the amber robe bowed, most formally.

"Warm greetings," she said as she straightened up. "I am Tredenta, Hand of Huroma."

The two dressed entirely in black stepped forward, short bows held in their left hands, a round shield strapped to their left forearms. At their waist hung a quiver of arrows. On their backs, they had a large case of short stabbing spears.

The male thumped his chest.

"Martar of Clan Zaland, he speaks for Clan Zalanad and Clan Pel'na, Tha'a'sa. He looks at you." He nodded at his companion.

She stated, "Brontil of Clan A'a'tar, she speaks for Clan A'a'tar and Clan Mu'antar, Tha'a'sa. She looks at you."

They stepped back.

The remaining pair stepped forward, holding great long bows in their left hands, large quivers slung on their backs.

"Far Shot, archer/scout-guide, Stonehold Perna."

"Mist Night, archer/scout-guide, Stonehold Turza."

The five formed a line and waited.

Rau'ke cleared his throat. "Warm greetings." He frowned slightly. "Er ummmm, why have you come?"

Mist Night smiled at him. "We two were sent by The First Blade." She indicated the others. "They joined us as we walked the wagonway."

"Sent? By Zak'ke?" Cant'al was staring at them, a very puzzled expression on her face. Why would Zak'ke do something like that?

Mist Night stared to the pair, equally puzzled. "You do not know?"

"No," stated Rau'ke.

Far Shot began to explain.

The Queen's twin, The First Blade, had suggested it to her and she had agreed. The Queen had given Far Shot a written document of her decision. He handed it to Rau'ke.

It explained that the Royal pair had decided that given the varied cultures and cultural values of the folk that she was gathering under her "banner" that a small Advisory Council should be formed so that any decision made would understand exactly how each group thought. The Advisory Council would help bring the various folk into an integrated whole.

"Mist Night and I speak for The Wild Fields." He indicated the others. "They speak for The Silent Woods and The Huroma." He spun around and waved.

A figure stepped from the dense woods and started toward them, walking softly and silently. "The Forest of Sighs sends one."

Far Shot turned back and bowed, an awkward bow, to the twins. "We are at your service, Majesties."

Tredenta nodded at them.

"I was sent," she explained, "by Verin'yashi for your Council as well as to rid Nu'vern of any who would follow or be part of The Dark Wind."

Rau'ke nodded at them. He wondered what additional surprises The Royal Pair would send his way.

"Please come with me and I will see to your accommodations and, eh ummm, find a suitable room where The Advisory Council may meet. Ahhh, can someone explain this Dark Wind thing?"

Iron Hammer.

The small group wandered through the central market of this northwest town on An'darl selecting food stuffs and the equipment that they had been told that they would require. Everyone that they had talked with had warned them against crossing the wetway to Farza and stressed the dangers of the inhabitants that lived there, "the crazed warriors."

After all, they stated firmly, the last pale skin of Nu'vern that had done that had never returned. But in spite of all that, they had been consistent upon what the party would need if they insisted on going to that land.

Sar'al had decided that the horses would be kept for them and cared for at one of the horse trader establishments. They had agreed on the cost and the duration of the care as the trader had argued that they might not return. And, if they didn't, how to send the horses to Nu'vern.

Now the party was walking down a narrow way in the market when a great commotion started somewhere behind them.

"MY QUEEN!" bellowed someone.

They all turned in that direction and stared at the folk that were leaping in all directions as a pair of horses surged through them.

She rode up, halted, and jumped down, and smiled at them.

"Viana!" gasped Sar'al

The other rider slid from his mount, hurried up, and bowed.

"Rid'linar?" Sar'al stared at him, frowning darkly. What was one of her Fast Riders doing here?

"He," explained Viana, "caught up with me as I entered Iron Hammer."

The Fast Rider straightened up and handed Sar'al a heavily wrapped document.

Sar'al took it. "What is this?"

"News of Nu'vern." He nodded. "All is well," he added.

Sar'al looked at the two of them.

"We are going to Farza," she stated. "Now it appears We shall need to properly equip you as well." She smiled at them.

Viana's eyes glittered. "The Tha'a'da prepare! And all seven clans greet their Queen."

Zak'ke laughed. "Good news."

"Clan Speakers ride for Nu'vern," stated Viana. She had set them to this. As The Spirit of the Tha'a'da she had the authority to do this, with or without the agreement of the Clan Elders. But all The Elders had agreed after they had heard about The Dark Wind as Viana had related from what she had heard while she had been in The Wild Fields with Sar'al and Zak'ke.

So the party walked back into the main market space and added additional food and equipment to their supplies and then led the livestock to the same horse trader and added them to his agreed upon care-taking.

When they were finished there and started down the way from the market, Viana looked at the other party members and said, "Viana, Clan Veronji, Spirit of the Tha'a'da."

The rest of the party introduced themselves and she nodded.

Zak'ke nudged Sar'al gently.

"Let us sit at that refreshment stall at the empty table. I wish to talk about your, eh ah, quest, My Queen."

Sar'al looked at him, then nodded, and headed that way.

Once they were seated, had purchased the beverage of their choice, and were alone, in a manner of speaking, while sitting in the middle of a very active market, Sar'al looked at Zak'ke, her eyes asking his the question.

"Ummmmm eh," he said. "I have been thinking about everything that we have learned since we first started from Nu'vern."

She nodded.

Zak'ke took a sip from his tall mug.

"The Ancient One," he stated, licking his lips, "told us that there was "a great and hidden enemy" of all the lands. That is the reason we are traveling and you are asking the various folk to recognize you as their queen."

She nodded.

"To my way of thinking, this great and hidden enemy is either rather, eh, unaware of the many cultural belief systems, or, is being very, very devious."

She nodded.

"Think of what has happened. That thing sent something that made the Azkar accept your claim. That hidden thing sent something that made the Tha'a'sa clans and the Second Royal House accept your claim."

She nodded.

"That thing is probably behind this Dark Wind group. And their behavior has brought The Wild Fields and Huroma under your banner."

She nodded.

Zak'ke smiled at her.

"So far then, everything that thing has done has been to insure that the folk will join with you in a united system." He shrugged and took another sip. "Thus, it does seem, to me, that this enemy is not all that clever. Or perhaps it is devious beyond understanding."

Verin'yashi looked at the twins.

"There is more," she stated.

All stared at her.

"More?" Zak'ke frowned at her.

"Most so! I was visited by a male of some unknown abilities, strong unknown abilities, who called himself Zarlar. That one warned me about the machinations of that thing and stated that we, in some manner unknown, had to lure it from its hidden place in order to destroy it. At that time, I believe, Zarlar will help us rid the lands of it."

Sar'al took a long swallow from her mug and banged it down on the table, her eyes scanning all her companions.

"It is becoming more complicated than We had

assumed!" She sighed. "So, it appears that Our endeavors are the lure to bring this hidden thing out of its hiding hole, eh ah, before anything can be done?"

Verin nodded. "I believe that is what Zarlar was saying."

Sar'al emptied her mug.

"Then We shall proceed the way We are going, We will!"

Zak'ke winked at her.

They rested one day and started across the wetway to Farza.

The party carried the necessary gifts, as explained to them by the local Trader-Merchant outfit, for the troop that guarded the entrance to Farza and for others.

The Crystal Palace.

He stood and stared at it, slowly turning around. It was the most amazing building that he had ever seen or could have ever imagined.

The sunlight struck refracted shafts of color in every direction as it passed through the structure.

It had been a surprise to find this place and the sense of wonder at its design. He had no idea how anyone could have constructed it in such a place on top of one of the highest peaks in the Sky Mountains. As he continued to slowly turn, he couldn't understand how or why this place wasn't shrouded with clouds. The rest of this mountain range was always capped by a thick cloud layer.

"My, my, my," said a soft voice speaking from behind him. "No one has ever visited here before."

He whipped around and stared at the speaker, eyes popping wide.

A short, young woman stood there, dressed in robes of an unfamiliar cut and design, colored a deep blue. She watched him with a curious frown above slanted, large oval eyes filled with the azure of the open sky above.

"Who are . . . you?" he gasped.

She smiled up at him and waggled one hand at their surroundings.

"I am the one that caused this place to be. Is it not . . . interesting, Alaine'an'dar?"

He frowned at her. "You know my name?"

"Most so," she stated. "Why are you here?"

There was something in that softly asked question that told him that an answer was not only asked for but was expected to be given.

He straightened up, realizing that he had been leaning toward her, and smiled.

"I was climbing, just climbing for fun, when I saw a lighter spot in all the cloud cover. So I came this way just to see." He shrugged. "So here I am." One arm pointed. "I will leave the way that I came. Most sorry to be a bother. It was not intended." He bowed slightly

As he started to turn to leave when she reached out and held his arm.

To Alaine it felt as if a metal shackle had been clamped around his arm. How could such a small female have such a grip?

"Ummmm?" he said, turning his head to look at her.

"We are going to have a little talk, eldest son of House Zilin Aacog. There is something that you must do! It is necessary and not exactly unpleasant, if you are successful. As I will explain, you will understand why it has to do with the very survival of all the folk of these lands."

She released his arm and pointed at two chairs, chairs which had not been there before.

"Sit! Be comfortable. And I will tell you everything that you need to know."

He walked over and sat, massaging his arm. He thought that if he pulled up his sleeve he would find black and blue bruising. Who, or what, was this female?

She sat and smiled at him.

Then she began to explain.

Palana Village.

Al'tana had been visiting and resting with the fisher folk of the northeast village of Nu'vern since she had returned home. At times she had sought the solitude of a small cove not too distant from the village to swim, or to wade in the shallows, or to just sit on the wide beach and listen to the soothing sea sounds.

At other times when she was in the cove she would visit with the Laterian, the great dweller of the depths, who had drifted south with her as she walked from Ea'na to her home in Nu'vern and then to this corner of the land.

This day, as she floated in the deep water of the cove, one arm thrown over the long neck of the Laterian, she talked with her about this and that and then told her that she would be returning to the main town, the seat of government, to rejoin her siblings in whatever all that activity was about.

Then she stood on the beach and watched as the great one drifted away from the cove and, with a last glance at Al'tana, sank from sight.

Thrallanaton.

The door, wood shining with a soft polished sheen, slowly swung in, here deep in the great cavern in the Thunder Mountain Range of An'darl.

Equi-veronik cast a quick glance at his twin, Bael'elyth, and stepped through the opening into a square tunnel carved into the black stone. The others followed him in.

The short, stocky male clad in grey armor of a design unknown to the small group, pushed past them, yanked the door shut, and dropped the several fastening bars into place.

He turned and stared at them, brow furrowing in curiosity just below the edge of his ornate helmet. He pointed. "You may drop your torches right there!"

"Visitors?" he rumbled from deep in his chest, fingers gently stroking the handle of the great axe that hung from his wide leather belt. He watched them throw their torches to the place he had indicated.

Equi nodded. "We are that."

"Why?"

Equi sucked in a deep breath and explained. He spoke of their research in the several places where they had found old documents and scraps of information and then why they had come here to search out the truth of that information. Then he identified each of his group, and explained, a little, about Gentle Smile and Dark Night.

The warrior thumped his chest. "Karlkarz," he stated. Then he stepped closer to Gentle Smile. "A Cure Person?"

The red eyes stared into his dark blue ones.

"This is One who saves." She indicated Dark Night. "This is One who does not." And stood as still as midnight.

"FOLLOW!" Karlkarz spun away and thumped down the tunnel which seemed to lead into darkness, almost darkness as they soon found out. In some way this tunnel was just very dim, the light just bright enough that the small group could see the warrior ahead of them clumping along with a slight rolling gait.

He was moving faster that he appeared to be.

After a number of twists and turns, they were led into a large cavern whose walls were riddled with dwellings and places of other activities of some sort. It was much brighter in here.

In the center of the open floor of the cavern sat a large square stone platform.

On all sides of the platform stood ranks of the

population, male and female, all armored and equipped much the same as Karlkarz although some carried large great swords. They seemed to have been listening to the one that sat on the platform.

In the center of the platform sat a single male dressed in ornate robes. The chair was plain wood. On either side of him stood a warrior holding a great sword, edges gleaming in the light.

Karlkarz stomped up the three broad steps and stopped facing the seated figure.

He bowed, straightened up, turned and jabbed a finger while telling who each of these "visitors" were and then related in the same detail that Equi had told him about how and why they were here.

The seated figure crooked a finger at them, beckoning them to step up.

The small party stepped up and stopped. Gentle Smile and Dark Night stood behind the twins.

The sword holder to the right of the seated figure bowed to them and announced in deep, rolling tones, "Here, before you, sits Markkarz Stone Fist, Ka'Thrall of The Thrall! He greets you. Step forward Cure Person!"

Gentle Smile stepped around Equi and stopped.

Markkarz Stone Fist stood and yanked his ornate garment open, exposing his chest to his waist. A great angry wound covered his left side from shoulder to hip. It was encrusted with blood and was seeping fluids from the red and swollen tissue.

Gentle Smile stepped toward him, Dark Night by her side.

The sword bearer raised his great weapon and glowered at Dark Night, blocking his path.

The pair stopped.

Dark Night glided between Gentle Smile and the warrior, scepter, now glowing a faint yellow, held in his hand.

"Do not tempt death," the deep, gentle voice said.

The sword bearer looked at the Ka'Thrall, who nodded.

The sword had barely begun to move when Dark Night lightly tapped the warrior on the chest with the scepter and watched the body collapse sprawling at his feet.

Bael gasped.

Equi stared.

Dark Night turned and started for Markkarz.

"No," said Gentle Smile's soft deep voice as she stepped closer to the Ka'Thrall and examined his wound. She reached over and gently slid her hand from his shoulder to his hip and back up.

He sighed as the pain left.

"Three sleeps," she told him. "You must eat much and rest long."

Markkarz turned to the other sword bearer and touched his chest.

"What see you here?"

"Heal wound, fast heal wound."

Markkarz turned back and bowed deeply to Gentle Smile and looked at the rest.

"Welcome, guest visitors."

He sat, eyes dancing from one to the other, then he indicated the crumpled form lying nearby. "It is understood."

Waggling one hand, he called for refreshments, leaned back in his chair nodding to himself at how well he felt, ignoring the body sprawled nearby.

"From where came you, guest visitors?"

Equi indicated Bael and himself. "Nu'vern." Then he indicated Gentle Smile and Dark Night. "The Heart of Darkness."

"Ummmmmmmmm. One is heard about, one is not!" He looked at Equi. "Is Nu'vern truly Royal led?"

"Most so," replied Equi. "Our older twins are The Queen and The First Blade."

"Once, in the long memories past, Royalty was so for the Thrall Sets. It is proper that Nu'vern still follows the Noble Way!"

He stood and smiled at Gentle Smile.

"Now I must eat much and rest long."

He looked at the sword bearer by his side.

"Talleraz will find quarters and comfort for all. Next First Meal we will talk." He walked from the stand and into one of the dwelling.

Talleraz pointed at a different dwelling and led them that way.

Strange Things

Hanalera.

She had followed the wagonway in its great arc around and through the farm fields. The perfume drifting from some of the fields had been quite pleasant.

Around the fields and up the long grade into the opening between the brown round hills she went. Then she drifted through the sharp curve to the right and along the high wagonway carving a very long, slow curve around the open grasslands below.

Finally she had halted and stood staring at the wagonway as it entered the narrow but not very long gorge in the mountain range crossing in front of her.

Clerian'tra looked at the sight beyond the end of the gorge. Something out there was flashing colors that appeared to be moving from one side of her view to the other. Whatever was out there, her view of it was sharply constricted by this high-walled crack in the mountains.

Frowning slightly, she headed into that tight space, very slowly, very cautiously. She had absolutely no idea what was at the end nor had she ever heard any tales that spoke of such a thing. This was becoming very a interesting land.

The Valley of Glar.

A large band of dark clad, heavily armed folk entered the valley from the narrow canyon to the south in the early morning light and encircled the small settlement.

Everyone in that settlement reacted quickly to this intrusion, at the first sight of those folk.

The heavy shutters and doors slammed shut and were barred and bolted from the inside.

M'aga, the Master Smith, working early as he always did, heard the commotion, set his drafting tools and materials aside, and looked out one of this workroom's windows just to see what was going on. He jerked back, dropped the massive shutter and latched it tight.

Hurrying into another room, he quickly gave his staff instructions.

Stomping back to his workroom, he thumped over to one of the long benches that lined the walls, and picked up a great long bow that he had built. Then he grabbed a thickly wrapped bundle and headed for the stairs that led up to one of the high platforms on his roof.

Once on the platform, he crouched, unwrapped the bundle, and then ever so slowly and carefully he unbent and peered over the edge of the low wall.

"Ahhhhh, mal!" he snarled softly. Who ever these folk were, they had come prepared to assault his town. He could see bundles set here and there which he assumed were probably their supplies.

He stood, arrow nocked, and drew back the great long bow. Seasons of metal working had overlaid his arms and chest with ranks of massive, corded muscles.

Ever since his last visit with Wind Sky archer/scout-guide he had practiced with this weapon, new to him, this bow, a copy of the one that she had carried. It had taken a great number of days to make it. He had done it from curiosity. In was in his nature to be curious about such things, being a Master Smith and designer of all manner of weapons.

The arrow flashed away and blasted through one of the black garbed folk, hurtling that one back and over the edge of the deep stream side wall.

Before that one's two companions could react to what they saw, they had joined him on the rocks of the more or less dry stream bed.

M'aga ducked and then hurried down the stairs.

At the bottom he set everything on the long bench and decided that he would wait for some time. Then he would take a peek from another of the platforms on his roof just to see what that bunch might be doing once they realized that three of their members were no longer among the living.

M'aga smiled and nodded to himself. That bow and those arrows, all designed, more or less, by Wind

Sky, were wonderful designs, very creative designs, ones that only a Master Smith, who designed some of the most lethal weapons produced in An'darl, could truly appreciate.

Then he sat on a stool and wondered who those folk out there were. From what he had seen, they only carried swords of some sort and nothing else. Not exactly the sort of things one would expect for folk coming to assault a settlement such as this one.

Every structure here was built of heavy stone blocks with very steep pitched roofs of heavy timber that supported a sheathing of dark stone. It was necessary for the heavy winter snow that fell here. It would appear, he thought, that those folk out there had no idea of this place before they had arrived.

He shrugged. The inhabitants would stay inside. There were no warriors here. And, he supposed, he would only be able to kill a few more of them before they finally took cover.

Sitting at the work bench he began to idly sketch a new design and thought about the settlement as the design began to take shape.

Every inhabitant had a great store of food and drink inside their dwellings. Winter for this valley was approaching and all were prepared to be buried in white for many long days of isolation. From what he had seen of those folk out there, they were not.

The Heart Of All.

He rode through the gate and jumped from his heavily lathered horse.

A groom that had been walking back to the stables took one look at the horse and came running.

The groom glared at the rider and demanded loudly, "What have you been doing? To treat your horse so badly?" He grabbed the bridle and gently led the horse away, glowering back over his shoulder at the startled rider.

Folk of the Armed Mass, having heard the commotion and loud voice, came running from several directions, all bearing weapons. None of them were sure what had caused the angry sound but none were willing to allow whatever it was to enter the Kingdom.

A small group poured from a nearby building.

The rider watched them and held his arm away from his side and the long sword hanging there from his ornately decorated leather belt. In this new group he recognized at least three warriors.

All those folk stood in a curved line facing him.

One stepped forward, eyes looking at his broad shoulders, fair skin, and grey eyes.

"Warm greetings, ah . . . cousin," he said. He bowed and said, "I am Rau'ke, King. Who might you be?"

Cant'al slipped an arm through his. "I am his Queen."

"Alaine'an'der Tan'dei Zilin Aacog." He bowed

in return. Straightening up, he frowned slightly at all those eyes staring at him.

"I came a long way," he explained, "to speak with Sar'al, The Queen of The Seven Lands."

He stared at Rau'ke and Cant'al. "King? And Queen?" His shoulder's slumped. "Is she . . . dead?"

Rau'ke stifled his smile and shook his head and waved a hand at that nearby building.

"Let us go inside and be comfortable and talk. This way, please. We have never been visited before by one of The Seventh Royal House."

He led the very puzzled Alaine into the main house, down a short hall, and into a room of comfortable chairs.

Turning, he poured a number of mugs, sitting on the small table, full of Beblue Berry juice and handed them around. Then he sat, took a sip, and looked expectantly at their "guest."

"It appears," stated Rau'ke, "that you have ridden long and hard to, ah, speak with The Queen who is not dead. Would you care to explain?"

Alaine took a sip, then he nodded.

He cleared his throat. "I was told to speak to her and to hurry and to do just that. So I did, ummm, hurry. May I speak with her?"

Cant'al leaned forward before any of the others could speak and asked, "Who sent you?"

Alaine looked at all the folk watching him, and nodded. Most of them must be siblings of The Queen.

He had been told about that.

Straightening up, he set his mug on a small table next to his chair.

"The Ancient One told me."

Then he explained what he had been doing and how he came to meet her and what she had told him, well, more or less. Some of that conversation was not to be repeated to anyone but The Queen.

When he finished, a tall, slim female stood, dressed in loose garb of a light purple color, her hiking staff held in one hand. She beckoned with her free hand to a shorter, rather compact female, wearing a jacket and trousers of a light brown color festooned with pockets, snaps, and straps. That one stood, a great long bow held in her left hand, bent, picked up a carry pack and a large quiver stuffed with arrows, and walked over to the other.

The Great Blue.

The upwelling was slow but steady. It was greater than any other on Farza. The water seeped into the surrounding sands until it became nothing but vapor. But before this happened a wide band of green drank deeply and flourished here in the very center of the vast desert.

This place was the home of The Troop of Many Fingers and the One Who Spoke For all, Vachannal The Insignificant. Here would all gather, all those who spoke for their separate troops, to meet and discuss matters of concern for every desert dweller. It was a large scatter of low houses around the pool of water.

Troop leaders, including the troop leader of this place, Kranz the Limber, jumped to their feet and stared. They had been in the midst of a long discussion.

Sar'al and her party had walked across the wetway to Farza and had stopped at the shield group of The Troop That Never Smiled.

She had handed the gifts they had brought to Quantar The Handsome, the leader of the troop whose face was a mass of scar tissue on the left side. It was the result of a misfortune at an early age.

Sar'al and Quantar had discussed long and hard why she had come to Farza. Finally, Quantar had selected four to guide her and her group deep into the interior where The Troop of Many Fingers dwelled.

There, he had told her, she might be able to speak with Vanchannal The Insignificant, The One Who Spoke For All. If he refused, she and the others would have to leave Farza.

Now, Sar'al and the others of her party stood facing Vachannal, surrounded by the warriors of The Troop of Many Fingers. Their leader, Kranz The Limber, and all the other troop leaders that had gathered here, watched these strangers carefully. Sar'al had already passed over more of the gifts to Vachannal.

Vachannal's eyes wandered over the various faces and lingered on Verin'yashi, Zak'ke, Rid'linar and then on Sar'al.

"I see light skins," he said. Then he nodded at them. "You are not the first one to come here. That first one walked unconcerned in our land. We named her *The Stranger Who Burned.* Her pale skin was untouched, never changed by the sun, always smooth pale skin, and light yellow hair."

He waved one hand at their surroundings. "The Elders and other females made that one a special robe that declared her as Bar'Farza, one who may stroll and visit all in Farza."

Sar'al smiled at him. "Does this female have another name?"

Vachannal smiled back. "That one said that it was, ummmmmmmm, Clerian'tra. Most strange a name."

Sar'al nodded. "She is my near-sister, one season younger. None knew where she went after her fourteenth season. May we speak with her?"

Vachannal shook his head and pointed. "She strolled the wetway to N'Farza and has not returned. Warriors are muttering angry. They worry that those of N'Farza did do harm to that one."

Zak'ke stared in the direction indicated, frowned, and mumbled, mostly to himself, "What was she doing?"

"First We will speak more with Vachannal, then We will find out," she whispered softly.

Turning back to Vachannal, Sar'al began to explain why she had come to Farza, The Land of Fierce

Warriors.

Demon Valley.

The quartet, Equi-veronik, Bael'elyth, Gentle Smile, and Dark Night, had passed down a long, very twisted, very narrow valley strewn with boulders and drifts of melting snow. They were headed, more or less, south and east away from The Thunder Mountain Range.

They had spent four days mainly in the company of Markkarz Stone Fist and his extended family, most of time answering questions about the Ten Royal Houses of Nu'vern and The Queen of The Seven Lands.

While these discussions were going on, Gentle Smile and Dark Night had wandered through the large settlement of The Midnight Cavern Thrall, stopping now and then to care for those that Gentle Smile felt really required it, those who would die otherwise.

News of their activities swiftly flew to the ears of Markkarz.

But, finally, Equi had explained, carefully, that his small group had to be on their way.

Markkarz, frowned darkly, glowered angrily, and grumbled loudly, but he had agreed and ordered supplies to be provided for them.

Just before they entered the gate opening to the great cavern, Markkarz gave each of them a ring with his sigil carved into the dark blue jewel set in the silver band.

Thanking him for everything, the small group headed back toward the outside and the howling winds.

Standing in a calmness of the cavern, Equi consulted a map the twins had made from their research and indicated which way they would be headed.

Now, many days later, they stood at the place where the icy stream entered the wide green valley surrounded by snow-shrouded mountains.

It was surprise, this valley, their destination.

All that they knew was what was on their map, and the few sentences, mostly obscure in meaning, found in ancient, faded documents.

They walked into moist and warm air and stared around at the lush growth. Then they saw and heard why this was so.

The valley, as far as they could see, was littered with pools of water and pools of mud, all hissing steam and bubbling loudly.

Reaching a small rise on the otherwise fairly flat valley floor, they stood on its top and looked in all directions.

Bael pointed. "There!" she said, "out there, more or less in the center of the valley."

Equi squinted at it. "Might be a structure, might be a natural thing of this valley.

He smiled at the rest and headed that way.

When they were close enough they began to make out details.

It appeared to be a structure of some sort constructed rather than being just a jumble of rock. Great slabs of rust-red stone leaned at odd angles making a rather tall shape with steep in-leaning sides. Steam drifted up from somewhere near the top.

The party wandered around it and stopped at what appeared to be a door, a very tall and quite narrow door of polished, red and grey streaked, wood.

As they stared at the door, it silently, slowly swung in.

A thick, rasping voice whisper hissed at them.

"Enter. If you wish."

After a long pause, it added, "Whether you leave will be our decision."

They stepped in and walked from one of the many alcoves to the central spot and stopped.

The being standing there was taller than anyone that they had ever seen. It was easily one-and-a-half times the height of Equi. It was dressed much the same as the small party were, in jacket and trousers. Its garments shimmered with an internal fire. They could feel the heat radiating from them.

Given this creatures stance, it appeared to have more than the usual normal number of joints in the limbs than the folk of the lands.

"This valley is closed to surface dwellers! Why did you come here?" A strangely jointed finger waggled at them. "You wear the Honor Rings of that pack of Thrall and they know better. We shall visit them and teach them a painful lesson about forgetting."

Equi stepped forward. "It is not their fault! No one knew that we going to come here or where we were going. They can not be blamed for our behavior."

"Oh?"

"Most so!" stated Bael, stepping to her brother's side.

The being leaned toward them. "Answer the why!"

Equi slipped an arm around Bael and began to explain their research. As he did, others began to slip from some of the alcoves.

One was dressed in black. Heavy smoke seeped from its clothes and puddled around its feet. It was joined by another dressed totally in grey colored garments from which steam drifted upward and out through the hole in the high ceiling and the small opening up there.

The one that had been speaking to them stated, "We are the Merphalan. We have been here since this world formed itself from the stuff of all out there." A glowing red finger jabbed at Gentle Smile and Dark Night. "Before your ancestral Father and Mother arrived. We watched what they brought into existence. We watched others as well. It was of no concern to us as your Mother in doing what she did, made a mistake. Her mistake was that she only saw three domains: The Domain of The Wet, The Domain of The Dry, The Domain of The Open. We are the dwellers of The

Domain of The Deep Below."

"We saw The Ancient One visit and watched her make her small changes."

It reached out a finger and lightly touched a nearby stone column. The spot touched began to glow yellow, then red, then white as the molten stone began to weep fiery tears.

"All," it stated, "of the force of the deep below are we. The stuff that raised mountains and split the dry land into the several lands, we are."

It stepped closer to Equi and frowned as Dark Night started forward and said, "We live as the very world lives. The Heart of Darkness has no sway over the land itself."

Dark Night stopped and looked back at Gentle Smile. She nodded and beckoned him back.

"We know," continued the strange being, "of you, The Seekers! And we agree with those of The Hidden Ones that you have visited." It waggled one multi-jointed arm at the small group. "You may leave our valley."

It stepped even closer, the glow fading, the amount of radiant heat dwindling.

"Show us your map!"

Equi reached into an interior pocket and yanked it out and unfolded it and held it out and up so this being could read it.

Fire flickering eyes studied the document. Then one hand reached out, fingers curled back except for one. The extended finger gently moved a talon over the map and draw a scorched addition on it and withdrew.

"Your map was not correct. The narrow pass I drew will be the best way for you leave this place. Go home, Seekers, go home. It is time. It is time. It is time for you . . . to . . . go . . . home."

The three creatures stepped back into the alcoves and the small group were alone.

The Valley of Glar.

The heavy thumping on his front door early in the morning jerked M'aga awake. He rolled from the cot in his workroom, he had cots scattered throughout the sprawling building, and headed for the door.

The cot he had been sleeping on was one of the many placed so he could do that in whatever workroom he might be utilizing. When he was deeply immersed in a project he would often just sleep on a handy cot until he finished that project. Then he would wander up to his real bedroom for a more comfortable and extended snooze.

He unbolted the door, a heavy hammer in one hand, and swung the door wide. And stood and stared at his visitors.

The four obvious Honglar stood there, dressed in grey archaic armor and helmets, large shields on their left arms, great axes for three of them, hanging from wide leather belts. The fourth stood, resting a great sword on one shoulder.

"WHAT?" rumbled M'aga in their general direction.

The four bowed to him.

When they straightened up, one stated, "Karlartz, Sa'Thrall, The Midnight Cavern Thrall."

The others introduced themselves.

"Jarlnarz, Sa'Thrall, The High Peak Thrall."

"Quarltarz, Sa'Thrall, The Deep Valley Thrall."

"Darldarz, Sa'Thrall, The Hidden Canyon Thrall."

M'aga nodded to them and stifled his surprise and astonishment. What they were saying to him was from the Honglar's most distant history and had become the stuff of legends and fanciful tales of great battles and conflicts. And yet, there they stood.

M'aga nodded, mostly to himself. He had studied all the Honglar history he could find, learning that history as well as searching for new ideas for weapons and armor.

"Would you come in?" he asked them. "I was just about to have First Meal." He stepped back. They clumped inside, smiling broadly at him as they passed.

As they finished the sturdy repast, sitting at the large table with M'aga, his apprentices and assistants, the four explained that they were walking down to Nu'Vern.

They were carrying the regards of the Ka'Thrall to The Queen there.

It had been, they explained to those at the table,

the termination of royalty in the government of Honglar those ever so many seasons past that had driven them to live in isolation. But now that they had been told of the still existing royalty of Nu'vern they were anxious to be allied with her.

The four smiled at the others and laughed.

As one of them explained, they had expected their travel to be a rather dull walk, but then they had arrived here and instead they had "fun" for just a rather short time, but it was relaxing for all of that. And it had broken the monotony of their hike. He laughed. "Those folk bothering you didn't think it was fun. But we did."

They stood, thanked their host for his hospitality, and clumped their way to the outside.

They called to M'aga their thanks for the meal and headed down the valley and disappeared into the narrow canyon that led south.

M'aga headed back inside and toward the workroom where his latest project was. He heard shutters and door banging open. Folk were coming outside to do something about the bodies.

The Great Blue.

"We have been thinking, We have," Sar'al said to Zak'ke as the many conversations swirled around them among the ever changing clusters of troop leaders that had gathered here to listen to her presentation as to why they ought to consider her as their Queen. It was an extremely alien concept for the warriors of Farza to grasp.

Zak'ke twitched, a very slight twitch. The twitch had nothing to do with her comment, not at all. It had been the tone of her voice that caused it.

"My Queen," he replied, softly and ever so gently. This time it was not a jest, it was serious.

She gave him a jab in the ribs with her elbow, just a small jab.

"Oooof!" He frowned a little. After all, it would not do to appear argumentative before the gathered Farza. "What?"

She sighed, heavily.

"Oh, oh," he whispered.

"It appears to Us, from all that We have seen since we left Nu'vern, that We were totally unaware of the true nature of the lands and its folk."

"Ummmm?"

"We have talked with a number of separate folk, have We not?"

"Most so," he agreed.

"Then this is what We have just concluded."

"Ermmmmm," he added, wondering where she was headed in this discussion, such as it was.

"As here," she stated firmly, "as everywhere We did visit, much the same. Every folk We visited was isolated in most respects from all the others. Most had little, if any, interrelationship with any of the others. Of course, there was some small contact, such as that of the scout-guides, the archer/scout-guides, and the Trader-

Merchants, who are more active but in a very narrow way."

She stared into his eyes.

"Brother Mine, some of the folk have never, in their histories, seemed to know, to truly know, or be concerned with any of the others, near or distant. Soooo. "

"So?" he echoed.

"So," she sighed even more heavily than before. "So what The Ancient One set Us to do is totally unique and unknown to any of them."

She shrugged, a slight shrug. "Those who have agreed with Us have chosen to do so because they have seen something from outside their group that was offering damage to themselves and are only, in a very slight way, aware of the need for true political unity. Each group in their own small space takes care of themselves, including an ability to protect themselves from the known dangers, what little there are. Just as have the folk of Nu'vern for many seasons"

She leaned gently against him and whispered, "We are engaged in the most unique event in the histories of The Seven Lands."

She turned and slipped her arm through his. "How can We do this?" Her shoulders slumped. "What if We fail?"

Zak'ke smiled, a very gentle smile. "I wouldn't mention that last point, if I were you. But do tell them about the uniqueness of it all." He leaned close. "Speak to them as their Queen. They will hear it in your voice."

Zaz'za'gaz Cavern.

He was sitting on the edge of the platform, legs dangling into space, elbows on his knees, staring out across all those quiet dwellings, and thinking.

Then he laughed, first softly, then louder.

She walked over and sat by his side.

"Zarlar?"

He turned his head and kissed her on the cheek.

"Hinili, that young Queen appears to have a certain talent after all."

She frowned. "Oh?"

"Um hum," he said.

He pointed up. "The Wild Fields and Huroma have joined her reign, such as it becoming. And not only that!"

"Eh uh?"

He laughed.

"The Huroma," he explained, "eliminated those of The Dark Wind that were attacking The Wild Fields. Sooooooo, she now has both Nu'vern and Sha'daine joined with her as well as those of Mart'den and is just now visiting those enthusiastic warriors in Farza. The Sinit is still watching her."

Zarlar mumbled to himself and picked at a loose thread on a seam in his trousers.

She slapped his hand. "DON'T DO THAT!" Then she slipped her arm around his waist. "Now what?"

"Someone, or something, has stirred up some of The Hidden Ones. It is not that dark one's doing. He is still keeping rather quiet and hidden."

She hugged him and kissed his cheek.

"The Lands are changing," she suggested.

He laughed.

Building . . . Building . . .

Three Drinks Green.

The small group had spent two hands of days with The Troop of the Fierce Continence, mainly waiting for a low enough tide to expose the sand of the wetway, Tide's Gift, so they could journey on to N'Farza.

All the troops, and Vachannal, had accepted Sar'al as their queen, an alien concept to all of them. But, they had decided that The Queen was just a sort of Vachannal only in a way that was sort of more than Vachannal. Den'tza had argued that whatever had sent the black monster to N'Farza required that all of them agree with Sar'al. So they had, after much discussion.

Sar'al had spent a number of the past days in discussion with the Elder females about their cultivation of the Yellow Flowering Red Sata Grass and their process for making the stop bleed powder. The Elders had given her a small bag of the seeds to plant next to her home.

Zak'ke had spent some of those same days talking with the Troop Leader, Den'tza The Gross, and admiring his shark-toothed weapon.

Glar-dogs and children had wandered

unconcerned in and around all these strangers. It was a new experience for them as well as for the adults. It was just that the adults were more restrained in their curiosity.

Then everyone received a surprise.

It was the sudden appearance of Nar'a'las, Wind Sky, and Alaine'an'dar, whose face wore as startled and surprised an expression as any.

"How" he gasped.

Wind Sky stepped calmly to one side and watched the Farza warriors who were staring at these three suddenly appearing strangers, hands fingering weapons.

Nar'a'las ignored all that and bowed to Sar'al. "My Queen. I bring you a visitor from The Seventh Royal House Zilin Aacog." She shoved Alaine roughly forward.

The Heart Of All.

Rau'ke was standing and talking with the gate guards early in the morning. It was something that he did every morning. It was his way of escaping, at least for a short while, the deadly duties, as he saw them, of being The King.

His twin, Cant'al, The Queen, was much more adept at all that tedious ordering and reordering of what seemed to be, to him, the ever expanding bureaucratic structure of The Kingdom.

A hand of days ago he had been doing much the same thing, talking with the gate guards when the watcher in the high tower had leaned over the inner wall and shouted down to them.

"TWO FOLK RUNNING TOWARD THE GATE!"

It had not only alerted the gate guard but had brought a number of Bows and Swords running from their practice fields adjacent to the gate plaza.

Rau'ke watched through the gate opening the pair heading toward them, running at an easy but ground covering gait.

They were dressed in loose over-shirts and trousers of cloth faded to a sun bleached white. A large shield was fastened to their left arms with a very strange weapon fastened to it in some fashion.

The two males ran up to them, stopped, and looked at all the folk gathering and watching them. They weren't even breathing hard.

"We are here to see The King," one of them said.

Rau'ke stepped forward and smiled. "That would be me."

They smiled back at him.

Then they explained.

They had been sent by Vachannal The Insignificant, The One Who Spoke For All, as suggested by Queen Sar'al and Her First Blade, Zak'ke, to advise on all matters relating to the Farza.

Then they introduced themselves as Inadat The Dower and Durtar The Sad.

Durtar smiled happily at Rau'ke and said, "It was a pleasant run. We have never seen that much grass before."

"Run?" Rau'ke stared at them. "From Farza?"

Durtar grinned even more widely and nodded.

Inadat also nodded. "Very pleasant." He didn't smile.

Cant'al joined the group, shooing the Bows and Swords back to their practice fields, and led the pair toward the main building, telling them she would find them a room, and then introduce them to all the rest of The Advisory Council.

But now, in the early morning of day coolness, Rau'ke was once again talking with the gate guards. All the guards has finally learned to relax when he did this as well as when they were around their acting King and Queen.

The high tower watcher leaned over the inner wall and called down to them.

"TROOPS MARCHING OUR WAY! UNKNOWN TROOPS!"

He blew a blast on the great horn mounted on that inner wall.

Bows and Swords came running from their dwellings hastily dragging on clothes with one hand while carrying weapons in the other. It was a day for relaxing not practicing. Once dressed and ready, a number of the Bows ran up and onto the upper battlements of the great guard wall. The Swords stood and began to drag on their newly acquired armor. Then they quickly formed up in ranks facing the just closed and barred gate and waited.

Three ranks of Bows formed up behind them. And all waited. Some patiently, some not so patiently.

Then, they could hear the stomp of heavy footsteps approaching and stopping.

"HELLOOOOOO THE GATE! MAY WE ENTER! WE HAVE COME A LONG WAY TO SEE THE QUEEN!"

Rau'ke nodded at the gate guards who quickly raised the iron bars and swung the gate outward.

Then those on the inside stared at those on the outside who were staring at them.

Those on the outside were obviously Honglar. But no-one in Nu'vern had ever heard of any Honglar who wore grey armor and helmets, carrying large shields, and having large axes hanging from wide leather belts, or carrying a great sword over a shoulder.

One stepped forward and bowed, then straightened up.

"Here stands before you, Karlatz," he rumbled, "Sa'Thrall, The Midnight Cavern Thrall." He bowed again and again.

"We are," he explained, "an Advance Party, Great King, and we have urgent matters to discuss. Where may we do this?"

Cant'al walked up and slipped her arm through one of Rau'ke's.

Karlartz bowed to her. "Great Queen."

Rau'ke pointed with his free arm at a great patch of grass where a circle of benches sat. "Shall we all gather there and talk. Refreshments and food can be brought, if you wish."

Karlartz beamed. "Food and drink! It would be most welcome."

Rau'ke turned and led them toward the benches as Cant'al talked with some others and sent them running toward the main kitchen. Then she followed the strange warriors toward the Discussion Circle.

Hanalera.

She stepped from the very narrow crevice in the mountain range, stopped, and gasped.

Before her was a vast, open, more or less, circular valley. She could see large areas of grass. Other areas that appeared to be crops of some type. Scattered about were dwellings, most of which appeared to have been built on the very tops of the gigantic, isolated, towering trees, soaring trunks capped with a green plateau of growth.

One of the rainbow glittering shapes zipped in her direction, stopped in front of her, hovering above the ground, feet clearing the tall grass, and stared at her.

She was wearing white and silver armor with a long sword hanging from her belt.

Clerian'tra judged her height to be at least a head shorter than any of her shorter siblings.

"Warm greetings," said Clerian'tra.

"Another of those," grumbled the being, great purple eyes scanning Clerian'tra's face.

"Ummmm?" Clerian'tra frowned at her.

"One of the light skinned ones!"

"Oh."

"How did you get here?"

"I am Clerian'tra. I came to this land via one of the Cargo Steeds, across the great sea from N'Farza, to the port," she waved, "way back there. Then I walked. Have you a name?"

"Teema!" she snapped. "Why are you here?"

"Curiosity. What are you?"

Teema settled to the ground and laughed.

"The Slynara call us Winter Sprites. No one knows why they do that. It just seems to be a peculiarity of their culture. We call ourselves The Wytera Aries. I am of The Warrior Class."

She touched her long blade on just the correct spot. It shimmered and became a thing of three blades, curved like the claws of a prey-beast. The weapon glittered sharp edges, top and bottom of each blade. The cross-wise handle had a glove-like grip which would support the wielder's wrist and forearm while the weapon was at work. The blades were as long as Teema's forearm.

"This is a Wraith Claw," she explained.

She looked up at Clerian'tra, touched her weapon, which shifted back to looking like a sword.

"Not long past, I met two very large warriors, very, very large warriors. They were with a short male, a cute short male who carried no weapon. Unfortunately that one had bonded with one of those Hakar females." She glared darkly at the grass. "All but

The Hakar were light skins."

"Ahhhh, ummmm?"

"What?" snapped Teema.

"Did these, errrr, light skinned ones tell you their names? That you remember?"

Teema twisted her lips back and forth as she thought. Then she nodded.

"The cute one was named Cereon. The great big ones were funny named. Ahhhhh, Altai'dorionasha and Hy'pherian."

Clerian'tra laughed. Then quickly stifled it as Teema frowned at her.

"No insult, Warrior Teema." She dampened her grin. "The, ummmm, cute one is my brother, my younger brother. The other pair are a near-brother and a near-sister. I laughed because I had never heard anyone call Cereon cute before."

"Oh." Then Teema told her how that trio had freed her and all that happened afterwards. She had watched from high above the Slynara town and saw them eventually leave there.

"My," said Clerian'tra. Then she looked at Teema's wings.

"You were able to fly all the way from there to here?"

"Of course! Do it all the time. I just got careless, that one time."

Clerian'tra nodded.

Teema pointed across the valley at a dark spot on a distant mountain slope.

"You will have to come with me and talk to the Leamageen!"

Clerian'tra smiled, and nodded. "It is a nice day for a walk."

Teema laughed gaily. "Oh, no need for that."

She wrapped her arms around the startled Clerian'tra and soared into the air.

Three Drinks Green.

The group was standing above the beach line and wondering how much longer it would be before a low enough tide would expose the wetway to N'Farza.

The Veleraine were still discussing weapons and tactics with the warriors of the troop. Two of them had caught up with the Queen's party, assigned to her by the Elders to be guards for Sar'al. All sides felt these topics were always subjects to discuss.

Sar'al was dragging one boot tip back in forth in the sand at the edge of the sea and wondering what was wrong with Alaine. He had said that he had to talk with her, but so far he was not doing that. For someone who claimed to be the next House Head he was awfully reticent.

Zak'ke stood near her and just waited, as patient as always.

Nar'a'las walked up to them and pointed at the mist shrouded lands in the distance.

"I could just move us there instead of all this standing around."

"Ummmm," replied Sar'al. "Perhaps we could

do that. But I feel like we ought to wait just a bit longer, just a little longer."

As the group stood looking at where the wetway was somewhere underneath the waters, one of the glar-dogs walked over and leaned against Sar'al's right thigh.

The glar-dog's back was just below her hip. Shar'al had to push, hard, with her left leg to keep from being shoved sideways.

The glar-dog was, as were all of them, white, a thick white heat reflecting fur. They were blocky in shape with deep, thick chests, and long legs. Running down the center of their skulls was a pronounced sagittal crest that anchored the massive jaw muscles.

Sar'al's hand lightly stroked over that massive head and then scratched behind the tall upright ears. The female glar-dog sighed deep in her throat and leaned her hundred twenty pounds just a bit more against the source of her pleasure.

Suddenly Zak'ke leaped in front of Sar'al, blade in hand, facing the water.

Just below and in front of them, the water was swirling, violently swirling.

"BACK!" yelled on of The Elders. "It must be a sea-raider."

The glar-dog growled deep in her throat, hair raising down the length of her spine.

The center of the swirling water began to rise and rise until it was almost as tall as Sar'al. Then it cascaded away.

A female stood there, on a rise in the water, her garments moving around her to a unfelt breeze, a billowing, cloud caressed soft white fog mist. She held a silver scepter in her right hand.

"Warm greetings, Sar'al Queen," she said, smiling at her, pale sea green eyes looking into pale grey ones.

"I am Blue Mist, A Daughter of the Moon. We have heard of your endeavors." She shook her hair back over her shoulders, silver cascades flowing in shining waves. "Why do you stand there?"

"Warm greetings, Blue Mist." Then Sar'al explained why.

Blue Mist smiled at her.

"A small problem." She waggled The Scepter of Delight.

The water parted, forming vertical shimmering walls, opening the wetway, the long sand spit to N'Farza.

Sar'al stared at her. "What are you, Blue Mist? If We may ask and know?"

"We are The Leumar. The Laterian that often spoke to Al'tana knew of your quest and some of the Laterian's folk told us. How they knew of this thing she did not explain. They do hold their secrets, they do." She shrugged.

She pointed.

"The wetway is open and will remain so until your party is all on N'Farza." She sank slowly from sight.

The Troop of The Fierce Continence gathered around the small group and stared at the passage to N'Farz.

Sar'al smiled at the troop, then headed down the sand spit toward N'Farza, waving the others to come along.

As they walked along, Wind Sky looked at Nar'a'las, who shrugged, and said, "No idea."

Alaine walked at the rear of the party and decided that The Ancient One certainly had not told him everything that he ought to know.

The Plains of Singing Grass.

It was mid-morning, a bright sunny day. The breeze floated gently toward the sea, the grass sang its soft song.

A prowling Grass Larpa stopped, head swiveling from side to side, ears flattening back against its long skull. It tensed. An unknown vibration could be felt beneath its feet.

The land just in front of its toes dropped. Dust boiled up in spurts around the hundred foot diameter three foot deep slump.

The Grass Larpa sniffed at the strange smell, hissed, snarled, twisted and bolted away.

It was mid-morning, a bright sunny day. The breeze floated gently toward the sea, the grass sang its soft song.

The Heart of All.

The Swords of The Armed Mass had been separated into smaller units, of varying sizes, to practice and train under the eyes and tutelage of Slinal, Hy, and Altai.

Cereon was standing to one side of the smallest group watching Slinal take them through one of their more complicated training routines. He was amazed at how smoothly the group swirled and attacked their imaginary foes, then broke into two groups and rushed at each other.

The contact between the two groups looked to Cereon like two groups of expert dancers spinning in and around each other, swords flashing, clacking and popping as practice swords banged off sword and shield, or in some cases, a body. At those times the sound was a very loud exclamation of one sort or another.

Slinal was smiling happily at her charges, correcting this one or that one, as required.

Cereon nodded to himself. They were certainly getting to be very good.

Suddenly, Slinal called a halt to all that activity, dismissed her group, and walked over to Cereon.

"Timder," she stated, touching him lightly on the shoulder with her gloved hand. "Lurin calls. We must go. Now!"

Cereon nodded. "We had better tell the others why we are leaving and all that."

"Most so," she agreed. In this case, her Timder

was in charge. After all, this wasn't combat.

They walked toward the main structure and saw Slinal's students merge with those of Hy and Altai.

As far as Cereon could tell, all The Bows and all The Swords were reaching very high levels of skill.

Down at the far edge of the practice fields, hordes of The Thrall were charging at each other with lethal intent, wielding long wooden staves.

After telling Rau'ke and Cant'al what they were about to do, Cereon and Slinal headed for the stables.

Suddenly a small being appeared in front of them, startling them both.

She was shorter than Cereon, a very slight, child sized, ethereal appearing folk.

"I am Baleliana, sent here by Treliana, to offer aid. Out student, Nar'a'las, told us of your endeavors."

"Warm greetings," said Cereon, puzzling over her comment. Nar'a'las certainly hadn't said anything like that or even mentioned that there were such a folk. And how could such a small folk offer aid?

"What aid?" asked Slinal. Hakar tended to be direct and pointed in any endeavor.

Baleliana smiled up at her. "You have the appearance of folk about to travel somewhere. I would aid you in this."

"Ummmm ah," mumbled Cereon, wondering how to explain how to find where they were headed.

"We travel to see Lurin," stated Slinal.

Baleliana nodded. "Oh, that one!"

The trio were gone.

The Tenth Royal House.

Sar'al and her party had clambered up the stairs carved in the rock and stopped in the village named "Those Who Trade With the Crazed Warriors." It was the village that stretched across the entry to N'Farza.

After greeting The Elder and presenting her with a gift box, Sar'al had explained why they were there, listing the groups that she had already visited and who had agreed.

Then Viana and Sar'al's Veleraine body guards had walked to the far side of the clearing with The Elder and held a long animated hushed conversation.

Eventually they walked back.

The Elder gave Sar'al a single sharp nod, and said, "We agree with our cousins. The Tha'a'ea greet their Queen."

Then she told Sar'al of Clerion'tra's visit and where she had headed.

Sar'al nodded and suggested that, when possible, she ought to send someone to Farza to tell them that Clerian'tra had not been harmed by any of the Tha'a'ea.

Now, the group augmented by four more warriors, two each from Tha'a'ea Clan Par'a'na and Clan Dur'na, one of each to remain as Sar'al's bodyguards, and one of each to be part of her Advisor Council, whenever she returned to Nu'vern, stood at the base of the long straight staircase on the rock wall and stared around the large cavern.

Sar'al, Zak'ke, Verin, and Nar'a'las recognized the Wood Steeds anchored across the open water from where they stood although none of them knew what that strange design was meant to be.

Alaine stared around him and, once again, marveled at what Sar'al seemed to do so easily, and wondered who lived here.

Sar'al led her party toward the far distance rear of the cavern, assuming that there had to be dwellings somewhere in that direction. There was no sign of them over near those docks.

And soon she saw that her assumption was correct. The back wall had many structures strung out along it, some of which appeared to her to be dwellings.

As they neared, a door opened and a male stepped out, and stared at them.

She stopped, not too close, smiled, and said, "Warm greetings. May We visit?"

"Ef a sartin," he replied, smiling in return. "Fair greetin's a thee."

He bowed deeply. "Fair Queen."

He gestured them to a small scatter of tables, walked over, and sat in one of them. Several males filtered over to the tables and began to set mugs and tall containers on the tables. He filled one of the mugs, took a sip, and cleared his throat.

"Thee be'en a sartin welcome from The Tenth Royal House to The First Royal House, and our Queen." He laughed.

"We'en do'en a'hear'd of ye and all thy siblings, we'en do'en. Tis some sarprise a se'en thee a'here."

Sar'al found his ancient dialect a surprise as well

as the fact that he had recognized her and knew of her siblings. The Tenth Royal House had been thought for long seasons past to have disappeared.

Then Tenil'an told her of their history, the same as he had done with Clerian'tra. Then he told Sar'al of her sibling's trip to the other land and of her telling them that she was going to visit that land and that she would be safe and would find her own way back.

Sar'al stared at Tenil'an who smiled back.

"T'were a'most self assured a'one, that a'one!

Sar'al nodded. Whatever Clerian'tra's gift might be, it apparently hadn't had any effect of that part of her. She had always been like that.

She took a sip and pointed across the water at the Wooden Steeds. "Would it be possible to have one of those take us back to Nu'vern from here? It would be much faster than us returning back the way we have come."

Tenil'an stared at her for long moments, then he nodded slowly. "We'en could be'en a'that."

Nar'a'las stood. "No need." She looked at Sar'al. "Now?"

Sar'al nodded, thanked Tenil'an for his hospitality and nodded. "Yes."

Nar'alas walked back to a clear spot and waved them all to join her. Then she had them grab each other's wrist, as Wind Sky grabbed one of her's, and one of the others.

Nar'a'las checked that everyone had a good grip on another wrist and that she had a continuous chain.

Tenil'an gasped.

The entire party was gone.

Zaz'za'gaz Cavern.

She walked from one of the rooms further back in the sprawling dwelling and into the open room to where he sat on the edge of the marble floor, legs dangling, gazing out and across the town, at all those silent dwellings. He sat where a fourth wall ought to be although for this room there had never been a fourth wall nor had there ever been one intended.

He was idly, abstractly, nibbling on a piece of fruit, kicking his legs back and forth.

As she sat next him, he gave a long, drawn out heavy sigh.

"I really hate to do it, Hinali."

"Then why?" she asked.

He laughed softly, one finger pointing toward the top of the immense cavern, so large that it was difficult to see the furthest walls.

"That Queen had managed to get all but the various folk in An'darl to accept her. It is rather amazing when you think about it."

"Ummmm?"

"She, and her party, were visiting her Tenth Royal House, once thought lost. She was asking them about her wandering sibling. It seems that she took a trip to visit that other land and is, apparently, still there."

"Zarlar?"

"What?"

"Why is that a bother?"

"It is not!"

She nudged him with a shoulder.

"That Queen has returned to her own lands. One of her siblings moved them there from The Tenth Royal House. A magic user."

"Interesting."

He nodded.

"And there she met the organization of antique Honglar warriors, the entire four groups of them. It seems that they have been living a rather isolated existence ever since the main Honglar population abolished their royalty. Somehow they found out about her reign and relocated to a political system that they preferred."

He sighed again.

"And so?" she asked ever so gently.

"I really hate to do this. But we will be needed."

He stood, walked over to a short metal pole anchored to the floor. It was waist high on him. It had a short arm poking out horizontally, ending in a small hook. A small wooden box was fastened to the upright shaft.

He opened the box, removed a slim metal tube, and hung it from the hook. Then he extracted a short wooden rod from the box and gently struck the tube, once, and replaced the rod in the box, and closed it.

A soft clear note sounded in the silence of the great cavern.

Zarlar sat next to her and sighed again.

He watched the lights begin to flicker on in the dwellings stretching into the distance below him.

The Heart Of All.

Rau'ke was standing and talking with the gate guards early in the morning. It was something that he did every morning. It was his way of escaping, at least for a short while, the deadly duties, as he saw them, of being The King.

Suddenly there they were, standing in a small group, Sar'al and a number of other folk, some of whom he recognized.

He stepped toward them, stopped, and bowed.

"My Queen? Welcome home."

Sar'al laughed at his expression and those of the gate guards.

"Sorry. Didn't mean to startle anyone."

Nar'a'las shrugged. She should have asked Sar'al where she wanted to come down.

Sar'al stepped forward and reached out and tugged Rau'ke by one arm.

"Let's get everyone inside and settled. Then we have to talk."

Once they were in one of the largest rooms, Cant'al joined them, and after being introduced to a number of them, led the new members of The Advisory Council in the appropriate direction to assign them their living quarters and then to introduce them to the rest of The Council. Well, she thought as she walked along,

Sar'al certainly had been very busy. And has certainly gathered together a rather strange Royal party.

In the room, Sar'al waved the rest to their seats, asked someone to fetch food and beverages, and began to explain to Rau'ke all that she had heard and had done.

She turned in her seat and frowned at him.

"Who were all those Honglar We saw, the ones wearing all that strange armor? Why are they here?"

So he told her about that.

"An army? One that has been hidden for countless seasons, in the more rugged, isolated mountainous regions of An'darl?"

He nodded. "Most so. Ahhhhh, you will have to meet with their umm, leader, Markkarz Stone Fist. His proper title is Ka'Thrall. He apparently was visited by Equi-veronik and Bael'elyth, The-Second-Twins-of-The-First, and two, ehm, strange companions. The twins told him of our political system, Royal Houses and lineages. They decided that this was the place where they belonged, ummmm, preferred to live. They are very eager to help in any way they can and are a very industrious folk."

She nodded slowly.

"Ask him, and who ever else he might wish to bring along, to have Last Meal with Us. We can talk, afterward."

Rau'ke stood, bowed, and hurried away.

Zak'ke leaned close to her and murmured, "It seems that you now have a greater Armed Mass that you thought." He stood and smiled. "I think that I will just wander about and visit with the various parts of that and see what it is, exactly." He bowed, straightened up, and strolled away, smiling happily to himself.

She crooked a finger at Alaine, and stood.

"Let us take a walk. We think that We need to have a little talk, you and Us."

She led him down one of the halls, headed for the outside.

The End? Of the Beginning?

Two Swords.

The warriors of The Avelerain, Tha'a'da, the warriors of the six Clans Nu'anji, Veronji, Czenji, Wizralji, Fa'dinji, Taurji, poured down the canyons and valleys of Mart'den and across the wetway to An'darl.

Clan Amenji, the Defenders of Mart'dan, moved into a blocking position at the junction of the continent and the wetway, after telling The Merchant-Trader outfits to pack up, take everything, and leave! NOW!

The warriors of the six clans streamed down the wetway, past the Market Place, down the wagonway toward the open grasslands of the Warrior's Hand. Frightened folk ran in all directions and barricaded doors and latched shutters over their dwelling windows, hoping that Two Swords wasn't about to be destroyed by those dark clothed forest folk.

The Elders of the Tha'a'da had gathered and decided that this was a necessary thing to do. They had sent the warriors racing toward Nu'Vern. Their myth omen made this something they had to do.

The Wild Fields.

The three sat in the small meeting hall.

Cloud Spirit listened to the report as Spirit Cloud

and Storm Sky, a pair from Stonehold Nalda that had been on go-about, told him what they had seen. The pair had hurried as fast as possible to bring this to his attention.

When they finished, he thanked them and urged them to go to their homes and rest.

Then Cloud hurried out the door and down the way to an inn that he knew was frequented by the archer/scout-guides of the various Stoneholds, a place where they gathered to talk among themselves about what they had seen on their go-about.

Inside the large open room, Cloud selected seven and told them to carry his message to the other Stoneholds. He watched them run from the place.

Deep in thought, he slowly walked from the inn and back to the large meeting hall. There he began to study a large map taken from the collection and to make plans. As he studied the map a wry smile came and went. It did seem that The Queen had told true.

Ranagaz.

He sat.

A great figure wrapped in shadow.

He sat, slumped and relaxed in a large chair.

It might have been a throne, that chair. But it wasn't. It was just a large chair. He had no need of a throne.

He knew who he was. Thrones were symbols of power. Totally unnecessary.

He was power. He was a power that was, so far,

unseen and little felt.

He had been aware of them for ever so many thousands of seasons, spreading and changing. Before he had come into existence and settled here, they had been given something. It could be a problem. But even if it was, it would not be for much longer!

The Dark Wind! He laughed. They were so expendable. They did watch and report and even kill a few of them. Those who belonged to that organization were gaining that which they were so anxious to have and sought: power and wealth. It made them ever so much more dedicated. But, in spite of that, they appeared to be rather incapable of doing what he really desired them to do.

So, now he would send things to do what they apparently could not. It was an easy thing for him.

After all, there could only be one Ruler of The Seven Lands. And whether they, or the other folk, understood that, or wanted that, it would make no difference. That Ruler sat here, in this large chair.

He smiled. His presence on the surface wasn't required. Yet!

This time his creatures would not be as weak as those he had put inside The Folded Lands. It had been a surprise that those peaceful folk had managed to get rid of them. And he would not just put one in place as he had done to keep those miners from working.

Exactly what things to use, to create, would take some thought.

He growled. That young Queen had, somehow,

convinced all those groups to agree with her. Now she had five of the six connected lands following her. In such a short time! How could one of those folk, at such a young age, be so charismatic! No-one in her lineage had ever shown such an ability, not once for all those many seasons.

It was unfortunate that those Dark Wind had been so inept.

He smiled and shrugged. Ah well, there would be no more weak folk expected to do what he was about to do.

Now there would be terror and destruction, starting with that Queen's towns. And then, while her folk were running about in confusion and fear, creating turmoil, all those who had decided to follow her would get their turn. To die!

He had waited too long.

Then he laughed, a deep surging laugh.

Terror . . . destruction . . .

Such wonderful thoughts!

Tammest.

They appeared.

Cereon, Slinal, and Baleliana.

Not far from the wide and open gate constructed of thick Hag Tree wood, noted for its strength and durability. On either side of the gate, high walls stretched and curved around the sides of the town.

Watch-guards peered down at them from the tops of those stone walls and the high towers.

Lurin stood just in front the opening.

Cereon looked around them, at the thick grass stretching into the far distance, at the dense forest of The Silent Woods to one side.

This," he stated, "is The Plains of Singing Grass, not one of The Folded Lands!"

He stared at the town and grumbled at Slinal, "What exactly is going on? Here?" Then he frowned darkly at Lurin and pointed at the town. "How did all this get here?"

Lurin strode over to them, golden robes flowing liquid sound around her, great golden eyes watching Cereon, then dancing from face to face.

"Welcome to the one that Slinal feels for. Welcome to Hakar Slinal. Welcome to . . . ?"

"Baleliana," replied the small, slender, delicate appearing being.

Cereon waggled one hand. "She brought us here?" He pointed. "That is Tammest, is it not?"

Lurin smiled at him, her poison fangs poking over her lower lip. She nodded. And sat in the short grass, and patted it.

"Sit! We have much to say."

Slinal did, legs tucked back and under herself, setting her shield and sword by her sides.

Baleliana dropped, legs crossed, hands in her lap, crystal clear eyes focused on Lurin.

Once all were settled, Lurin looked from face to face, and stopped on Cereon's.

"I told The Guardian to move my town to this

spot," she said.

"Told?" mumbled Cereon. "The Guardian?"

Lurin nodded at him.

"There is much you must know, selected one of Slinal. And much that you think that you know that is not, zzzzzz, accurate."

"So, sit still and listen carefully!" she ordered.

She began to carefully explain that much of what he had been told by the folk of Undil Village was wrong.

Andercal, The Great Protector, did not direct them to tear apart the An'others. In fact, that term was rarely used to mean anything other than one who was an "outsider," that is not Slynara.

That term was a corruption of the name An'Thar, the name the Slynara used for an evil, magic user.

Long many seasons past, Andercal met and visited The Guardian who was, at that time, creating The Folded Lands. "As you have experienced," she told Cereon, "The Folded Lands do not show much variation. They are lands of quiet living folk."

She shrugged. "Perhaps The Guardian used up all its imagination creating itself in its current form."

During that visit, The Guardian told Andercal of a great threat to the lands and the folk of those lands far many seasons ahead.

Andercal offered to help in this matter, if The Guardian gave her a space inside The Folded Lands. It was agreed.

Andercal created her folk, The Slynara, and the

town of Tammest for them.

And over the many, many, many seasons, The Slynara studied the way of the warrior. They studied ever nuance, every aspect, every movement, little piece by little piece by little piece forcing that activity to be as pure and as lethal a martial art as it was possible to create.

Their craftsmen did the same thing with the warrior tools, their armor, their shields, their weapons.

Andercal watched those in the valley called Honglar'a'at who were following a different path and told the teachers of the Slynara everything that those folk had studied and improved. She told those same teachers of everything that any weapon wielding folk knew.

The warriors of The Slynara are a distillation of all that knowledge gathered from everywhere.

Lurin smiled at Slinal and nodded at Cereon.

"You have seen," she said to him, "your Hakar fight. From that you have some small understanding of what I am saying."

Lurin pointed. "Out there is The An'Thar, the one seen by The Guardian all those many, many seasons ago. The Guardian misjudged how many seasons would pass, and was attacked to prevent it from seeing its error, before The An'Thar became active."

Lurin nodded at him. "You and your companions restored The Guardian to its full abilities. It was a good thing to do."

She flowed to her feet.

"Tell your Queen of The Seven Lands that the evil of which she was warned is soon to erupt!"

Lurin gestured at the town.

"Tammest is now of The Seven Lands, and her warriors are ready. We, The Favored of Andercal, The Great Protector, have prepared and prepared and prepared for seasons beyond counting. And now . . . we . . . are . . . ready!"

She nodded at Baleliana.

"Take them back. They have work to do!"

Baleliana stood and smiled at Lurin.

They were gone.

Lurin walked through the open gateway to call her warriors to action.

The Heart of All.

Sar'al and Alaine were standing on the highest platform of The Tower of The Soaring Dragon.

She had dragged him up there right after he had explained what The Ancient One had told him what he was supposed to do, what he had to do.

Her response to that had been, "WHAT!"

Then she had hauled him to the gatewall and up the tower to its very top, after she had paused and fetched her lance.

Peering over the back wall she saw Cereon, Slinal, and Baleliana appear.

Cereon looked up and shouted, "WE NEED TO TALK!"

Sar'al waved at him. "SOON!"

She turned, sucked in a deep breath, and barked out the call toward the sky. It roared outward, anger laden words glaring red fire.

The call crashed into her chamber.

She leaped to her feet. "Oh, oh."

Then she was there, a short young woman dressed in robes of an unfamiliar cut and design, colored a deep blue.

Her slanting, large oval eyes, reflecting the azure blue of the sky above, frowned at Sar'al.

"Young Queen?" she hissed.

Sar'al glared at her, her hand clenched white knuckled around her lance.

Alaine pressed himself back against an outside wall. It was as far away as he could get.

Sar'al jabbed the point of the lance at her.

"How dare you send . . . *him*, to tell me that We are supposed to make him Our King! If We had a dungeon, and We thought that We could keep you there, We would put you in it!" She was beginning to crackle and sizzle.

Alaine began to sidle slowly along the wall toward the stairs down. The air around Sar'al was beginning to faintly glow.

The Ancient One's eyes popped wide.

"Careful, Sar'al, careful! You are beginning to pull power from your lance!"

"What?" she snapped. She had just felt the tower twitch.

The Ancient One snatched them to the ground. "OUCH!"

The Ancient One shook her hand, the one that she had grabbed Sar'al with. Steam was rising from it.

"I should know better," she grumbled to herself.

Sar'al stepped back, staring at that steam. Then she looked at her free hand. It looked all right to her, other than the faint glow around it.

"Explain this!" She waggled that hand, and pointed at the steam still rising. "And that!"

The Ancient One smiled and pinned Alaine's feet to the ground. He had been about to bolt.

"You are The Queen of The Seven Lands, Are you not?"

"We are that, We are!" she snarled.

The Ancient One waved her hand at the Bows, Swords, and Honglar warriors running in their direction.

"Do send them back to their practice. We have things to talk about, now that you are capable of drawing power from your lance."

Sar'al waved everyone back to their activities and frowned at The Ancient One.

"Come with Us," she stated. "You also, Alaine. To a small private room." She stalked toward the building.

Alaine was staring down at his feet, his face going more and more pale.

The Ancient One followed Sar'al, tugging him into motion as she released his feet.

Entering the building, Sar'al bellowed at the top of her lungs, "ZAK'KE!"

As they headed down the hall, there was a puff of steam and smoke on the plaza near the gate.

The soft breeze blew the cloud away, uncovering the four folk standing there.

One of them still held a map in his hand.

He stared at his surrounding and then looked at Equi-veronick, his twin sister, totally confused.

"We just stepped from the mouth of that small, narrow canyon." He indicated that spot on his map. "And now we are here?"

Bael'elyth shrugged and looked around. "We are certainly here. Those things must have been responsible, somehow." She looked at their two companions who were standing so still and patient.

"Unknown," said Gentle Smile

Dark Night looked around, gently tapping his scepter against his thigh, watching a gate guard hurrying toward them.

The gate guard stopped and smiled at them.

"Welcome home! Many of your siblings are already here." He indicated the main structure.

"The Queen probably has many things to discuss with you." He spun of his heels and hurried back to his post, wondering who those two strange folk were.

Equi nodded and sighed softly.

"Might as well. Maybe someone will have an idea."

"Those . . . Marphalan told us to go home,"

stated Bael. "It would appear that is where we are." She laughed. "Certainly saved a lot of walking."

"Let's go talk with The First Twins, find out what everyone has been doing." She waved an arm.

"I see many changes here."

Equi nodded. He didn't want to think about how those things had moved them from the upper edges of An'darl to Nu'vern so easily.

Prime Shield.

Ran'dyal was just signing a contract to sent a caravan to Iron Hammer when the door to his office slammed open and bounced off the wall. He had just thought to himself that life had been good for the last two hands of days.

He spun around and stared as An'tarna hurtled inside, banging the door closed.

"WHAT?" gasped Ran'dyal, squinting anger at the red face of his long-time friend and the Second In Command of The Dark Wind.

"Time to leave!" snarled An'tarna. "How fast can you grab some clothes?"

Ran stood, frowning darkly, and pointed at the other chair in his office. "Sit! Then explain! What is all the excitement about?"

An'tarna dropped into the chair and sucked in a deep breath, and nodded.

"Fon'talar was a holding a meeting of his Fist in that small meeting hall we acquired, the one close to the north gate. They were getting ready to leave, ready to travel up to The Valley of Glar."

Ran'dyal sat in his chair and leaned forward. "Why?"

"Mir'dlar and his Fist didn't return, ah, from there. So, Fon'talar was going to head up there with heavier weapons. He wanted to make sure that they could control that forge."

Ran stared at him.

"What is going on out there? Do you know? That is the second Fist to, emmmm, disappear."

An'tarna shook his head.

"No one knows for sure."

Ran'dyal leaned back in his chair and shook his head.

"And that is what all this bother is about?"

"NO!"

"Ummm?"

An'tarna hands were clenched tightly on the arms of his chair.

"No," he repeated in a soft tone of voice. "Fon'talar and his Fist are dead!"

Ran'dyal stared at him, mouth hanging open. It snapped shut. "How?" he hissed.

An'tarna cleared his throat. "Um'am told me. Fon'talar had posted him to stay across the way and watch, just to make sure that no-one might be getting curious about them meeting there." He sucked in a deep breath, exhaled slowly, and leaned closer to his friend, finally releasing his grip on the arms of the chair.

"He told me that he saw a tall, very large warrior

wander through the north gate and then casually step into that meeting hall. He was wearing black armor, black everything, holding a gigantic black sword."

"Black? A black warrior wandered into that meeting?"

An'tarna nodded, licked his lips.

"A few moments later, he walked out the door and strolled south, headed for the gate and the wetway to Shar'daine."

He swallowed loudly.

"Um'am walked across the way and stepped inside, just to see what that warrior wanted. Then he ran and told me!"

"What?"

"In those few moments, that warrior slew the entire Fist!"

"Not possible! They were armed?"

An'tarna nodded.

"I hurried there and looked. All true. All dead. Good thing that the ownership of the structure was in Fon'talar's name."

"And that is why you want to run and to hide?"

An'tarna shook his head.

"Um'am saw that warrior's face. It belonged to no folk that he had ever seen, dark brown eyes, dark brown skin."

"Farza!" snapped Ran'dyal.

"No! I sent two of my most persuasive members to talk with the Farza. They are brown skinned, but much lighter. They wear loose, baggy white garb. That male was dressed in black armor. The Farza do not use armor of any kind."

He waggled his hand. "Beside, they told my pair that they had everything that they required and that they didn't need anything else. Then they walked them to the wetway, and ever so politely told them not to return. My pair left, knowing full well what would happen to them if they tried to return. That black warrior wasn't from any group of folk out there in the lands that I know about or ever heard of! And I visited most of the lands we trade with as a member of a great number of caravans."

"And?" gently urged Ran'dyal, knowing that there was more.

"I was part of the caravan that traveled down to Nu'vern, as you ordered, as it was time to move some of their produce. From what I saw, Nu'vern has built up a very large warrior structure! They have never in all their long history done something like that. On the way back I saw, off to the west, a town. It wasn't there when we traveled south a minor hand of days before. There were swarms of armor clad warriors assembling in front of it. None of them wore black. Further north, we passed a long column of archer/scout-guides walking south. And, as we crossed the wetway north, six great clusters of those northern forest dwellers ran past, headed south, fully armed."

He stared at Ran'dyal.

"I have no idea what is happening down there, but I am leaving Prime Shield. I have a dwelling way up in the mountains west of here. No other folk live around there. No-one knows about it, no-one!"

He stood.

"You coming?"

"Ummmmmm."

Ran'dyal slowly stood, and looked around his office, and shrugged.

"Perhaps you are correct. We can take some horses from here."

An'tarna jumped for the door.

"We better not waste any time gathering up things. I do not want to be seen. I do not want anyone to know where we are going."

Ran'dyal nodded and hurried after his friend.

"Ran," An'tarna said back over his shoulder, as he hurried for the outside door, "something is eliminating The Dark Wind! I am not going to sit around here, hoping that it won't happen to me!"

The Heart of All.

Zak'ke burst into the room, sword in hand.

Hy'pherian and Altai'dorionasha were right behind him, weapons in hands.

The three looked ready to hack something to bits.

They stared at the others in the room.

Sar'al seemed to be glowing.

Alaine had his back pressed tightly against one of the walls, watching her carefully.

The Ancient One was glaring at Sar'al as she waggled her hand. It was steaming.

Sar'al spun and pointed at the three just inside the doorway.

"Zak'ke, you stay!" She nodded at the others, smiled, and waggled her hand at them. "Nothing for you two here. We will speak later."

The pair backed out and shut the door.

Sar'al spun back, glared at The Ancient One, and snapped, "Explain!"

The Ancient One beckoned over a chair and sat. She nodded at Sar'al.

"I made that lance, long many, many seasons ago. It was passed, as I instructed, through your lineage. You are the first to be able to do what you did."

She smiled. "Now you have to learn how to control it."

Sar'al dragged over a chair and sat close to her. Zak'ke walked over and stood behind her, weapon still in hand, watching The Ancient One carefully. He shrugged. It probably wouldn't do any good to attack that one, but he would try, if necessary.

The Ancient One leaned forward, carefully not touching that glow, and began, ever so carefully to instruct her student, the young Queen, in what she had to know.

During the long, long discussion, Zak'ke walked to a chair, slid his sword back into its scabbard, and sat down.

Sar'al was carefully repeating what she was told. The glow vanished, reappeared, vanished, reappeared, and vanished. Over, and over, and over, and over.

Zak'ke leaned his head back and closed his eyes. Might as well, he thought. It was always good to rest when you are able to do so.

Alaine shoved a chair into a far corner and sat, and stared at Zak'ke, now sound asleep. That was not something he was about to do.

And the low conversation went on . . .

Zak'ke's eyes flew open. He was wide awake.

"Sar'al?"

She stood in front of him, gently kicking one of his feet.

As he straightened up, he realized several things. She was no longer glowing. The Ancient One was no longer in the room. And Alaine was sound asleep.

"What?" he asked.

She walked over and shook Alaine awake.

As his eyes popped open, she snapped, "You will go with Zak'ke!" She spun around. "Shadow, take him to Slinal and tell her to test his skills, then to train him until he falls over. Stay with him! Make him stay with you, at all times!"

She grinned at her twin and shrugged a shoulder.

"See if you can keep him alive. Please?"

Clenching her lance in her right hand, she stalked from the room.

The Silent Woods.

The sun had risen on a new day.

The warriors of the four clans of the Tha'a'sa

were gathered in loose ranks inside the dense shadows of their forest, watching.

Across the tall grass to the north, they could see something forming all around that shallow depression.

The scouts had all sped back, and quickly, softly, told what they had seen.

Warped, bent creatures, holding strange weapons, were appearing, smoke becoming solid. These things were not from their myth worlds, explained The Elders. These were things of evil intent.

It was good to know that Viana had six of her clans positioned on the far side.

The Plains of Singing Grass.

They stood to the northeast and not too far from the depression, robes casting amber glow on the surrounding grass.

The four Touched of Huroma had done as Verin'yashi had instructed.

All around them, sitting in the deep grass, watching the same spot as the four, were Grass Larpa, ears erect, silent and still as statues, fur-clad statues.

No folk had ever seen this number of the great predators gathered in a single group, not even during their mating season. This group was mainly comprised of senior males, larger, more lethal than the females. But, here and there, sat a female, older, scarred females, unafraid.

Suddenly, in a great, silent rush for the sky, fire shot upward. And disappeared.

A charred circle, fifty paces larger than the edge of the shallow depression, had become a bare, sterile, burned black space.

High pitched, tinkling laughter drifted across the plains.

Whatever had been forming around the edge of that depression was gone along with the grass.

The Heart of All.

Sar'al stood in the plaza near the great gate in the early morning sun and carefully checked all the folk standing around her.

She nodded at Zak'ke and Alaine as they walked through those folk and stood next to her.

Zak'ke smiled and said, very softly, "I did as you asked. Slinal said that he was fairly well trained and then started to train him. When she was done, she said to tell you that he has a stout heart and great strength and determination. And that she was surprised that he lasted as long as he did, ummmmmm, before he fell over."

He thumped Alaine on a handy shoulder and grinned at him.

"He slept until just now."

She smiled and indicated all those standing around them.

"Markkarz Stone Fist is in charge of all security for Nu'vern. We are taking one-third of the Bows and Swords, and one-half of the archer/scout-guide and the Deep Valley and the Hidden Canyon Thrall warriors.

Slinal, Cereon, Altai, Hy, the triplettes, Nar'alas and Wind Sky, and all those assigned by the several folk as my personal guard!"

She pointed over the heads at a small folk patiently waiting.

"Analiana said that Lurin wished Us to come. The war is starting!"

Equi, Bael, Gentle Smile, and Dark Night walked from the nearby building and pushed through to stand near Sar'al.

"We are coming," stated Equi.

"We will be safe," added Bael.

Sar'al looked over at Analiana. "Can you move this great a number of folk to Lurin?"

Analiana smiled as Baleliana joined her.

The Plains of Singing Grass.

Al'tana stood not far from the edge of the water. From the high rise at this spot she could easily see into the great depressed circular scorched area, a black desert surrounded by tall grass.

The Laterian had brought her here.

She had been surprised at how fast her companion could move through the water.

The Laterian had allowed her to straddle the long neck and wrap her arms around it just below the head as she was held high above the water.

As they had surged along the coast line, the bow wave gurgling white along the Laterian's side, Al'tana could see great numbers of others, not just Laterian, surrounding them.

She had tried to count how many there were but it had been impossible as they weren't always visible, not all at the same time.

But here she was, standing on a relatively high spot for the plains, eyes scanning that dark spot.

Black vapors were beginning to seep upward, long, thick dark vapors, that appeared to be forming into . . . things.

Tammest.

Lurin smiled at her and those clustered around her.

Sar'al began to point. "Those and those and those are now under your command. These folk will stay with me."

Her arm swung and pointed toward the northeast. "We will stand just there."

She started her group in motion as Lurin's enhanced might started toward the east.

The Silent Woods.

The Tha'a'sa, dark shapes set back from the edge of the shadow dappled, dense forest, watched the scorched bare depression and the black creatures taking shape there.

The thick vapors pouring from the ground swirled and eddied and things began to appear, packing the space with tall things clenching strange weapons in clawed hands.

Obeying a silent command they poured from the spot and swarmed toward the slightly used horse trail at the edge of the forest and hurtled along it toward the east.

Clouds of arrows erupted from the woods, pouring into the flanks of the horde lumbering past.

Bodies fell, thrashing, howling, dying.

On the creatures ran.

Short bows whispered death signs.

Bodies fell, thrashing, howling, dying.

The column raced on, a single mind focused on a single task.

Destroy the great gate to Nu'vern!

They churned on, bodies dropping.

Tireless. One mind, one goal.

These were the shock troops of Ranagaz.

As they destroyed the gate and gate structure, flights, clouds, of winged beasts would fall on all the towns and the main village, The Heart of All.

The great fire that had killed the last King and his Queens should have ended that family and ruling class.

But the offspring had already scattered into the lands and places unknown.

Wave after wave of arrows poured into them. Creatures staggered, and died.

Deep in the forest, unseen, shadows flickered, shifting, changing, moving.

The horde reached the wagonway and flowed south, toward the wetway, toward the gate, toward terror and destruction in Nu'vern.

The gate, the gate, shouted the voice in their minds. They ran faster.

Shadow Dancers ripped into their flanks as they charged from all edges of The Silent Woods.

Red claws ripped and shredded the horde.

The gate, the gate, shouted the voice in the creatures minds.

They ran faster.

Onto the wetway, into the light.

Outrunning their attackers.

The gate, the gate!

Into The Forest of Signs.

The survivors lurched into the meadow and ran toward the gate, ran on Aydel's Track.

The gate, the gate!

They disappeared under a wave of silent Azkar, pounded to a halt by heavy wooden clubs.

The Plains of Singing Grass.

Lurin's Hakar stood in a great arc just inside the scorched opening, facing the depression, rows of armored clad warriors, glistening color in the sunlight, curving around the western side. Spaced within their line the Honglar stood, ranked in their battle orders, eyes watching.

Behind the ranks, facing arranged gaps in the line, stood rows of archer/scout-guides, the Bows and Swords of The Armed Mass brought here from Nu'vern.

From the south, Tha'a'sa warriors slipped silently from The Silent Woods, holding stabbing spears, followed by those carrying short bows.

Across the north, the Tha'a'da stretched in battle order, blades glittering.

At their eastern edge the grass shown amber from the glow of flaming robes. All around this handful of Huroma the tall grass was moving.

In the depression vapor poured upward, swirling, boiling, angry.

Things began to take shape. Things began to attack those that faced them.

And died.

Nu'vern.

Clouds of winged beasts appeared.

Over every town.

Over The Heart of All.

They were bringing terror . . . and destruction.

They were here to eliminate the challenge to the power of Ranagaz.

Markkarz Stone Fist stood on the top platform of The Tower of the Soaring Dragon and watched. He smiled.

From near and in the distance he could hear the warning bells. And he knew. The population would race to the prepared shelters as the carefully hidden troops waited for the onslaught.

His job was done.

Everything had been prepared.

Everyone knew what to do.

All he could, now, was watch.

Ranagaz.

He sat.

A great figure wrapped in shadow.

He sat, slumped and relaxed in a large chair.

It might have been a throne, that chair. But it wasn't. It was just a large chair. He had no need of a throne.

He knew who he was. Thrones were symbols of power. Totally unnecessary.

He was power. He was the power that was, so far, unseen and little felt.

He had been aware of them for ever so many thousands of seasons, spreading and changing. Before he had come into existence and settled here, they had been given something that was making those changes.

"After all," he said to himself, "there can only be one Ruler of The Seven Lands. And whether they, or the other folk, understand that, or want that, it could make no difference. That Ruler sat here, in this large chair."

He smiled and shrugged. Those folk were of no concern, other than a bother to be ended.

Now, he had sent terror and destruction to fall upon that so-called Queen's towns. Now, her folk should be running about in confusion and fear, creating turmoil. Now, all those who have decided follow her are going to get their turn. To die!

He had waited too long. He relied on others. It

was time for him to do what was needed.

Then he laughed.

Terror . . . destruction . . .

He sighed. Creating all those things, those monstrosities, those short-term necessaries, was consuming great amounts of energy.

But.

It was necessary. A means to an end.

No opposition would be allowed, none at all.

He nodded. Soon his hordes would eliminate Nu'vern.

Now, it was time to remove all those gathered to oppose him on The Plains of Singing Grass. Now, it was time to see all the wonderful chaos that he had turned loose.

The Plains of Singing Grass.

Sar'al stood and watched the turmoil of battle boiling around that depression. Waiting.

Her personal guard stood, watching for anything that might come in their directions, anything that might escape the carnage taking place not all that far away.

Bows had sung death songs. Bodies had piled up in front of them. Anything that had managed to run past had flown in pieces as glistening blades had flashed and chopped them into beast morsels.

Zak'ke stood close to her but not too close, sword in hand, smiling, waiting. But he kept a careful distance from his twin. She, or the air around her, was beginning to glow. The tip of her lance was shifting color, becoming more silver, a pulsating silver flame. As the war waged on he talked softly with Alaine, pointing at this or that with his sword.

The Hakar were engaged in a fluid, complicated dance. Black things were piling up in front of them, thrashing, twitching, whole or in parts. Honglar were tearing into anything that escaped.

Clouds of arrows arced over the heads of the warriors and plunged into the dark mass surging, struggling, pushing, driven to break free.

Those that broke around the east flank of the Tha'a'da swords along the north line of defenders disappeared in the tall grass laden with Grass Larpa.

Verin'yashi jerked. Someone had just stepped to her side as she stood a short distance behind Sar'al and her group, watching that nothing would be able to circle around and attack The Queen as she stood watching the battle.

"Zarlar?"

He smiled and waved a casual hand at the raging battle and carnage.

"That Ranagaz is a nasty one."

He indicated those standing some distance behind him.

"I woke them from their sleep."

She turned and stared. They were vague shapes, standing in a rather loose group. She looked at Zarlar, eyebrows rising.

He nodded.

"My folk." He laughed, a soft sound barely heard

over the noise.

"The Cavern of Zaz'za'gaz," he added.

He patted her on a shoulder. "Perhaps we may talk later." And strolled off to rejoin them, now a vague shape, hard to see.

Ranagaz.

He knew a great battle was taking place above his head. He was creating horde after horde, wave after wave. Their purpose was to kill that young Queen and all those that would get in the way.

By now, he felt, Nu'vern should be on its way to becoming a smoking ruin as well as a portion of Shar'daine.

He shrugged, ah well, everything can be rebuilt. He would have all the populations that survived to see that this was so.

More things were created. He felt the fatigue seeping in. It was a war of attrition. He would rebuilt his forces faster than they could.

The rock around him thumped.

He shrugged.

All this efforts must be disturbing the environment around him. The surface had already dropped, a little. The force he was releasing must be causing shock waves in all directions.

One wall cracked.

He jerked.

Yellow orange molten rock oozed into his space. Steam and foul fumes seeped from the floor.

He nodded.

Time to go up there and finish what his warriors were doing. He had enough energy left to do that little chore.

The Plains of Singing Grass.

A runner charged up to Sar'al.

"Lurin says that the great evil is coming up . . . " he pointed, "to the surface."

Sar'al stepped forward and spoke to her personal guards.

"Make a wider clear space around Us, please. We want an opening between Us and the great depression!"

They side-stepped and did.

The Honglar warriors began to drag bodies and remnants of things away from in front of her, working their way towards the depression, casting careful glances at her as they did. She was The Queen, their Queen, and this seemed a dangerous thing to do.

He appeared.

A dark shadow standing there, radiating hate.

He stood and looked around the depression, admiring the carnage on all sides, on almost all sides.

He stared at her.

A single female was standing there, on a high rise of ground right at the edge of the sea. She was dressed in trousers with a slight flare at the ankles, an over-blouse that draped to her waist, both a soft sea-green color, and watching all the warfare, apparently unconcerned. None of his warriors had paid attention to this one, standing so calmly, just watching.

He shrugged and turned away. Battles had spectators, it appeared.

He spotted her. And her companions and guards.

He pointed across the battling lines of combatants at her.

"It is time to die, young Queen."

His voice carried to her, easily heard, clear as a chime, undisturbed by the din of battle.

He saw her eyes glare at him.

He laughed and raised his wand high over his head, ready to start the great downstroke that would remove her and a rather large amount of the surrounding grass lands around her.

It snapped from her lance and blasted through his hand, sending the wand flying up high above him.

Spinning around, he searched for it, reconstructing his hand as he did.

That watching female picked it up and stepped back onto the high piece of ground. She examined the wand and looked up at him.

"Very pretty," she said.

"Toss it to me and you shall live!" he snarled. And stared.

The sea was rising behind her, a great mound of dark water, rising higher and higher, high above the land, surging, towering above her.

A thin edge of water began to flow onto the land and around the mound she stood upon, a gentle flow which barely disturbed the tall grass.

"You want this?" she asked.

"NOW!" he roared.

She began a high toss and somehow the wand flew up and behind her.

"Oooooooops!" She smiled at him.

A long grey-green tentacle ending in a wide fleshly wedge snapped from the sea and wrapped its tip around the wand and jerked back.

She shrugged. "My friends thought that they should have such a pretty thing."

She waggled one hand, indicating the vague shapes of large creatures just visible in the black waters.

"Of course, you could just fetch it yourself." She nodded at him. "Ummm, if you wish."

"RANAGAZ!" boomed a voice.

He jerked around, water swirling around his ankles, water seeping into the cracks and crevices forming across the face of the depression.

A rather plain looking male walked through the on-going struggle, totally unconcerned with it, untouched by it.

"We have waited for you."

Ranagaz peered at him, saw the energy and power billowing around him, pouring into him from a large cluster of hard to see folk standing well behind the lines of struggling warriors.

Ranagaz pointed north. The bolt flashed from his finger and disappeared.

He laughed, and laughed, and laughed. A final gift!

Zarlar gestured.

The dark being was blasted into a cloud of black fragments swirling into the air, rising higher and higher into the sky, dissolving into nothingness.

All around the depression, black creatures fell where they stood. Everything, whole and pieces, dissolved, making dark stains, marking the circumference of the depression.

Steam began to erupt from the crevices and fissures as cold sea met molten lava deep below the surface.

Zarlar turned, walked back, and bowed.

"Young Queen, you have done well."

He was gone. All his folk were gone.

Combatants began to collect their dead and injured and head back toward their homes.

Sar'al watched, then jerked, and glared.

Zak'ke came towards her, limping from a cluster of Honglar warriors, one arm around Alaine's waist, more or less dragging him along.

As the battered pair staggered up to her, the glow around her vanished.

Clenching her lance tightly, she snarled, "We told you to keep him alive, We did!"

Zak'ke released his grip and laughed happily.

"He hasn't died. Yet!" He shrugged and winked at the badly tilting Alaine.

"I told him," stated Zak'ke, "no heroics! But he is a thick skull! I had to run after him." He sat in the grass. And looked up, nodded at her.

"Ah well. I think that Slinal's training helped keep him alive as much as my aid did."

Zak'ke laughed again.

"So, you see, Sister-Queen, we might be rather battered, but we did survive." He grinned, a happy warrior's grin, up at her.

"As you did so order, Your Majesty."

Cast

(so far met)

The First Royal House – Noriyon Zacog.

The King – Zerta'ald'ver The Observant

First Queen – Salanda, House Cueron Tacog

The-First-Twins-of-The-First

    Sar'al Rada'doa Noriyon Zacog   23   ♀

    - The Queen of The Seven Lands

    Zak'ke Elias'dea Noriyon Zacog   23   ♂

    The First Blade

The-Second-Twins-of-The-First

    Equi-veronik Rada'doa Noriyon Zacog   22   ♂

    Bael'elyth Elias'dea Noriyon Zacog   22   ♀

    - the twins have become know as

    - The Seekers of Truth

    - marked as special to the Zarnarz

The-Third-Twins-of-The-First

    Rau'ke Elias'dea Noriyon Zacog   21   ♂

    Cant'al Rada'doa Noriyon Zacog   21   ♀

Second Queen – Runsda, House Melta Nacog

The First-Daughter-of-The-Second

    Clerian'tra Rada'doe Noriyon Zacog   22   ♀

    - made *Bar'Farza* by The Farza

The-Triplets-of-The-Second

    Verdorion-elvershair Elias'dee Noriyon Zacog 21   ♂

    Caevelas Rada'doe Noriyon Zacog   21   ♀

    Cer'alda Rada'doe Noriyon Zacog   21   ♀

    - all trained by the Adepts living in Two Swords

The-Second-Daughter-of-The-Second
> Nar'a'las Rada'doe Noriyon Zacog   20   ♀
>> - trained in The Vale of Treliana

The-First-Son-of-The-Second
> Cereon Elias'dee Noriyon Zacog   19   ♂
>> - trained in the encampmernts of Warrior's Hand

> Third Queen – Oanna, House Oalen Hacog

The-First-Daughter-of-The-Third
> Verin'yashi Rada'doi Noriyon Zacog   22   ♀
>> - Senior *Hand of Huroma*

*The-Second-Daughter-of-The-Third**
> Altai'dorionasha Rada'doi Noriyon Zacog   21   ♀

*The-First-Son-of-The-Third**
> Hy'pherian Elias'dei Noriyon Zacog   20   ♂
>> *trained by The Six as warriors

The-Second-Son-of-The-Third
> Neverishan Elias'dei Noriyon Zacog   19   ♂

The-Third-Daughter-of-The-Third
> Al'tana Rada'doi Noriyon Zacog   18   ♀
>> - trained in Ea'na

The Second Royal House – Beran Sacog
> The House of Philosophers/Historians
> House Head – Arma'fa Zalna'dei Beran Sacog   ♂

The Third Royal House – Cueran Tacog
> The House of The Stewards of The Land.

The Fourth Royal House – Melta Nacog
> The House of The Stewards of The Seas.

The Fifth Royal House – Oalon Hacog
> The House of The Stewards of Commerce.

The Seventh Royal House – Zilin Aacog

The House From Whom New Kings Arise.

The First Son

Alaine'an'dar Tan'dei Zilin Aacog   23   ♂

The Tenth Royal House – Aadon Dacog

The House of The Traders of The Seas.

House Head –Tenil'an   ♂

The Avelerain

The Bera'ar'ander

The Tha'a'da Clans of Mart'den

Viana Tivean Tru'ert of Clan Vernoji - The Spirit of the
Tha'a'da. ♀

Clan Amenji - The Defenders of Mart'den.

Clans of Valleys and Mountains.

Tuarji, Czenji, Veronji, Nu'anji, Wzralji,
Far'dinji.

The Tha'a'sa Clans of The Silent Woods
Zaland, Pel'na, A'a'tar, Mu'antar.

The Tha'a'ea Clans of N'Farza.
Par'a'na, Dur'na, N'dara, Sin'tu'ar,
Bindulin.

The Archer/scout-guides of The Wild Fields

Stonehold Anda

Cloud Spirit ♂ - Senior archer/scout-guide, advisor,
counselor.

Wind Sky   ♀ (friend, companion of Nar'a'las).

Swift Wind   ♂

Bright Sky   ♀

Stonehold Nalda
      Spirit Cloud ♂
      Storm Sky ♀
Stonehold Derda
      Far Shot ♂
Stonehold Turda
      Mist Night ♀
Stonehold Onda
      Dark Wind ♂ (friend, companion of Al'tana)

The Slynara - The Favored of Andercal, The Great Protector

Tammest - the home of the Slynara
    Lurin - The Guide of The Slynara
    Slinal - Hakar - bound to Cereon

The Farza

- called by many *The Crazed Warriors*
Vachannal The Insignificant
    - The One Who Speaks For All
The Troop of the Fierce Continenance - Three Drinks Green
    Den'tza The Gross - Troop Leader
The Troop of Many Fingers - The Great Blue
    Kranza The Limber - Troop Leader
The Troop That Never Smiled - Guards of the Wetway
    Quantar The Handsome - Troop Leader
The Troop of Slow Feet - Blue Small Drink

The Baine'lar

Dark Shadow ♂
    The Baine'lar of Evil Warriors - warrior
Clear Shadow ♀
    The Baine'lar of Evil Magic Users - caster
Pure Shadow ♂
    The Baine'lar of Evil Intent - warrior

The Hidden Ones

The Forest of Sighs

    The Azkar - *The Ones of The Forest*

The Vale of Treliana

    Treliana - Master Caster ♀

    Baleliana ♀

    Analiana ♀

The Zarnarz - *The Shadow Dancers*

    Drakar Zarta - a large place

        Sha dar ♂ and Sha zar ♀ - Heads

        Jina dar ♂ and Nima zar ♀ - guides

The Heart of Darkness

    Soft Touch - A One Who Saves ♀

    Final Touch - A One Who Does Not ♀

    Gentle Smile - A One Who Saves ♀

    Dark Night - A One Who Does Not ♂

Thrallanton - The Thunder Mountain Range

    Markkarz Stone Fist - Ka Thrall

        Ruler of The Ancient and Forgotten Warriors

    Karlkarz - The Gate Keeper

    The Midnight Cavern Thrall

        Karlatz - Sa Thrall (Field Leader)

    The High Peak Thrall

        Jarlnarz - Sa Thrall (Field Leader)

    The Deep Valley Thrall

        Quarltarz - Sa Thrall (Field Leader)

    The Hidden Canyon Thrall

        Darldaz - Sa Thrall (Field Leader)

Demon Valley - The Domain of The Deep Below

    The Merphalan

Zaz'za'gaz Cavern

    Zarlar

    Hinali

The Mythological Beings - The Development of the Populations

The Merphalon

- came into existence with the creation of the planet.
- live in the Domain of The Deep Below

The Father Of Us All; The Mother Of Us All.

The Heart Of Darkness

- The Mother Of Us All

  - populated the three domains:

    The Domain of The Wet;

    The Domain of The Dry;

    The Domain of The Open.

- The Father Of Us All

  - created the end of life.

Two Daughters:

The Lady Of Life - grants the gift of healing and health to her favored ones

The Lady Of Death - grants the gift of death to her favored ones.

The Goddess Zmarmarzl

The Zarnarz - among first dwellers

The Ancient One.

- created The Crystal Place
- gave special capabilities to the main Royal line of Nu'vern as she watched the growth and change in the populations of the lands.